AN UNENDING LANDSCAPE

AN UNENDING LANDSCAPE
TOOMAS VINT

Translated and with an introduction
by Eric Dickens

DALKEY ARCHIVE PRESS
CHAMPAIGN   DUBLIN   LONDON

Originally published in Estonian as *Lõppematu maastik*, by Varrak, Tallinn, 1997
Copyright © 1997 by Toomas Vint
Translation and introduction copyright © 2012 by Eric Dickens
First edition, 2012

Library of Congress Cataloging-in-Publication Data

Vint, Toomas.
[Lõppematu maastik. English]
An unending landscape / Toomas Vint ; translated by Eric Dickens. -- 1st ed.
    p. cm.
"Originally published in Estonian as Lõppematu maastik by Varrak, Tallinn,
1997."
ISBN 978-1-56478-736-1 (pbk. : acid-free paper)
I. Dickens, Eric. II. Title.
PH666.32.I5L6713 2012
894'.54532--dc23
                    2012013728
Supported by the Estonian Ministry of Culture and the Cultural Endowment
of Estonia

Partially funded by the National Lottery through Arts Council England, and a grant
from the Illinois Arts Council, a state agency

www.dalkeyarchive.com

Cover: design and composition by Sarah French, painting by Toomas Vint

Translator's Introduction

Painting and intertextuality are two of the leitmotifs of this novel. Its author, Toomas Vint, doubles as an accomplished professional painter of landscapes in which there is always a tension between nature and the vestiges of human activity. So too in this book.

Toomas Vint was born in the Estonian capital, Tallinn, in 1944, the son of a budding Soviet economist. He was brought up in the villa suburb of Nõmme and spent his youth as an amateur sportsman. He then studied biology at Tartu University, but by the 1960s was already editing programs for Soviet Estonian Television, then gradually adopted his present dual career as painter and writer. He did his military service in the polar region of Russia.

During the next thirty years Vint gradually broke through as a painter in Soviet Estonia, independent Estonia, and abroad. He has a special, instantly recognizable style. He evolved from painting abstract compositions to landscape painting, often with trees, where the grass, heather, or foliage is painted in great detail. But in nearly every painting there is a trace of human life, such as a pole or rod painted in red and yellow stripes, a mysterious building, some ornamentation from a park, or—less frequently—a human being.

From the early 1970s onwards, Vint has been writing both short stories and novels. He started publishing collections of short stories in 1974, and from the early 1980s to 1994 published many individual stories in literary magazines. On his website, Vint says that the themes of his early work include "games and play, the interweaving of the unreal with the real, loneliness, contradictory states of mind, eros." There is also an ever-present irony.

The period 1995 to 2005 was especially fruitful. During that time Vint wrote this novel, another about the lives of artists, and a trilogy featuring his protagonist Helger Tepner, intended to capture the mental and psychological life of Estonians between the 1960s and the present day. During that period Estonia changed a good deal, from the hopeful times of the Prague Spring, via the grim Brezhnev era to emerge at last, relatively unscathed, from the ruins of the Soviet Union as it broke up between 1989 and 1991. Vint now began to use postmodern narrative techniques.

*

This particular novel—not surprisingly given the above—involves art and painting. But the influence of Derrida, however ironically tackled, also shines through. The story and text incorporate various key concepts, such as undecidability and iterability. The novel is structured as repetition of a plot. The characters remain undecided with regard to gender, sexual proclivities, and their view of their own lives, looking back.

Toomas Vint is rather critical of some of the trends of modern art, with its installations and performances, and the contemporary exploitation of culture for commercial purposes. So this novel refers indirectly to a whole host of international personages from the world of the arts. Vint's acknowledgments to those who have inspired this book are as follows:

> *The author of this book would like to thank the authors of other books, but would especially like to credit the following authors with direct influence: Irma Truupõld, Iris Murdoch, Anton Chekhov, Tõnu Õnnepalu, Roland Barthes, Milan Kundera, Tõnis Vint, Virginia Woolf, John Fowles, Anton Tammsaare, Pentti Linkola, Jacques Derrida, and of course my sincere thanks to you, Good Reader, the most notable of all authors.*

The four Estonian names in that list may not be familiar to foreign readers. Anton Hansen Tammsaare (1878-1940) was the most significant Estonian novelist between the wars. Tõnu Õnnepalu wrote the gay novel "Border State," under the pseudonym Emil Tode, which has since been translated to English. Tõnis Vint is Toomas Vint's graphic-artist brother. And Irma Truupõld (1903-1980) was a children's writer, specializing in a romantic vision of a green world, and author of "The Land of the Green Sun". The Finn, Pentti Linkola was a radical environmental activist and author.

A couple of names omitted from this list of acknowledgments are those of Joseph Beuys and Jacques Lacan. Part of the novel's humor involves bringing up the names of various of these intertextualized figures as the names of characters. These names are distorted to reflect the way an Estonian would pronounce them, so I will draw the reader's attention to the fact that the farm where the novel is set is called Teeriida (Derrida; an Estonian multi-pun involving tea, roads, and quarrels); the main female protagonist is named Maria

Laakan (Lacan; pun on bedsheets); and the socially inept installation artist Joosep Vaino is called "The Boy"—Poiss, in Estonian. This is a pun on Joseph Beuys. And indeed, the fish-and-mushroom dish suggested by Maria Laakan is called a "dölööz-guatari" whose provenance will be obvious to those familiar with postmodern theory. There are hidden hints of other authors, such as the Estonian postmodernist author Mati Unt, whose novella "An Empty Beach" has appeared recently in English translation in a British anthology.

As mentioned above, the action of the novel recurs—twice over, in transmuted form. A case of metafiction of the nested fiction brand. The first narrator is writing an autobiographical piece recounting the way an old schoolmate, now a minister, attempts to recruit Vint's alter ego—the writer So-and-So—to spy on people suspected of being covert environmental activists, working under the cover of running a group of summer houses for tired city folk. This author So-and-So then proceeds to write his own novel, *Informer to the Estonian Republic*, on the strength of his experiences, and soups up all the details of what he has himself gone through. He is writing this novel at Teeriida Farm, which is also an allusion to the various farms featured in the novels of Tammsaare. And Vint himself, in his painter guise, appears under the transparent pseudonym of Vennet, a man always full of advice, good cheer, and a bit of philosophy, now a teetotaler after years of drinking and somewhat bohemian living in what was still the Estonian Soviet Socialist Republic. And within this novel the writer So-and-So writes a third text, a novella entitled "A Novel For the End of the Century," that hints at Chekhov's "The Lady With the Lapdog". Once again Vint shifts perspective and point of view, and creates another story out of the same basic plot, with changed components. And giving Vint's penchant for examining Derrida, the status of these three stories is subverted, so that it is not entirely clear whether these stories relate to one another like Russian dolls or are three takes of parallel narrative validity.

Toomas Vint likes playing around with the concepts of the self and perception. The writer So-and-So, both in the first story and the novel-within-a-novel sections, is a somewhat nervous, slightly paranoid man who has just split up with his wife. None of these men are fully conscious of life around them as something straightforward. There is distorted perception of what goes on in their presence, and the status of dreams and waking life are called into question. A similar aspect is the idea of the game. When acting out their various roles in life, people are indulging in play. (Vint returns to this aspect of human behavior in his 1999 novel, "At the Weekend—Playing Games".)

Within this weft and warp of intertextuality, Vint deals with a number of basic themes and leitmotifs: town and country life, road accidents, sex and vomit, romance, political skulduggery, farming and fishing, drink and cigarettes, moonlight and the night, the sea and the beach—and sunshine, plenty of sunshine, as much of the action takes place during the late summer. Toomas Vint spends his own summers at a farm outside the seaside resort of Pärnu in western Estonia, so there is a link between the descriptions of life in the countryside in this novel and the reality that Vint himself has experienced when fishing and looking after the farm.

"An Unending Landscape" won the Estonian Cultural Endowment prize for literature in 1998.

ERIC DICKENS, UPPSALA, MAY 2011

AN UNENDING LANDSCAPE

"When I wish to find out how wise, or how stupid, or how good, or how wicked is any one, or what are his thoughts at the moment, I fashion the expression on my face, as accurately as possible, in accordance with the expression of his, and then wait to see the thoughts or sentiments that arise in my mind or heart, as if to match or correspond with the expression."

EDGAR ALLEN POE
"The Purloined Letter"

This is not a pipe

"And Roland wouldn't blow [the horn]—swore that no enemy could ever make him blow. A big brave fool. In war one always chooses the wrong hero."

GRAHAM GREENE
The Confidential Agent

First Chapter

He's gotten fat, I'm thinking from the comfort of the leather armchair I've been shown to by the minister—soft, like sinking into
a fresh haystack. And then I remember that nerves make you fat.
Nerves or a stressful job make you nibble, run to the fridge, sneak
into the kitchen at night and munch a chicken leg (yes, a chicken
leg!) in secret. He looks taller and slimmer on TV, with his belly
conveniently hidden by the desk. What if I pretended not to recognize him—pretended that I can't see what was once Specs Leo
in what is now Minister Leo? It would be interesting to see if his
wry smile would broaden, if the feeling of hurt would show in his
eyes. (Nonsense! He hasn't the time or temperament for feelings,
emotions—he's always been a psycho-brute).

"Want a smoke?" asks the minister, and I feel like someone under interrogation, someone who's gone without a cigarette in his
cell for days on end, and I want to cry out: You bet I do!

"I prefer to smoke my own, I'm used to the lighter ones," I say
rapidly in reply, putting my hand in my pocket to retrieve my
cigarettes. This is my last chance not to be on first name terms
with him, to clothe my replies in formality, but I don't want to
make things unnecessarily difficult for myself, curiosity is egging
me on, and I simply can't wait for him to reveal the reason why
I'm here. As I sit in this soft armchair the minister controls the

temperature of my self-esteem—he can watch it rise or fall, as if on a thermometer.

I pull my hand from my pocket and bring my packet out into the open, while he, as if he hasn't heard me, slides a gold (gilt?) cigarette case in my direction. He should smoke himself—that might reduce his weight.

"Is your mother still alive?" asks Leo, quite unexpectedly, and continues: "Look, even ministers can sometimes allow themselves a bit of sentimentality. Since I knew we were going to meet, I had a look at a few childhood and school photos yesterday evening, and concluded that your mother had played a significant role in our upbringing. At any rate, you'll always have a great mother," he says in a soft, somewhat sing-song voice, and I notice a glint or glimmer of roguishness in his eyes.

"For a couple of years now she's been . . . " (what I'm about to say is "with the Lord," but my lips seem to stumble over such an alien expression, and I manage to swallow it at the last moment, and continue) " . . . pushing up daisies."

"I see," he says, hesitating a little, not knowing how to catalogue, systematize, comment upon my reply. I feel him look searchingly at me, without embarrassment, and I allow him to assess me, my gaze slides off towards the wall, to a landscape painting behind the minister's back, where a woman dressed in blue and with her back to the viewer seems to be going off somewhere. The yellowish-grey sky is reflected in the white cap the woman is wearing. She is wading through the juniper bushes, across a large meadow, toward the horizon, where a patch of forest or scrub stands shrouded in mist, from which a kind of white luminescence wafts towards her. The blades of grass seem to have been painted one by one. The painting radiates an inexplicable anxiety, a secret significance which we, the lookers-on, will never know. It is as if, within this painting, another is hidden, whose disturbing message must be concealed from the viewer for as long as possible.

I know who painted the picture.

"Look," says Leo, with unconcealed disappointment in his voice, because this evocation of common memories is starting (for some reason he can't quite grasp) to unsettle the old schoolboy camaraderie he's trying to conjure up, because the intended school-chum atmosphere (I have to smile) just isn't working. "Look," he repeats, in a different tone of voice now. "We've decided to encourage you to take a short break from your creative work. A couple of weeks in a nice place out in the countryside. If you like it, you'll be able to stay even longer. Live your own life, we'll pay your daily allowance as if you were on an official trip."

("Look" is a throwaway expression. The minister would do well to keep his language under better control; it's interesting that he wants his old childhood friend to get wistful with him, to start reminiscing—does he suppose that I find him agreeable as a politician? And what damned break in a nice spot in the countryside?)

"Since when has your ministry been encouraging writers?" In asking this I begin with a certain recalcitrance, then grow more cautious, thereby exhorting the minister to follow my lead.

"Look (!)," he says, "it isn't actually a break. More like a kind of assignment for the state. You'll be just like a secret agent, a 007 or a Stirlitz." He begins to laugh as if coughing, the tip of his tongue visible between his teeth. I understand that my facial expression has caused this laughter, so I smile graciously and tell him how, years back, the KGB tried to recruit me; words flow from my lips, Leo listens patiently, but his face reveals no interest in my tale, and I myself have grown weary of telling the story for umpteenth time.

"Oh you intellectuals. Always in opposition, never quite seeing the difference between the KGB and the Estonian Republic."

*

I have no opportunity to think the whole thing through until the afternoon—no chance to clarify my thoughts as to what was being openly offered, and what was being said between the lines. I take a coffee sitting outside on a plastic chair at a sidewalk café, put on the expression of an urban citizen—bored indifference (as if I myself have grown bored *with* indifference).

Not that Leo has it easy now, I think as an ordinary citizen, many things aren't easy at the moment, because we've never learned to take responsibility, because we aren't used to it. In times past personal responsibility was masked by an all-promising collective responsibility, and only yesterday the majority of those now in power were insignificant civil servants, or even mere students; they have managed to climb to the top, skipping quite a few rungs.

As if feeling somewhat ashamed Leo had said: "Look. You can refuse, can make it look as if state business is none of yours, since you're a well-known author; but then the state, in turn, will take no interest in how you're getting on, and won't raise a finger should you get into a real mess."

This was said with slight embarrassment (feigned) or as a joke, but the threatening undertone was not concealed by the amicable tone of voice—the facts were what they were.

At any rate, when he finally looked in my direction in a questioning sort of way, I imagined him lying in his (the minister's) bed, with his head resting on the pillow and the (embroidered!) edge of the sheet pulled up right under his chin. "This is blackmail, pressure," I let out jokingly, pretending to go along with his plan while at the same time trying desperately to work out what they wanted of me.

On the face of it, nothing special.

The waitress (girlish, her makeup too provocative) brings a mug (not a real one, transparent plastic rather than glass, but a mug nonetheless) of beer, and I'm thinking that what they wanted of me was merely to take a trip to the country, a couple of weeks' holiday, to relax and write—to do just what I want at state expense. On the face of it this would be no nervy, life-threatening secret agent's assignment, no humiliating snooping around, just the usual stuff, dull, mundane. I said that, as I understood it, I couldn't really be of any use to them. "That's our business," said Leo.

The weather toward the end of summer is warm and sunny enough, the beer is chilled and pleasantly bitter. Life is tolerable enough, even pleasant, and I don't really have anything special to do in the dusty (cliché!) city.

Give Satan a few of your fingers, he'll take your whole hand—that would be a rather clever variation on the old saying, and might be a good description of my immediate prospects. It's only natural that when someone is prepared to do a small job for the state (play the overture), soon enough he'll be asked to make greater efforts (indeed). So I told Leo what I thought of the whole business.

"Still, think it over and phone me," said Leo suddenly, a note of visible (audible) indifference suddenly appearing in his voice, which made me all the more agitated (am I not so important to them after all?).

"Fine," I said as I rose and pushed a piece of paper with someone's name and telephone number into my pocket. "I'll think it over and then phone."

Considering this from an ethical point of view, I think—taking a swig of my beer—that any self-respecting author should stand in opposition to the powers that be; being a fellow-traveler, being in their pocket, isn't exactly the most honorable of positions. In actual fact *Names on a Marble Plaque* (Albert Kivikas; nationalist) and *Red Carnations* (Johannes Semper; communist) are one and the same novel. When a writer accepts a ministerial portfolio or sits in the President's chair, then, with regards to writing, we can speak of him in the past tense.

When you weigh it up from an ethical point of view, the secret police of every state comprise one and the same institution. When some upright and honest little man or other starts assiduously serving the interests of the secret police, however decent and right the assignment, he will suddenly discover (overnight!) that he has become a tool of Evil, that he is unable to break off these work-relations or pretend they never existed. At any rate, it would be ethical for an ethical man to steer clear of all of this. Phone and say—writer So-and-So has considered the matter and concluded that it would not be ethical for him to cooperate with the powers or structures of the state.

I can certainly imagine myself phoning in a few minutes, like a well-paid whore, and agreeing to everything. Then I will meet some civil servant or other who will get me to sign an oath of silence (!), whereupon I will be instructed, (only) some cards will be laid on the table, and soon I will find myself being winked at conspiratorially from all directions, as all my colleagues will have been secret agents or, in common parlance, informers, for ages. From tomorrow onward I too will be an *informer*.

I imagine that in actuality things will be much simpler than that. No secretiveness as in the movies, no spy romance. They regard me as someone suitable to do certain jobs for them, and it is only natural that I do what is to our mutual advantage, and I will have no reason to start (now you are going to read a completely ordinary, hackneyed cliché, but an exact description) dodging or wriggling out of things like a prostitute feigning innocence.

A colleague (a writer) plonks himself down next to me and puffs and blows, he is portly, the heat of the summer city does not suit him, but he has no choice but to rush around (like a squirrel in a wheel—I try to imagine him as a squirrel!) between the buildings of the city, earning his keep and relaxing with a beer on rare occasions. My colleague is wheezing, and I worry that maybe he has some hidden disease, and I ask him, as if by the by, whether he would agree to do business with the structures of our beloved security apparatus (what an expression!).

I ask him this unexpected question and at first he is clearly startled, he seeks an evasive answer, dodging the question, and orders a beer from the waitress. No doubt he's one of them already, I suddenly think, no doubt he's been an Informer to the Estonian Republic for ages.

"I understand the ulterior motive of your question, its hidden irony. But the problem with all of us lies in the fact that we're used to mocking the people in power. People tend to avoid joining the armed forces or becoming police officers. But they cannot be free until they get it into their heads that freedom needs to be defended," my colleague explains with a dead straight face, and in a slightly didactic tone.

I listen to his ratiocinations and arguments and know that no direct answer to my direct question is forthcoming, and I get the inappropriate (but no doubt well-founded) impression that this is that selfsame ministry spiel that Leo had given me earlier; it could well be that the text had been written by this writer colleague of mine, then learnt by heart by the minister. Suddenly (I would like to, but . . .) I pluck up the courage to ask where this colleague of mine actually works, because he has to work somewhere, he could never keep a family on the proceeds of freelance authorship; this feeling of alarm is ridiculous, as in the past we used to get on very well (. . .)—used to.

The expression "used to" pops up unexpectedly out of the flow of my thoughts, gets stuck, stranded, as if behind a rock on a beach, and is now quite visible to me.

*

It is curiosity, sheer curiosity, that makes me dial the number. Maybe that is indeed what's urging me on when I announce my name to the unknown and seemingly uncouth young man's voice and say, after a short pause, that I would probably be prepared to do business with them. "Fine," says the voice, with no nuance of feeling. "I'll drop 'round, just say what time suits you."

He could at least have sounded pleased, I think as I replace the receiver, somewhat dazed. One short sentence—and that was all. No information, nothing definite, simply a couple of extra hours of unknowing. (Idiot! Should have asked him to come immediately.)

"I'll drop 'round," without even asking the address, without enquiring whether or not I want to receive him at home (give them your finger . . . and they'll take your whole hand). Though I'd said I would *probably most likely* agree to cooperate with them, any reservations on my part were either not understood or ignored. I feel my heart growing cold and my stomach hollow—I am now under their authority, there is no going back, in fact it was clear right from the start that I was given just the one chance and one seeming choice.

All of this becomes clear to me in a split second, my fingers are still gripping the gray receiver, my gaze is still fixed on the pencil with its eraser. I will try to describe it: a pencil sharpened for the first time (freshly), white, rounded, a pinkish-red eraser, whose edge is worn down and smudged with graphite, fixed to its end with a small strip of brass. I have no idea how such a pencil got onto my desk, there is no manufacturer's mark. It is not my pencil.

I could cry out: "Listen, how did this pencil end up on my desk?"

My feeling of unease slowly changes to panic, the images in my imagination are like shots from a film—killing, persecution and at the very center a middle-aged, pampered author with urban habits, whose appearance is nothing like that of a spy or secret agent, a man without a shred of bravery or rashness in him, more the psyche of a coward whose heart begins to pound when he goes out in the evening, let alone during the sort of extreme situations in which a secret agent can find himself when at work.

(But: maybe the information I acquire will prevent something terrible from happening, maybe thanks to my efforts many people's lives will be saved and the state preserved, though at the same time my information will be fateful for someone—someone will be put behind bars, someone could even lose his life.)

I am thinking that such a situation would be worth writing about, letting the protagonist fry in the fat of ignorance, having him balance on the edge of the abyss of his forced loyalty to the state.

I roll the white pencil with its eraser between my fingers until the telephone rings. I pick up the receiver, and a moment later I hear an even humming tone.

It feels as if my peaceful existence is going to be filled with adventure from today onwards, to become more complicated, more exciting (or more repugnant). Of course someone could have dialed the wrong number, dialed a number they didn't want, but realized their mistake immediately and cut the call before I managed to answer. But I suddenly find this very hard to believe.

I turn to the next blank page of my large-format exercise book and write along the top—*Informer to the Estonian Republic*. There, that is the title. Intriguing enough, and the large capitals suggest a hidden double meaning, giving the title an ironic undertone.

I write: Is love of one's country sufficient motivation for a thinking person to sell his soul on the marketplace? To be or not to be an informer? An ordinary citizen who has to identify with a subject of the State; compulsion; self-justification; non-existent choice; an unfamiliar post-socialist situation—a sincere, heartfelt love for the State.

And why not also use the opportunity presented to me on a plate (silver salver? plastic dish?) to turn the situation into something useful for myself, write a story, develop the unpleasant situation in which I have landed into a novella or novel, it would be like a documentary or, in other words, literature standing with both feet (wearing soldier's boots, nicely polished and creaking) firmly on the ground.

The telephone rings again, cutting through my newly awakened wave of inspiration, and I suspect that when I pick up my writing again in a short while, it will not look as good as it did a moment ago. "Is Mrs So-and-So available?" asks a man's voice with intrusive familiarity—the voice is completely strange to me and I can't place it. "Oh, you'll have to wait a while, she's in the States and will be back at the end of the month," I say in a voice expressing deep sympathy, at the same time emphasizing the ambiguity of the word "available." Where do people get such expressions, I'd like to ask.

*

He looks like a bank official—that new species of Eastern European that has suddenly rained onto our street-scene as if from the heavens (it's completely out of the question that the humble Soviet bank clerk could have developed into the likes of him). He's a businesslike man, who not doubt knows what he's doing (I hope). I cannot guess where the glass ceiling of his career might be, but he is at any rate doing everything he can to get there as quickly (and while as young) as possible (and when he's arrived, who knows what happens then).

I don't bother asking whether he wants tea or coffee, I ask whether, at the end of our conversation, I will still be able to refuse collaboration, as everything hitherto has been like buying a pig in a poke.

"In what way a pig?" he says with suspicion, distrust; his eyes begin to dart to and fro, suddenly his face brightens—he now gives the impression that not for one moment did hesitation ever cross his mind, and says: "Naturally, you'll have to sign a form indicating that you won't make unwarranted use of any information received from me, then you can forget all about it."

"OK," I say with satisfaction. "Do come out with your concerns, you know I am most curious." (What use of language! I feel as if a wry smile has formed on my lips, but I let it rest there. The intelligence officer can think of it what he likes.)

"What we're concerned about is green terrorism," is how he starts, sighing (probably unintentionally) before the word "terrorism." "Over the last few years extremist environmental campaigners have become ever more active. They will stop at nothing to achieve their goals. Disruption, acts of sabotage, even murder. Unlike other terrorist groups, they don't go in for boasting about their actions afterward. They like to give events the appearance of accidents—you can see where that seemingly innocuous environmental activity is leading. We have good grounds for believing that such groups are gaining ground, and we are at pains to set limits."

"Well," I say. "If you take into account the latest review of my latest novel, I ought to be a suspicious person from your point of view because of my own green thinking."

"That review was commissioned by us," he says, lowering his gaze as if ashamed.

It's all very well for you to be ashamed, I think, hurt but also astonished, gloating with Schadenfreude: this means that one of our more respected critics does jobs for the secret police!

"But maybe I'm an ardent proponent of radical ideas?"

"We know that you're not."

And indeed I am not, I think, downcast, and I suddenly see in my mind's eye how I exchanged ideas with Teodor about an environmental catastrophe in quite vehement terms ten days ago or so at the Artists' Club.

I say nothing.

"Have you ever heard of a firm called 'Full-Blooded Recreation'?"

I don't even want to open my mouth. I can image that someone has made great efforts to undermine the ground beneath my feet, so that without my knowing I've been taking part in things (they have, no doubt, consulted KGB files), so that the knot around my throat has been tightened by stealth and then—abracadabra—the unfortunate creature is in the bag.

"A while back a married couple, the Ummals, Enniver and Alma, returned to their native Estonia from Germany. They bought up twenty or so farmhouses in some borderland parish, did them up, and started renting them out. The business plan is that people taking a break can live there without the usual creature comforts, and will have to expend a good deal of physical effort doing the farm work, running the farm's economy.

"The motto of the firm is: 'Only when someone draws water with a pail and chops wood with an ax to feed himself does he feel that blood is flowing in his veins, rather than Coca Cola.' Despite the steep price, such vacations have been a success.

"We have collated information on the Ummals' green background and their links to extremist circles. We have to keep an eye on them, and to that end it is necessary for you to infiltrate their set-up. Our assignment is for you to make yourself visible, to act as a decoy for the Ummals, so that they get the concrete urge to get in touch with you."

*

Once I have seen my guest to the door, the wall clock begins chiming at full pelt, I count the strokes (out of habit), my brain registers them exactly with the result: it is five o'clock, about the right time to end my working day—to pack up and go home. I don't really have anywhere to go, as I'm already at home. By now my guest will no doubt have hit rush hour traffic; it will take him the best part of an hour to cross to the other side of the city to the other side (no question that's where he's heading), there are so many private vehicles these days, no one can be bothered to walk anymore, or take the bus. Something has to be done: some chemical compound will have to be discovered, so that if twenty or so grams are added to the contents of the gas tank the gasoline within will be ruined, and the automobile rendered useless—the engine all clogged up, the cars standing there at the edge of the road like warning monuments for clouds of smog.

"I can't help it, in my heart of hearts I feel such tremendous warmth toward the greens." (Try again.)

"I can't help it, somewhere in the pit of my stomach I have the feeling that green terror is perhaps the only thing keeping us from the terrible end approaching at an ever-increasing pace." (Again.)

"I can't help it, rational thinking suggests that green thinking may be the only thing that can supply any kind of future prospect for mankind.

"And yet it isn't possible to do the right thing by way of the wrong methods. Well, it is possible, but it just shouldn't be done. It's not a nice way of doing things.

"When I exchanged ideas recently with Teodor on this subject, I did stress that no one should have the right to decide who or what constitutes excess in our world today. There is no acceptable criterion for such a decision." (That could be the theoretical approach on my part.)

Well, there we are! That little conversation with Teodor will have been an adequate check on the way the future secret agent will be thinking—I can now approach our conversation from a different angle. What I mean is that one of our leading art critics lives (an interesting? a profitable?) double life, and is informing (no point in looking for a nicer word) on me. He is surely, in his own estimation, doing the good and honorable thing, with a microphone in his buttonhole and a tape-recorder taped to his belly button.

But. From today onwards I myself am in the same boat. So as to (I must, rapidly and accurately formulate a justification, in order to let myself off) . . . I refuse to think the thought to its logical conclusion, dial Teodor's number, hear his whining (no better word for it) voice and ask whether he couldn't tell me something about Joseph Beuys. He doesn't ask why I'm interested in Beuys, he says that I can drop round at his place this evening, then I can hear everything that interests me. I ask what time evening is for him. He says (I understand what he's hinting at) that by nine or ten he wouldn't mind a glass or two of the hard stuff.

When I look back at our conversation it seems that Teo (don't try it on with any Vincent / Theo associations!) had quite radical ideas: only thanks to the indescribable misery in which most of the population of the world finds itself do our type of people have the opportunity to squander, and because of such inequality, life goes on, at least for the time being. It is not possible to foster fecundity while promoting welfare. We are incapable of understanding where humanism and the brotherhood of the whole of mankind is leading us in the long term, what the point of aid and educational programs to less developed countries will be in twenty years' time. It should not be forgotten that natural and food resources are limited on this planet.

He gave a good performance, I think to myself, smiling wryly, but at the same time the thoroughness with which he had prepared my recruitment amazed me—as if the whole business really did constitute one great big danger. I could boast about my own importance in the matter, but instead I gradually grow worried: maybe my vacation at "Full-Blooded Recreation" will be no vacation at all, but instead (good reason to let a couple of Bond films pass before my mind's eye) . . . And I can't really imagine the everyday life of an informer . . .

*

As I step though his door, I could look my colleague Teodor conspiratorially in the eye, but think it would be more stylish to shake hands with my friend (informer) heartily as I'm on the point of leaving, and whisper: We'll win anyway! Now I fish the bottle of whisky out of my bag, which brings a smug smile to the lips of the art historian and makes his wife grow gloomy, which (presumably) means that I shouldn't have brought anything, but I imagine (by way of justification) that nothing much can go wrong when two informers do a bit of tippling together.

In actual fact, Teodor has in recent years begun making a name for himself as an installation artist, and if I call him a gentleman artist as a joke, his eyes may sparkle even more than when he saw the bottle. I'm not really at home in the field of fine art, which means that I've never bothered to immerse myself in artists' problems (which are, on the face of it, incomprehensible even to the artists themselves), and I cannot judge Teodor's status in the art world, even though I have seen the corners of one or two men's mouths quiver at the mention of Teodor's installations. I would imagine that even that secret policeman I spoke with is better oriented in the world of contemporary art than I am—at any rate, in connection with Enniver Ummal and his links to the Fluxus movement and his friendship with Beuys, he did talk about such things as if mentioning names generally known.

Teodor has had someone do renovation work during the summer (or has he done it himself?), he seems to be proud of something about his home, though I can't really fathom why, as the interior strikes you with its lack of style (deliberate?), and I grow embarrassed at the thought that the owner of this apartment assesses the work of other artists. But then Teodor's daughter Ulrike comes in from another room and stands flirtatiously on the threshold and a thought flashes into my mind from thirty years back, as this girl is dressed in a neat Pioneer uniform and the three stripes on her sleeve reveal that she is the chairperson of the Higher Students' Brigade council.

"A silk neckerchief is good for your throat," explains Teodor. "Keeps your neck warm." Ulrike turns on her heel and looks coquettishly over her shoulder at me. She has shot up over the summer, will be starting to wear a bra one of these days. "Come on," Teodor says to me, inviting me to Ulrike's room, which is straight out of *Pioneer Illustrated* from the 1950s. "A living illustration," says Teodor laughing, as if filled with joy. Ulrike pulls a face (you must understand, Dad's a bit you-know-what) and sits at the desk with the computer. Above the desk hovers a model airplane.

"Joseph Beuys is the greatest German artist since Dürer," Teodor pronounces after a good swig of his whisky. "Just imagine back in the 1950s, when people were debating about figurative and non-figurative art, when artists were wrestling on canvas with problems of form and color, Beuys was interested in the relationship between crystalline and amorphous life, the heat properties of fat, wax, and honey as organic substances, and the role of heat in general in works of art.

"He was indisputably the first to understand the deeply artistic nature of *process*. For him, a sculpture in fat was a dynamic process, in which the potential for melting and solidifying were both embodied. Depending on the amount of energy or will he possesses, a human being influences, or doesn't, the substance of life, and thus creates living or dead sculptures, where a dead one contains the eternal potential to come alive, to become amorphous. Consequently—the meditative and stimulated state of humans creates non-linear time and super-space, gives life and consciousness as materials the ability to flow outwards beyond birth and death."

(*Bullshit*—I am thinking in American terms, then in Finnish: *hevospaska, perkele* . . . without being able to penetrate the flow of words to reach the thought behind which would render them logical, but I can't just—I grow embarrassed, don't dare—ask Teodor to give his spiel again, this time more slowly, I have the stupid feeling that I'm listening to a foreign language, where the meaning of the words escape me.)

"Try to conjure up, visually, Beuys's 'Siberian Symphony, Part One,' for piano: small heaps of clay are put on the piano, previously a dead rabbit has been hung on a blackboard; a small twig is pushed into each heap of clay; Beuys begins to play a free-form piano piece while his assistant takes a wire from the piano to the blackboard and removes the rabbit's heart; the music starts again from the beginning . . . Here shock and provocation serve as stimuli to expand the essence of human existence; the symbolism indicates the mysteries of death and birth, life in its eternal cycle; the way of using symbols nonetheless gives the theme an unexpected power and brings it into consonance with the consciousness of civilized humankind; the myth stuck in the human subconscious in dark times is revived in artistic language adequate for the technocratic world."

*

Teodor pours himself a glass of whisky, a mechanical gesture which fails, no doubt, to register with his conscious mind. He doesn't even glance at my glass, he is so wrapped up in himself—and I smile when I notice that he runs his palm across the neck of the bottle before he pours. This is habit whose (murky) background I am unable to fathom, but the movement is in harmony with Teodor's outward appearance: his robust facial features, caricatured by sensual lips, and a special (lecherous?) glint in his eye (at first glance the image in my mind is that of a pervert peeking at a young boy who has just entered the public toilets, though I have never heard such things said about Teodor), his body is more like that of a sportsman (which he was, at a respectable level, in his youth) than an intellectual. And he is trying with his choice of clothes (in the appropriate Marxist-Maoist manner of the Sixties) to be the proletarian, beyond fashion, especially with the checked shirts and creased suits that distinguish him from his class. With all this he seems to be shouting in people's faces: I am not like you, you damned little intellectuals.

The way that Teodor deals with his opponents resembles a brawl where the only and ultimate aim is to put the other person down. No fair play—a kick in the balls, and that's the end of it.

The energy and obstinacy with which Teodor realizes his ideas is also unintelligent, there is something of Jack London in it, effective and vital, as if constantly driven by some inexplicable thirst or hunger. In the 1990s, he managed to become one of the leading art critics—he had himself become an institution, one that attempted to overthrow other institutions, and he didn't waste time—some artists had managed, amidst the absurdities of Soviet times, to make an international name for themselves, and Teodor's primary aim was to wipe the slate clean of them and trample them into the dust. He did what he liked because he knew (had the inkling) that no one would stop him, and the mutual envy among his colleagues gave his own articles a sneering undertone. Someone (maybe

Vennet) compared him to a character in Dick Francis's novel *Nerve*, where the television reporter Kemp-Lore, who is himself unable to race on account of an allergy (to horses), begins constantly (in the literal sense of the word) to wreak revenge on top jockeys, ruining their careers and their lives. One evening, Vennet drew the attention of his table companions to the human ghost of a drunk Teodor, citing Francis: Look, all of his life-energy, all of his brilliant talent is being wasted in order to hurt people who've done him no ill.

He has the gift of the gab, and is witty, especially when he's whispering details of some new intrigue into your ear.

I like him—he's a real jewel for our young republic, someone who's able to shape his surroundings at his pleasure, and I'm not well enough acquainted with the political nuances of the art-world to be able to censure his actions. His penchant for alcohol—like that of other social climbers (and Teodor is indisputably a cultural climber)—is like an infantile disorder, but in his case (I could be wrong here) it seems to have gradually shifted and become a chronic sickness.

*

I'm listening to the art critic frothing on (emitting foam like a fire extinguisher), but I haven't come all the way from home merely to rank the power of his words, so that what is unimportant becomes important and what is important takes on a special significance.

"Beuys aims to liberate people from a methodology of cognition totally subsumed under rationality, in order to achieve a harmonious existence again," says Teodor, "and the dead rabbit's heart turns into a glittering diamond."

Deeply infatuated—I think to myself as I listen to the tale—that's how people talk about women they love. Teodor's swollen face has begun to become flushed, as he pours himself another whisky. As his voice grows louder, Ulrike comes to stand in the doorway, staring fixedly at her father, who doesn't even notice her.

In the kitchen a plate (saucer, bowl, tureen) falls to the floor and smashes to pieces.

"But what link is there between Beuys and the green movement?" I ask, to move the conversation over to the patch that interests me.

"Interested to know where you got that from. Not much said about 'The Organization for Direct Democracy.' Beuys's ecological ideas tend to remain in the shadow of those about art, but 'The Rose of Direct Democracy' is hardly ever mentioned—as if it didn't even exist."

"I've heard that someone with 'green views'—the former Estonian exile Enniver Ummal—is supposed to have been a big buddy of Beuys'ss."

"Ummal? Haven't heard that. With dead greats, it's often like that—anyone who's exchanged three words with them must have been their big buddy. But none of them are worth the dirt under Beuys'ss fingernails. During the 1960s he was already a man of the next century, and has achieved, in recent decades, a complete renewal. What Beuys actually meant to his contemporaries can be seen by the over three hundred students he had at the Düsseldorf Academy of Art, who all, when he was sacked, left with him. By the way, Enniver Ummal's wife happens to have been one of those students. Even in those days, Beuys status as a prophet was greater than his status as a professor."

"Teodor, my dear, could you help me with something," his wife twitters at the door like a sparrow. Teodor stubs his cigarette out in a coffee cup and rises, tripping almost immediately (not over anything), and takes a couple of steps to right himself.

He doesn't know Ummal, yet he does know the fact that his wife was a student of Beuys'ss (!). I will now have to interpret that. Presumably Teodor has been given orders not to know anything about the Ummals. But for what reason? Maybe he's being prepared for infiltration as well. An alcoholic can function as an art critic, but a secret agent has to have a clear head, so as not to blurt things out.

Teodor does not reappear, hushed voices can be heard coming from the kitchen. Teodor's love of alcohol is known all over the city, and it's unlikely the secret police want to exploit that sort of person. Even the KGB left alcoholics alone. I know that the wise thing to do now would be to get up and go. Leave the family to their own devices, leave Teodor to his well-deserved alcoholic haze.

*

The evening is mild, a warm evening in early September, it is not yet late, in the concrete walls of apartment blocks hundreds of windows are lit up, windows open to the warm evening, from which the sounds of voices and music waft—a monotonous thumping, not the tinkling of the piano or accordion music; ahead of me is a gang of youths, I cross the road, not wanting to tempt them to ask me for a cigarette or a light.

The feeling of unease that the youth gang gives me will not leave, rumors of violence are amplified into sinister imaginings: I am already twitching in my own blood, gurgling, crying soundlessly for help as in a dream, but blow follows blow, they need twitching flesh for the *sheer delight of beating*—and all of this without a pang of conscience. I can already hear rapid footsteps behind me, breathing, my heart is pounding louder than anything else; then the safety of a taxi light heaves into view, I take a few brisk steps on the pavement and wave an arm.

"This is the house where they held their hostages," says the taxi-driver and slows down. "On the second floor, the end windows," he explains glaring out at the building as if there could still be something interesting to see there.

There is nothing to be seen, everything is peaceful, ordinary. "A friend of mine who lives across the way said that he heard gunshots yesterday evening, and he looked out the window and saw more police cars racing up, there were people running, shooting, just like in a real Hollywood film, but then this friend of mine felt that something was missing . . . and only a while later did he realize that it was the background music." The taxi-driver laughs in a carefree way at his own joke, but I think that now that I've driven past the place where it happened, that hostage-taking will become more special (will affect me more) when I hear about it on the radio or read about it in the paper.

"In the old days, there weren't so many corpses at the same time," says the taxi-driver, and he has the voice of a reporter announcing a fantastic sports win.

When I open the (three) locks of my own empty apartment and shut the door firmly behind me, I feel that my feeling of unease has become sheer fear. My heart hurts—my heart is pounding, beating restlessly—and physical pain is not far off either. I switch on the TV set and lie down on the sofa. The late news is about to begin, there are advertising smiles and the unreal sparkle of products, the greens too green, blues too blue, whites too pure white.

"Kitty, kitty, kitty, come on, come on . . . " I invite it, and wonder why it didn't rush up to me in the doorway and say in a commanding voice "Food's ready," and it hasn't drummed against the fridge door with its paws either. The cat isn't answering. There was shooting among the wooden houses of the Kalamaja district, some youth killed someone with an automatic weapon and wounded five others his own age. The perpetually jolly woman director of the National Library announces the Great Catastrophe: some hitherto unknown insects have eaten up meters of books—no, the exact amount of damage is impossible to describe, suffice it to say there are dangerous insects in every depot.

Horrible things happen in my home town and it would be nice right now to have the cat on my chest, to be stroking it, listening to its breathing and purring, I can't understand where the cat has got to. Have I left a window open and allowed the creature to jump out into the evil world? The windows are all shut, it is sleeping under the kitchen table. Sleeping, and is impossible to wake. It is dead.

My dear old cat, now grown cold and stiff! At first I feel no sorrow or regret, I am thinking that if I now go away for a longer period of time, I won't have to bother the neighbor's girl, to ask her to look after the cat; won't have to rush to the market in the morning to get fish for the cat. One less problem in life, life has become easier.

I stare at the cat's corpse—I don't want to throw it into the trash bin, will have to drive out of town and bury my dear pet in some nice natural spot. But better do it tomorrow, or whenever I travel out to the "Full-Blooded Recreation" farmhouse.

I put the cat's corpse (long, as if stretched, stiff) in a carrier bag (I don't like touching dead things, I wrap it in a sheet of newspaper, so as not to have to touch its fur), tie up the bag with a shoelace (can't find any string) and put the whole thing in the fridge.

Then I wash my hands long and carefully under the faucet.

Second Chapter

Some sound awakens me (a muffled thump, as if a heavy object has fallen: metal, maybe the cylinder from an automobile?), in my imagination I see a blurred metal cylinder, weigh its unexpected heaviness in my hands, its fall to the floor—a dull thud, a dent in the floorboard that I spot later on; I can't link my unexpected memory with anything concrete, it's possible that it is simply the continuation of a dream, but suddenly I'm wide awake, tensely awaiting a new sound, agitated, listening with every fiber of nerve.

Then another thump, amplified, dying swiftly away, as if someone had kicked the front door with his heel. I jump up, want to rush to the spyhole in the door, then stop, open the door of the bathroom and let it slam shut—I've not yet looked through the spyhole, I *don't want to do so*, since what I see there (the ugly faces of some brutal thugs) will begin to oppress and haunt me. I open and close the door a second time, walk with heavy step across the entrance hall, so that anyone standing outside will understand that there are people inside, which will complicate his criminal plans and hopefully render them impossible to implement, so that he'll realize it would be better for him to move on, find a better apartment, one whose lock he can break, and then burgle the place.

I should get a recorded dog's bark (the rough barking of a Rottweiler, or the sharp angry bark of an Alsatian), is what I have thought on several occasions. Then I heave a sigh and put my eye to the spyhole.

In the (formal) light of the corridor a half-open door can be seen, leading to the stairs, on the floor lies a whitish pink lump (long, blunt ends, looks as if it's covered in fabric, wrapped in fabric) and I can't work out where it's come from or imagine what it is used for. When I retreat from the door, the whitish pink object is still in my mind's eye, and I go and take another look, but it's no use—the four doors to the apartments on this floor are nocturnal, dead (!), the door to the stairs is half-open. I am not so inquisitive as to open my door and go and take a look at what's lying there on the floor. Caution is the mother of security—I don't want anyone opening that half-open door fully and attacking me.

When I am back in bed, I feel a strong yearning for my cat. In its old age (I can guess how old it was, maybe twelve years old, my daughter was ten when we got it) it had become something of a teddy bear, it couldn't get to sleep unless it had its head resting on my shoulder and its body in my armpit; it would purr itself and me to sleep and the breathing of the little cat's body (heavy with sleep, just like that of a human being) always fended off loneliness.

It is possible that the need of animals and human beings for each other is close to love, although looked at superficially it appears to be purely altruistic. As if they don't demand anything from each other. They never ask questions such as torment human couples: Does it love me? Does it love anyone more than me? Does it love me more that I love it? Maybe all these questions about love, which measure love, put it to the test, examine it, interrogate it, all destroy love at its embryonic stage. Maybe we are incapable of love because we want to be loved, in other words we want something (love) from the other, instead of approaching the other with no claims, simply wanting them to stay with us.

Now it is in the fridge, where it used to have the (pretty tiresome) habit of jumping in after food, and on some occasions I failed to notice and left in there for some time (I've read somewhere that cats can stand very low temperatures; I can imagine that tests have been done in freezing chambers: someone watches as the cat is covered with rime and gradually turns to ice . . .).

In my mind's eye, on a muggy day in August we are traveling back to town from the countryside, and stop off to say goodbye to the milk lady; two weeks in the artist Vennet's summer cottage have passed in the twinkling of an eye, my daughter strokes a cat (one of many) and asks the lady how many there are on the farm. "A couple dozen wandering around," she says—she opens the door to the barn, and lying on the hay are four tiny kittens. "Let's take one," the child begs. "Take two," says the milk lady. "You can't imagine how nicely they play with one another." My heart goes soft all of a sudden (the pleading eyes of children + sweet little kittens). "Oh, alright then," I mutter a promise, the lady fetches some milk from the pail cooling in the well to take with us on our journey. And cats come from all over when they smell the milk.

The milk woman (lady?) has never killed a cat (kittens are usually put in a sack with a number of stones, then placed in a bucketful of water till they stop writhing, then buried in the sack in some deep hole; smaller children are told that they have been given to a new owner, older ones have to face the fact that it isn't that easy to look for new owners, and they don't always succeed in finding one), she either couldn't or didn't want to get rid of her first brood of cats, and so there ensued a progression whose mathematical inevitability is impossible to stop without decisive action being taken.

Destroying life is cruel, but it would be just as cruel to other species (e.g. songbirds) were we to let cats breed unchecked.

Well, I think, won't be taking another cat.

Those two weeks in Vennet's summer cottage were the closest I've been to nature in all my life. I'm not ashamed to admit that I am a city dweller. There are city people and country people and those in between (who don't feel happy either way). I like city life, both my present and former wife like the city, and our type is a pure, developed strain of human being.

Those like Vennet are amphibious, so to speak—summer in the country, winter in the city—but that is presumably necessary for painters. I was looking at a catalogue of Vennet's paintings only the other day, where he depicts the Schnell Pond in the park— the pond's green edge, reeds, a path across the grass, and suddenly amid the green grass there is a red cabin. The title of the painting is "Cabin in the Park," but is given in English in this catalogue as "Dressing Cabin in Park," which adds an unexpected nuance— there is a cabin in the park, where people can dress and undress— and the painting is suddenly coded differently, as the cabin now receives a specific context, which wouldn't otherwise enter the heads of the viewers.

By the way, the pond isn't depicted where it actually is in the surrounding landscape.

I think that I ought to call Vennet, and draw his attention to the significance of the "dressing cabin" (the artist himself is hardly likely to have picked up on this nuance or thought about it), that I ought to take Vennet along for a few days to this summer cottage, because it's easier there to adapt. Vennet is not in the country right now, I saw him walking in town recently—he's supposed to have rented the cottage out to some French people.

As pre-sleep images (the blinking yellow traffic lights, the whitish-pink object creeping towards me) glide past my eyes and sleep enfeebles my body, making it seem lighter, suddenly, with unexpected sharpness (like a slap in the face), the change that came over Teodor (behavior, stance, way of speaking) when I hinted at his connections with the secret police springs to mind. He suddenly grew wary (almost sobered up, even) and my unthinking chatter made him understand that I in particular had been given some tasks to fulfill by the secret police. That could have been interesting news for him. Especially if he himself had nothing to do with spying and the informer was someone else sitting at our table.

Well, so what—I try to be above such things—but a vague feeling (shame? fear?) keeps bothering me, driving away sleep, getting me back on my feet.

I drink a glass of water, and without putting on the kitchen light I fumble my way (actually it has grown so light that everything in the kitchen is clearly visible) toward my cigarettes and lighter (a Zippo—an expensive present from my wife), the kitchen momentarily lights up (must be quite visible from outside), after which the glow of the cigarette is the only sign that betrays me (a sniper would no doubt be easily able to pick me off).

It has been raining, the asphalt and roofs of cars shine, it could be late (or early?), only a few windows are lit up, there is a party again in the third-floor apartment across from mine, where a married couple of roughly my age (or a little younger) live, who are always rummaging in the garbage bins; the man is now sleeping with his head on the kitchen table (or has he been murdered?), something is happening beyond the uncurtained window of the room next door; some man is eagerly exercising between the legs of the lady of the house, a second, a young man with cropped hair is going through the drawers of the clothes closet.

Just like any other day, I think, as I extinguish the cigarette under the faucet (can't find an ashtray), after which I put the half-drenched cigarette on the edge of the table, fill up my tea glass and drink some water tasting of the city. That woman has an unpleasant, a repulsively sleazy appearance, bright red painted lips making her face look like some parody; her idiotic smile making her look so innocent, and yet she seems perfectly natural when rummaging through the garbage, half her body in the bin, trying to fish out all manner of things as if they were treasure.

When I looked through the spyhole again, the whitish pink object has vanished from the floor (presumably it was some wrapped-up object forgotten about by the neighbor and later retrieved); I'm thinking that the sound that woke me up must have been the lift, then my neighbor's door slamming. I could go and see what time it is—find out my exact location in time—but instead I look up at the blueish color of the ceiling, and think that Greenpeace must be well financed to be able to afford its own boat and bureaucracy.

The TV images of police officers welding through chains with which housewives have attached themselves to trees, then carrying them off to waiting police cars, is a clear instance of sentimentality; the green idea acquires a halo of martyrdom, and at that moment thousands of viewers, feet tucked into their slippers will be all for the greens, and against the forces of law and order (the damn police!). The bodies of dead fish in the water by the shore, oil-covered birds floundering, a Greenpeace rubber dinghy pushed out of the way of a whaler—all of these things influence people, and no one is in any doubt that the greens are fighting for a good and just cause. (But!) If some Greenpeace branch office runs out of money, some huge corporation or other will start doing things: you bastards, polluting our nature. If you won't install purification plants that'll cost you tens of millions (the most modern kind, of course) by next year, we'll do all we can to bring your production to a standstill. Of course, there is another possibility— support our organization with a couple of million, so that we can finish our current project—and we'll leave you in peace.

I imagine that such a thing is not entirely impossible. Seen from a distance, many ideas are wonderful and just. But often the wrong methods are used to solve problems, and people shut their eyes to reality in the light of their ideas. After all, the lefties of the Sixties were still filled with enthusiasm, though the tanks rolled onto the streets of Prague with Moscow laughing up its sleeve (maybe this was taken to be "our" show of strength?!). Or how can you understand how Mao, that great swimmer, won the support of the left-wing intelligentsia of Europe, when even an idiot could see what was hidden behind such grand ideas during China's Cultural Revolution.

I remember an article about some poststructuralist (Julia

Kristeva?), where a number of instances of binary opposition were examined: night/day, light/darkness, nature/culture. At some point, unexpectedly, a pair of words you once noticed (and instantly forgot) affords the Cultural Revolution in China a new meaning: culture opposed to nature, through "green" eyes.

That man from the secret police talked about a (theoretical) threat that the greens would come to power in some small state or other, inevitably start to implement anti-human projects. "In Kampuchea, for instance" he said worriedly, "a very bloody project was called into being,"

I cannot escape the thought that behind the information intended for my consumption there are quite different things, which I have no access to. All that's clear to me is that in some way or other they need me. Unseen threads are being tied behind my back, and without my knowledge, and someone is pulling them so that writer So-and-So will begin to dance like a puppet.

The fact that my own world, the one in which I live, is quite different from that of Minister Leo, is of no interest to anyone. I have to be manipulated in such a way that the elements of Leo's world become part of mine, so that our differences become (when all is said and done) similarities.

The apparent (our) worlds are fragile—for instance, I constructed an image based on some association, in which Teodor was the epitome of an informer for the secret police, one who had been assigned to probe my way of thinking. Once this image was complete, I never doubted for an instant that it was true, and my subsequent behavior was attuned to this (unverifiable) situation (which appeared as a fact in *my* world).

During our recent debate Teodor tried to claim that natural

selection had been brought to an end by medicine—those who were unfit for life suddenly achieved the right to live, weak people breed other weaknesses, the end result of this being that mankind, now unfit to live, will die out. This argument had a ring of misanthropy about it, but (in fact!) it was a humane one. While I first assumed that Teodor was defending his ideas for the sheer hell of it, and later believed that this was the acting out of a provocation set up by the secret police, I have now (at last!) realized that Teodor actually did think this way—only now do I remember his furious performance some time back, acted out in the pages of the press, where he censured the work of the National Cultural Endowment which allots pensions and subsidies to older artists, and which is entirely a problem of social welfare, and where he claimed that all the money in question should go to subsidizing contemporary art projects.

In my mind's eye I see a darkish room in the Artists' Club, the noise of a restaurant (the clinking of cutlery and crockery, the murmur of voices, the loud replies), cigarette smoke hanging in clouds above the tables. It is the same room where, some ten years previously many incisive thoughts and words were collated for KGB files, with which your best drinking-pal and colleague would try to lighten his own burden of sin at your expense. In reality the provocation came from the mouth of someone I didn't know, someone with an unassuming appearance, a bland face (probably?), someone whom Dinner knew: "Ecological reality has never supported any form of social or societal progress. It would be ghastly if India or China were to develop as welfare states. The super-consumers should no longer help anyone else to join them. Development aid should be limited to birth control programs."

Teodor's claim that AIDS is no tribulation, but a blessing for mankind, that only sickness and hunger can save mankind, poured oil on the flames.

In fact it was Dinner himself who, along with a friend of his, came to our table and offered me work: "Listen, in my opinion you're the right man to translate *Trout Fishing in America*," is what he said.

Dinner was one of the younger generation of authors, who, after a couple of pretty bland collections of short stories, had devoted himself to publishing. I didn't really know him very well, we were nodding acquaintances, and of late I had heard that he'd taken to playing the saxophone at night, thereby angering all of his neighbors. The fact that a younger man was offering me the chance to translate *Trout Fishing*, dragged me up by the ears, momentarily right into the clouds. I had read Brautigan's *In Watermelon Sugar* about a year before, but I didn't really think any more about it, other than that it was a very good book.

I asked whether this book was the novel that ended with the word "mayonnaise." "Exactly," said Dinner. "An early dream of mine was to publish a book that ended with the word "mayonnaise."

Third Chapter

I have to go through the door of the main office of "Full-Blooded Recreation" at exactly 11:05—meaning five minutes after the Ummals; they have a habit of visiting their firm at the same time every day and staying there for an hour or so. It is a very welcome trait (for an informer) when people have regular habits.

The office is right in the center of town, earlier the building housed a small and cozy bookshop, whose owner (a well-known bibliophile) was found beaten up last year in the stairwell of a fourteen story apartment block (he'd been visiting his sister). His wallet (with the couple of hundred *krooni* he'd borrowed from his sister) and coat had been taken, and for a long time he hovered between life and death, and was never the same again. The book-shop (which was deep in debt) was declared bankrupt, and the Ummals were at the right place at the right time to rent the rooms. It is eleven o'clock—the secret agent (snoop) has just enough time to stroll across Raekoja plats—Town Hall Square—buy a news-paper, light a cigarette and observe a helicopter whirring above the city. It is windy, so I have to waste several matches to light my cigarette (I left my Zippo at home on the kitchen table), and when I try to open my newspaper, the wind prevents me.

164 people in hospital! Terrible railroad accident! Cloud of poison gas over the marketplace!

On the arts page there is one of Teodor's articles, where he "takes to task" one of his regular adversaries. I skim the first paragraphs and identify a familiar theme—Beuys is the greatest German artist since Dürer—but I haven't the energy to read the article in more detail, as I suddenly see a woman I know coming towards me, but whose route is being obstructed by a group of tourists in front of the Town Hall, so that I'm able to nip round the corner and am just in time for my appointment.

At exactly 11:05 I step inside "Full-Blooded Recreation." The doorbell rings like in any good grocer's. Ting-a-ling. The room is furnished in a ponderously farmhouse manner (*my homestead has a black ceiling . . .* that sort of thing): furniture made of beams, fish net (!) drapes, one wall covered with household objects like a display at an ethnographical museum, spinning-wheels in the corner, a massive (oak?) table with a computer, like something from quite another century; a pretty and (no doubt permanently) smiling blonde like in an advertisement; at the ringing of the bell, three pairs of eyes turn to look at me.

At exactly 11:05, I am standing perplexedly before the crossfire of three pairs of eyes, the ting-a-ling has just died away, leaving my ears free for the soughing of the sea (from loudspeakers), which gradually subsides, becoming so quiet that it no longer prevents speech; my gaze records the first picture (the flash of a flashgun, the shutter opens for a hundredth of a second), then focuses (a revolting word !) on a man whose appearance makes me start—the mythical hero Kalevipoeg, our very own Kalevipoeg, is peering at me—but then I realize that it isn't him after all, it's a short man who has stepped from the pages of a folk epic like a little souvenir;

and the woman who straightens up is strikingly small, her brown (penetrating) eyes are sizing me up (age, weight, height, dress), you can see from her face that she's making instantaneous decisions about me (price?!) which will be very hard to change later on. The woman smiles coquettishly (alluringly?), which, given her age, strikes me as comic, and for a moment I think that when young she must have been a prostitute and her grimace is now beyond her control, but then a sweet smile appears on the face of the man too, he comes toddling forward and stretches out his hand.

The three smiles say that I am welcome in this room and may proceed without fear or further ado, and the extended hands shake my own. I utter my name and now hear that I am dealing with Enniver Ummal, the owner of "Full-Blooded Recreation," who wishes to be of service to me.

I let them know that I want to stay for a couple of weeks away from the noise and bustle of the city, to enjoy the fall in my native land, and work without being disturbed. "I am the writer So-and-So," I explain. "This darn city never allows you to concentrate."

"Yes, indeed, unfortunately I have not yet got 'round to reading your latest novel, but just a day or so back I happened to see a review, from which I concluded that you had done something rather special," says Ummal in clear (accent-free!) Estonian, but on hearing that I'd like to travel out there today or tomorrow, he spreads his arms dramatically: "I'm really sorry, but we're booked up until the end of November. We'd like to help but really can't. You see, we're planning to renovate Saagna Manor and turn it into a house of creativity, where writers, artists and musicians can create together—it would be a sort of commune of mutual inspiration, and with such a building we could make cultural history."

Then the telephone rings: someone (who can it be!) cancels his booking, the place (a farmhouse near the sea) is unexpectedly free, Enniver Ummal is genuinely delighted, and starting tomorrow I can begin my "new life" (as he keeps on stressing)—he asks hesitantly whether his visit wouldn't disturb me, as he'd like to see personally whether my new life is "happy." "I do believe that we have a lot in common," he intones, tapping meaningfully on the page of the newspaper where huge letters are shouting the message: "Cloud of poison gas on the marketplace!" Then he shakes my hand in farewell.

*

"You know," I say to Vennet. "I'm going to start a new life tomorrow."

"Going to stop smoking and drinking. I know, I've heard things like that innumerable times from friends. I no longer believe them and I don't know why they bother mentioning it and boasting about it. As if they want to shuffle their problems off onto others. But they don't get anywhere with me."

"That's where you're wrong," I shake my head theatrically. "I'm going to be living in a house by the sea, where's there no TV or telephone or newspapers or central heating or electricity or running water or bathtub, the nearest bar thirty kilometers away and the Artists' Club one hundred and eighty-five.

"I'm going to stoke the stove and the cooking range with logs, whisk myself in the sauna, pick mushrooms and berries in the woods to the best of my ability, and fish a few fish from the sea."

Vennet decides to laugh loudly and I know that my story amuses him: the townie, the street urchin of yore, the man of the city. You were brought up in the city, and that's where you ought to stay!

*

"This one's called 'An Unending Landscape,'" says Vennet, and puts a square meter of green onto the easel, which at first glance looks to be a harmonious composition, a rolling landscape above which hovers a lone cloud in a clear sky, but then I realize that the cloud is green and the sky is green and the whole landscape is a congealed green, through which, from the bottom left-hand corner and across the hills to infinity, there is a trail drawn through the green with patches of white blades of grass, forming a dotted line as in the middle of a carriageway, as if a white-line-painting vehicle has driven over hill and dale.

The painting is fascinating, the picture only begins to affect you after you've been looking at it for a while, and I realize that the effect is increased by a paradox of thought—the green cloud, as if made of moss, the green sky and even the white line seem natural somehow, as if that is what the world should look like.

"This, on the other hand, is 'Closed Landscape,'" says Vennet and shows me a painting with no sky, just a green lawn with a strip of trees and bushes painted in a scale from green to black on the horizon; in among the sunshine and shivering shadows there are unusual tubes or pipes painted in red and yellow stripes, at the horizon stands a red and yellow pole, to which blue balloons are tied, or balloons that reflect the blue sky and the clouds. Some of the clouds have glided (as if the wind has pushed them off the balls) into the green background.

"They're Magritte's clouds," Vennet explains with a smile, "They suit my picture and I need to use a quote from Magritte to give the work concrete significance, which would push the viewer straight into the picture."

"You're starting to talk an awful lot," I have to point out, whereupon Vennet spreads his arms wide. "Nowadays talking is a pretty important part of art," he says and opens (a random) exhibition catalog and points to the winning work from the Graphic Art Trienniale in Osaka, with a woodcut relief by the Chinese artist Zhang—an indisputably exquisite work. Then Vennet lets me read the artist's description of what to see in the picture, and it turns out that the artist, when creating the work, took into account Mankind's struggle with Nature as well as with environmental pollution; the picture symbolizes the strength of the Unity of Mankind, where traditional Chinese dance figures are struggling, despite many setbacks, for the Progress of Mankind (and so on, and so forth), and to cap it all—amidst his struggle Mankind believes in a bright future.

"In the olden days, a work of art had to speak for itself, people looked down on those who tried to explain things: What a loser, you can't explain by artistic means what you're actually trying to say. Commentary was left to the critics, Art lived a quiet life of its own. The avant-garde was the avant-garde, which was explained later. But then art dealers began to realize that it was dead easy to produce the avant-garde: all you had to do was find some obscure but interesting artist, do a long-term deal with him, pay him a couple of thousand dollars for a painting, an enormous sum for a starving artist, and get him to fulfill the terms of the contract by doing a couple of dozen paintings on the cheap within a year, something which at that moment would seem a miracle to the artist. Now the art dealer will drum up several critics (at least one well-known, but bribable), whose mission is to make the artist (using his skill with words) into an avant-garde phenomenon—a part of art history—and in no time every self-respecting art gallery will regard it as their duty to have items of his work. At that point the dealer can add five noughts to the price while the artist continues to slave and grit his teeth under the terms of the contract.

"For some while this system worked perfectly and made several art dealers rich, but the whole business began to be seen as a disease, and one fine day avant-garde became kitsch. Theoreticians had no choice but to declare an end to art history, because what kind of avant-garde is it that is sent triumphantly to galleries and bought for large sums of money by art museums.

"But the verbal circus had taken root, the torrent of voices became part of an artwork.

"Circumstances were created whereby anyone who was hungry enough for fame and sufficiently ambitious was able to declare himself a great artist, without having a scrap of talent or making any effort to obtain professional skills. In our artistic province your friend Teodor has managed to become a master at creating installations. People tend to become art critics as compensation for the fact that they lack talent as artists. I have heard that Teodor had great difficulties at school when trying to draw, but instead he would build models in the Pioneers' room, some of which once ended up at a national exhibition of pupils' work. An extraordinary sex-drive will make people start dabbling in all manner of perversions. Sometimes these are anti-social, and the perverts end up in prison. Teodor has become an art pervert, but no one is not permitted to tie him up, instead he is allowed to make a fool out of people. Yet people like him have driven art policy so far that making fools of others is now regarded as a very spiritual and elitist pursuit.

"One evening I happened to see an interview on TV, where a theoretician from the USA and one of our own were saying that the beauty of an art object prevents us from seeing social inequalities, those places where society fails us. I had the horrible suspicion that I was listening once again to two communists from the GDR who were promoting their circumscribed ideology in the shadow of their slogans for equality and tolerance. Teodor writes in the paper today that Beuys is the greatest German artist since Dürer! And this he serves up as the plain truth, without citing any sources or context, where this has been said. It would be the same order of garbage were I to say that Teodor was the greatest Estonian artist since Wiiralt!"

I have never seen Vennet get so angry before. Watching him makes me feel uncomfortable, and I can imagine how any moment now he'll start throwing things (paintbrushes, tubes of paint, cans of varnish) and attacking his own canvases, and ripping them to bits with his teeth. Vennet rests his hands on the windowsill and looks out at the city's roofs, a trumpet can be heard in the silence— the sorrowful tones of a lone trumpet—I realize that this sound has slipped from the adjoining music school, slipped in through Vennet's open window, and I say that I too am surprised at Teodor's aggressiveness (don't myself know why I'm using that word here).

"This Fluxus movement with all its avant-garde ideas is typical of the left-wing terror that emerged in reaction to the commercialism of art. The plans of the Fluxus people, which were quite advanced, were to abolish professional art and artists, to gradually demolish traditional art and replace it with life art. In the 1960s they revolted, made a lot of noise and prepared the ground, without themselves knowing it, for an ambitious generation that had nothing to do with the ideas of the Fluxus people, who merely declared the Beuyses, Vostells and Paiks as classics and took over the world of art. And all that art-teaching rubbish, where Beuys got thrown out of the Düsseldorf Academy of Art, took root on the west coast of the USA and spread from there all over the globe like cancer. Now you can graduate from such academies without any professional skills, but with the gift of gab. Art, using the yardstick of Memling or Picasso really is dead now."

*

I explain to Vennet that I have followed what has been going on in the art world as a bystander. What resembles a farce has not worried me unduly, as I'm sure that everything will soon be back on the rails. "But I have often had the feeling that especially on account of my ignorance I can't grasp the whole business, so that my uninformed state means I simply don't understand much of it all," I say (rather long-windedly) by way of an excuse.

"Very good! This is exactly the opinion that these people rely on, and most sensible people think like you do. Many people feel guilty—they've missed the boat, can no longer catch up with the *development* of art, but at the same time they make no effort to understand the situation. And not one major city would refuse to subsidize some pompous contemporary art exhibition or other, people point at those that refuse—they don't understand the spirituality and profundity of contemporary art, they are stupid uneducated people. Every government official is afraid of being made to look the fool and naturally has no compunction about spending city money (not his own, but the taxpayers'!), though he is left with a painful feeling when the galleries are filled with bleak and pointless works of art that nevertheless make huge claims.

"It's possible that you see in me an old grumbler, but when I'm robbed of my favorite criteria for value—such as ethics, originality, honesty, aesthetic pleasure—and they now get called, deprecatingly, "modernist myths," —then I at least want to end up with something roughly equivalent. I long for the time when music, art, and literature were created by people to whom God had given special gifts."

*

I reckon Vennet is about ten years or more my senior—let me be more precise: his fiftieth birthday was a couple of years ago. He looks quite young for his years, and not bad withal. When I was still sitting on my bench at school, he was already a famous artist, and for the past quarter of a century he has remained a respected figure in the eyes of the general public and critics alike. Vennet is supposed to suffer from vertigo, and he is said to have explained that the fault lies with writer So-and-So (me)—when they (we) were at a North Korean socialist fairground, and he had the urge to tease writer So-and-So (me) by getting him to go on one of the attractions there. The nearest one was some "American Mountains" thing, but of more or less modest dimensions—two-person gondolas would rush up and down, right and left, at great speed. Vennet had hoped to sit behind the protective back of the writer, keeping his eyes shut, but the writer was too quick for him, and climbed into the back seat. The whole thing started moving: steep, squealing curves, then a steep descent, the safety belts were broken and the speed was dizzying.

At the end of the ride, Vennet looked wretched—his face green, his eyes bulging from their sockets, he had managed to buy himself a lifelong fear of heights, which steadily became more and more unbearable—even standing on a third floor balcony would make his knees tremble.

Sitting in the plane that time on our way to North Korea, we were already nodding acquaintances, and since we had no friends among the other members of the tourist group, which consisted principally of actors, we ended up roommates for a couple of weeks, and went around together a lot for a few years after the trip.

It turned out that our lifestyles differed a great deal, and without our noticing our great friendship (brotherhood? liking for each other?) abated. My environment was the city and its cultural circles. Vennet, on the other hand, wasn't keen on cultural life. Once they wanted him on some board or other, whereupon he flailed his arms about and yelled that he had withdrawn his candidature, saying that he had the reputation of an alcoholic, and had two dogs back home—the latter fact served as an irrefutable argument.

He probably was an alcoholic. I've often seen him knocking back the vodka—as if he could, glass by glass, reduce his aversion to other people, as if dissolving some clot of feeling that the surrounding reality had generated in him. He had the sincere (romantic) mind and temperament of a true artist, which underwent a curious change a couple of years ago.

"One day I simply started to call things by their proper names," he would explain to those who had not quite managed to be amazed by the fact that he had become a teetotaler overnight. "The epoch of modernism has come to an end, contemporary art needs new types of practitioners," he said, smiling to those who were irritated by his articles on art. Indeed, Vennet really did stop drinking and plunged headfirst into the thorny thickets (quagmire?) of art problems, so that he ended up becoming quite well oriented in the landscape of art, even better than some of our professional (provincial) art critics.

*

This Vennet was (once) the eternal mongrel, a hedonist of the brothel, a self-sacrificial workhorse—moving from one extreme to the other, always wholeheartedly and thoroughly. Strange, but sometimes it struck me that a bohemian lifestyle simply didn't suit him, it was like a protective layer over an urgent rationality, like a layer of insulation that didn't allow the world to penetrate through to his soul.

People told (used to tell) jokes about Vennet which (at least one, that I know for sure) he made up about himself and then eagerly (like a heap of manure for growing crops) spread about town.

Once Vennet had supposedly chained himself up, stark naked, in front of his dog's kennel, and barked there convincingly (a couple of decades later a Russian called Kulik did the same thing in Stockholm within the framework of an art performance, but he overdid it a bit and bit one critic in the leg). [Aftonbladet, 27 June, 1998]

Another time, Vennet had let himself be painted white all over, and had adopted the pose of a javelin-thrower by the Harjumägi fountain on the square—for a very long while, passers-by hadn't realized what was going on, and when Vennet finally threw his javelin and walked down the steps onto the street, the initial panic evolved into a huge scandal.

Once Vennet had painted a picture in which a girl in a yellow dress was walking among the trees and bushes and by one bush a man was standing (with his back to the viewer). The picture was entitled "Little Liisa Walks Through the Woods Near Town." When some top officials came to view the exhibition before the launch, the picture caused such embarrassment that they stood for ages in front of it, squirming in silence. One of them finally asked: "What's that man doing by the bush?" When the exhibition was opened, the title had become: "Little Liisa *and Her Father* Walk Through the Woods Near Town."

"Yes," I am thinking, *"Vennet's paintings are pretty, their (distressing) beauty strikes the viewer, but they seem like a deceptive surface, behind which there is a mysterious lost (closed) paradise, full of tragic premonitions."*

His paintings are like wandering between reality and dream, a labyrinth where the beautiful scenery hides a catastrophe. It is an existential game, where the bet is placed on the indifference of

nature for nature, and an (illusory) impression is conjured up in the
viewer, as if his soul has been expanded.

Yes, I am thinking, a pretty little poem to Vennet, maybe for his birthday, would no doubt make him happy that his old friend the writer So-and-So has finally reached the source of meaning of his work.

Yes, I am thinking, it is very likely that the pretty landscapes he has created are a joke, a mystification, a double game. That the whole meaning lies, in fact, in that double game.

***

"This time, I want to stage an exhibition of ideas, where I exhibit (present) paintings of landscapes (representations) as bearers of information," says Vennet with bravado, grandly, just as he (once) did when treating people to the bubbly.

"I will have a number of my paintings enlarged as photos, will frame these in gilt frames, and exhibit them as landscape photos. For instance, 'View of Leevaku Hydroelectric Power Station,' where the power station building is the real one, but instead of having the foaming river, there is a billowing landscape like that of an English park. I will give the date of the completion of the painting as this year, but will add the explanation: photograph of the painting 'Landscape With Object' (1982, oil on canvas), is housed at the New York Public Library.

"Or then there is 'View of Rahukohtu Street on Toompea Hill,' where instead of asphalt, grass is growing, and depicted in it is the photograph of a painting, 'Old Town,' from 1986, which is in the collections of the Tretyakov Gallery; or 'By the Schnell Pond,' where there is no pond in the picture, and there is a red changing cabin on grass.

"In this way I will manage a degree of multiple meaning—self-irony plus a smirk at the criteria for contemporary art (or lack thereof). Next to the photos in their expensive frames I will exhibit modestly-framed virtual worlds painted on canvas: a mown lawn in the form of a billowing sea; green pyramids rising up over an Estonian landscape; a painting where among the juniper bushes a green egg, as if from Sooster, rises, or out of an autumnal landscape of linden trees, a huge green cone. Out of my sunlit fields rise Magritte's pinkish matchsticks with yellow sulfur heads like pylons, and around a courtyard roll Magritte's cloven spheres," says Vennet as he pours peppermint tea into the cups.

The new aroma (close to the soil, to the fields) momentarily conquers the smell of turpentine and paint (which always overwhelms you as you enter a studio, but which you get used to, so that in the end it disappears). "So too the peppermint aroma disappears," I am thinking with strange sadness, and to avoid slipping into sentimentality, I ask: "What are you trying to say with those spheres of Magritte's?"

"Those? Oh, with those cloven spheres of his I mean cloven spheres, what else?" says Vennet with a shrug of the shoulders, and goes on to explain: "In my own opinion, I have always painted surrealist landscapes, and I have achieved this notion or feeling without using any kind of special or intrusive symbols, the metaphysical moment arrives in an ordinary landscape by way of the surreal coloring, while in our superficial world this never happens.

When you add to this landscape a recognizable citation, however tiny, like a motto or epigram for a story or novel, the whole thing soon becomes clear to the viewer, and after that even the art critic can manage to insert my art into one of his categories—the citation will give him a foothold, he will see something familiar, something he learned about in school, and only now does he understand why my paintings have made an impression on him for years."

*

"Sometimes I get the feeling that the end of the century has brought with it a mystical conspiracy against culture. Culture must be compromised and crossed out of, the human consciousness," says Vennet sadly, as if he had given in, and shows me a couple of his latest works.

On one of the canvases is depicted a beach in the light of evening, and in very pure and bright colors two changing cabins have been painted. A yellow one and a red one. On one of the cabins someone has scrawled *FUCK YOU*, on the other, *DO IT*.

The other painting depicts a park in summer, with bushes that have been pruned very carefully like topiary, and in the midst of which is a hoarding full of graffiti. When you examine the hoarding more carefully, you will discover words in Russian and English, a blue-black-white Estonian flag, the carelessly written name Jean Baudrillard, and a primitively stylized "babe," which hints at the fact that (the famous artist) Keith Haring has tried his hand at art in this park as well. The center of all of this is dominated by a word in (garish) purple: *UNDERWORD*.

"Shouldn't that be *UNDERWORLD*," I ask discreetly, because I get the feeling that next to this hoarding there are stairs leading downwards, and furthermore Underworld plays pretty interesting music.

"No, the word written there has to be *underword*, something like *subword*, or perhaps the basic words with which you form a sentence," Vennet explains importantly.

We drink our tea and listen to how the trumpet repeats the same phrase again and again. (OK. The author needs at this point to mark a longish pause. He has just remembered that earlier on he was talking about a *sad* trumpet melody. There's nothing wrong with using the trumpet again here, this time simply repeating the same phrase. The reader (or critic) can at this point ponder the *significance* of the use of a trumpet.)

"That is a fucking lefty thought—i.e. that aesthetic culture is not something that human beings need, but a luxury, something to destroy as a pointless expense. To be more specific it is pure green thinking, which envisages general thrift, saving, stinginess. Art is only necessary in as much as it can warn about the impending ecological disaster. Music, on the other hand, is simply not necessary at all, it is enough to have natural sounds—the purling of a brook, birdsong, the soughing of the wind," says Vennet, shutting the window.

Fourth Chapter

It's a fox, I am thinking, as I see something russet by the road slipping into the bushes, or even a cat, I decide a second later, and let my gaze rove over the open space right up to the horizon from the rich colors of the marshy ground glowing in the sun, and it seems to me that I have seen a landscape like this before. Then I see, in my mind's eye, Vennet's painting, with its strikingly similar colors, except for the fact that in Vennet's painting there are dried-out birches in the foreground, a couple of white tree trunks, which give the painting an anxious undertone (quite unfounded), the premonition of an accident, which carry one's thoughts to the approaching horror, the inevitable catastrophe, which can in no way be avoided—simply have to press your hands hard over your eyes and wait in despair.

There seem to be people ahead, I slow down gradually, and there are indeed people—two youths kicking a third who is lying on the asphalt, then (presumably because they have spotted me) they drag the lying youth to the roadside and *wave* to me. In the background is a hamburger kiosk (open 24/7) and it looks as if the windows are smashed.

It's their business, I think to myself, in low spirits, and the horrible premonition begins to slowly gnaw at my heart—gnaw-gnaw, such a natural gnaw-gnaw, where you feel something with dread and know that nothing can stop it from being *set in motion*. What you feel very clearly is your own powerlessness.

The weather is surprisingly warm for the beginning of September, high summer all around, Indian summer, as they say, a ridge of high pressure is pushing in from the south, it was already forecast yesterday and was confirmed this morning. Usually, weather forecasts leave me cold, but this time I even stopped in the middle of doing something (gnawing? chewing?), in order to listen to everything very carefully, so that no nuance would escape my ears. But now for the first time I catch myself worrying about what I'm going to occupy myself with these next couple of weeks, as I lack the opportunity of reading the newspaper, listening to the radio, let alone watching the news on TV. I won't even know what kind of weather it will be tomorrow, I think in an uneasy panic. If things carry on like this, I soon won't even know which party is in power—I say to myself, highlighting my own disquisition.

Immensely beautiful nature, the phrase slips into my head and I begin to form sentences about the image of the landscape: obscenely beautiful nature, abominably beautiful nature, bleakly beautiful nature. I know that all those epithets have their own precise meanings, and I have to think about Vennet's paintings and (a little uneasily) about Vennet, who has gone a bit far with his disquisition, has found a number of conveniently intriguing ways of linking facts together, and keeps trying to find more suitable facts, so as to exploit them. A very typical brand of paranoia, an objective viewer could think, no one wants to compromise culture, there is no world plot. Things are simply as they are.

A number of vehicles are standing on the road, and the nearer I get to them, the bigger the crashed dump truck becomes, it is lying on its roof and has broken in two; ochre-colored sand and stones have formed a pile on the dark asphalt. Three vehicles are waiting by the roadside, and there are men standing around the cab of the truck. I drive up to the scene, you can't see ahead because of the overturned truck, a man in a red checked shirt stares at me vacantly, although he should understand that I can't see ahead to continue, and he ought to indicate to me, whether someone is approaching the other way or not.

The accident has happened recently, a few minutes back; I know that I can't be of any assistance here and drive carefully round the wrecked truck, out of the cab a face stares at me, pressed against the glass, chalk white, no longer that of a living being. When I get to the other side, a vehicle with blue and white flashing lights stops, out of which emerges a grim person in uniform, who looks at the scene with aversion—he is already middle-aged, a village constable or something similar, he neither can nor wants to actually do anything here.

*

The road has suddenly come to an end, run to sand, and I cannot drive any further, it's a good place to turn round, as it's clear I won't get anywhere this way. The sea is glittering beyond the pine trees, I interrupt my consultation of the map, step out and walk down through the pine copse towards the sea—the sea, *meri*, the name of the president, Meri! ("A Stormy Shore," the Tuglas long poem, "The Sea" ("*Meri*"), the president, the sea abloom, blessing the sea, and so on, and so forth.) The sea is before me and behind the boulders, bright blue, smooth, to the right an islet in the haze, on the horizon the (lone) gleaming triangle of a sail. Clearly an idyll, but the wrong place for an idyll—this is not a seashore where I should be planting my feet. The wisest thing to do would be to find the village store, where I can ask the way. In the countryside (I believe) they know everything and everyone in the local store.

"I see, they couldn't direct you to the Teeriida farm. Many people don't know it. When the *firm* bought it, they started calling it that. It was up to the firm how to call it, before it was called Värniku, after the name of the owner who drowned himself last spring, people round here still call it Värniku, but the firm gave it a new name—Teeriida. They said that was the right name for this place, but people round here still know it as Värniku, and plenty of them have never heard the name Teeriida."

The storekeeper is a tall, thin man and pants (asthma?), he pauses to think before starting to speak, and then, once he's opened his mouth, you get the impression that this faucet of words will be impossible to turn off again. But I'm not stopping him from talking, I have nothing against the fact that he knows this and that about the village (I can hardly call it my home village), my aim is simply to pour oil on the flames and ask where (this) Värnik drowned himself, because if I'm told *where*, then the *why* and *how* are sure to follow, and it is pretty certain that the next person to enter the shop will get a long description of what the new guest at Teeriida looks like.

"This Värnik tied himself to some huge lump of iron or other and then drowned himself in the canal near Vaariku harbor, and when the men went down to the sea in the morning, he was staring at them, it was a still morning and clear water and Värnik was smirking up at them from the seabed, Värnik was always such a scoffer, would pick fights, too, no wonder his wife left him, she went to live with a taxi-driver in town, but this got Värnik down, he threatened to cut his balls off, but never managed, and drowned himself instead. He was a townie himself, too, only moved here with his wife a few years ago, Värnik was a good fisherman, but he couldn't be bothered to do any other work. His wife couldn't even milk the cows, she'd been a hairdresser, while Värnik had worked in an office, the local farmers didn't care for them, Värnik couldn't get on with other people, was always getting into arguments, and no one wanted to go to sea with him. That farm was his grand-father's and when his wife later sold it to the *firm*, people started saying all kinds of things.

"So you're the new tenant, there seems to be an Indian summer this year, but it's not right when a woman drives her husband to his death and then profits from the use of his farm."

I tell the storekeeper that it's exceptionally fine weather today, must be over twenty degrees Celsius, and that the weather station forecasts high pressure for a number of days running.

"The delivery truck comes at around twelve tomorrow, we can't store much here, it won't keep, but this truck comes on Mondays and Fridays, if you do need anything then you can order it, and if it's in stock they'll bring it to you right away, things are getting better for us since the firm took on those new tenants in the early spring, all sorts of people have dropped in, when people have money I always think, Why don't they go off for their vacations to some warm land or other, but maybe you know better. And what do they say there in the firm about this woman and her daughter, do you know?"

I ask *which* woman, the door behind me opens, but I don't yet look inquisitively to see who has come in, though I know that in ten seconds or so I will be looking, observing, confirming, locating, etc.

"I mean the woman who was the firm's tenant before you, I remember how she came into the store, small, shy, the daughter was exactly the same, almost like twins, and they say she was a professor at the university. She didn't really know what to do, I don't understand why such a person would want to come out to the countryside from the city, Jaak always went over to her place to get the stove going, otherwise she wouldn't get any hot food, oh you know nothing about all this, do you, they probably don't talk about it in the firm, the whole thing's a cover-up, as if it never happened, they're certainly capable of that."

"Listen, could you give me three beers," I hear an unexpectedly familiar voice behind my back, and when I turn around, I see Kandiman's beard and large paunch. Wherever I go in town—to the theater, to a bar, to the opening of an exhibition, the President's reception, on the trolleybus, to the editorial office of the paper—wherever I go, Kandiman is already there, greets me with gushing friendliness (always squeezing my arm) and the greeting is so sincere that I have to embrace him for a moment.

*

The name of the farm is Teeriida, I am thinking, now turning off the road into the juniper bushes, this word *teeriida* could mean various things in Estonian: *tee* (i.e. tea) and *riit* (a stack or rick) or *tee* (a road) and *riid* (a quarrel, though the genitive is, in fact, *riiu*), *tee riid* (a quarrel after drinking the drink), or even *teerida* (a row of teas). And so on.

Teeriida is, at any rate, better than Värniku, as *värnik* doesn't mean anything at all (whereas *värik, värin, värd, värnits, värdjas* are real words). Where could such a name that doesn't mean anything come from; for instance, the writer So-and-So is a very good name, you know immediately who you are dealing with, you know you are dealing with such and such a person. I, at least, am satisfied with my name, nor do I have anything against Teeriida, and now the house is coming into view—a white chimney and a dark roof, the house itself is yellow. Even back at the store, all the houses around were yellow, some ship with yellow paint aboard must have run aground here and the waves washed the pots of paint up onto the shore; or people think that yellow makes life more sunny, the weather may be cloudy, but the house still glows with the light of day, heartens you immediately, when you see it from afar.

What a funny feeling you get as you approach! At any rate this isn't the same as entering a hotel room with indifference, see how your heart has begun to beat faster, somewhere in the lumber room of your consciousness, some feelings of your home farm are stored, which rear their head even in the mind of a lifelong apartment dweller.

The writer So-and-So looks around him: *here a juniper, there a juniper, further off a third, to my left a fourth, to my right a fifth, and behind them a sixth, a seventh, and more. Between the juniper bushes there are meadows and a number of buildings, farther off the wall of the woods.*

One such field of junipers will now become home for him, the writer still sitting in his car (and perhaps it is there he will end his days).

For some reason the writer's heart contracts painfully in his chest. The pain spreads downwards, reaches all his organs, which seem to be bunched around his navel.

Yes, he'd never imagined that he would ever have such a home. Up to today, he has always imagined homes in buildings of several stories and on broad streets—the big city that bustles in the bright evening lights. But where would you go here if you wanted to get a breath of fresh air? Would the junipers listen to his ratiocinations?

*

Teeriida is a well kept, neat establishment, you get the feeling that the family has just popped out to church or to the store and for that reason it makes you feel a little uneasy that, in reality, they are not coming back. I open the window and let the late summer sun shine onto my face. It is quiet, so quiet that I can hear the flies buzzing, like low planes over the city. The silence will now become my companion, and it will be a while before I cease to notice it. Once in Wrocław I spent a week sleeping in a room which was near the spot where the streetcars turned. At first it was as if the streetcars were running straight into the house, it was as if your brains were being turned inside out. The first night I didn't manage to get a wink of sleep; by the fifth I was sleeping like a log.

You can probably get used to silence, I say to soothe myself, and go and sit on the steps. The yard is neatly bordered by a lilac hedge, the path leads to a building like a sauna, and no doubt is one, in the flower beds long-stalked brightly-colored dog daisies (or cosmos, as I later find out they're called), there is a millstone resting on three stones that can be used as a table and in the middle there is some flowering plant (moose hemp). To my own surprise I immediately realize that apart from dandelions, I know virtually no wild flower names, I have never needed them for my texts, as the flowers available in the flower store, such as roses, tulips, carnations, have been sufficient for my purposes, and when I read the following in a review (which, as it turned out, was commissioned by the secret police) of my latest novel: "What is especially captivating is the author's way of looking at nature, making the grayness around us glow thanks to his deep understanding of nature and the environment . . . " I couldn't help laughing to myself for some time.

Anyway, when I was writing my latest novel, I needed some allusions to the plants and flowers surrounding Anton's childhood home and I wrote a good episode where little Anton was examining a (unusual, rarely occurring) striated butterfly. I had never seen one myself, but I could not pick the most rare one from the handbook of butterflies (that I had seen at the natural history museum), and the other butterfly seemed more believable. I cherish the thought that I will now be able to write not from a book but from nature itself, and can genuinely note in my text that I have a "deep understanding of nature and the environment"—I notice that on the shelves in the main room there are a number of books about fish and birds and butterflies and flowers.

I bring in a bottle of beer from the car, thinking in passing that I ought to put my whole stock of them in the fridge, and that means finding the fridge—which, at a cursory glance around, is not in evidence, but when I go outside and open the bottle on the steps, I realize that there is no point looking for a fridge since there is no electricity in the house. The thought that all fridges run on electricity and there is no main supply here suddenly strikes me with dismay.

I then remember that in a bag I have a coffee machine that runs on electricity, an electric razor, and a portable computer (!). I did, after all, come here to work! I have to translate *Trout Fishing* into Estonian and write *Informer to the Estonian Republic*! Fucking hell! (When someone utters the name of the Prince of Darkness or his habitation, then Satan can slip into his opened mouth—a text I once read springs suddenly to mind . . .)

"Fucking hell!" I say again. Around a meter away, a dried leaf that has alighted on the grass suddenly opens up, and I see the bright blue wings of a striated butterfly, shining as if luminescent.

The road I've been traveling along has ended in the farmyard, I get out of the car, open the gate and drive it into the yard. It is now impossible for me to drive any further.

From the moment I shut the gate I am no longer the man I was before—a person is a bundle of habits, of which I am suddenly bereft. The fact that Teerrida is my (temporary) home occasions the difference. The writer "So" separates from the writer "and-So".

Writer So-and-So is now a bundle of differences.

In the kitchen there is a long table, and when you sit on the bench at the middle of the table you can see the view: in the foreground the end of the wall and a well made of chunks of local stone, behind the stones juniper bushes (two of them with long stalks like chrysanthemums), bushes of reddening berries, a table made of gray planks, where large silver spangles (?) glitter, a glowing ridge of dried grass ends in a dark strip, which is the shadow of the taller trees on the ground, the trees form a green wall (an unusually precise expression) indented along the edge of the sky. It is the end of summer, cold nights have not yet colored the leaves. In the sky a large bird is flying, making huge efforts with its wings to move ahead. I feel particularly happy. I don't even have the urge to smoke.

*

A magpie flies onto the gray outdoor plank table and starts pecking avidly at some silvery spangles—always one at a time, it munches for a while, then spits it out. Ten minutes or so later another magpie comes to the table, now they are both strutting about, as if in some ritual dance. A quarter of an hour later a large gray bird flies onto the table and starts driving the magpies away. It must be a hawk, I think, as I catch sight of its powerful beak. A fledgling hawk, no doubt.

Am I now someone else, I think to myself as I eye the spangle-strewn table, now birdless (I ought to go outside to take a closer look at these strange objects). If here, now, at the Teeriida farmhouse, I am someone else, am I then in the city, in my own home, also someone else, am I different enough that when I get home I will be someone else, or is it simply that the writer So-and-So, who was staying at Teeriida, was *someone else*.

In the end I get to my feet, kick my shoes off on the steps and go in my stocking feet to have a look at what these strange spangles on the outdoor table actually are. The ground has been warmed by the sun and is soft under the soles of my feet like a carpet, the spangles are transparent fish scales, about the size of five cent pieces, and look as if they are coated on one side with nickel. Someone has recently been scaling (and gutting) a large fish, because there are piles of scales around the table on the grass. (I wonder whether this professor lady, who couldn't even manage to get a fire going, would have been tough enough to go fishing?)

I go to the car to fetch a file (in Russian: *delo*, in English: *file*) which has hard covers with a bunch of papers, directions, instructions, between them. I leafed through it yesterday evening and became convinced that there is enough wisdom in this file so that even *that person* who is abandoning a centrally heated flat in the city for the first time wouldn't run into difficulties. In actual fact, I can't even imagine a person who has never held a box of matches or an ax before, but there are probably plenty of people in the modern world who belong to that category, and the number is increasing; I feel an urge to describe in some story or other such a *helpless person*, and in order to do it as well as possible I would have to pretend (to myself) that I am one of them. That I'm not who I am, but someone else.

It turns out that in the slope covered with heather there's a storage cellar, so I take my bunch of keys from the house and open the (massive) padlock. When I open the door, a clammy chill wafts into my face—the air of a burial vault—and on the shelves are rows of jars (jam or salted fish?), and I notice there are even a few beers and packets of butter and a hunk of cheese in cheesecloth and (on closer inspection) eggs—the previous occupant left an enormous amount of provisions behind. Or have these things *been abandoned*?

If I hadn't bumped into Kandiman in the village store, the storekeeper would maybe have furnished more details about the lady professor. Now there's a vague suspicion or premonition of evil (a crime?) hanging in the air and I don't quite feel safe in my new dwelling. In the file it says how safety and security are maintained in summer houses, and when I go back inside I immediately search out the buttons of the (emergency?) alarm system. There's one next to the bed in the bedroom, a large red button like the stop button on some machine, and another similar one in the kitchen, behind the window drapes. In case of emergency, all you have to do is press the button.

I let the drape with the pattern of liverwort fall back into place, and now the red button is hidden from sight, but a second later I draw the curtain again and goggle at the button like an idiot: if there's an alarm system, then on pressing it I must connect it to an electrical circuit. *An electrical circuit.* But there isn't any electricity in the whole place, there's a petroleum lamp on the table, and there aren't any power lines on posts leading to the house.

It is very likely that the house had electricity, but the Ummals had the cables ripped out, leaving the client without such creature comforts. So it's up to me to find some length of cable and a loose socket (must be able to obtain such things from the village shop), then I can get my computer working . . . have a shave . . . make my coffee. If I rummage around in the shed I may even find some cable, so that I can pay the Ummals back for their trickery. This whole summer house is a kind of mild survival test and you have to be smart to get through it.

But there is another possibility, that the red alarm button is merely a dummy, press it as much as you like and nothing will happen, but it nevertheless gives everyone a feeling of security, knowing that something (in actual fact nothing at all) is protecting you. It's like swallowing placebos (tranquilizers, sleeping pills). Sleep comes and you calm down. You feel safe until it enters your head to unscrew a couple of screws. I could now go and take a screwdriver (tip of a knife) and open up the junction box and have a look, but I'd rather leave it till later.

*

The house is a good deal larger (roomier) than it appears at first sight. The lower story has a main room and a bedroom, and in the attic there are three smaller bedrooms. In the long, corridor-like entrance hall there is a coat-stand with all sorts of garments— padded jackets, parkas, waterproof fishing pants and jacket—and beneath these clothes, rubber boots of various sizes. While the upper story, the kitchen, and the entrance hall have been renovated recently, the main room bears traces of a living-room from a century ago. I sit at the massive writing desk, in an upholstered leather chair that feels comfortable, the desk is just big enough to accommodate everything you need, and it would be pleasant to write here. Through the window you can see the front lawn, then a gate through which the track winds off between juniper bushes, leading away from here, back to where you came, else- where. To the right of the gate lilacs are growing, but here and there the hedge has grown sickly, and behind the low and sparse foliage and the lilac flowers you can see whitish-yellow grass, and a couple of hundred meters away a fir tree rises up, and deciduous trees too, and a stone wall can be seen. In the distance between the trees, a stretch of flat land (sun-bathed) can be seen, which could be a hayfield.

Beyond the trees are the neighbors (the Laakans). That's where you fetch the milk from. A path leads there (according to the map). There is also a path to the shore. To get to the store, you follow the path, ditto to get to the mushroom woods. There are paths in the landscape like a rhizome. I look at the names on the map: Laakan, Vikati, and Tupp, those are my neighbors. There's a cluster of buildings around the store, but these are not indicated by name. The sea is perhaps a couple of hundred meters distant, and I want to go there soon, but I first have to move in properly, spread books, (my) diaries, and papers on the writing desk, then make some coffee (light the stove!), fetch some milk and make my acquaintance with Laakan (or are there more than one?).

Next to the table there is a sparsely filled bookshelf, where there doesn't seem to be any light reading material, mostly books on fish, birds, and flora, the "Dictionary of Ecology," a Finnish book covering the thought of the 1990s, "Johdatus 1990-luvun ajatteluun," the "Pioneers' Guide" (!), a copy of the "Gardener's Handbook," another Finnish book, this time "Toisinajattelijan päiväkirjasta," i.e., "From the Diary of a Dissident." I cast my eye over the books there, and find nothing written by myself, and think it would be nice to leave one of my books, maybe the last one with its "green" sub-text, as I always have a couple of copies in my bag—just in case. But then I realize that there's no fiction on this shelf and maybe there isn't meant to be, so that when you need relaxation after a physically wearying day, you won't start watching TV or reading a crime novel (there aren't any there!), but will instead read about the realm of fish, think about the end of the century, or exchange serious thoughts with your family.

I am thinking: evenings in the fall can be long and dark.

In the bedchamber (I don't know why I have termed the room thus, perhaps because there used to be "chambers" rather than rooms on Estonian farms) there is a closet with a mirror, and shelves with sheets, pillowcases; I take my clothes out of my suitcase, lay them on the shelves, setting my stamp on the pieces of furniture and storage spaces like a dog marking out its territory with bushes or posts. When something of mine (a jersey, a jacket) hangs on a clothes-hanger, the closet itself has somehow become my own, as has the house where the closet is located, and the plot of ground with its fence where the house has been built. When, however, I pull open the bottom drawer, I smell an unexpected whiff of perfume, and find a pile of women's underwear.

Look what someone has left behind, I say with a smile on seeing the soft garments; in hotels you now and again find some intimate trace of the previous occupant that the cleaner has missed; and someone whose daily bread is earned by fantasizing will not be ashamed of letting his fingers stroke the cloth, of taking the panties and bras out of the drawer and into the light, sizing them up and conjuring forth their owner; and it is not surprising that desire suddenly paralyzes the finder and he sees in his mind's eye the (pink) buttocks of the woman and her pert pink breasts with their nipples covered by the lace of her bra. Then the whole of the owner emerges life size (wearing a pink tracksuit)—she is blond, with a voluptuous rump, wears spectacles, and is an angel without wings. But my desire does not allow me to get into the spirit of the game of fantasy, because of a strange disturbing thought, the fact that the storekeeper alluded to the lady professor and hinted that *something* might have happened to her, which now throws quite a different light on the underwear *left behind* in the drawer.

*

I decide I can do without coffee this time round, fill a mug with milk and cut a slice of bread: the milk is cool and rich, quite different from that bought at the store, and the wall of the jar has become coated with a white film, which is presumably the cream. When I went to fetch the milk and I reached my neighbor's door, no one answered my knocking, so I tried the door, it wasn't locked, it opened when I pressed down the handle. In the room lay a man with a bare rump on a divan and a woman in a white smock looked at me in astonishment.

I excused myself and closed the door, and had the strange impression that they had been playing—like children—a game of doctors and nurses, and a text sprang to mind where a little girl who is starting to strip off, says to the little boy: *"Doctor, you must examine me."* And the little boy says: *"But my dear little girl! I'm not a doctor!"*

Laakan, my neighbor, has made a strange impression on me, I'm not using the term "strange" in a loose way, but as a pretty accurate way of characterizing Laakan, a man in his mid-thirties, with a soft feminine face, small hands, a voice that sounded like a whisper—he hadn't anything manly about him—and when he went over to the well to pour the milk into my glass jar, wearing his tracksuit trousers, he seemed to be wiggling his (feminine?) bottom in a provocative way.

"What professor?" he asked in (genuine?) surprise. "Before you arrived, the Riis family were staying there over the summer, and if I remember rightly the husband was some sort of construction entrepreneur, they were very content, would have liked to stay longer, but the children were starting school and nowadays a businessman can't afford more than a few days off from his job, the woman was in effect alone with her children and didn't know how to cope—it was, after all, their first time without electricity—but I suppose that people soon get used to it."

This wasn't the way a person from the countryside would speak, I thought, and asked him if he had a large family.

"No, just my sister and me," he said hurriedly, took off his spectacles and began to polish them with his handkerchief. "You can get eggs from me if you need any," he added. "Vegetables are there already. Rolli will take you down to the sea to fish, I don't go out to sea myself. If you need anything, then ask us, the firm said you are here on your own, and I don't know how you are going to deal with cooking your meals, but if you do need help, my sister can make you a hot meal once a day, but you'll have to pay extra for that. It would of course be better if you don't say anything to the firm about that, because they have a principle that everyone should fend for themselves and that village folk should only help you when you're in dire straits. My name is Jaak and my sister is called Maria," and quite unexpectedly a kind of grin passed over his face. Ironic and provocative. I said my name.

"The firm has already mentioned this, their boss should be coming on a visit any day now, but without announcing his arrival beforehand. I don't read fiction, I don't care for things made up about other people's lives, I do browse in travel literature and memoirs, if I feel like it and have the time. Maria, on the other hand, is an avid reader and would be only too pleased, no doubt, if you would present her with a book with a dedication."

I am chewing the milk-soaked bread for a long time and notice to my astonishment how enjoyable simple fare can be—a taste which city life simply cannot offer, I mean: simple food, a simple life; a cat jumps up onto the fish-scaling table, almost the same as I had at home, the one that is now pushing up daisies. I can't hear, but can see, how it is meowing—it is opening its mouth and complaining about something. I fill a saucer with milk, go to the kitchen door and call: Kitty-kitty-kitty. The cat comes from the corner of the house, stops and looks at me diffidently. I stretch out my finger, the cat approaches shyly, then nudges my finger with its muzzle, meows as if in greeting, purrs, and wraps itself around my legs. When I put the saucer on the ground, it dances for a short while then begins to lick the milk happily. This cat is surprisingly similar to my own, just a tiny bit larger, with a more brutal face. A farmyard cat, for sure. I stroke the cat with the back of my hand as it laps up the milk, and it doesn't let itself be disturbed one bit, and I think, with a start, that I have a dead cat in my fridge at home.

*

I can't get the thought of the dead cat out of my head, wondering whether it might start smelling in a few days' time, maybe a week. It would be foolish to travel all the way into town, but I don't dare burden my neighbor's daughter with the cat's corpse—I can't anticipate how a fourteen year old girl might react. And as there isn't a man in their family, as she lives there alone with her mother, I wouldn't dare to entrust the burial to these women. At the same time it just wouldn't do (initially, at least) to just throw the dead cat out with the garbage. But how can I arrange the cat's burial in town? You do at least have to have a spade and somewhere to dig a hole.

I now have two worries in my head at the same time: how to make the cat's corpse in the fridge disappear, and how to bury it. I am afraid that I will have to give up the latter despite everything (all those wonderful years with my cat!), and let the mother of the fourteen-year-old throw the cat into the garbage bin. I can't imagine that anyone would want to bury my cat (despite promises to the contrary).

I imagine Evelin (that's my neighbor's daughter's name, the one who my wife asked to water our plants while she was away in the USA—she didn't trust me with the task) finding the cat's corpse in the fridge. A scream? Retching? Would she pass out? Not really sure of that. Evelin is free of complexes and is at home in our flat, almost like a child of our own. But she is beginning to bloom, becoming too big, and one day (or overnight) you'll notice that she has grown up—that she has become an adult. Then you'll think twice about addressing her informally. You will notice that she's become someone else, no longer the dear little child you've got used to. I experienced this myself when our daughter (from my first marriage) grew up one fine day. When we divorced, my wife took our daughter, I our cat. Now our daughter is married and the cat dead. We have both lost something.

A very lively image (as if it happened a moment ago, a glance over your shoulder), a very lively image reaches my mind's eye of one late summer's morning: sunlight flooding in through the window, washing over those in the room, specks of dust like a shower of silver, and Evelin in a short dress watering the ferns, stretching up in order to reach the bunch of thick fern leaves with the green (black-and-green) watering can, then sighing in relief, and on suddenly noticing the cat, bending down to it: Well, kitty-kitty, how are you; stroking the cat pussy-wussy, picking it up and slumping down with it on the sofa, the sunlight stroking her slender legs, the cat purring earsplittingly . . . *Evelin dropping a slipper, rubbing the heel of her foot without her slipper and with her sock round her ankles against a pile of old newspapers, to the left of me on the sofa—and every one of her movements, every change of position, helps me to achieve the secret meeting of beauty and the beast, the sly, lecherous monster hidden within me secretly joins this pretty body, which is covered above the hollow of the knee by the virginal chastity of her cotton dress.*

No, I decide, that cat is not ending up in the garbage bin. The only alternative is that someone brings it here so that I myself can bury my beloved Katarina (nicknamed Kati) in the earth. Right. Vennet promised (if the weather was suitable for fishing) to drop in and see me. Let him bring the cat with him. He will understand my wish—not everyone would understand it without making fun of it. All I need to do is ring him, no, better to write to him, nowadays letters are delivered more quickly, and in a couple of days we can arrange a fitting burial for Katarina, we will invite all the local cats to the wake, which means getting loads of fish from the sea.

I will now start for the village, the store should still be open, and from the storekeeper I can perhaps learn what happened with that (non-existent?) lady professor, and near the store there must be some sort of post office, where you can phone the city and send letters. It's about a kilometer's walk to the store, I lock up the car and start walking.—I have never allowed myself to drive after a few swigs of beer, even on village roads, and today I've had a few already.

I lock the door to the $f\Omega$ like the owner, there is a mat for the keys and I put them under it; the cat accompanies me to the gate, then sits down there and only follows me with its eyes—it is, after all, the cat belonging to this particular house, and its world is such that new faces appear every two or three weeks, people who take things out of the fridge. In the countryside, the cellar serves as the fridge. When my own cat got hungry, it would walk up to the fridge and drum with its fists (paws) on the door. Here it will thump against the cellar door, which, for cats in the rural world, is the only constant thing.

The expression "country life" springs to mind again as I spot near the store, between the store and the shed (barn?), on the well-trodden earth, a gang of men (four, five—I haven't the time to count them exactly, they're all grey and similar), who are holding bottles of beer or wine and stand looking at me. I am an alien in their world—a little green man.

This "little green man," as I imagine myself in a humorous vein, is now taking on a new symbolic significance—Ummal's little "Full-Blooded Recreation" house is a kind of green oasis and those hiring it at enormous cost in order to make their lives miserable are just like little green men with their green way of thinking.

A green way of thinking is associated with green lettuce—in a white bowl, the leaves freshly cut.

Behind the counter in the store I see a woman who must weigh at least a hundred kilos, who on seeing my confusion (the storekeeper, where's the storekeeper?) and not understanding it says challengingly: "Well, what's it to you?"

I say that I'm the new occupant of Teeriida farm and that I need to phone.

"The communications center is a kilometer further on, on your right, open from ten to one. Closed on Sundays."

"But can't you phone from here?" I try to be a little bolder.

"No, that's not possible, you place your order and then have to wait for half an hour for a connection, and we don't allow people to phone on principle, because you can imagine what it would be like with strangers hanging around in our back room. Who can tell whether you have evil intentions? Who can say whether you're really from Teeriida? Do you walk into a store in the city just to phone someone?"

I ask for a bottle of beer, step out of the gloom of the store, then into the shade of the store, where the villagers have clustered. A few meters of Estonian space separate us, but in actuality this is a huge chasm, and I have no idea how to bridge it with words. I know that whatever I say now, it will sound like a joke in their ears. I know that I'm not a hundred percent sure of this, but I'm not taking any chances by opening my mouth.

By the time half the bottle is gone my presence (standing there) has become uncomfortable. It's as if the ground is burning under my feet. I feel I have to say something, that I have just walked into their space and I am obliged to make myself known, to say something, show what I am by my tone of voice, tell them some news (good or bad).

"Around lunchtime there was a man serving here," I say as if continuing a conversation, but it is actually a sly question, which is designed to pump the men for information, especially considering that my facial expression is one of expectancy, eyebrows raised, lips parted.

There is silence for quite a while, one of them takes a few gulps and his Adam's apple moves, glug, glug. Another rummages in his pocket, a third spits on the ground, and the fourth says: "Sure, there was a man." And that in such a way as if he, like me, has noticed that there was something out of place or unusual around lunchtime, with a man behind the counter, and now he is wondering how that could possibly have happened.

I would like to take my packet of cigarettes out of my pocket and offer them to the men, but that would be like buying them over, trying to bribe them, like . . . I drink up my bottle and think with envy how someone like Kandiman would have easily made friends with these grim-looking men. When the bottle is completely empty, I suddenly don't know what to do with it—to put it in the garbage bin with them watching would be an insulting waste—I must (as I imagine the custom is round here) take the empty bottle in to the storekeeper and sell it back.

"Here you are," I say to the woman behind the counter, holding out the bottle. "Thanks," I say as I receive the deposit from her.

Fifth Chapter

When I open my eyes, I can't really make anything out at first; the cosmic feeling of "not being anywhere" lasts a while, before the world takes on its familiar contours. I go over to the window, pull back the thick drape, which had prevented the moonlight from flooding in during the night (as light out there as during the day!). And I see a landscape painting, with the morning mist, the sun's rays penetrating the mist to the ground that glows golden, the junipers which look like ghostly human figures in the mist. When I notice that one of the junipers is moving, this fact does not seem odd or require explanation, I'll ponder on that later, in the future, in an hour or so.

Mr. President, I think anxiously, you don't have time to admire the sunrise of your native land, do you?

I pad through the main room in my bare feet, through the kitchen, and push the creaking outside door open. The morning is crisp and so beautiful that it takes your breath away. I walk down the concrete steps and urinate onto the grass. My pee steams—the surface of the earth has grown chilly during the night and the frost isn't far away. I shake off the last drops glittering in the sunshine and think anxiously that the President cannot enjoy such a morning pee, neither in the presidential palace park at Kadriorg, nor in his house in the suburb of Nõmme, nor even when in the country, because he is always under the watchful eye of his security guards. Presidents neither shit nor piss, they give stirring speeches for the people, travel around the world, and send their former colleagues postcards at the New Year. Ordinary people shit. I once had a sentence in my novel about the lyrical poet: "Marie Under wrote a wonderful sonnet and then hurried off to have a shit . . . " When the book appeared in print, Marie Under's name had been changed to "the poet." Even Marie Under doesn't shit, let alone the President.

In North Korea we went to look at art, in the museums watercolors (!) several meters in length were hanging, in which the life of the leader was depicted. One picture showed a train moving through the snowy night, its windows lit up, and in the window of the last carriage (number 10) the central figure of the painting holding up a lantern was a girl (the station signalwoman?). And behind her, ten or so people, one of them a man with bared head, another a soldier saluting with his hand up to his cap, and women standing to attention in awe . . . The title of the watercolor was: "Whither are you bound tonight, o dear leader?!" (!?).

I don't know what you're eating for breakfast this morning, Mr. President—I think anxiously, but for myself, I decide to warm up a Wienerwurst (known nowadays as a weeny)—such sausages have undergone a major development (also technological), so it is unlikely that they tasted the same at the end of last century as they do now. Now I have to correct myself, stop all the prettifying decorative descriptions and get the "weeny" out of the packet. This involves two different things—*and an unending series of differences*, when you compare someone this century with someone a century ago. It is *impossible* to imagine anything that is exactly the same as it was *a hundred* years ago.

I haven't left enough firewood by the kitchen range, and when I go to fetch more I see, behind the shed, a woodpile, and a sharp ax embedded in the chopping block. While chopping the first log into sticks of firewood (no problem for me) I think about Enniver Ummal, while chopping the second one, I think anxiously that the President has quite a problem to make his nest in the hearts of all Estonians. Estonians neither fear nor respect God or the Devil, let alone the President.

When the fire starts crackling down in the grate and the kettle, filled with fresh water from the well, begins to boil, I feel a strange kind of peace, as if I have exchanged the Coca Cola in my veins for blood, just as prescribed by Ummal. A strange state of mind envelops me as I close the squeaking door of the grate and listen to the crackling. I am sitting on a comfortable little bench (stool?), and I want this moment to last and last, but then I reach out for my packet of cigarettes and wonder anxiously whether you, Mr. President, have a packet of cigarettes within reach.

*

Looking out of the window, where dozens of small birds are flitting about in the sunlight, between his fingers a cup of steaming coffee, sits the writer So-and-So at a farm on the edge of civilization, trying to create immortal works or art, or, in fact, if we are pedantically honest, simply enjoying himself in these surroundings. The lawn in front of the house and the leaves of the lilac bushes are like green gold.

Yes, Mr. President (I think anxiously), you can't get up early in the morning, go to your writing desk and start writing novels.

I once wrote a story where someone dreamt that he had been elected President of the USA, and there follows a gloomy description of the morning mixed with a hangover, where the drunkard discovers to his delight that he has not been elected president in reality, otherwise it would have been quite impossible for him to go and drink his first the hair-of-the-dog-that-bit-him beer behind the kiosk and wet his insides. On that occasion, they rang me from the publishers and apologized for having to remove the reference to the USA, their publishing regulations didn't allow any aspersions to be cast on the presidents of foreign nations. But now I am thinking (anxiously) that it is not the best thing for a writer to have the post of president. Like that Havel—always in opposition, always critical, but then suddenly all that endless praise. It would drive an honest writer crazy—choosing every word that falls from his lips. Thank God that Mario Vargas Llosa lost the Peruvian presidential elections in 1990, which finally opened his eyes (like those of a kitten!).

It seemed to me that I could glimpse under the high trees, between the bushes or the young alders, some strange color, nothing definite, something in shades of light and dark green, with dark shadows underneath. I ought to get up and go out onto the steps to have a look, as the lilacs are hiding most of the landscape outside the window, but I just can't be bothered—perhaps someone (Jaak or Maria) is coming along the path through the trees, I think apathetically, and leaf through the texts on the table that I found on the shelf the evening before. They are articles or speeches by unknown authors with foreign names (Finnish, German, English), originating from green meetings. Translated, copied, and neatly placed in files, they stand there on the shelf of this rented summer house and anyone staying there can read them during the long evening hours: . . . *the world scraped free of ethical syrup is the bedrock of the coming centuries, in as much as nuclear war does not annihilate this one chance of survival . . . not many individuals willing to risk their lives for mankind without the support of the raging masses are born in every millennium. Andreas Baader and Ulrike Meinhoff are the bravest people that the history of mankind can offer . . . those with any sense are very small in number, a grasp of reality is a most rare thing among people . . . the fiercest struggle in nature is always one within the species—man is wolf to man . . . at any rate, Andreas Baader and Ulrike Meinhof will show the way to mankind, not Jesus of Nazareth or Albert Schweitzer.*

*

When I look out of the window for a little longer (and also begin to see what I am looking at, because people often glance out of the window, but thoughts prevent them from taking anything in, and they stare like blind), the sun has been moving across the heavens for several hours and has produced a shadow in front of the house. It is around lunchtime, reading and making notes has made time pass without my noticing it (like money in the bookshop), this fresh countryman has not managed to get outdoors, and the former city dweller has not managed to feel joy at the fine weather.

I am focusing on a field with a clump of junipers and pale yellow (yellowed) grass, through which a dark strip, a line, a path leads to the trees which right now are without deep shadows, are in the full sun, when suddenly something glints like the reflection of the sun in glass.

This reminds me of how one of the junipers was moving this morning, the junipers were dark like human figures in the mist, and one of them was a walking figure.

I look at the row of trees for a long while, but there is nothing special to be seen. I believe I now know that someone is keeping an eye on me, someone is spying, playing at reconnaissance, this may be some little boy or other (who should be in school but isn't), though it could be an adult. For a moment he (or some part of him—binoculars, the sleeve of a jacket) comes into my field of vision, then vanishes, only to become visible again moments later.

And there he is—this time, between the junipers, I can definitely see the flash of binocular lenses. A spy, a secret agent, or a birdwatcher has left his mark there.

My privacy has been disturbed, and there are two things I can do: either let myself be disturbed or not. I can feel my heart beating more rapidly, and I am no longer myself. The next moment I see with relief that the space under the trees is not the same either, and someone emerges, a woman wearing dark clothing, I can make out the spectacles on her nose, and am even more relieved when I see the glint of her lenses. The woman is not coming in the direction of the house, turns to the left a few moments later and disappears behind the lilacs. She is not coming to visit me, merely going down to the sea. She could be a neighbor. Yes, she almost certainly is—and my neighbor is skirting my house to get to the sea. I feel slightly regretful that she didn't drop in for a chat.

Now my field of vision is empty of people again, as before, but I am thinking that soon the beach will no longer be deserted.

Presumably, the woman went down to the sea, she could hardly have gone anywhere else walking this way, only to the sea. Anyone local would hardly go to the beach, they wouldn't have the time, as rural tasks never come to an end. She has something to do by the sea. I suddenly begin to wonder what a countrywoman would be doing down by the sea; I'm about to sneak after her, but then stop myself and carry on sitting in my comfortable armchair—I suddenly see myself from an informer's point of view—an informer must (wants to) inform from morning till night—and this makes me grow uneasy.

When I focus my thoughts again (I look out of the window at the landscape beyond, not seeing anything there), Vennet's painting "An Unending Landscape" springs to mind, and at this point in time it is not the contents of the painting that interest me but the title. When Vennet told me the title, I interpreted it as a whole list of different meanings: an endless / never-ending / everlasting / unfinished / repeated (the same, different) as a sequence / remaining / (even) immortal landscape.

I have no preference among these alternatives, but regarding a concrete interpretation, I must utter my preference, and make a final decision. Vennet left this to me.

The previous evening (as it was growing dark—my watch had stopped and I didn't know what the time was), as I went to bed and wallowed in my pre-slumber thoughts, the desire overcame me to write a story in which the author writes a story and presents that as well. In a story within a story, I deal with (real) things in an extremely arbitrary manner—I am no longer chained by one hand to the real world. Since this story is billed as a fiction, it makes it possible to write, for instance, that the art expert Teodor (or whatever other name you use) catches stray cats, tortures and kills the creatures (in the name of art) in order to make an installation of cats' corpses at a seaside resort, an installation with a voice-over intended to shock the visitors—a child (his own daughter?) is begging for him not to torture the animals, to let them live. Or I could make a real historical figure do the torturing of cats, for example Joseph Beuys. At any rate, the author of such a fiction is no longer the writer So-and-So but someone completely different—a person invented by the writer So-and-So, someone who (himself), as an invention, does not have to be bothered about the truthfulness of the facts described.

In this way you can reduce the burden of responsibility—it is a story where the author writes about an author writing, where the author writes a story which consists of the writer writing a story. An endless sequence of stories, with each story ending / breaking off where the next one begins. This would be the "Never-Ending Story." The cover would be Vennet's painting, "An Unending Landscape". What a book that would be!

Some film or other (it echoes in the depths of my brain) had the same title, there was a song (which is already ringing in my ears), but this doesn't matter, because I cannot give my book an English-language title; the title would have to be "Lõppematu lugu" (i.e. the Estonian for a never-ending story), no, even better "Mitte kunagi lõppev lugu" (i.e. a story that never ends), no (fuck it!) the English title is better, but how the hell can you give an Estonian book an

English title? And who would buy a book that never ends? After all, when it boils down to it, books are bought because the reader wants to know (on page 2,001, or in instalment 2,001) what happens to the hero in the end. It's not the process that is important, but the final solution: a *never-never-end* the ideal solution, making every reader happy.

*

The sea spread out before me is glowing rather than glittering in the low September sun. Now there is no wind, the sea rests quietly on the beach, its surface is almost devoid of fringed waves and foam. Towards the horizon it has become a beautiful mirror, shot through with dark fissures. At the horizon the sea is cobalt blue. Near the shore, where my view is framed by pale, cold green wild rye, the ragged stripe is lighter, icy, clearly less shiny, more opaque than translucent. We are in Northern Europe, and the shining sun does not penetrate the seawater with its rays. Where the quiet waters lap the rocks, the surface of the sea retains its hue. The cloudless sky is a very pale cobalt towards the horizon, where delicate silver stripes are drawn. Near the zenith, the sky takes on more quivering blue color. But the sky is cold, even the sun is cold.

The seascape could be varied in my novel, creating a mood, tying up actions, forming the basis of the story, separating into tales, as if seen by different people. *I feel that this is a good idea. The sea. I can fill the whole volume simply with pictures of it painted with words. I would like to record a realistic overview of the surroundings, its flora and fauna. That could be of some interest, if I do it with persistence.* That's what I'm thinking, so why not call the book "An Unending Landscape."

Indeed, that *ought to be* the title of my book, it is like an excursion (years ago, experienced in the polar regions by the White Sea) in a landscape strewn with conical hills, a landscape where, with each hill he climbs, the wanderer is seized by the expectation that from its top he will see something special (the sea?), something that would be the destination of the whole journey, but from the top of each hill he sees merely the next, to whose top he must climb, in order to *see* . . .

I look out over the seascape, the iridescent water and the empty beach, I step onto the shore grass, under the pine trees, lichen and sand under my feet, I'm not yet right by the sea, I am in the woods near the sea, each spot has its own mark, one spot does not reach the next, simply blends into it; now the shore opens up—a wide bight on whose right-hand edge you can make out the wider curve of the coastline, to the left you can see the lighthouse, quite a long walk away.

One day I will go there (to the lighthouse), I think calmly, as if in a well-lit art gallery (plenty of time) strolling from picture to picture; in my mind a strange (unusual) silence, where nothing can now upset (it would seem) my balanced state of mind; I walk right down to the water's edge, where the seabirds line the water like feathers of foam in the bathtub—I play with the distances and the strength of the wind, which would blow the feathers up like sails.

But there are real sails on the horizon—what else can they be— boats a few meters in length with blinding white sails, bearded sea dogs trimming their sails, humming snatches of Irish or Scottish shanties. Before the horizon, the open sea, before the water, wet sand, where someone has left footprints—when I press my own footprints next to them, they are surprisingly similar in pattern, mine are bigger (unlike) but not so different really, and I imagine that the neighbor—who else could it be—and I have footwear produced by the same factory. Her feet are larger than the average woman's feet, mine are smaller than the average man's, and the dissimilarity of our footprints isn't so important, the same can (maybe) be said about our bodies—she is tall for a woman and I am short for a man, we would only differ a few centimeters in height, were we to stand together our various body-parts would almost be level.

Those feet made their own imprints in the sand, and suddenly small paw prints appear, those of a cat—I have never seen cats on the sea shore, I can't even imagine them sitting or standing near the water; I stop in surprise and say *Kitty-kitty-kitty*, but no cat appears, and I now remember in a flash that I have forgotten to go to the post office, and tomorrow is Saturday, and who knows whether I'll manage to phone Vennet before Monday or write that my poor little cat is in the fridge, and that I'm very afraid it could start decomposing—all you need is an unexpected loss of power and the process would accelerate significantly (especially to the nose).

Unexpectedly, I discover that the cat's corpse is perhaps the only thing linking me to my former city life, that if Vennet brought it here I wouldn't even think of the city for days on end. And should it appear before my eyes, it will be vague, its details distorted, and I will have to prise out the (un)real places and events by force.

When the footprints stray suddenly over from wet sand to dry, I too step inland, along the path, and when their traces mix with others (at some point, recently, there have been a lot of people here), and I lose my way and wander aimlessly between the dunes covered with lye grass.

And there, in front of me, I see a human being.

For one horrible moment I think I have stumbled upon a corpse. But it is a sleeping woman.

My first instinct is to get back out of her field of vision. I cannot see who she is. I stand there helplessly looking, but not seeing, the beautiful landscape opening up in front of me. I hesitate, want to step back, but curiosity urges me on.

The woman is lying there on her back in a deep sleep. The flaps of her coat are open and I can see she is wearing an indigo woolen dress whose severity is softened only by a white collar. The sleeper's face is turned away from me, her right arm is thrown out over her head like that of a child. There is a largish bunch of rowan twigs lying next to her. Lying there she radiates something boundlessly gentle and yet harshly sensuous—her dress has pulled up somewhat, one bent knee is thrown aside. Between the woman's legs a curled cat is sleeping. It is the same kind as the one at Teeriida, as the one in my fridge.

*

I can see from far off that someone has come to visit me—there is a bicycle leaning against the gatepost, and when I approach I see that its owner is sitting with his back against the wall of the house. "Hi," I say breezily, in a friendly way. "Are you looking for me?"

"So you're the new man, they said you were desperate to go fishing, so let's get going, the days aren't too long in the fall."

"I'm not really desperate to go fishing, I wouldn't mind a trip out to sea, but I'm not really up to it today. Perhaps some other time," I say lightly. I don't like this man, I can't imagine why I should suddenly go fishing with someone I don't like. I smile apologetically, the man looks at me in silence, straight at me, in a dull and immobile way, the afternoon sunshine is shining on him, he's pulled the peak of his cap down over his eyes, and half of his (unpleasant, bearded) face is in shadow, and if it has any thought or feeling this is concealed from me. The man simply doesn't budge, I stand there for a moment as if waiting for him to do something so I can wish him farewell, but then I turn (uneasily) my back on him and walk towards the door. The key is under the stone. I am thinking that if I am now playing the role of the master of the house here, then I am responsible for everything. For the jars of jam in the cellar, the apples on the trees, the books on the shelf, the vegetables in the plot.

Fuck this politeness, why should I be so servile and sycophantic (what a word!) toward the locals? I am the firm's client and the firm no doubt gives some villagers extra trade. If some man wants to sit by the wall of my house, then let him.

If someone sits silent and immobile, leaning against the wall of your house (I can't see him, but feel him with every nerve in my body), then that someone is getting on the master's nerves, and in the end the latter will have no choice but go out and start a conversation: "D'you want a beer?"

"If you happen to have one to spare, I'll say yes."

I get some beers out of the cellar, cool, pleasantly cool, it's nice to look at the surface of the bottle—you never get the right temperature in the fridge, I think, taking a long swig.

"So today's a good day for fishing, like," I say, wiping my mouth with the back of my hand. The word "like" (as in the translation of Faulkner's *Light in August*) crosses my lips inadvertently, with that word (like) I seem to want to get onto the same level as the villager, to turn myself into someone else, erase at a stroke my townie background, education, circle of friends, to get friendly with someone I knew nothing about only moments before.

"A good day like," says the villager obviously aping me, but seeking to demonstrate by his intonation that the whole thing is now fixed.

*

I am on my way to meet my wife, who has just come back from some trip or other, walking (there's still plenty of time before she actually arrives) along the path by the railroad track, I am saying to my companions, one of whom is my wife, that I am on my way to meet my wife, who has come back from a long trip.

When I wake up, the light of the dream (murky, almost dark, far-off orange street lights are glowing) stays in my memory as if it were something I have really experienced, then (a few seconds later) I realize that I'd explained to my wife that I was going to go and meet her. In actual fact she hadn't traveled anywhere, was walking beside me, so I wasn't in fact going to meet anyone.

In actual fact my wife had gone off on a trip (USA, Colorado, Denver) and the person I was telling that I was going to meet my wife was someone else, maybe someone I imagined to be my wife.

Suddenly I hear a noise near the bed. I am thinking: as if someone has banged his foot against it. Then I am wide awake and holding my breath, listening.

Cold air seems to be blowing in my face. The floorboards seem to be creaking.

A good while passes during which nothing happens; I realize how helpless I am (in a strange house, a dark room, without the electricity needed to extinguish the darkness), my helplessness makes me angry, my eyes begin to make out vaguely the rectangle of the window (hell! what words for deconstruction!), by groping around on the floor I find my jacket (smooth synthetic material that rustles under my fingers), a lighter in the pocket (reassuring cool metal) and my cigarette packet (rustling cellophane). The lighter lights up the area around me, the far corners of the room are still hidden in darkness, and when I go over to the table to light a candle, there is light in the room, but when I look up, I see the candle flame and my naked body reflected in the windowpane.

I take a couple of avid drags on the cigarette, then stub it out in the ashtray and blow out the candle—I am thinking that, were anyone to look inside now, they would see an Estonian writer with a swollen member; at the same time I mumble half-audibly to myself that smoking on an empty stomach is very bad for you. Now there is darkness all around me, much darker than before.

I know I will not get back to sleep, back home I would switch on the light and read until my eyelids began to droop.

Some feeling or other (I can't really explain what) won't let me sleep. If I should decide that it is the excitement (an inheritance from my forefathers) that accompanies hunting or fishing—on this occasion the anticipation of a catch, since the three nets I put out in the sea might be catching fish right now—I could simply leave the whole job to the fisherman and sleep through till the morning. If it is cowardice that is gradually becoming fully-fledged fear, then there should be enough logical arguments to calm me down, and all I have to do is get up and go and check the front door, thus allowing the habitual urban method (my house is my castle) to give me a feeling of security and lets me get back to sleep.

I get up again, go to the front door by the light of my cigarette lighter, pee into the night, turn the key twice to lock the door again, drink a few mouthfuls of water in the kitchen, pull on my jersey, go and sit on the table and light a cigarette. Holding the ashtray in my hand, I take a long pull on the cigarette. Meanwhile, my eyes take in the light and dark of the landscape outside. It seems to be thundering in the distance. Suddenly I realize that the sky must have clouded over, as otherwise there would be lots of moonlight outside.

My fishing instructor, leader, and assistant Rolli (Roland—not Ronald, and Rolli—not Ronni) held a long (lasting four bottles of beer) and thorough talk about net-fishing skills, which ought now to be the one real joy of my stay here. After this fraternization over a few beers I shouldn't (like) have any reason to dislike Rolli, but I just can't begin to like him, I feel some indefinable antipathy—he just isn't my type. But I don't have to go to bed with him! It'll do just to go and empty the nets in the morning and then do everything myself in future.

Rolli left the city with his wife Julia back in the 1980s, and by way of angling (!) had managed to reach the *kolkhoz* norm for armored fish (read: pike). When fish-nets with weights and fishing line from Ceylon came onto the market, Julia began to make (construct) nets and sell them. It took a year before they themselves began to use them to fish. Now the two of them go to the sea and the nets have become the meaning of their lives (as well as their livelihood). So they weave, braid, and catch, and Ummal has decided that I too should now fall into their nets.

When I went with Rolli to the shed to choose a net (there were several dozen hanging there to dry), Julia, who looked like an Amazon, joined us (cap on her head, wearing a Maoist "party jacket"), and I got the impression that Julia (who had, by the way, "studied something" at university) wears the trousers in the house and Rolli (seeking solace in vodka) is the carpet-slipper hero.

We got the nets in the water by sunset. The calm sea was showing off with all manner of evening hues and the lighthouse sent out its regular portions of measured light. Rolli did the rowing and Julia and I sat astern (?) on the bench.

"This summer, something rather complex took place here," the otherwise taciturn Julia suddenly said, in a clear, rather didactic voice, as if making a speech.

"The village idiot—well, he wasn't an idiot but a weirdo—a thirty-year-old man, whom people call Poiss—i.e. The Boy—though his first name was Joosep, and Joosep was a more suitable name for a man of his age anyway, this Boy fell off the top of the lighthouse and was killed instantly. But people started whispering around that they didn't believe that he fell. If you prefer the accident theory, then you might think that he managed to climb up the lighthouse drunk, but people started saying that it all happened quite differently and that the poor old Boy jumped deliberately. And it's not unthinkable that somebody even pushed him, though there did not seem to be any reason for suicide or murder.

"The Boy never got into arguments with anyone, he had tried to get into art school several years running in his youth, but had never even managed to pass the exams; they say he wasn't even capable of drawing an ordinary pitcher; it's like musicians say—someone trod on his ear—in this case it would be more appropriate to say that someone trod on his hand. People always have the urge to do something that God didn't intend them to do! But latterly he had begun to regard himself as a great artist, the whole village was filled with all sorts of stuff he collected and put up explanatory signs for—now he was supposed to have become an installation artist. Anyway, me and Rolli said that you might as well stick a sign on every piece of junk, it will immediately take on significance. I even planned to write about it in the local newspaper, but then he fell from the lighthouse.

"When they buried The Boy, quite a lot of people came to the funeral, it was the time of year when there are lots of flowers in bloom, and everyone brought white lilies, as if they'd agreed to do so, but one man from the city—he lived near the lighthouse during the summer—brought a great big bunch of red roses. People said all sorts of things, even that this man from the city was gay, that they had often been seen drinking beer together.

"If you look at the story from the angle that The Boy himself jumped, then in a particular context," (!) (damn it, surely Julia hadn't studied literature at university!) "you see the story in a new light, and people do tend to gossip . . . " said Julia, and it's possible that she would have said more, perhaps about the people who had stayed at Teeriida, but that was the end of the sea for that night as far as we were concerned, and the boat glided noisily onto the reeds.

I want to light another cigarette, but decide to try to get to sleep. Rolli will come in the morning and get me out of bed, as otherwise the gulls will peck our precious catch to bits, and you can't eat fish that have died in the water—as Rolli has explained.

I have been truly caught in a net myself, I think ironically as I pull the covers up over my chin. A few days ago I would never have imagined myself to be a fisherman. At times, certain hours, minutes, seconds change a person's life. Sometimes a person can drop dead in an instant.

I feel how the hints that Julia dropped about the Boy affair are beginning to spook me, and will do so until I've written them down. I begin to imagine a contextual gay novel, in which a queer man seduces the village idiot installation artist, fucks him up the ass, and the idiot, filled with pangs of conscience, jumps off the top of the lighthouse. (Everything has its price, as the plaiter of nets, Julia, with her hidden agenda, would say.) However, the story should be committed to paper without the slightest hint of homosexual union, pangs of conscience, the boy would simply lie there with a shattered spine on the sharp rocks. That's all. The true tragedy emerges from the contextuality—being a homosexual, homosexuality as the key quality of one's identity and existence. But then I would have to be gay myself.

I remember, during our university days, how I was coming from some party very early in the morning with my roommate, we were pretty drunk and hadn't picked up a bit of skirt—the girls (prick-teasers) had got us nicely horny and then gone off somewhere else. My bed in the student dorm was occupied, someone was sleeping there, so I had no choice but to creep in next to my roommate; when he started to feel my cock I didn't pull his hand away, when he pulled down my briefs I didn't jump out of bed. There I was, later, squatting in the communal toilets of the dorm and waiting for the other man's sperm to drip out of me, and it is hard to describe my feelings of depression, shame, disgust, and the physical pain I had in my anus. Through a crack in the door (the locks were eternally broken) I saw how my bedmate came to wash himself, how he was rubbing my *shit* off, in the ice cold water for quite some time.

I am thinking about how many texts have been written over the past few decades justifying, even praising, homosexuality. I would never write such a text, I didn't become gay that early morning and my bedmate standing there at the sink struck me as particularly comic; at the time we both forgot about what happened or pretended not to remember.

But I still remember to this day the sickly smell that rose up from the toilet.

***

Sixth Chapter

Rolli gets on his bicycle and is pedaling off, I shut the gate and am left holding the fish. Staring at them. I will give them the knife. And all at once suppressed joy bursts forth.

It was quite a spectacle (at least for me) when large orfe fish were thrown into the boat one by one—I had already felt the noose of the net tightening, and suddenly shimmering silver emerged from the darkness of the sea and began to fill me with a surge of triumph. Rolli's own nets were relatively empty—a dozen or so perch, a couple of small pike and a handful of sprats. This time I was helping Rolli. "You don't have to do anything with them really, salt them and smoke them, a dozen fish will do, but you can take some more perch to smoke," he was saying to me, as we were hauling the fish from the boat onto the shore.

It's such a fine feeling, as if goodness knows what heavy work has been achieved. As if goodness knows what big deal has been accomplished.

I am surprised how genuine my joy is, as if it isn't my joy—some fisherman centuries ago is lugging home his catch, and his family gets food to eat; the children no longer watch him with starving faces, and maybe he'll have the energy himself to take a tumble with the wife, and bring into this world one or two more children.

A strange feeling of regret darkens my joy—there is no one to boast about my catch to, there should be at least a wife to admire her man, Vennet could drive up to the gate, some Artists' Club friend (like Kandiman) could happen to get lost in the area, climb out of his car, and ask me the way while the fresh catch of orfe are doing their dance in the washbowl, and the friend would ask whether there is anywhere round here to buy such beautiful fish. Whereupon I'd say breezily: I don't really know, the villagers haven't caught very many, if you like, take a couple of *mine*, I've got plenty for myself, and to share out to others.

Ah well. The rumor would soon be about that the writer So-and-So is a good fisherman.—Lo, a miracle! Wouldn't have thought it of him, looked like any other townie. But you never can tell . . .

However, I can't find any admirers anywhere, the cat runs out from under the shed, its tail erect like an antenna, rushes up to the bowl of fish, glances at it, and starts to wind itself round my legs, wheedling, playing at being (God rest its soul!) my own kissy-missy. One of the fish has been pecked at by gulls, its innards pulled out, I cut a piece of the underbelly off for the cat, and it grabs the piece and disappears back under the shed with it.

Now I'll have to gut and clean the fish, fillet them, salt them, I've done such things before, I feel at home in any kitchen, I have no problem making any dish (following the instructions in the cookbook), boiling, frying, braising, but at the same time a man like me (and there are many) could just as easily behave in the kitchen like a lady looking at a car engine that refuses to start; and such a man would rush off to fetch help without delay, ask some expert, beg others.

When I go off to see Laakan with a milk pitcher, I am no longer myself, I am another, someone who cannot make food, who has not done more in the kitchen than boil a couple of eggs that (for some reason) look bluish in their shells.

If I now repeat this thought, then I, who can cook perfectly well, am someone else, who cannot cook, but at the same time as being someone who cannot cook, someone who cannot make food, I can prepare (really well) whatever dish you like.

(Now I have written a sentence, which ought to be read one more time. Have you read it through? Is the sentence the same as on your first reading, or is it now another sentence? Suddenly you would be reading the *second* sentence through again . . .)

*

When Jaak goes to fetch his sister (Oh, don't worry, Maria will soon teach you, Rolli has already told us, we immediately thought that you wouldn't be able to cope on your own), a cat climbs down the ladder from the loft and it is indistinguishable from my own cat, both the one I saw at the seashore, and the one in the fridge at home. Here in the village all the cats must be brothers and sisters, of course you can see the differences if you begin to look closely, but I can't think the thought through to the end, as someone is at the door who doesn't look to me like the woman lying on the beach yesterday.

She looks surprisingly similar to her brother—and why shouldn't she—they are twins after all, I now remember that Rolli told me, and there are one or two more clues as to what this talkative woman (and I as a writer at least have nothing against that) would be willing to tell. When Maria (who it undoubtedly is, this time) comes across the yard to meet me, as I sit there on a bench by the well, rolling a cigarette (something I rarely do, but which is an exact sign of the act of smoking), I take in these striking brother-sister differences, which are especially noticeable in the color of the hair (the woman lying on the beach had a headscarf, so I couldn't see her hair), and now I realize that the sister is a little taller than the brother.

"Hi, I'm Maria," she says in a deep (but extraordinarily familiar) voice.

Suddenly and with unexpected clarity I know that I've bumped into Maria once before. I look with close attention at the expression on her face, in which I can read no recognition. Not even faked recognition. This face is now like a foreign language to me, a language whose alphabet I cannot decipher. Like a coded text, with which you have to wrestle for several sleepless nights running before its system begins to become clear. A system is usually based on logic, but sometimes it is the very lack of logic involved that makes the whole thing so undecipherable. Naturally, no code can be completely without logic (as every system of language has its own logic), not even if its significance begins to reveal itself by way of a completely different system of logic, which is ambiguity.

*

Maria walks a few steps ahead, a narrow path has been trampled into the yellowing grass, the background is a good deal darker in general, many feet have trodden it, and although two people could walk abreast, the path restricts their freedom and forces them to walk shoulder to shoulder. I slow my step a little, the distance between us increases, the full length of her body comes into view, and the curve of her buttocks attracts my attention (the wandering glance lingers for a moment and, instead of moving elsewhere, feels as if it is tied to a single spot). Packed tightly under her clothing, which hides nothing—quite the reverse, her clothing accentuates the tautness of her body, its litheness—there are what look like small, fully-inflated balloons—no, not filled with air, but with flesh and blood—which begin to make my own blood quicken, my own flesh swell.

(I am talking here about my lust, as an Englishman would about his home . . .)

Maria takes a fish from the bowl, it writhes, resists, but Maria stuffs her fingers in its mouth, scrapes the scales from its sides, so that they fall glittering in the sun; the fish without scales lives on, even when the sharp knife cuts open its belly and Maria (who has rather large hands for a woman) rips out its innards with her blunt-tipped fingers in order to stop the fish writhing; I turn my head aside, the whole scene makes me retch, Maria doesn't seem to be particularly affected by the agony and suffering of the fish, she tosses the gutted fish into the clean, white, and shiny enamel bowl, and says that I should now attempt this task myself.

My fingers aren't that nimble when it comes to dealing with fish, it all takes time, I fumble around, but I do make a start, and the next one is easier, the next even more so; every time I have a fish between my fingers, its tail lashing, the fish trying to wriggle out of my hands onto the grass, I feel a stab inside me—an unpleasant feeling—as if my conscience is leaping, doesn't want to follow orders, but none of this is evident from the outside. Maria smiles encouragingly, she has a tiny scar on her right nostril, I think I have kissed it once, as well as her pursed lips, but it must have been years ago, and when I cautiously (so as to avoid touching the poisonous spines) pick up the umpteenth perch, put my hand inside and (carefully) press it down on table, already dark with fish blood, Maria turns around abruptly, disappears with swift steps (runs) out of sight round the corner (between the apple trees and the berry bushes), and vomiting can be heard. I can't see, but I can hear, how a woman is puking at the other end of the sunlit garden.

When Maria returns a short while later, I feel embarrassed to look at her, as if I know her sordid little secret (I shouldn't, in my dealings with people, exaggerate small details, that creates pointless tensions, prevents me from being natural), but when I finally raise my eyes from the table dark with fish blood, and see Maria's dull, indifferent look as she scrapes up the scales, and imagine I can smell the faint odor of spew, I consider two options—either the woman is pregnant, or are these the after-effects of alcohol poisoning.

Large blue-spotted and smaller greenish mud flies try to attack the fish.

The cat drags the entrails of the fish (roe, liver, stomach, heart, intestines, fat) out from under the bush. Intending to eat it all up. Our own city cat (God rest its soul) didn't eat fish entrails, wouldn't even take the trouble to investigate (sniff) if you threw them right in front of it. I'm thinking that if I'd had it stuffed, it would have been nice to take around with you. Then I think that the post office (communication center) should be open, that I'll still get a chance to phone Vennet today, or to send him a letter.

*

It's well past midday and the sun has moved on by the time we're finished with our task. I take (the last) bottles of beer from the cellar, and now it is time to try some fresh, quickly salted orfe, which can also be called "lightning salted," and has been prepared some way or other. I like the vague expression "some way or other"—it explains nothing, doesn't go into details about the method of preparation, leaves everything to your imagination, as each and every one of us has lots of his own images in his head. The expressions "quickly salted" and "lightning salted" also explain nothing specific, refer vaguely to previous experience and recently read information: If I say that freshly salted fish (here there is also a paradox—salted fish implies storage, canning, requires salting over a longer period of time, so that the salt can penetrate into the body tissue) tastes wonderful, I have not said anything about the fish, but about myself: that under certain circumstances the fish tastes wonderful to me, personally. The word "wonderful" does indeed mean something positive, pleasant, and certainly superlative. I think to myself that the word "wonderful" has a superlative meaning (only, of course, if I use it under specific *conditions*).

While Maria, who is sitting across from me (and who is right now drinking beer, putting the glass down on the table, wiping her mouth with her handkerchief, taking another piece of fish out of the bowl on the end of a fork and putting it in her mouth) should become the heroine of my story (I have after all come to Teeriida to write) I don't really want to describe her at all. Every single hint (the tiny scar on the nostril, blunt-tipped fingers, nice backside which isn't hidden by her clothes, but accentuated by them in a provocative way) will conjure up in the mind of the reader some-one else who has just such qualities, and Maria is sketched out before his eyes on the basis of such similarities, so that he doesn't want to know about the *differences*, which are in fact more important when thinking about the (real) prototype.

When I describe how Maria, after taking a swig of beer, wipes her mouth with her handkerchief, I am bringing forth a difference—a situation which does not gel with the stereotype (in the countryside you wipe your mouth on your sleeve or with the back of your hand), and with a single movement of the hand Maria stands out from all the other Marias that we know in the countryside, although I have given no hint of her appearance.

I take a few swigs of beer, put the glass down on the table before plunging my fork into a piece of orfe, and draw my hand across my mouth.

"Are you going to start writing anything?" asks Maria.

I reply that I have the intention of doing some more translation work, but that (unfortunately) one pretty interesting idea for a story has been lurking for several days now in the (empty and bleak) corridors of my mind. I think to myself that I ought to suggest to the neighbor woman that we can be on first-name terms, since that would be easier, but then I think, as in a dream, of how in my story the protagonist will still address Maria in a formal manner, and do so with embarrassing persistence even after they've sported together in bed (or somewhere else) on several occasions.

I don't suggest being on first-name terms with Maria, instead I complain that I didn't bring along my typewriter but my computer, which I can't use without electricity.

"But there is electricity," she says, and takes me into the other room. Next to the writing desk, behind the bookshelves, there is a socket. You can only see it by moving the shelf a little and lifting the loose edge of the wallpaper.

*

I wake in the darkness, weariness floored me toward evening, I went to lie down straight away, and have clearly slept for several hours in a row. Nothing or no one is forcing me to do anything, so I can allow myself this luxury. I have no idea of the time, and that thought doesn't disturb me—I should be quite indifferent to it anyway. I find a candle by groping around, and my lighter (have to get a flashlight), and I can see myself in the closet mirror.

After I've drunk some water in the kitchen (the salty fish!) I go and sit at my writing desk, light the other candle, and plug in my computer.

The writer So-and-So is tapping the keys of his computer by candlelight.

If I were to write such a sentence in a story, it would sound like overdone nonsense—and I simply don't dare to write such things— but right now it is patently true. When Maria had gone I rummaged around in the sheds but didn't find a single piece of cable there, let alone a table lamp. So: computer by candlelight. (The light of a spill lamp would have been even better!) Tomorrow, tomorrow, already no doubt, I will drive to the nearest small town (only 60 kilometers) and buy some extension leads and table lamps and some sort of radio and will thumb my nose at what Ummal wants.

I think like a schoolboy that I will have to black out the windows, otherwise the whole village will know how I am squandering electricity. But so what if I do, I'm paying Ummal (that is to say the secret police are paying for me) through the nose for this place, and it is entirely my affair whether I accept his restrictions or not.

To a certain extent, the ideas that Ummal proclaims are like playing a game of blind man's buff with blind people. (I've used this comparison earlier in one of my texts, but I can't remember which, or the context.) The blind men are given blindfolds and have to find one another. The blind men have a lot of experience (their natural state) of finding things by touch.

A game of blind man's buff is one situation where circumstances allow a blind man to appear to be sighted; for that reason he will be prepared to have himself blindfolded before the game starts (though this will serve absolutely no purpose), and during this game he will have the advantage over those who can see. But when a blind man plays hide-and-seek, and has to hide somewhere in order not to get caught, then he is at a disadvantage vis-à-vis a sighted person—he will (unexpectedly) knock some object or other over and give himself away.

I've plugged in my computer and should now start work, should write a text or translate someone else's text. At present my text simply doesn't exist, but the other man's text is in the book I'm holding. But I'm not yet ready to start work, I've been enjoying the unusual situation (computer + candle) for several minutes now, and have switched the computer off again, I now wait for more fruitful times and start reading something which has already proved to be fruitful.

```
I N
G   A
N   M
I   E
H   R
S   I
I      C
F      A

T
R          a novel by
O
U              RICHARD BRAUTIGAN
T
```

You can see right from the start that the layout of the title is going to lose its forked shape in translation, it won't be the same thing. Richard Brautigan shakes himself free of the hook, and he (the fish) is gone.

The sun has long since risen as I end my reading (P.S. *Sorry I forgot to give you the mayonnaise*), and I know that I am not going to be the translator of this book. You simply can't translate the American flag into the Estonian one. Turn the Sixties into the end of the twentieth century. To keep the significance of the text, Benjamin Franklin's statue in San Francisco should become old daddy Jannsen's statue in Pärnu town (maybe?). And in the same spirit you would have to alter the whole book and the end result would be (a really) absurd text, which would make poor old Richard spin like a top in his grave. Of course you would be afforded the opportunity to comment on things—allusions, puns, historical names, place names, idioms, and so on, everything would have to be annotated in detail, you would have to chew the text for local consumption, but even this doesn't necessarily explain the meaning (context) of words and phrases and make them comprehensible. The educational level and intelligence of the reader—everything will play a role, and only Brautigan himself can read Brautigan, if even he can (!), since whatever he planned at the moment of writing might not be the same the next day.

When I step outside, the sweet smell of smoked fish from the vestibule fills my nostrils. I look for a long time at the golden brown fish, then I break open a perch and crumble a little bit of its white flesh between my fingers. The Laakans were supposed to be coming to taste the smoked fish in the evening. Maybe they came when I was asleep. In my opinion the fish has come out quite well—just enough salt, and doesn't seem too dried out. That especially uplifting pride (about work that I'm not used to) touches me again, brushes pleasantly against my cheek, and I feel I must share this pride with someone. The cat runs towards me from under the shed and demands to be fed. And gets what it wants.

*

(CECI N'EST PAS UNE PIPE)

I line the events up in a row: In 1926—the same year as Pol Pot and Michel Foucault were born—René Magritte painted the first variation of the painting "This is not a pipe" (*Ceci n'est pas une pipe*). (The painting depicts a carefully-drawn smoker's pipe, under which is written in the handwriting of a schoolchild the words "Ceci n'est pas une pipe".) In 1968—when the world was shocked by student unrest and Warsaw Pact tanks rolled onto the streets of Prague towards the end of the summer—Michel Foucault published his essay "Ceci n'est pas une pipe," which has points of reference to *Les mots et les choses*, which starts with a detailed description of Velázquez's "Las Meninas." The people represented in the painting (one of whom is the painter Velázquez himself) are looking with interest at something happening in front of the canvas, outside the space of the picture—where in all likelihood someone interested in art (and not those individuals sitting for the artist in the painting—the royal couple, revealed to us by a *mirror* positioned at the back of the room) is standing, admiring Velázquez's work.

I can imagine a mirror in which I look intently at myself, and I don't (usually) think that the other (my mirror image) is in turn studying my appearance: gray hair, a face already wrinkled, the skin of my face growing slack. I can also imagine a situation where there are mirrors in front of and behind me, where I suddenly notice with surprise that I have been copied an infinite number of times, although to first appearances it would seem that we are only looking at each other (my mirror image and I), sizing one another up both front and back.

(I see that it is now late afternoon and I have been sleeping through a beautiful Indian summer's day. Maybe there won't be any more days like this for the rest of the year, so that one would have to wait very many days before something *of the same order* were to occur.)

I am thinking that although I decided in the early morning that you couldn't translate the American flag into the Estonian one, I now reckon that it's possible, and that the end of the century *is* the Sixties. A Brautigan style counter-culture is the culture that holds sway right now. The Fluxus artist Yoko Ono is very rich and owns expensive works of art that depict reality. John has been shot dead. Brautigan's books have sold copies by the million. He's now a classic. The doors of the drawing and painting departments at the Düsseldorf Academy of Art are adorned with the names of Russian academics—the free world is beginning to relearn artistic skills. The cultural terrorist, Nam June Paik, who has become well known as a composer, is now an art professor and a classic. One member of the Fluxus movement, founded in order to counter bourgeois values, the composer of the music of gesture, Vytautas Landsbergis, has become the President of Lithuania. The homosexual Foucault has died of AIDS. Julia Kristeva, who fled the Socialist Bloc in 1966 and started up as a Maoist in France, now sits on art exhibition juries. My male member has grown hard while I slept, its swollen impatience and lust disturb me, are becoming a bother. I am not thinking, do not want to think about anything sexual just now, but my flesh is operating against my wishes, my flesh has begun to revolt.

I sit up on the edge of the bed and light a cigarette. Something is moving outside—someone's shadow is sliding along the wall. I drag on my pants and go over to the window to have a look. A woman is busying herself at the shed, and on the wall of the shed a net is spread on nails. The woman (it is Julia, she was going to teach me how to clean the nets) is fiddling about with something, she is presumably weaving together some of the ripped mesh, she is dressed for sunbathing (the weather really must be as warm as summer), and I can't help admiring her body. The clumsy fishing wear had turned Julia into a fisherwoman, and now it makes me grow all hot to see how feminine this person who's hatched from the fisherwoman is. Like a butterfly that has sloughed off its chitin cocoon. She awakens lust, the desire to possess, I can can't help the fact that she is now bursting with sexuality, she agitates and rouses, she is like an unearthly object, something from heaven, which has landed unexpectedly in my world, and I feel the irresistible urge to touch the arousing body, to feel it, stroke it, violate it.

Oh, Julia, Julia . . . I moan, throwing myself back onto my bed, but suddenly her *face* is before my eyes: narrow lips, ironic, cold-eyed, power-hungry, almost masculine. Not a whit of softness—as if the body whose back is facing me as she deals with the nets belonged to someone else, that body is like a picture in an erotic magazine and her face like something off the cover of a political weekly.

I glance in the mirror and drag a comb through my hair. When I step outside, and call out a greeting to Julia in a lively way, she silently picks up her dress, goes round the back of the shed, and when she emerges, her alluring body is almost completely hidden.

"You were sleeping so sweetly that I hadn't the heart to wake you," she says, her voice sounds free of tension, mild, I look at her face in astonishment and see that this woman is a complete stranger. "I'm Julia's sister, Kristel," she says with a smile. "We're all sisters round here."

***

Seventh Chapter

I am now quite near the lighthouse. It rises up over there, rigid and straight, blindingly white (a white bulge with a railing around it surrounds the semicircular dark top, from which light bursts, on pitch black nights, in the form of rays), and you can see how the surface of the sea, smooth as a mirror, reflects the stones and pebbles at the foot of the lighthouse, large and small alike. For a moment I want someone to emerge from the lighthouse and look at me with a spyglass, but the stiff tower rising up against the sky has congealed, with its dark window apertures, from one of which you can clearly see a small white patch of light . . . I keep looking at the lighthouse, growing ever larger, and am thinking of nothing at all (. . . as soon as someone tells me what something means, it becomes repulsive to me).

I pull the prow of the boat between the rocks, throw out the anchor and press it down into the low, rough grass (with a surface like a beard that has not been shaved for a few days), although with the sea so calm this is not necessary, but this way of acting like a (real) fisherman gives me satisfaction, and I don't care if I can't or don't want to examine the motivation for this satisfaction.

The lighthouse is situated at the tip of a grassy rise. The door is locked with a padlock and I have no way of climbing up. There are several boats on the sea, the sea is glittering—the slightest splash of a wave contains the sun (that is to say a reflection of the sun), and now I am thinking mawkishly: a sea full of little suns, the sea is swarming with little suns. I am thinking that the answer to the question—when is it art?—is very simple: art is when the village idiot squats down and says he is making art.

On the cream-colored foot (worn by the tooth of time, yellow in places and crumbling away) of the lighthouse a blue-black-white Estonian flag has been painted, under which is written in large (red) letters:

JOOSEP VAINO (THE BOY)

ONE MAN SHOW

The whole of the area around the lighthouse has become (may he rest in peace!) an art exhibition.

There are ten or so holes, which resemble graves, and at the bottom of these there are plates of glass, on whose underside, from the observer's point of view, are pasted pictures cut out of newspapers, showing famous singers, politicians, sports people. Short planks have been tied together to form crosses, with fragments of mirror in the middle. On the door that has been dug into the ground the word GRAVEYARD has been written in large letters and under it in smaller ones: anyone can die.

There are a few dozen or so window frames propped up against the rocks, behind which are hung tatters of fabric (and even some newer pieces), ripped underpants, blouses, a veneer board with MUSEUM written on it, under which: anyone can be an artist.

There is a stack of logs, driftwood, bits of planks. This is the ESTONIAN FOREST, which means: anyone can saw wood.

There is a ring of flat stones, on which are lying (glued on?) fish bones and those of birds and animals. RESTAURANT, along with the inscription: anyone can eat.

There are rusty parts of engines, car bodies, with fluttering blue-black-white flags painted on them; this is the GARAGE, with the explanation: a rich man can drive a car.

There are all manner of pieces of junk with ribbons tied around them, and this is the SHOP, with the inscription: anyone can buy presents.

I pay great attention to The Boy's installation (me—member of the public at an art exhibition) and deliberate on the fact that many of the objects here could very well be in the art galleries of the capital, only the words (inscriptions) would need to be adjusted somewhat and then the whole thing would take on powerful social significance; whereby the GRAVEYARD is a ready-made (and a very profound) work of art, according to whichever criteria.

It is possible that The Boy (was) is a reasonably powerful artist in a contemporary art context, and were he still alive he would have been discovered, in the same way as Sunday painters were once discovered (in Yugoslavia). He *could have* become famous (feeble-minded, a homosexual!), but why shouldn't he attain fame even after his (tragic) death, if only some knowledgeable theoretician (Teodor) would plug his reputation? The Boy himself (may he rest in peace) would no longer have anything to do with the matter, but Little Estonia could feel proud of its Great Man.

I push the boat (conjuring up a serious face) out onto the smooth water—now I really will have to phone Teodor (still haven't been to the post office, oh damn! the cat could disintegrate there in the fridge), must phone tomorrow (without fail!), let him come and examine the most interesting art objects (according to Julia, the whole village should be full of them) and mold a great figure in our suitably flat artistic landscape.

*

I let the mild south-westerly (?) breeze drive the boat towards the harbor, and pensively exhale smoke into the sea air. There was quite a new padlock on the door of the lighthouse—clearly the villagers were afraid that someone else could climb up and jump off. Earlier anyone used to be able to go up and have a look over the surrounding area. I imagine a couple ascending the narrow spiral staircase, groping at each other's genitals, pressing slobbering kisses over each other's lips ringed by rough stubble. I felt (if I'm honest with myself) a strange excitement as I reached the lighthouse (as if peeking out from the bushes at the lovers), and images ran willy-nilly through my mind, which depicted two complete strangers' indecent act (which their behavior undoubtedly was). Kandiman once told (when quite drunk) how, when he enters a hotel room, he immediately rips the sheets off the mattress to see how many sperm stains it's covered with. If the mattress seems to be clean, Kandiman is filled with disappointment, as if he'd been somehow deceived.

I can imagine that some kind of latent homosexuality lurks within me, which rises to the surface when thinking of the licentiousness of others, releasing tensions and giving my mind room to think (pure) thoughts. This (the previous sentence) is a nice justification, on which can be erected an artful myth, so that when I describe (to my reader) endless perversities, murder most foul, horrible (psychic and physical) violence, then I am doing my reader a big favor, freeing him from the propagation of subconscious evil, and at the same time doing society a favor, protecting it from (hidden) evil being unleashed.

This (the previous piece of text) gives one (for example) the freedom to make films whose content consist of various types of killing, and in which the myth is born that people need to see horror, so that people then begin (themselves) to believe in the myth, giving rise to a new myth that people want to see it . . . etc., though in reality they long for romantic love, noble feelings, etc., yet in reality . . . ?

People probably don't brood (nowadays) over what they really want, merely take what is given and, as the givers are many, swallow what the (most powerful) giver pushes down their throat.

Interesting to know whether that townie (I'd like to see him, look him over—wandering around here sometimes on the weekend, relaxing from city life) endeavored to get The Boy to make his installations, praised him, patted him on the shoulder: "You, my Boy, are one great artist," is what he (maybe) said.

I gradually drift into the harbor, the clear water reveals the rocks on the seabed, covered with seaweed. Right next to the boat the spine of a large fish appears and vanishes beneath the bright blue membrane covering the sea. Then another fish cuts open this membrane. I take my spincast rod and cast, the hook lands some distance away, and I feel good about the fact that I'm beginning to get the hang of this sport. I am thinking—sport—and smile, wondering whether fishing with spincast tackle is really any more of a sport than net fishing, and it does seem quite impossible for a fish to end up on the hook simply because of the glittering bit of tin on it. It is possible that this (the possibility of catching a fish by angling) is, once again, one of those myths that are crammed into people's heads, because those who produce spincast rods and reels want to get shut of their products one day.

*

I am trembling all over, as if I've been indulging in passionate sex, and have then released a powerful spurt of semen. At the prow— the bottom of the boat, right in front of my feet, is a large green and gold fish, I try to pick it up, to free its mouth from the choking line, but a couple of wild thrashings ward off my hand, and the line flies as if spat out onto my trouser cuff.

I daren't touch it, the huge mouth is full of sharp teeth, insolent eyes full of hatred are bulging in my direction; I have nothing at hand to whack it with in order to stun it, I look helplessly around, there's the anchor at the front of the boat, I grab it, almost falling over to get a grip on it, and feel a sharp blow to my leg, but I'm already holding the anchor, and now I can wallop the fish with it.

The first blow misses, the second hits its target, and the creature begins to tremble as if suffering an electric shock. The third blow finishes it off, its head is bloody but its eyes are exactly as before. Grimly accusing, promising revenge. But now I have the courage to pick it up, and its body might weigh several kilos. I cannot explain to myself how I got the thing on board. Everything happened as if in a dream, as if someone else did it.

One of the oars is bobbing a dozen meters away in the water, I take hold of the other from the rowlock and, paddling from both sides, I finally reach the stray oar. It's not a great distance to the harbor, and when I steer the boat in the right direction, I notice several men watching me. Well, you're getting a free performance, I think bitterly, and try to imagine the victory of that other person with the fish. Yes, several parts of the whole performance have been rather ridiculous. Especially intriguing (to the spectators) was the scene of the murder of the fish. The writer So-and-So smiles wryly. He cannot explain to those watching on shore that it was someone else that did that. Everything will be blamed on him.

Every man who has never read even one line of my prose knows who is in that boat. The whole village knows. Every movement I make will be blamed on (proper name, written as one word) *Estonianliterature.*

When, by some miracle, I manage to reach the harbor without any great bungling on my part and am standing there with two feet on the ground, I hear an appreciative murmur, which means that my catch has met with everyone's approval, and that I have now caught a big fish for Estonianliterature. The legend that So-and-So is a *good* writer passes from mouth to mouth, family to family.

*

There is a car standing at my gate, someone's (unfamiliar) car is standing at my gate, and the evening light is reflected in its glinting, dark green roof. I cannot imagine who this could be, and equally strange is seeing smoke rising up from the sauna chimney, but the tires of my bicycle are already revolving at a greater speed and the heavy rucksack (filled with the fish!) feels as if it's filled with feathers (what an crude exaggeration!). I am joyful—there is now someone here to whom I can brag about my exploit.

The nearer I get to home (Teeriida is, at present, my home), the more my wish to boast about the fish begins to fade and a worm of protest creeps out in my mind—who the hell has taken over my household, has stoked the sauna and is having a party at the table outside my house?

It turns out to be Ummal, who rises from behind the table and extends a hand in my direction—and when I recognize him everything falls into place, my momentary irritation changes to unease (I'd already forgotten that I'd been placed here to spy on others, and now the time is ripe for me to start taking my task seriously), and I'm now in such a funk that as I get off the bicycle I trip against the frame with the fishing rod still tied to it, and there I am sprawling in the flower bed. When I lift my head, I notice to my horror that I've fallen only a few centimeters away from a sharp line of edging stones.

"Well, so you see, instead of driving around comfortably in his car, a real man rides a bicycle, even though he may put his life in danger by doing so," Ummal points out to the others, using me as an example of a model vacation tenant. I get up from the ground, am grateful that those standing around are not snickering at my mishap (popular TV program—someone falls over and the whole studio audience bursts into laughter), so I don't bother to explain that I only went down to the beach on a bicycle because the car wouldn't start, as the battery was (probably) dead.

"And what's that in your bag?" Ummal wonders. I take my rucksack from my back, open the flap, and tip the fish out onto the grass.

"Well, fuck me!" says one of them in admiration.

"Great photos you could make of that!" yells another.

"We were thinking, if you have no objections, we'd do an item about you for the papers. It'd be a kind of advert for our firm, but at the same time it would give you a chance to expand on the principles of what the weak points of our society or state actually are," says Ummal, looking me attentively in the eye.

I pull the bicycle out of the flower bed and lean it against the shed, then I take a seat at the table, open a bottle of beer and quench my thirst. I can imagine that the newspaper story would be an exposition of their ideas through me, if indeed all of this (founding a green state? terrorism?) corresponds to the truth. The story will be done while I am kept here, and when the paper is published, I will be able to read, to my surprise, all that I've said. At the same time (given the real reason I'm here) I should not begin to refuse their requests and avoid appearing in the paper. I realize that I have been nicely maneuvered into this corner (for a moment I even admire this expression) and can't wriggle out of it.

"Wow!" cries Maria, who comes up with a sandwich tray in her hand, her mouth open in admiration at my fish. For one moment I have the stubborn urge to say that I bought it from Rolli, but then I am already posing with the fish, and I pose and pose.

"I think that'll be enough now," I say putting down the fish, or rather giving it to Maria (who has clearly been assigned the task of hostess), so that Maria can free it of its scales and entrails, so that Maria can chop it up into small pieces, which will then begin to dance nicely in the pan on the fire. "OK," I say. "If necessary, then we'll do that story for the paper."

"Let me do the introductions. This is Walden the journalist, he became famous for exposing Russian spies, KGB people, and doing exposés on environmental disasters. It is to be hoped in the near future—let us say at a suitable juncture—he will be igniting little fires under the backsides of certain top Estonian politicians."

I shake the hand of this man who seems to have lacquered hair and is thin and lanky, and think for an instant of the expression "at a suitable juncture," but only for an instant, just enough time to register it in my mind; then I shake hands with the photographer (who I've already known for some while) and the hand of a woman, slack, without feeling, and cool. Ummal says, introducing her: "And this is Tuulikki." Sure, this is simply Tuulikki, around thirty, looks like a feminist, and is Finnish.

*

"So you seem to like it here," says Ummal, running his finger along a shelf as if to check for dust, and sure enough he brings his finger up to his eyes, inspects it (!), and I begin (for some reason) to feel embarrassed and look aside, out the window, where the guests at the table are drinking beer and laughing loudly (audible even here in the room).

"I feel this is a quiet place, perfect for writing, I haven't felt so good for quite a while, as I've only been staying here for a few days," I say, honeying my words for Ummal's benefit, and those are the expected phrases. "Just a pity I left my typewriter at home and I brought my computer instead which, as far as I know, works on electricity—I bought it second-hand but it didn't have a battery. Turns out that a computer is pretty useless really under these circumstances."

Ummal runs his finger over the computer, his finger traces a circle in the thin layer of dust, and within it two dots for eyes and a downturned mouth. This is Ummal's idea of a joke, I smile a suitable smile, and Ummal understands that I've gotten the joke, so he redraws the mouth, this time with the corners turned upwards. "I have a problem, because I can't write with a pen or pencil, got used to writing on a typewriter right from the start, if I don't move my fingers those thoughts just don't flow into my brain."

"Never mind, we'll bring you a typewriter tomorrow," says Ummal, he doesn't say, Look, behind that shelf is a socket, no, he says, We'll bring you a typewriter tomorrow, maybe he doesn't know anything about the socket (which is presumably the case), but it's interesting how concerned they are about my work (earlier, the secret police, now Ummal).

I say that there's really no point in bringing a typewriter, because there are only a few days of my stay left and I'm quite happy just to read and potter about. Ummal sits down at my place at the writing desk and lets his fingers roam over the literature there (the series of "mildly green" periodicals), and I notice that one or two things have been added to the shelf; Ummal drums his fingers thoughtfully on the desktop then suggests that I work here as long as I have to.

I sigh: "Unfortunately, I can't really do that." These couple of weeks are technically over my budget, but I don't regret anything, I'll get an advance, and already said so in my interview.

"We think that you could work here without paying," says Ummal.

Everything has its price, I think, looking Ummal inquiringly in the eye, the interview (although they're going to twist the truth every way they can) isn't worth those thousands in revenue that the firm wouldn't get; if anything needed to be bought from me then it would be said immediately, because Ummal hardly regards me as such an idiot that I'd believe in noble (disinterested) charity.

"What do you think of these publications?" asks Ummal, moving some of the "green" books on the table from one pile to the other. I can say that I haven't yet had time to take a close look at them, that leafing through them is far too superficial to give me any idea of their contents.

I could say that everything here is a grim, and ever accurate, reminder of what the future holds in store for us. That it is all true and that abandoning humanism is maybe the only way out. I could nod enthusiastically to him about everything written there and then everyone would be happy. (All the Ummals of this world, plus every secret policeman.)

I could say that it is all a load of garbage that stinks to high heaven of fascism. After such an utterance, Ummal would be in an awkward position (just having offered the writer So-and-So free accommodation), and the secret police would also be in an awkward position, as they had just forked out for the wrong man (can imagine that Ummal would lose faith and interest in such a man). The only winner would be the writer So-and-So, who had been honest and straightforward and could continue to marvel at his own honor and lack of compromise. He could sit in front of the mirror of his thoughts for hours on end, the way a beauty could sit in front of a real one.

If I am completely in agreement with him I will immediately raise suspicions (I don't think he regards me as a sycophant); if I give a wishy-washy answer, seemingly going along with what he says, he might imagine that I was keeping something from him and withdraw his feelers like a snail; if I go on the attack, seeking in his truths (if these truths are really his?) his Achilles heel, his weak spots, I'll give him the opportunity of affirming his positions, in which case I would be able to retreat and even use the "yes" word with him, which always seals every agreement (and marriage) nicely.

"I can't really give an answer off the top of my head," I say thoughtfully (though there isn't much time for thinking). "Up to now the rules of the game have been the diametric opposite. Mankind has eagerly believed the grand tales of progress. Missionaries have run schools and extended humanitarian aid to the dark continent. If someone said openly that a sick or disabled person should be left to his own devices, he would be lynched without further ado."

"Yes, those are the truths that the world of today has to accept," Ummal intones. "They are pleasant and comfortable truths that have helped mankind survive up to now. Everyone's happy to hear about such things again and again, and when some writer or other starts defending such truths against an Antichrist or other, then that is a worthwhile occupation."

(The word *Antichrist* gives me a pain in the pit of my stomach—I don't know whether Ummal said it without thinking, but if *this* is the embodiment of evil, which he wants to put paid to before the end of the world, then you can see many things in a different light.)

"We have come around to the opinion that you could become one such praiseworthy writer," says Ummal smilingly.

(Again he has said "we," I think in panic.) I should say something back, he's looking me straight in the eye, as if wishing to reach my thoughts with his glance, see what's going on inside me, I slow my words as I ask: "You would like writer So-and-So to expose the Antichrist?"

"It isn't important to us whether the writer So-and-So, or some other writer, e.g. Such-and-Such, does so. What we want is that a story emerges in a big enough edition that everything written in these books," (he moves a number of the books from one pile to the other as he ruminates) "would be blown to smithereens. A crime novel, a horror novel, a sex novel—the easier to read the better—the main thing is that the writer explains in detail *what it is* he wants to expose and destroy in his book. The writer must show that there are a number of very evil characters who don't respect the rules of our civilization. The writer will not end up opposing anyone, he will expose the Antichrist and quietly let the end of the world take its course. He will be a very social writer, whose heart bleeds for us, and he will have humane ideas."

So, Ummal has ended up on the hook, I think mournfully, Ummal has swallowed the bait laid out by the secret police. The writer So-and-So is doing the dirty work for both sides but will himself emerge unscathed (at great profit to himself). Outside the window it is growing dark as evening approaches, and Maria brings a dishful of fish (the fish I caught) to the table. The golden brown pieces will no doubt taste wonderful.

"Think it over," says Ummal. He rises from the desk and lightly squeezes my shoulder (in a friendly way). I cannot stand men touching me, I would have hit him if I were anyone else—but the likes of me swallows the unpleasantness. The Finnish woman Tuulikki lights the candles on the table. It is a still and beautiful evening. It'd be interesting to know why they've brought her along. Ummal says that I'm thinking about *the thing*—I am in fact thinking that my wife will soon be returning from her trip to America and that she'll no doubt like Teeriida. We can catch fish and pick mushrooms.

*

"Mankind has always lived with the thought that tomorrow will be better than yesterday. Every human being wants his child to have a better life than he himself has had. Usually people understand 'better' as meaning 'easier,' i.e. that their child will not have to make so much effort and slog as much as their parents," Ummal is saying, and crams logs into the fireplace with the poker; he is not helping the fire, simply preventing it from burning properly, but I won't say anything.

"The belief that things are going to get better has helped mankind for centuries. It has created the myth of progress which was supposed to ensure that machines do our work for us, leaving us to enjoy life. But one fine day, let us say that that day just happens to be today, people notice that, thanks to progress, the morrow will be bad and gloomy. Those few individuals that have grasped this fact have tried to explain it to others—that things have changed, that what awaits us now, if we don't change our relationship to progress, is all negative. But they are ignored, it's too easy and pleasant to carry on living in the old way, telling made-up yarns about a happy ending, yet moving inexorably towards a catastrophe, the foreboding of which is increasing day by day.

"If you look at the whole matter from the point of view of the individual, what is most important is to survive, to save oneself biologically, so that one's child becomes a new version of oneself, in the same way a book comes out in a new, improved edition.

"So let us say that at this crazy point in time—when it could still prove possible to postpone the catastrophe and assure coming generations of a life worth living—one part of mankind has opened its eyes, and knows pretty clearly how we should live in the future; but against all common sense, no one wants to listen. Too many people are interested in turning a blind eye to the truth, and think only of today's advantages. Too many are easy-going and lazy and can't be bothered to think what will happen tomorrow. The vast majority are so self-centered and uneducated, they don't give a damn what the future holds in store for their children.

"In such a society, those that know better could create islets where people are oriented towards values and a way of life that promote rationality and not consumption. The easiest way would be to go out with your family and live in the bosom of the forest, ignoring everything going on around you, but at the same time, this family is not protected from what is happening all around them, so that one morning they'll open the door of their hut only to see that all the surrounding forest has been felled. To survive, you need a larger number of people who think in the same way, and maybe the most beautiful solution would be to turn our dear native land into a great mini-state. A green state, which can serve as a model for the rest of the world, which would prove the worth of green ideas, and thanks to this way of life survive the centuries.

"The most important thing of all is that people get to know what awaits them and how, by making small sacrifices, they can turn the current. Mankind must bravely effect a change in what are termed humanist ideas, we must brace ourselves and think of nothing but our own survival. No point in rushing to save the weak in the flood if you don't know how to swim yourself—that would be tantamount to death for all.

"In actual fact, living life is very easy, natural, if you get rid of the unnecessary ballast that mankind has amassed with its so-called culture. I will gladly repeat here the words of my Finnish friend: Whatever catastrophe—the release of radioactive pollution, or anarchistic hunger marches, or even the collapse of society—occurs, *if one building remains standing, then from that building some famous tenor will sing out loud, some musician will play the cello, and a lion-maned conductor will conduct the orchestra.*

"Back in the Sixties my good friend Joseph Beuys had maybe found the right road to follow, a way that would save and support the nature of mankind only if one destroyed the age-old cult of creation. If everyone can become an artist, the profession will gradually lose its meaning and mankind will have gotten rid of one unnecessary expenditure, and the same goes for music—what experiences you can get from a minimalist Jew's harp being played somewhere deep in the woods, around a campfire. The circle of friends won't mind if someone who lacks a good singing voice amuses himself and the others by droning out a song. It isn't the architect but the builder who knows best how to erect a cottage that's strong, cheap, and durable. There is nothing more pleasant, towards the end of the afternoon, than when a family begins to act out a play in their own home, a play they can give full voice to and skip around in without some expensively educated critic seeking meaning and significance in what they're performing.

"I can't understand why, in our small and poor state, we build a stinkingly expensive musical conservatory or—even worse—an art museum! If you want impressions, travel out to our lighthouse, where a certain Joosep Vaino, a simple child of nature, has constructed his work of art entitled "Graveyard," which in the world context we can see as a paraphrase of an installation created by Yoko Ono in the Sixties—and indeed, Vaino has developed the idea by placing mirrors at the bottom of the graves."

I clear my throat and say: "Actually, his mirrors were stuck on crosses, and in the holes were pieces of glass to which were taped the photos of prominent people from Estonian life."

"Even more social, more true, more artistic. Have you seen them? A very good example of how you can achieve something on the periphery, in the provinces. If the statesmen had any common sense, Estonia would be just right to become the first Green State in the world. There is urgency to this. Much has to be done in a short space of time. The European Union would be the end. The end of dreaming. The end of the Estonian state.

***

134

Eighth Chapter

When I open my eyes it is light outside, the ceiling is white, not yellow, from which I conclude that the sun is not shining today, and I try to think what day of the week it could be—Ummal came here three days ago, or is it already four? Time has begun to pass quickly out here, it has got up to a good speed, and during one day I get as good as nothing actually done. I'm not even able to get down to writing anything, although I have a great desire to do so, and ready sentences loom before me as I fall asleep.

Have to get up, but I'm not doing so yet, no one is forcing me to, I don't know what day of the week it is, I haven't a clue what's happening in the world and the Estonian Republic, I haven't read the papers for some time, I don't have a radio, my car has broken down, and the kitchen smells of the mushrooms I marinated the previous evening.

The thought of marinated mushrooms makes my mouth water, but not so much as to get me to rush into the kitchen, I continue to lounge there with open eyes, staring at the ceiling, listening to my thoughts and to the silence, which is suddenly cut through by the sound of a gunshot.

The report is a loud one, as if someone has fired a shot right outside my window; without thinking I rush to the window into the other room and near the gate see a car and two men getting out. They are wearing camouflage outfits, one of them has pushed twigs into the ribbon of his hunter's cap, they are so close that I can see their red faces, I can sense from their staggering gait that they are half or completely drunk, they stop by a large juniper bush, look down at the ground, one bends down, looks at something lying on the ground, then puts the camera hanging round his neck up to his eye, the flash flashes, then there is another flash of light, the other man opens his fly and pisses, after which he shakes his long, thick prick for a long time and with pleasure, as if right in my face (though in fact in the direction of the house).

The man with the camera, hunter's cap, and stout body takes from his pocket a flask, and both take a swig, then he lifts something up from the ground—the legs of a roe deer, takes hold of the animal and lugs it into the car, the second man opens the trunk, and both of them heave it (the body) in.

*

I am sitting by the kitchen table, watching how the magpies are munching the silver fish scales on the fish-gutting table. I have pushed the head of my big pike over the tip of a juniper bush (letting the head dry out, I'll take it home later and nail it up on the wall). Now the magpies start pecking at it, they stick their heads into the wide open jaws, with no fear for the hundred of sharp teeth visible there in rows. Today the fledgling hawk is nowhere to be seen, he is occupying himself with field mice.

I take a gulp of coffee and light another cigarette. In my mind there's an unpleasant feeling of unease—the foreboding that something is going to go wrong pretty soon, though I know that this is the result of this morning's gunshots, not on account of some heartache about anything or anybody. I can't explain to myself why I went straight outside after the hunters had left and strode over to the large juniper and looked for a long time at the blood stains on the yellow grass beneath it, at the crumpled cigarette packet (green Form)—(this is the brand they use to promote Form, focusing on the colors: bright ochre, blood red, and "soothing" green) then I look back at the house, and it seems to me that someone is sitting at the window, where I work, at my desk. I think (for a moment) that this is what the hunter saw when he'd finished pissing. For some strange reason I feel I need to go too—I haven't had one since rising from bed—and when I shake off the drops what goes through my head is that that man could not have seen me sitting at my writing desk, because I watched them standing several paces away from the window.

I am now thinking that what I have seen is the image of my future self, that every morning in the future (when I don't need to go out to sea, to the nets) I will be sitting at my writing desk and writing a tale about how Ummal gets the Informer to the Estonian Republic, who has been sent out to spy on him, to write a tale about how Ummal wants to turn the Estonian Republic into a Green State. He is unaware of the fact that at the same time the Estonian Republic has recruited the writer as the Informer to the Estonian Republic who ought (by exposing Ummal for what he is) to hinder the implementation of Ummal's plans, and the writer is performing his duty as an informer at the same time as writing Ummal's assignment and writing a work condemning (but at the same time promoting) green fascism, so that all parties—the Estonian Republic, Ummal and the writer—end up happy and satisfied with the result.

I feel a little ashamed of myself when I think about how I (perhaps) should have written a report about Ummal's visit, or given an account of it—that is my concrete (paid) task as an informer. I should be writing a letter full of details about our conversations, writing down information about the people who were with Ummal. But I don't have anything against Ummal, not in the slightest—he has a bleeding heart for the future of the planet, so what if he exaggerates a little, who'd take his exaggerations seriously? There are people who are against joining the European Union in every country, and both parties have a right to air their arguments. Every point of view has its good and bad sides. And so on.

In actual fact I haven't chosen sides myself—the fact that I'll be informing for money (a free vacation, per diem) still doesn't mean that the other party can't pay me better, which they are no doubt very keen to do if they can use me as a double agent. I can play with the thought that my choice would be influenced by purely financial considerations, especially given the fact that Ummal wants nothing but good for the Estonian Republic.

That man from the secret police said that they'll get in touch with me when necessary—they surely know Ummal's movements, but hardly anything about our (Ummal's and my) plans for me to stay here longer. I can imagine that other villagers have been commissioned as informers, and it's possible that some villager has been assigned by Ummal to keep an eye on me. In a village every movement is, after all, under scrutiny, as if under a magnifying glass.

I suddenly feel like an outcast—I've been given the task of spying all on my own, with no one to seek help or advice from. I haven't even been told what it is that's hoped and expected of me. If I suddenly discover the plans for an act of terrorism, I can't get in touch with anyone, because phoning from the communication center (I have the man's number, the man who came to visit me at home) would be tantamount to announcing it to the whole village.

And the fact that they never gave me any address (!)—is what I'm now thinking, with growing fury. They recruit me as an agent, then I get the assignment from Ummal (I infiltrate), and could actually be of use already, but they've planned the operation with little thoroughness, clumsily, without taking their own informer (me) into consideration, so that everything, as we say in Estonian, could "draw water.".

"Drawing water" is an interesting Estonian idiom. It means that something planned fails, ends up achieving the opposite of what was intended. I can't see why drawing water would necessarily mean failure. Or are we talking about drawing a line (with your finger, with a stick) on the surface of the water? You draw, but no trace is left. Hence the planned informing operation will leave no trace either. But there can't be any activities that leave *no* trace (in people, events). Yet in this case, it has to be said: the spying operation is passing with no visible (tangible) results—it's drawing water.

*

The day is half spent, and it's drizzling; when the day is half spent, evening is no longer far away, when it grows dark, when you have to light a candle, or get your bed ready for sleeping in.

*

"You're a right Charlie," says Vennet, shaking his head. "You whizz off to the countryside overnight, you leave your dead cat in the fridge, and don't give any sign of where you're actually staying. The firm called 'Full-Blooded Recreation' knows nothing about you. The neighbors in town believe that you've gone off to America. You did say to me that you were starting a new life, you promised you'd invite me to go fishing, but then you go off and disappear and no one hears a thing about you."

I have nothing to say to that, I'm really pleased that Vennet has turned up, I'd like to start dancing around right away, but my temperament won't let me show my feelings, all my nature allows me to do is smile wryly and utter: "I did want to phone you earlier, but we have a communications center here that's only open a couple of hours a day, I keep on going there when it's already shut, and I sent the letter a few days ago, didn't you get it?"

"No I didn't," says Vennet, peers out at the landscape, spots the pike's head. "Ohoh!" he cries. "Caught it yourself, did you?"

I tell rapidly and verbosely about the key moments of my fishing expedition. Vennet regrets the fact that he can't stay on, and mentions that he's come to fish in this area a couple of times, and that the waters here are teeming with fish. My mood saddens and I ask why he came to "bring fire" (another Estonian idiom—dropping in for a short while).

"I came to see you," he says evasively. "To bring you a few letters and fresh newspapers. To tell you that Evelin buried your cat and asked me to smash your face in. I hope she only meant it as a joke."

I regret my sin. I try to explain it away. Then I see that the letters are from my wife, and from someone I don't know, but I'm not going to open them right away, I glance at the newspapers and already know (shaking my head) what to expect there. A long story spread over two pages, color pictures. The big fish looks even bigger in the photo than it was in real life, or in my mind's eye.

"You can read it out aloud to me," says Vennet bitterly.

I don't start doing that, I let my eyes roam over the columns where the writer So-and-So airs his points of view: "I consider that unbridled growth with limited resources will lead to destruction. We are now living in an epoch where putting a brake on things is the way out, there really can't be any more progress the way we lead our lives. Stability is the key to the future.

"People are incapable of resisting the charms of technological invention, they accept everything offered quite uncritically. The fertility of man and his need for consumption increase by the day, by the hour, on this planet.

"Mankind gladly shuts its eyes on reality. Everyone acts as if they were alone on the planet, as if there were no rules governing resources and raw materials, as if economics were an abstract branch of science. Thanks to the specific way Estonia was occupied by the Soviet Union, it has been damaged far less than other European countries with a market economy. We are an educated people, capable of thinking, a northern nation whose urge for self-preservation is especially well developed. What, I think, is most important for our nation is that it has kept its common sense regarding how things stand in the world at large.

"A small state like Estonia can (and must) stop during this final stage of the transitional phase, and ask its people where they're rushing off to. It must be asked by way of our propensity for common sense if we really wish to increase the speed of destruction. It is still possible to discover a new way, the road to survival. A poor country must live like a poor country. The same goes for a poor person. Being a spendthrift and enjoying consumption above one's means was the way a socialist economy was run; a free country thinks of its children and grandchildren."

"You could explain to me what this is all about," interrupts Vennet. I'll have to give him an answer. I clearly can't tell him how things stand at present. All I can do is curse (along with Vennet) at people who have (sneakily) exploited my name—but cursing is merely a disguise concealing other things, and it's pretty obvious that Vennet understands that, that Vennet understands that I understand that he understands . . .

I read: "Culture is, in essence, a question of money. In our small country, small should mean beautiful. We have to think seriously about whether we really need the type of culture that requires large rooms, expensive furniture, and paid personnel. Every time we spend something, we have to ask ourselves: what do we get out of this?"

*

"What do you mean, 'Full-Blooded Recreation' knew nothing about me?" I ask hesitantly, and I am genuinely worried that I may not be able to show my face in town after this article.

"I raised this question last week when some exile Swede, someone called Ummal, came to my studio for some pictures. I got the impression that he hoped to convert me to some belief or other. He said of my paintings that they were the quintessence of a 'green' way of thinking. He said some muddled things about supporting culture and about alternative cultural projects, in the context of which he mentioned your name. In the end I was quite confused as to what he really wanted—none of my paintings, at any rate. I imagined that you might know a thing or two, and since I had business in the Läänemaa province, I went to 'Full-Blooded Recreation' and asked where this house was actually located, the one where my friend was staying. A nice young lady clicked away at her keyboard and then said there were no clients with your name. Then I went along to your neighbors in town, but they knew nothing either— you had left your keys in their letter box and had asked Evelin to water the flowers. Evelin was surprised that I hadn't asked about the cat. She had gone to look for it and, on failing to find it, had looked in the fridge, as it had the habit of jumping in there—then she found it, but dead and wrapped up in a plastic carrier bag.

"All I could imagine was that you'd gone off to see your wife in America, but then this morning I leafed through the newspapers and there was this letter to the editor, which said that my dear friend was being put up by that very same firm of Ummal's, 'Full-Blooded Recreation,' and was expressing his pretty dubious opinions about life, the arts, and the future of Estonia. When I opened the newspaper, I found your location pretty quickly; they even provided a route map.

"Yes, maybe you could tell me what it's all about," says Vennet, and I see that he's become unusually curious about things.

I can't explain everything to Vennet in a couple of sentences, and after reading the article in the newspaper I can't even explain everything to myself. I take Vennet into the living room, show him the kind of literature standing on the bookshelf; I want to discuss things in general terms, I open my mouth, but then shut it again: I am suddenly overcome by helpless fear, the knowledge that walls have ears—the same feeling that held sway (for us all?) in the 1980s when the KGB was especially interested in the arts.

"Let's go outside instead," I say to Vennet and listen to how odd my voice sounds. And when I start telling Vennet about the whole episode, it has nothing to do with the real truth of the matter.

*

I'm genuinely sorry that my good friend Vennet has to go already, but he'll be opening an exhibition in a few days' time. Tomorrow he'll have to hang the pictures, and can't afford to relax right now. I see him to his car, am told (for the tenth time) that he promises to go fishing with me once the exhibition has kicked off; as he gets in, I notice a newspaper open on the passenger seat and the bold headline "Interior Minister Resigns," next to which is a smaller headline, "Leonhard Sammalpõlv: I am leaving politics for good."

"Here, what's this?" (I bawl this out, or at least that's how it sounds to me.)

"The usual Estonian postmodernist politics," says Vennet, shrugging his shoulders indifferently. "The umpteenth scandal . . . true, you're lucky to be cut off out here, a happy man, one who can think about the Estonian Republic in a blue-eyed way, since you can't listen to the radio or read the papers. Well, it's just the umpteenth scandal and already fading away. Can you imagine a high-up government official suddenly starting to think ethically (though behind this there's little you could call ethical) and exposing a whole string of Sammalpõlv's escapades? For instance, how he blackmails politicians. First he drags them into some shady business, then keeps them trapped.

"It's not clear how much of all this has come out into the open, since now they've decided to stop exposing him, to bury the whole story. At any rate, the story about a high-up government official spilling the beans was part of a plan hatched by Sammalpõlv to get money for some anti-terrorist struggle. Well, as you can imagine, plenty of money around, but he won't be getting any, because Estonia hasn't got any terrorism. If there isn't any, thinks Sammalpõlv, then we'll have to pretend there is. Really does sound a bit creepy! This official claimed that when there was money available for the fight against narcotics, the same game was played: an impression was created that Estonian farmers were growing cannabis plants and poppies and that Estonian narcotics dealers were rushing about all over the globe."

"Ahah," I say, on hearing Vennet's tale.

"Do come again!" I shout after the disappearing car. "What will happen to me?" I ask myself, spreading my arms.

There's beer in the cellar, plus a bottle of vodka (for making compresses); my dear old friend from my childhood days, my schoolmate Specs-Leo, has started doing ugly things. It would seem that he wanted to use me as well, but he didn't succeed, poor guy. Ummal too has his own grand plans, and I'm a pawn in his game—a pawn with which the opening move has been played. I have taken a step forward on the chessboard. If I am valiant, I can quietly move to the other end of the board, then I'll be made into a queen or knight or bishop—precisely the chess piece that's needed at the moment.

When I open the door to the cellar, the cat flies at me in a horrible way—it is lamenting its sad fate, it blames and curses me. "Why all the fuss?" I grunt angrily, with no pangs of conscience whatsoever, as I see on the ground a piece of smoked fish that the wastrel has not yet managed to gobble down.

*

I sit at the kitchen table, drawing on a cigarette. There is an open newspaper in front of me, I should read the whole story from beginning to end, but I just can't, I have that kind of feeling you get when forced to rummage about in a smelly garbage bin for some valuable object you've lost. Although there's nothing in this article that could belong to me.

When I picked up the paper, I was hoping to read something about Leo, but to my amazement there isn't a line about him. Presumably, the newspaper lying on the seat next to Vennet was yesterday's, or from the day before, and I really regret I didn't ask him for it. I'm thinking that I ought to ask the Laakans for some newspapers, but I'm not sure that they get any delivered. Or I should go and take a bottle with me to Rolli's place, nowadays the whole village is usually on the ball regarding politics, and there I would hear stories about politicians that well-informed journalists only dream of hearing.

I push the newspaper aside and the letters appear from under it. One from America, but the other from Estonia, and on the back is an unknown sender's name and address. I rip open the envelope and read:

"Dear Mr. So-and-So. With regard to your promise to collaborate with us, we are expecting your short pieces at the following address: Samblamaa 12, apartment 16. The name is Geiermeier. The matter is urgent, so would you be so kind as to complete the assignment as soon as you get home? We are especially interested in details about your visitor and everything about the firm. Our telephone number has changed, so if you have any questions, please contact me at this same address. Telmo Geiermeier."

What a name, I think to myself. This letter was sent after Ummal's visit.

When this letter was written, they already knew about Ummal's visit, and the scandal with Leo must have been at its height. Leo is resigning, but the informer operation will remain in full swing.

I think: my status has not changed, I am still an Informer to the Estonian Republic. And it is indeed nice, I think: I can take revenge on Ummal for that article. And maybe I can also take revenge on Leo Sammalpõlv (and also get someone else!)!

I open my wife's letter (neatly, with a knife): there I read that she'll be staying longer in the USA, that she has thought about a number of matters, has thought that life with a writer doesn't suit her, she is not that self-denying, living for someone else, she wants to enjoy life herself, and so on, and so forth.

I can't really see what she is trying to tell me. I do understand (or am I wrong?) that there's somebody else.

Somebody that isn't me. She no longer wants to live for me, but wants to live for someone else.

*

It is beginning to grow dusky, and despite the fact that the whole day has been gray, the horizon is growing red in a threatening way. I want to light a candle, and discover that the Zippo (a present from my dear wife) is empty, dry, and I haven't got anything within reach that I can fill it with, nor even one match in the house or in any of my pockets. I know that if I don't get what I want very, very soon, if I don't light up a cigarette, I will start to be tormented by tobacco cravings. As I step outside to go over to the Laakans (to borrow matches, newspapers, or anything whatsoever), I suddenly realize that this business with my wife has Ummal's prints all over it, that he needs complete control over me and therefore had some exile Estonian whisper sweet nothings into my wife's ear. Very likely, I think, as I turn the key of my home in the lock.

*

A new morning, I don't know how many I've now spent here in the country, with the sun shining in at the window, golden on the wall of the room, and I go to the front door to have a pee and notice a glittering spider's web between the twigs of a bush. "Like delicate crystal, that web, how utterly beautiful," I sigh.

"That web has been woven to catch someone," corrects the other, the writer.

I plug in the coffee machine and watch the dark brown liquid begin to drip. Then I open the lid of the typewriter that Ummal brought me. It is an Olivetti with a pleasantly light keyboard. They probably don't sell typewriters any more, I think to myself, as I put my computer in the corner by the bookshelves. Once upon a time you used to present manuscripts to the literary museum as fodder for researchers. Now your text comes ready, straight out of the printer. No one will get to know what the writer wrote in his first flush of enthusiasm. Real creation (conflagration) remains a mystery to the machine memory. What is written on a computer is like plastic writing, I think as I roll in a sheet of paper.

When I type the title on the first page, I am not thinking, just pressing the keys: INFORMER TO THE ESTONIAN REPUBLIC—at that moment in time I already have in my head a complete story about a writer who is employed as an informer—what needs to be done now is to render it visible on paper.

****

Informer to the Estonian Republic

Contemporary art is like a symphony concert, where a group of musicians appear on stage who have no ear for music and cannot play their instruments, and on the conductor's rostrum stands someone wielding the baton who cannot read the score or convince the audience that the noise they are hearing is music.

RICHARD BONNAIRE,
Introduction to the 21st Century

The telephone snorts, and snort it does, you cannot call this sound a ring, and this is the way countless phones scattered around the world sound, also when a phone rings in a film on TV, the sound often forces the viewer to jump up and rush to the other room in order to silence the impossible snort, to render it harmless by lifting the receiver, so that it will keep its mouth shut until the next time.

The snorting does not abate, the dreamlike state—some seemingly impossible activity (piloting a plane?)—is broken off abruptly, the bright day changes into the dark night room, I raise my hand above my head, grope behind my head until I can feel the surfaces of book covers and newspapers, the slightly bumpy bedside table; and when in the end I reach the plastic body of the telephone, my fingers crawl like mountain climbers onto the receiver, grab it, and my wife's fresh and brisk voice replies to my sleepy mumble, she sounds as if she is in the next apartment (I cannot justify the expression to myself when I say it to my wife), I ask whether she is phoning from the airport and she starts to laugh, saying that she's phoning from Denver—for a brief moment the name says nothing to me, the word simply slips into my ear, then onward, but no image is projected on my mind as to what this word could mean. "Where?" I ask, almost shouting for some reason.

"What you yelling for, I can hear you perfectly well, are you drunk or what?" says my wife with familiar suppressed irritation.

"How is it going?" I enunciate clearly, in a calm tone of voice which is supposed to suggest: OK, so what's with you?

"I'm going to be staying here longer," she says. "I've had plenty of time to think about my life, and I feel that I can no longer play the role of your wife."

"Did you play it up to now?" I ask gently, trying to hide the bitterness behind my tone of voice, at the same time thinking, What the fuck is she doing over there in Denver, it could at least be New York or somewhere on the West Coast.

"In my opinion the PEN Club could add an international organization of writers' wives to its brief."

"So let it," is my reply.

"I think that I'm going to drop out of the whole game," she says.

"What are you saying now! Have you bumped into someone who's nice, caring, thoughtful and all the rest?" I ask at random, surprised by my own question.

"I don't know . . . I'm not sure . . . maybe . . . I'll write you about it. No point in talking about it on the phone, things we've tried to put right ten times over."

"I'm going away for a couple of weeks," I say, just to say something. She doesn't ask where I'm going. I listen to the silence for quite a while, then I say that I'll phone when I get back.

"Why bother?" she says icily, and I can see her face in my mind's eye: the face of someone peering from a cliff into a chasm. "I'm sorry to say that there's nothing that binds us any more, I snapped the last thread one day without even noticing."

I could say something sarcastic, I would like to scar her soul with a blunt knife, I want her to feel humiliated and sit in tears at the phone, but what I say is: "Look after yourself"—and nothing more.

A short while later, when I've replaced the receiver, I cannot even remember in what tone I said those last words.

"It would seem that this marriage is over as well," is what I mumble, as I get up; I don't yet want to switch on the lamp, I feel ashamed to see myself in the light, I can feel my guilt, my true pettiness, which has brought our marriage to the brink of this abyss, and the fact my wife has pushed over the edge what little remained of the marriage we had (didn't need any pushing, the touch of a finger was enough to make the whole thing tumble down) is her bit of derring-do. Self-sacrificial derring-do—and I burst into laughter: a theatrical volley of forced laughter that lasts for several seconds, then cuts off abruptly, as if a pillow has been pushed over the face of the laugher, as if the laughter-teeth have been knocked from his mouth.

"It would be interesting to know," Kandiman once said, "if more tires than marriages burst during a single day. In the first case, you simply change the wheel and carry on driving—later on the burst tire is mended, and will save the driver from trouble next time there's a flat."

Kandiman himself isn't married, though he has had four children with three women. On a few occasions the women have come to blows. They all belonged to the same cultural circles and therefore bumped into one another pretty frequently. Kandiman didn't get worked up about this and was getting all lovey-dovey with a fourth woman, one with whom he hadn't yet had a child.

I go into the kitchen, take a packet of cigarettes from the table, and am about to light up, but the compulsive thought that I must drink something first stops me (at least a glass of water that will soothe my stomach and internal organs), I fill the glass from the faucet, but then something inside me starts to protest: damned coward, it says. I'm not a coward, I say back, and go and open the fridge door—the light made sharper by the darkness of the kitchen shows me the bottle of beer. Look, you, I say as I flick off the top with a click, what are you moaning for, and open my Zippo lighter. This is a present from my wife, I think as I draw on the cigarette, this is no doubt her last gift to me.

"Fucking cunt!" I yell, now realizing that our marriage is over, once and for all. I'd like to be Kandiman—I'd like to be the person I usually take him for. I don't want to burden myself with any more worry, I want to have a wry smile at everything, or even better: a laugh, a snigger. On this earth there is no tight spot you can't wriggle out of, it simply depends on how you take each situation, how you're capable of handling it.

In the building across the way all the windows except for two are dark. Parasoolin is having a party, the curtainless windows reveal a group of people sitting around the kitchen table with a bottle of vodka. Parasoolin himself is sleeping at the kitchen table, resting his head on it. Now two men are dragging his wife off to another room. The woman is as drunk as they are. She collapses on the floor like Jell-O and they pick her up and push her onto the bed. The men seem young, hardly more than boys. One of them pulls up her dress, pulls off her panties, spreads her legs. Parasoolin's wife is a good deal older than her husband, at all events she looks like an old woman, both of them root around in garbage bins, start out from home in the morning, have no shame any longer— when the Parasoolins greet me, the wife always speaks loudly, with her red-painted mouth wide open, stretching round to her ears. But for these boys the woman seems to be quite satisfactory. One of them is already wading around between her legs. The other is rummaging around the underwear closet and throwing its contents onto the floor.

They're thieves, the rascals, I think to myself, thieves, if there's anything there worth stealing. For a brief moment the thought enters my (a decent person's) head that I should call the police, but I'm soon smiling at the thought. Only a few years ago, Parasoolin wore a tie, and his official car would be waiting at the door each morning. Then something happened. We greet one another but never have a conversation. Just exchange cool, polite greetings. We were in the same class at high school for a couple of years. I can now see that one of the two youths has discovered a bottle of vodka, whereupon the other one climbs off the woman, pulls up his pants, and the two of them sit on the edge of the bed and drink from the bottle. Parasoolin is no longer at the kitchen table, has presumably slithered to the floor. This is apartment-block theater. I suddenly feel disgusted, draw the curtains and see shining through the curtains two rectangles of light, one larger, the other smaller.

I just have to smile at the thought that Parasoolin used to sit on the same school bench as Leo. Once upon a time, he and Specs-Leo were big chums. Now one of them goes around rummaging in garbage bins while the other is lolling in his minister's seat. It would have been fun today to lure the present minister to go and visit Parasoolin, his old bench mate, after all, I am thinking, and try and imagine us popping across the road to his ravaged apartment with a cake in a box and a bottle of wine, and what kind of expression there would be on the face of the minister when he saw it all.

I am thinking *today*, but actually (given the fact that the windows all around are dark) it was already *yesterday* that the minister invited me to his office, even sent a car for me and devoted quite a bit of time to my affairs. It would seem, on the face of it, to be a meaninglessly small jump in time that I seem to be making. That moment during the afternoon when Minister Sammalpõlv asked me to sit in the guest armchair at his desk, has now become the past, history (the previous day). If I bring forward our meeting to this day, much will be added that didn't happen yesterday— the intervening hours will have additions and subtractions, some details will have receded into the background, others will have become more important. An endless process of falsifying reality will have begun, one which gathers speed (over time).

Yesterday, when I stepped into the spacious office belonging to the minister, I did not see Leo sitting behind the desk, but opened my eyes wide at his office, which was like a clip from a Soviet era film: pleated (?) silk drapes at the windows, a massive writing desk with uncomfortable armchairs on both sides of it, a long runner like the road to Golgotha from the door to the desk. Then I spotted Specs-Leo, who was smiling at me—and as I approached he rose from his seat, and when I reached the desk he was at full height and stretching a hand across the desk to be shaken.

I had not seen Leo face to face since our schooldays. The brightest lad in our school did of course go off to Moscow to study, finished his postgraduate work there, and didn't come back to Estonia until the end of the 1980s, and then not to earn his daily bread as a researcher, but to serve as a government official. I was surprised at how disproportionate he had become—on TV you couldn't see this, his paunch was hidden by the all-concealing desk, but now that his jacket was unbuttoned, it was disturbingly obvious. I can't help it, short fat men abash me, I feel embarrassed and uneasy in their presence, I cannot take them seriously, because the knowledge of their unbridled gluttony turns you immediately against them. (It's the same as with kleptomania—you know you shouldn't take something, but you still take it.) Nonetheless, now that I'm sitting in front of the minister's desk, I realize my wavering attitude towards fat people is my own affair, at any rate it has not hampered Leo's career.

"No doubt you're curious what your old school chum has in store for you," said Leo, placing the fingers of one hand on the opposite wrist and looking at me roguishly. I could imagine how much he was enjoying the fact that I didn't know, and I thought about how much more he *enjoys* things beyond his meals. His present position and post offered many opportunities. During our schooldays, I got on fine with him, but surely (I try to remember, but no one does) he had enemies, boys who bullied him. I entertain the thought that, were I to need a short fat man of power for one of my stories, I would undoubtedly elaborate on his urge to avenge—compensation for all the jeering that he himself suffered during his childhood and teenage years (how cruel children can be!) on account of his physical shortcomings. But Leo, thanks to his brilliant mind, was in fact popular during his schooldays, and although he became a Komsomol organizer, which meant wielding real power already at school, he never, as far as I know, played anyone any really patently dirty tricks.

In fact, it should perhaps be me who has a bone to pick with Leonhard Sammalpõlv. My mother, who was a teacher, always used him as a model that I should emulate—he was an epitome of wisdom, cleverness, assiduity, willpower, doggedness (etc.). He possessed all those qualities that I lacked. My boy's brain promised him cruel punishment, if I were ever to get into a position of power.

Then the Minister got down to business—he mentioned (under a veil of secrecy, of course) that in our small but most cherished republic certain groups of people are consolidating—groups that could be a serious threat. Data is available showing that terrorists are using green ideology as a cover, people who want to demolish our international reputation, quite apart from the serious harm that their actions could inflict on our peaceful population. He spoke generally and in very muddled terms, though gradually describing tighter and tighter circles around the problem, already approaching the kernel of the matter with concrete accusations. I was listening but at the same time letting the (unimportant) words flow in one ear and out the other, and noting the way that his babyishly chubby fingers stroked his hairy wrist. I tried to imagine Leo having sex (I have heard talk of several woman who worshiped him, both at party meetings and in bed) with a woman, I tried to play an indecent mind-game, imagining the naked Leo through a woman's eyes; I knew that if I ever wanted to describe in some story what was going through my mind, there would be a real witch-hunt once the story was published: How dare the writer So-and-So insult fat people! The fat minority will rise up thirsting for blood, and turn the writer So-and-So into a gob of spit to be smeared across the floor of the public toilets with a muddy boot.

I watched my schoolmate stroking the back of his hand and decided that his fingers were gentle and sensitive, that they could give a woman no end of pleasurable thrills. At that moment I would have given anything to know that Leo was envious of me. Why shouldn't he be. Maybe just a little. And why not envy a popular writer who has made significant contributions to the cultural history of his little nation, who looks like the positive hero from some film or other, about whom people always say with a tinge of jealousy—He's devilishly handsome.

"What we would need is for you to infiltrate their circles, your latest novel would provide excuse enough, and with sufficient imagination you could wind the likes of them round your little finger."

"I always keep my fingers crossed for the greens when they're defending baby seals on TV."

"Exactly—exactly, baby seals, cough-cough-cough," said Leo, starting to laugh. "When you hear the word *green*, it's always some story about whales and baby seals, but when this same seal-defender uses chemical weapons in the metro, taking out hundreds of people, the press just shrugs its shoulders and issues muddled statements; and when your whale-defender wants to foment bloody revolution and institute a green dictatorship, then this is called lunacy, not even considered worthy of a press bulletin. The fact of the matter is that the whole business is much more tragic than people realize."

Suddenly I realized that he really meant what he said, that I hadn't just been invited to come along, but that they really did want to make an informer of me.

"Ahah," I said, prevaricating. "In the 1970s, I was also invited to an office, was told that exile Estonians took an interest in me, that they really wanted to know things, so do tell us how you'd describe life over here to them. 'I've always been an obliging sort of person,' is what I told them on that occasion. 'What I'll tell such people is what they want to hear, I'll go and say that goats graze on the central square in Tallinn, that we share women, but that it's illegal to have intercourse with another man. Then you'll get put into prison.' I was offered some nice sweet grapes for my opinions, but they still didn't ever let me travel abroad."

"I think that your type of intellectual should finally come to an understanding of the binary opposition—the secret police of the Estonian Republic, and the KGB. When a republic is created, each and every thinking person ought to feel himself a subject—which, by the way, entails loyalty. And when some danger threatens a Free Republic, then a man must, if necessary, give his life for his country."

"A well-known artist told me about his meeting with a foreign ambassador. The artist had brought up the subject of the complex situation in which artists find themselves, their concrete financial worries, to which the ambassador replied that in the new situation artists should make compromises. 'We're not going to make compromises, our previous way of life was one huge and conscious effort to reject compromise and we were not keen on doing what was expected of us and what was financially advantageous.' 'Well, it's quite understandable that you didn't make compromises with the occupying powers,' said the ambassador.

"This demonstrated the strange fact that the ambassador didn't really grasp what it meant to have an uncompromising creative nature. I think that you're more understanding, that you grasp the fact I don't want to cooperate with any intelligence organization, even one belonging to the Lord God himself."

"OK—if we ignore that trip of yours to Sweden in 1986," he said, as if in passing, while at the same time doodling very childish little flowers on a sheet of paper.

He is clever and crafty, I thought to myself, as I lit up another cigarette. (This is not Specs-Leo, this is the Specs-Serpent—I muttered through my clenched teeth.) He did not look up to see what effect his mention of my Swedish trip had had on me, he continued to be engrossed in his little flowers, then he said that I need not make any decision right away, he suggested I think it over until the next day (i.e. today), and then phone a colleague of his, who would give further instructions, were I to agree to the assignment. "Terrorism is appalling. A terrorist nearly always strikes at random, hurting totally innocent people. Because of terrorism, no one can be sure that they will be alive tomorrow," said Leo, thumping my conscience with his fist.

He rose from behind his desk, in so doing giving a sign that he could not waste any more time on me. I was trapped like a mouse, like a fish in a net, a fox in a trap. I was still alive, but was no longer free in my actions. I couldn't tell Specs-Leo to go to hell, I had to go along with what he said. I had to do what *he* thought necessary.

"Our guy will give you instructions, and please do be careful. The person you'll be replacing when you go to that farm met with a little accident, nothing serious, you understand, but now that you're being sent as an alternate I really do hope there won't be any excesses," he said as he showed me to the door of his office, and I knew that he knew what my answer would be, and he knew that I knew that he knew.

I stub my cigarette out in the ashtray, open the drapes and look over at the building opposite. Parasoolin's windows are now dark. I remember how, back in school, in the last class at school, we performed "Pygmalion." The play was immensely popular, and we played it five or six times to packed houses. It was a big event for the Estonian provinces. I played Pickering. Parasoolin was the perfect Higgins. Teodor played Mrs. Pearce, but best of all was Leo playing Liza—the fact that two of the female roles were played by young men made it a crowd-puller. This happened over twenty years ago. Nowadays, Leo is a minister, Teodor is one of our leading art critics; Parasoolin—who played Higgins to a T, and ended up with a silver medal from the school—Aleksander Parasoolin, is now rooting around each morning up to his waist in garbage bins right in front of the apartment block; and I—an author of ten perfectly decent books—am an Informer to the Estonian Republic.

***

I stare at the rectangle of white paper lying on the table in front of me on which is written a seven-figure telephone number. For me it is an anonymous number, one which I cannot connect with a human being who has a voice and a brain, walks on two legs of flesh and blood. Instead, the number represents some organization, some grouping, some state cell (or, in fact, cluster of cells), some monster that can penetrate any group of people with its tentacles and enter the brains of citizens. It is of no importance whether it is called the FBI or KGB or the intelligence services of the Estonian Republic. They all deal with more or less the same problems, so their differences are minuscule compared with their similarities. They all employ government officials who use ordinary citizens, inveigling them into working for them for a whole variety of reasons. When blandishments don't work, they resort to threats. Government officials are indifferent to whether the citizen is cooperating against his own better nature or not.

When Leo said to me that I had to infiltrate some criminal (?) group, he did not have to explain to me what that meant. People who have had no dealings with the police or crime can get a good idea about them from books and movies. Nowadays, everyone, whatever their age, knows something about nearly everything, the whole world is at their fingertips (as long as they're prepared to accept the information).

In my imagination, which is largely shaped by American movies, a life of "infiltrating something" has its inevitable dangers: cars race around, people run about, pistols are fired. Leo hinted that someone had suffered an accident (oh, nothing serious!) and asked me to be careful.

I'm now sure I've memorized that phone number. (A secret agent must commit everything to memory.) I could throw the piece of paper away, burn it, rip it to shreds (swallow it!) and pretend that nothing has happened—neither the conversation with the minister nor any kind of recruitment. When they phone me I can say that the writer So-and-So is traveling. They're always in a hurry, they change their plans, make use of a new variant, in which I would no longer play a part. I would be out of the game. I'm not just going to start doing my duty as a citizen in a blue-eyed way. I don't like the party in power right now and don't want to help people whose points of view and faces are unacceptable to me.

But I have a number in my head, have the figures there in my visual memory, plus a real experience of meeting the minister who, among other things, reminded me of my trip to Sweden (during which there was an awkward misunderstanding, which led to unpleasant consequences). They have let it be known that they have information on me, that they've begun dealing with me, that my past has been scrutinized and that they plan to use my present-day self. I know that the whole misunderstanding back in 1986 had been planned beforehand, that the unpleasant consequences were a professional victory for certain people. At the same time, those now dealing with my life should understand that I was manipulated on that occasion—but it's not useful for them to understand that, they prefer factual material, because this time around they are planning to manipulate me too. An ordinary citizen is defenseless, helpless, if the State wants to exploit him.

I dial the number, and a pleasant woman's voice answers without revealing who she is, saying hello in a vague and impolite way, and I'm already sure I've dialed the wrong number, but just in case I give my name and say that I was asked to call. "How nice of you," she says. "Have you made your decision?"

I say that I can say neither yes nor no, as I haven't received all the details.

"Of course," she says. "But we need your agreement in principle."

"Well, in principle I've nothing against collaborating with you," I say, hesitating, choosing my words carefully.

"Very well," says the anonymous woman's voice. "If it suits you, I will call round in about half an hour."

I say that that will suit me fine. "Suit" is a suitable word here, though it reminds me of a store where they sell hats and caps. "Does it suit me?" asks the customer in an uncertain voice. "It suits you very well," affirms the store assistant, who is keen only on getting shut of the goods, and nothing else.

I once wrote a story where the protagonist was an informer who had a bad dose of the clap, and this made being an informer particularly onerous. My attitude towards my informer was one of sarcasm, and I felt true joy at his ailment. Society has never viewed informers with any great sympathy. The lower layers of society despise informers, while the upper echelons feel that they're necessary to preserve the status quo, but no one in their own circles would get involved with such (degrading) activities, so they haven't really formed an attitude toward such people. There is nothing noble about informing. A pretty dirty business—using people, building up their trust so you can do the dirty on them.

I haven't written anything for quite some time—true, I've translated a couple of average novels, but I haven't produced anything original, not even a short story. When I think about it, it really has been a long time, some seven months now. To keep in practice, I'd have to start on something new. If I accept the offer the minister has made, then I can devote my efforts to writing in the quiet of the countryside, and material will flow in automatically—landscapes, types of people, the circumstances of an informer. People have two positive qualities: they try to exploit every situation, and to justify each and every decision they make.

When the doorbell rings sometime later I am at peace with my role, not angry that they want to use me, since I have the feeling that I myself want to exploit their arrangement; but standing in the doorway is not my (new) colleague from the secret police (she wouldn't have been able to get here in such a short time), but my neighbor's daughter Evelin, who has come to water the flowers.

"Hi, Evelin," I say with a smile. "How's it going at school?"

We both have a good laugh (I myself laugh a little louder to hide my nerves), because this question about school is our own little private joke, one which—like all such jokes—never gets boring or becomes annoyingly banal. When you insert such a private joke in a literary text, it doesn't usually work, because it is the context—the innumerable tiny details—that makes the joke funny, and explaining it would be too complicated.

Evelin starts to water the flowers—this is a big and systematic task that my wife would not entrust to me. I can sit there in an armchair, sip at my coffee, smoke a cigarette, and watch how the young lady who has grown up over the summer is watering the green plants. You can get used to things as well as people, and this very familiarity can make them all grow invisible. Evelin is like one of our own children, and it was quite startling when I one day *noticed* her again—noticed that, for me, she had (unexpectedly) become a young woman. From that moment onwards

I began to be afraid of myself because the lust that (quite) un-intentionally affected my body was too unambiguous. My body was no longer under my control, I was thinking of Evelin as a woman and was preoccupied, captivated, and had to subdue the complex negotiations with physicality, had to get my body back under control. Drinking another mouthful of coffee, I take an-other swift look at the young miss in her short skirt as she stands on tiptoe watering the fern on the shelf, and think with relief that before long I'll be traveling.

Evelin has just finished watering the flowers when the doorbell rings and a largish woman enters the room. "I'll be going, then," Evelin cries out, whirling past us both, as if she's suddenly in a great hurry. The women size each other up. For a fleeting moment both register the presence of the other, make lightning assess-ments, record them in their memory. "That's the neighbor's girl," I say, almost apologetically. "She comes to water the flowers."

They (and especially the woman) know everything about me, and this suddenly makes me nervous. They have browsed through the old KGB files and have no doubt spied on me extensively. They even sent a woman to instruct me, as they know my weakness—my three official wives and an (unending) series of mistresses. For them I am an open book with all the pages cut. I am their prop-erty, like the knife on a chain that you find on the tables of some canteens in Russia. I can imagine how my materials were handed over to this (attractive) woman, how she was also warned that I want to screw everything that moves.

"My name is Barbi," says the woman with deadly seriousness, looking around in a professional manner for somewhere to sit down. For a moment I imagine her parents, try to think what their motivation might have been for giving her such a name, but then the sun shines through the gray mists of my mind—this must be a false name, her secret agent's pseudonym! (I wonder what code name they'll give me!) and I can't help asking her whether only little girls are allowed to play with Barbie dolls, or whether . . .

She brushes aside my banal joke (though one that's perfectly suitable for informer circles, in my opinion) and sits down at my writing desk, and I have the urge to spill (in an exceptionally banal way) coffee on her well-fitting light gray costume, but say instead in a placating tone, "You appear to take your work very seriously."

"When dozens of innocent people die or get maimed for life thanks to some criminal or other's cruelty and thirst for power, you lose your sense of humor. Reading your books I get the impression that you take the things of this world seriously too. I was pleased to be about to work with you, and hope I wasn't mistaken."

I am disarmed, I summon up a serious mien and ask a business-like question. She answers professionally, explains the situation, has me sign something, then another paper, keeps on talking about terrorism, radical "greens," and the direct threat that this extremist way of thinking poses.

"In my view, a 'third way' has to be found."

"You could call that Marcuse's brand of deconstruction, if such designations should be used at all. On the other hand, it's mostly the thirst for power that conceals itself under a noble exterior. A suitable excuse in a suitable situation is made and the matter is sewn up. If it can't be done democratically, it will be done by force. Joining the European Union scares them, time is short and they are in a hurry. Various unfortunate links have been established—a number of political careerists are now under their thumb and are waiting for their moment to arrive. At this very moment they are probably plotting a huge election campaign with the slogan: 'Estonia as the first Green country on Earth.'

"Nowadays, people no longer speak of a green dictatorship, they speak enthusiastically of Estonia as one great big national park. There are two ways these days to draw the attention of the world—either by being at the forefront of technological advance, or lagging behind to an extreme degree. Some guy or other is dreaming of Estonia as one enormous museum, where plows will be drawn by horses, harvesting will be done by hand, and tractors will be turned into plowshares by the blacksmith hammering away at his anvil. Such people claim that the world is waiting for a return to paradise and that a never-ending stream of tourists will bring wealth to the ethnographical Disneyland."

"But how do you know that I myself am not someone who fights for such a Disneyland, as one review of my latest novel suggested?"

"In such a dangerous situation as this, we are not going to take risks—I hope you don't feel offended, but we did of course check out your credentials and convictions, and it was we who actually commissioned the review of your last novel, in order to make Ummal take notice of you."

"Who is this Ummal?" I now ask to cover up the awkward silence: I cannot allow my pride to show my shock at the fact that the secret police have commissioned a review of my novel, and that a leading critic is doing the reviewing.

"Ummal is the person who interests us most in the context of the promotion of 'green' values," says Barbi, and pulls a sheaf of papers out of her briefcase. "Right now, the Ummal family owns the firm called 'Full-Blooded Recreation,' which provides a large variety of vacation opportunities. Canoe trips, horseback riding holidays, vacations in boggy areas, on farms, where families can take part in manual labor, camps where adults experience extreme living conditions or train to become ornithologists. The last of these—training camps for partisans—interest us the most, though up to now there have been no signs that their activities are directly connected with politics or any radical ideology. It's simply that people pay money and learn how to take care of themselves. At the end of the camp there's an exam which in essence consists of a tough type of war game.

"We know very little about the Ummals' past. They have no links with the usual émigré circles. Reports about them are conflicting, as if about two different people or sets of twins. What we do know is that Enniver and Alma Ummal were connected to the Fluxus movement back in 1960s West Germany, and that they were among the founders of the Green party; but later on they were no longer on the membership list of the German Greens. We can imagine some big ideological spat having taken place, but there's no trace of one in the minutes of their meetings. This gives the impression that nowadays the Ummals have nothing to do with the green move-ment, and I reckon this impression is deliberate. If some Ummal type gets caught, he won't besmirch the name of the party."

I admire Barbi's fingers, soft and presumably quite unacquainted with any physical work, so well-manicured and clean, I imagine these fingers giving me pleasure (I can't help it that such fantasies plague my subconscious, that I can't even look at the fingers of children or old people without entertaining such thoughts), and I sigh, probably aloud, as Barbi raises her eyes from her papers and looks up at me.

"Let's go and have lunch somewhere," I suggest. I like large serious women and imagine that a sexual relationship between secret agents could only be to the advantage of everyone concerned.

"Not until I've given you a complete overview of the situation," she says with an (ambiguous / knowing?) smile, and starts to speak about sending me off to a farm on the west coast, where (presumably) villagers under Ummal's special guidance (presumably) follow his orders, and where I will have to be on my guard and extra careful.

"Isn't someone exaggerating here?" I ask, getting to my feet to empty the ashtray. I'd prefer to joke around with Barbi on lighter topics, since I don't really believe that the likes of Ummal would stage a "green *coup d'état*."

"Unfortunately, no one is exaggerating. We have reason to believe that the accidents that have occurred over the past few years—accidents that the press tends to describe as environmental disasters—are the handiwork of terrorists. They try to give the impression that there are businesses behind these accidents which, on account of their environmentally unfriendly production and carelessness, are committing crimes. It's easy for them to manipulate public opinion this way, to sow the seeds of confusion, preparing the ground for a takeover. We have data that they personally use cruel and violent methods, even murder. All these fine ideals conceal personal ambition. They want to set their most inhuman programs into motion under the cover of humanist slogans."

Barbi is speaking with such zeal that I don't doubt she believes her spiel and wants to see the world as a place of goodwill. She's hoping that her enthusiasm is mine as well, and that I share her ideas and thoughts. That her truth will become our common truth, and that the truth will spread in geometrical progression—by word of mouth, from ear to ear—and now I can see in my mind's eye (as if in a film) the Germany of the 1930s, where raving crowds of people accepted the one sole truth which seemed to be of great advantage to the nation.

"But this is a very delicate matter—a captured 'green' terrorist is compromising 'green' ideas, while at the same time green thinking essential to ensuring the survival of the planet," I say, hinting at the ambiguity of the situation.

"But of course. You'll remember that horrible cloud of poison in the metro with hundreds dead, and the authorities accusing the group of conspiracy, but no one said *what kind of* government these people were aiming for. Nobody wants to compromise the 'greens,' and they are *very* aware of the fact," explains Barbi, and says that now it's time to get down to brass tacks regarding the operation.

On hearing the word *operation* I imagine a scene in an operating theater, a bloody wound in which rubber-gloved fingers are poking with nickel instruments. An operation is an activity where you cut something open in order to sew it back together again. Especially dangerous are the complications that can arise after the operation. One of my friends developed an imbalance in his serous fluids, after which he passed away.

It is already growing dark when Barbi goes; she has done her job and refuses to go out with me as I've suggested; she is rushing home to her kids, her family. I gnaw on a piece of smoked sausage and watch how the lights in the neighboring apartment blocks come on like candles on a Christmas tree. Apartment blocks are themselves Christmas trees. After a while they are tossed on the garbage heap.

On the table in front of me is a newspaper where my latest novel is reviewed. This time I read through the article unhurriedly. I try to immerse myself in the hidden meanings behind the surface commotion of the words and phrases, but I get the impression that someone who thinks too much of himself is tottering across the paper, someone who thinks he is handsome, clever and healthy, though I see that he is in fact crippled and needs crutches to get along, crutches he's picked up here and there and has even given names to: Michel Foucault, Neil Evernden, Julia Kristeva, Roland Barthes, Jacques Maria Lacan, Glen Love, Cheryll Glotfelty, Georges Bataille, Jacques Derrida . . .

I'm thinking that if some of the names on that list were replaced with others, it would emerge that I'd written a splendid and highly important feminist novel. And if more are changed, we would have a review analysing a novel that tackles the problem of dark-skinned people in the Estonian Republic.

The review is long, takes up a lot of space, and the photo of me that adorns it was taken some ten years ago. Not only I myself, but my *novel* as well, has become—in the direct, literal sense of the word—an informer. Has taken its place among practical activities. NB! A singular postmodernist *literary* process (which needs a more profound theoretical analysis) has occurred.

***

The writer So-and-So has been recruited as an informer, he is strolling along a street in the Old Town and pondering on the subject of *good* and *evil*. In principle, informing on people is a dirty business, it means poking your nose in other people's affairs and ratting on them. For someone who has lived their whole life under foreign occupation, an informer is certainly a tool of Evil. But when circumstances change (the country is now a Free State) an informer becomes an instrument of Good. The dirty business has now become noble, although the means by which the information is obtained remain as immoral as before.

When an informer's motivation for informing is an idea, when he informs with dedication, believing that he is serving the Good, then he embodies Good. When an informer is only out for personal gain, then even when serving Good, he embodies Evil. When (during the Soviet occupation) Good was Evil, then the status of an informer was the opposite: passionately serving the idea, he became an embodiment of Evil.

But what happens when what seems on the surface to be Good is in fact Evil underneath? Should an informer then play a double game: seemingly fulfilling the demands of Good, but at the same time offering services to Evil, since he knows that Evil can damage Good, which is in actual fact Evil, and Evil becomes Good (Evil) by doing Good . . .

When I spot an advert for "Full-Blooded Recreation," a pleasant surge of recognition flows through me for a moment (ahah, I know that building, there used to be a bookstore in there), but this soon changes to a strange unease—I remember how the owner of the store was beaten within an inch of his life, and after that the bookstore went out of business, and then Ummal started renting the premises at low cost. I knew the owner of the bookstore before he was beaten up, he had indeed run into financial difficulties, but he surely didn't intend to close the store down. I simply can't help thinking that Ummal had something to do with all this. And for the *first* time the thought strikes me that the business I'm now getting involved in could be physically dangerous.

With each step I take toward the shop's protruding sign, my idea of the future grows grimmer—the name "Full-Blooded Recreation" takes on a new meaning: a vacation filled with blood; the text I should begin to write will turn into a horror novel, in which a trail of blood leads to the House of Evil, decorated with blood-splattered wallpaper. My pace slows down, but I do not stop—there is no convincing reason (sudden sickness, an unexpected disaster in the family) to hold me from my goal. And probably (I can imagine) someone's (unseen) gaze is (already) following me, fixing my every move—by scribbling a little signature I have squeezed three drops of blood out of myself, signed a pact with the Devil, from which there is no going back.

As I open the door, a little bell tinkles as in a village shop, a small workshop, and at first I imagine I've wandered into the exhibition hall of an ethnographical museum, but then I hear birdsong, a cuckoo in the early morning (I automatically try to remember whether I had breakfast, automatically I count my years) and the dark room is suddenly illuminated, and the far corner turns into a green forest in the sunshine, and the ceiling into a summer sky with white clouds. "Welcome," intones an incessantly smiling blonde, and I think that the life of someone who smiles like that must be filled with sunshine, without any trace of a cloud.

All of this is nauseatingly overdone, I decide when I walk towards the barrier, which looks like a bar in this room, and is in fact a counter where, instead of bottles with bright labels, they're selling green trees, birdsong and white clouds. Apart from the smiling blonde, there are two other people here: a sporty-looking tall older man and a woman wearing a pink costume. "Fantastic," is what I say. "Stepping in here is a truly unbelievable experience." The lady smiles happily and I imagine that she's the one who came up with the décor. Her name is Alma Ummal—she has the habit of being in the office with her husband for an hour or so from eleven in the morning. I know quite a lot about them, and now they have to know more about me to render me visible to them.

"How can I help you?" the blonde springs to my aid. She has long slender fingers, her nails are painted with pink mother-of-pearl nail polish.

"I've come about hiring the Teeriida Farm," I say looking stealthily at the Ummals (I can't imagine that I'll look so fit about twenty years from now, quite the opposite), and they consult their files behind the small oblong desk and sip from small cups of coffee. The blonde has a coffee cup in front of her too, but it's markedly larger. I explain in a business-like way that the booking is in the name of a friend of mine, that I am the writer So-and-So and I need to be able to do my work in peace and quiet. That every little thing in the city has begun to annoy me too much, and that I haven't been to the countryside for some time now because someone who does a lot in town needs real motivation to get out of the squirrel's treadmill of everyday life. That my friend will be traveling to Paraguay this week, that he'd planned his time badly, and nowadays nobody can really take any time off. This friend is quite happy for me to take over the booking because—as he says—there's quite a long waiting list for such vacation spots. I just happened to be free—being a freelance means you tend to be your own boss, although people nowadays often can't afford to live the life of a freelancer . . .

I deliver my spiel in a quiet tone of voice and at moderate speed, so that no one will be able to interrupt, I look the blonde in the face with a sincerely naïve expression, as if testing her patience the whole time, I imprison my conversational partner's eyes with my glance, follow their every move, don't let them back off into a corner. This way of conversing is sheer psychological terror—always a suitable method when dealing with an official who doesn't have the time (or desire) to get involved in other people's affairs. Now I begin to feel sorry for the delectable blonde—she isn't a bit interested in what I have to say, she has found the necessary data on the computer and is waiting to begin to process it.

"Welcome," says a voice speaking in accent-free Estonian, and the blonde can now take a breather. "My name is Enniver Ummal, and this is my wife Alma. We're the owners of "Full-Blooded Recreation," and we're really glad that you want to spend some time at the Teeriida Farm. Teeriida is one of our most exciting properties, especially if you're interested in fishing."

I say my name again and shake both their hands. Although he's quite heavily built, his hand is noticeably cold (like a fish), while Alma Ummal's doesn't even attempt to hide her temperament—

she appears eager to get to know as much about another person via this brief expression of physicality as possible. Mrs. Ummal reminds me somehow of Yoko Ono, I can't tell how old she is, I can only avow that the likes of her would never keep any beauticians in any part of the world idle.

"I just happened to be reading a review of your novel recently—I haven't had a chance to enjoy the book itself, but I'll find the time soon. Oh yes indeed, enjoyment is just the right word; nowadays there are so few writers who want to regard themselves as part of Nature. I think that we should become better acquainted, it is entirely natural that people who think in a similar way stick together."

I feel an unexpected surge of happiness, and rejoice inwardly, as if I've just got some onerous task out of the way. I'm making progress in my new role—matters are moving according to plan, the actors are speaking their texts as written in the script, and are acting as is expected of them. The strange feeling of bliss doesn't even leave me as I shut the door of "Full-Blooded Recreation" behind me, the little bell tinkles briefly and I am back in the familiar surroundings of the Old Town. I would like to describe in detail the whole episode of meeting Ummal for Barbi, in order to earn her smile of empathy or praise.

That afternoon, choosing which books on my shelves to take with me, spy novels seem to stick to my fingers, and I wonder whether I'll be able to turn my recent (and future) experience as an informer into adventurous episodes in stories I might write. I can imagine the confusion of the critics when there appears a decent work of fiction (I imagine myself to be writing a decent book) which, due to its external qualities (a spy story, horror or pornographic novel), should not actually be regarded as quality literature.

At around five my bags are packed and I ring the artist Vennet and ask him whether I can drop by at his place. "Not for an hour," says Vennet, who is working in his studio despite the fine weather outside. He has even hired out his summer cottage to some Frenchman and abandoned his ideas of fishing and mushroom picking, so as to produce new paintings for the exhibition in October.

I got to know Vennet during a trip to North Korea, where for three weeks we shared hotel rooms and had long chats. For a couple of years after that trip we would mix a great deal, but then the friendship began to cool off—we probably got fed up with each other, our attitudes toward life and toward ourselves were too different. Looking back, the early 1980s had their charm—even for Soviet citizens the world had begun to open up, and we *seemed* to have a greater choice. We chose to be bohemians, and lived life to the full. It must have been in 1982 that my family and I spent three weeks out at Vennet's cottage by the sea. For my type of urban cockroach that was a very long time without the creature comforts of the city. I was not exactly wringing my hands because of what I had to do without, but for the next fifteen years I never tried anything of the sort again. I can't imagine how I'm going to occupy my time out there in the country for two weeks (and alone too). I'm unsure of myself and want to try to persuade Vennet to come and visit me for a day or two.

I'm annoyed that my wife has to be in America right now. It would have been much cozier to have her here at Teeriida Farm, and then I feel ridiculous for having allowed myself to forget last night's phone call—my brain has been so full of my role as informer that I've forgotten all about my (new and old) bachelor status. I remember that when my first wife and I decided to get divorced after a series of nerve-wracking quarrels, I (probably?) felt like a passionate hunter who had been given a permit to shoot game in a nature reserve.

That time, against all expectations, I began to overdo the drinking, and a couple of months later I was married again. The permission to shoot in a reserve had extinguished the urge to hunt and I no longer bothered to raise the gun. Hunting had lost its edge. My second marriage was more of a short joke-marriage, neither of us took it seriously, it was more of a societal game than an attempt to start a family.

Since my boyhood days I have always been conscious of my sex drive, restlessness, dissatisfaction. It's as if I have always wanted to get close to all the women in the world, not put off by the fact that they were more similar than different, it was like a tourist's passion to discover something special in each city, town or village he visits, something that has remained hidden to the eyes of others. This same urge to wander means that I cannot stay and enjoy one place, I am driven on to discover what lies ahead. I have, however, had enough common sense not to make my passion the essence of my life, and have managed to divide my time sensibly. I would describe myself as a Sunday hunter of women, as there are Sunday painters and Sunday anglers.

I can make decisions about myself, but daren't apply them to other people. In novels, stories, tales, the characters feel hunger, weariness, cold, but when someone has an urgent sex drive, that isn't the suitable kind of thing to write about. I get the impression that it isn't a problem for people to be burdened with, and anyone who thinks of his sex drive in the way others think of hunger or cold will end up in a kind of bleak isolation, will start to see it as sickness or evil exaggeration, he will not be able to see himself as on an equal footing with other members of society, and may have a breakdown or die in the cross-currents of an inferiority complex. But the older I get, the more I begin to value my urges; I think I talk about my desire as an Englishman talks about his home—my lust is my castle . . . I think that my life would be as ugly and entirely without meaning in the absence of lust as the work of some dauber at a contemporary art exhibition. Only my lust can set off the thousand emotions that arise when I look at a woman.

On top of the cake of my lust, love is merely the creamy rose decorations that usually remain uneaten because of the fear of obesity, of those extra kilos.

When my wife went off to visit her sister in America last month, a kind of lull after the storm held sway in our family, and the sun was shining in a cloudless sky. All was well. My latest escapade had come to an end and I promised myself that I wouldn't go in for new adventures (in the near future), since they make life uncomfortable and complicated. Home felt (as always after trips, military campaigns, exile) pleasant and safe. I had not prepared myself for such a night call. I had not secured my rear. I had not given my wife any reason to treat me as she did. We had no reason to get divorced: at least I didn't have one—I was used to looking at our marriage only from my own vantage point, the thought never entered my head that some motivation would arise in my wife (and in her alone) that had been (unfortunately) concealed in past conflicts, and which would give rise in me to an illusion of guilt that I would immediately embrace.

In actual fact (if I am honest with myself) I am a jilted husband, a male who has lost out in the competition, whom some fellow male has trumped. My vanity is too great merely to regard myself as a loser—I must immerse myself in illusions, create new backdrops, new speculations that will help me to rise above the whole thing; I guess and know that what you can't have becomes desirable, what is lost becomes priceless; only when you lose something does it become truly dear to you.

The doorbell rings: once, twice, three times. I hope that standing outside my double door (the outer one made of metal) is some woman. Someone I have forgotten, but who has remembered me. Someone I made vague hints to about dropping in, as my wife is in America and I am suffering from desperate loneliness. No, after such a vague hint no one would be likely to drop in (a woman is not a man, one who would visit old flames when drunk); that would be a planned operation, already arranged by phone. A military campaign, with every move anticipated. No woman would come over to visit a man like that unless she had some urgent business. When I open the inner door and peek through the spyhole, I'm pretty sure it's going to be Barbi—but there's no one there. Just the endless corridor with curving walls and, somewhere in the distance (there where the lift door should be), something red on the floor. I am not interested enough to open the door and see what it is.

The ringing is repeated—tee-linn, tee-linn. Damned kids! I curse, running to the door so I can grab their coat tails and give them a tug, but it isn't a little boy, it's Teodor—my former classmate, now a famous art critic. He's trailing a banderole behind him with a Red slogan on it, and holding a well-polished trumpet; he is very happy, very pleased with himself. "We've just had a post-socialist communist action nearby, and I've brought you a present. Your wife can make this banderole into a little evening gown, and your neighbors can do their morning exercises to the sound of the fanfare."

Teodor is one of many who like to play around with Soviet symbols, show his superiority to the color red and to five-pointed stars, as if they constantly need to affirm the correct attitude, all the while forgetting the respect they themselves paid to these symbols and objects only a few years ago. It is said that Teodor's house is like a Red shrine, his daughter's room dedicated to Lenin, and when they happen to have visitors, their teenage daughter walks around in a red Komsomol scarf. If you didn't know this was retro mockery you could almost start thinking that Teodor was a real, full-blooded Stalinist.

Once I happened to read one of Teodor's investigations into perspective (always interesting to know what a former schoolmate is writing about), and it pointed out a tendency—highlighted in bold—in older art to have several viewpoints, as if the artist wanted to describe all the space surrounding him. Not the space before him, but the space around him. When in the Pioneers, Teodor would amaze everyone by building models. Spatial models of the town he lived in, models of Pavel Matrossov, Kortshagin, and Morozov as heroes—everything was constructed with loving care and displayed at exhibitions of pupils' work from throughout the whole Estonian republic. In the lower grades he had often received praise for his drawing skills, but it turned out that his mother (presumably) had done the drawings for him, which gave rise to a big scandal. They had various paintings on the wall at home and his mother exhibited as an amateur artist. The fact that Teodor wanted to become an artist wasn't surprising. He had drunk in a love of art with his mother's milk. But for some curious reason he was not even allowed to take exams. Despite several years of effort he failed to land a place at the academy. He took this in stride and studied art history instead. In no time at all he became a leading art critic. He had found his feet in the world of art, but recently people had also begun speaking of him as an installation artist. He knew what to do: the models he'd made at school now grew into large installations (could he ever have dared to imagine, when working in the Pioneers' rooms, that his models would one day fill large halls in the Art Museum?), and as an expert in perspective he achieved the aspirations of the old masters—and pretentiously designed the rooms around him.

I like Teodor, the monotonous landscape of art is crying out for the likes of him: Please come to us, shake us up good and proper, show us what you can do! During his schooldays he'd practiced sport, and now he could show the aesthetes a thing or two with his sportsman's urge to conquer. As if he wanted to yell: Enthroned talents of art that I admired as a boy, the time will come when you'll be eating out of my hand, when I'll be the one who decides who'll enter history! I go to the fridge to get couple of beers, and try to think why Teodor has come to visit me—he's never been the sort simply to drop in and ask how you are; every one of his movements has an ulterior motive, there's a reason behind every tale he tells. I can't imagine how I can be of service to him.

"The world is cruel and unjust," says Teodor. "I should have the opportunity to make it show justice towards me, but the cruelty of the world won't let it happen. Just imagine how many people there are on this Earth that snore, and how many there must be who would give anything to stop the person they share their bed with from snoring. Now imagine that I've found a method—not medicine, but a method—to cure people who snore. But I can't sell my method, so I'll have to make do with the pittance I earn with my art research."

"And what does this method consist of?" I ask, feeling a kind of selfish interest in what he says. "Do you have anything else here apart from beer?" Teodor replies, and I imagine what kind of impression he would make in beer halls or wine bars.

When I've filled his glass up to three finger-widths, he begins to chat pleasantly: "My wife—you know her, of course—snores like an asphalt crusher, as soon as she's lying on her back, and so loudly that the neighbors start banging on the ceiling with a broom handle. So I got the idea to tape-record it and play it back—you know how it is—no snorer will admit that he makes even a peep when he's fast asleep. But then I found out that it wasn't so easy, after all. As soon as I switched on the tape-recorder, the snoring stopped. I tried and tried for over a month before I got a tape-full. You should have seen the wife's face when she heard the snoring. Eyes wide with shock. Hand pressed in despair to her mouth. And that was it. A couple of months have passed now, and not one snore."

"You ought to consult a psychiatrist," I suggest in a friendly manner.

"You think I'm crazy, just as my wife does," says Teodor, jumping to his feet and beginning to pace the room nervously.

"Now listen, I think that a skilled psychiatrist could maybe, on the basis of subconscious ploys, explain why your wife stopped snoring on hearing the tape," I say, trying to smooth over my last comment, to put a humorous gloss on it, and I ask him whether he's not afraid I might describe the method in one of my novels, in order to increase sales with that very tale.

"What can I do, I'm defenseless in the face of a cruel world. I've suffered injustices all my life, others have always done better than me—I can't help trembling noticeably with sheer envy every time I hear that somebody has done well."

I can't work out whether Teodor's joking or whether he's offering me one of his rare moments of frankness without ulterior motives, but I pretend not to be too concerned about what's being said and add that he's just like any other typical Estonian.

"Yes," says Teodor, "I've heard that you're going to some nice place to relax. If I had such a sum of money at my disposal, I'd dash off to the Maldives. I didn't know that a writer in our country could allow himself such luxuries. Especially a freelance one. Even Ristikivi had to work in a bank over there in his Swedish exile to be able to write in his free time."

I've clearly hit a raw nerve with Teodor, pressed some painful button, for him suddenly to have become so personal, but Barbi had anticipated that question and so I was able to explain the matter truthfully (and with playful jocularity). Noticing with what interest Teodor looks at me, I suddenly realize that my classmate has come to spy on me, that he's the same sort as I am, but that it is Ummal who has sent him.

**

When I finally get shut of Teodor, hinting that there's some woman that I'm going to go and meet (I don't want to say that I'm going to drop in on Vennet instead, as I know that those two play a game of cat and dog involving mutual rivalries), Teodor gives me a knowing look, walks off with his self-assured proletarian step, and I have to try and remember what links him to Ummal and what his motivation could be for spying on me. The idea that he's come to inform on me strikes me as more and more plausible; he was observing my state of mind, provoking me to be candid, letting himself be thought of as someone who criticizes Ummal, because our conversation turned to Ummal rather quickly—he said quite a lot about Fluxus, about Ummal's role as an ideologue in the Direct Democracy Organization, and, of course, about Joseph Beuys, with whose work he appears to have a special relationship. Now, as I walk across the square that has been turned into a parking lot, toward the House of Art where Vennet's studio is located, I try to imagine Teodor as a terrorist, armed to the teeth, hijacking trains, ships, or planes simply to save one ginkgo tree in downtown Tallinn.

It's quite impossible to imagine Teodor as a terrorist. When still at school he and Specs-Leo sat on the Komsomol committee and conducted their affairs from comfortable armchairs. Leo was tougher than Teodor and always got more votes in elections. Leo always managed to outwit Teodor. Teodor did, it's true, compensate for his lack of success in Komsomol by indulging in sport, where he received his halo. For someone from a provincial town to gain a spot on the national Soviet Estonian team was no mean feat. Maybe it is power that spurs Teodor on, I think as I press Vennet's doorbell. If they ever create a Green Estonian Republic,

Teodor will at least get the post of Minister of Culture. (And I the Head of the Writers' Union, if I manage to suck up to Ummal, and my links to the secret police aren't exposed.)

"Would you be able to tell me what connects contemporary art with the Green Movement?" I ask Vennet, who thwarts my attempt to shake his paint-stained hands by hiding them shyly behind his back.

"That isn't an easy question," intones Vennet. "But I think that I can understand *why* you're asking." As he turns the painting now on the easel to face the wall, I manage to glimpse the familiar red-and-yellow-striped posts and poles that made Vennet famous some twenty years ago, then disappeared from his work (it's possible that they moved from his paintings into the surrounding landscape: lots of metal border posts and even playground constructions were suddenly adorned with the same red-and-yellow colors); but the white clouds escaping from the sky, reflected in balloons and floating off between the bushes, are something new.

"I dare say that both these phenomena are a latter-day reflection of the radical left-wing ideas of the 1960s, now we've reached the turn of the century. There is also a clear similarity to the previous turn of the century, when the ideas of Marx and Darwin reflected in the Sixties originally represented—or to be more exact: transformed—the ideological landscapes of the new century. The current end of the century is ruled by people who were young in the Sixties and took part in student unrest, but have themselves now become institutions. In the previous century there was the slogan, "workers of the world unite," but during the following century we have had the dictatorship of the middle classes, which entails a program for the total unification of thought. No deviation from the norm—both geniuses and freaks require help to be normal people in a normal society.

"When Darwin taught that human beings hadn't been created, but had evolved, a number of basic human values became suspect, whereas today's analysis of our world as a fragmented organism renders invalid *all* value judgments. Information technology gives everyone equal chances, and against that background a kind of redistribution of intellect occurs."

Vennet puts the kettle on and asks whether I want peppermint, or raspberry, or cowberry tea, and he says this in exactly the same voice he used to ask, a couple of years ago, which alcoholic beverage you'd prefer. This is a pretty surprising change that Vennet has undergone since one fine morning he chucked his bohemian lifestyle into the corner like a sweat-sodden shirt.

"And when I sobered up," (Vennet's own words) "I noticed that the whole world had changed. I was really surprised—I saw to my horror that my coevals still hadn't noticed, that they were living in the former world just as they always had. Two quite different worlds exist in parallel, people talk to one another but fail to communicate, because even the simplest words take on different meanings. I was seized with a boundless curiosity, I had to get an understanding of the language people spoke together nowadays, and what was even more important, I had to understand why things have become what they have."

I watch him as he strides purposefully around. I have the strange feeling that he has become a good deal younger during his two years as a teetotaler. Suddenly, the picture is there in my mind of how he used to sit trembling in the corner of some bar, his face swollen, and it takes some effort to realize that these two very different people have fused into one.

"I can't really say anything profound about the green movement, I haven't gone into the matter, though I imagine that (maybe) they've undergone the same sort of development as in art, in which case there's very little about a green way of life that is encouraging," says Vennet, and I know that he won't leave it at that. Recently he's been bubbling with scraps of information and ideas, as if his head is a pot in which the soup is boiling over.

"By the 1970s, injustice in the art world—on account of greedy businessmen who were exploiting equally greedy critics—reached the pain threshold. Every day, key works of avant-garde art were being created: yesterday's talentless loser could become tomorrow's star. It was high time for art to be freed from the yoke of commercialism—and it was. But no one could imagine that the alternative to the rather kitschified avant-garde would soon begin to operate the same way as its despised predecessor, and even more so. The thing is that the present-day theory in all of its basic truths aspires to openness, but in actuality we've arrived at a bewildering epoch where truth (as a rule) precedes practice. Let me explain: whereas earlier an artist would create a work of art that theory was meant to investigate in the cultural space, now an artwork shows how theory performs in cultural space.

"A shocking metamorphosis has taken place: the developments that were pursued in the name of greater freedom for the artist have turned the artist into a pawn on the chessboard of the curator. While theorists busied themselves a decade ago with the promotion, analysis, and interpretation of art, nowadays a whole theoretical army has been built up merely to secure its own exceptional status.

"The situation has been arrived at where the world of art can be compared to a well-oiled machine that produces the required products without hindrance, and there is no sign that it will be going in for repairs any time soon. It seems to be a perfect machine. The ideal machine. When you examine this machine more closely, what strikes you is that for a couple of decades now it has been deriving its energy from the same set of ideas, which ultimately stem from the left-wing radicalism of the Sixties.

"I can now return to your question, and I'll say that I don't really see any difference between an official pumping money from some contemporary art fund, and some branch-office employee of Greenpeace doing the same. The idea that they should have been serving is long forgotten, they served ideas when they were young and poor. Now they thank their lucky stars that they're able to take advantage of an idea."

Vennet pours out the cup of tea—it's this year's heather tea, and if you add a teaspoonful of linden blossom honey you are reminded by the aroma of the heath in summer, as if you are lying on the warm earth and following a white cloud in the sky and listening to the buzz of bees.

"Are you trying to tell me that the right kind of art these days is that commissioned by the art critics with the most clout, and that all the artist has to do is follow the rules of the game and receive recognition in the competition—like in the days of Stalin or Hitler, when the artist knew exactly what was expected of him?"

"Yes, exactly the same sort of prostitution," says Vennet

"And on the other hand, you, old fellow, with your more conservative type of work, are in an honorable opposition, while the younger artists who are supposed to oppose the powers-that-be complete commissions with submissive diligence."

"Yes, however paradoxical it may be, perversely conformist relations have arisen in the art world. The honesty and originality of the artist has been declared a romantic myth. Top culture, just like business, considers opportunities, and in my opinion it makes no difference whether the person commissioning the work is a rich grocer, or the state, or a highly trained critic using private capital."

"The ones who did what was required of them in Russian times were despicable because they sucked up to the Commies, but those who are on their knees to the curators nowadays and lick their asses are highly-esteemed elitist creators of art. Anyone working for the KGB was regarded as a slimy toad of an informer, but now that he's snooping and betraying others for the good of Estonia, he's become a noble and honorable informer to the Estonian Republic. As if sucking up to those in power in the independent Estonian Republic were more ethically justified than sucking up to those in power in the Estonian Soviet Socialist Republic."

"Yes, and what's saddest of all is that some of those artists that think and create in a modernist fashion have become turncoats and produce all manner of hideous daubs, partly in order to do what the curators want with no demur; they bow and scrape in order to exhibit—even I, when necessary, use contemporary art jargon, partly out of a blind desire to be topical. Such people have been struck blind and do not realize that they have, in effect, demolished both the form and content of all that they once stood for. They are openly betraying their own epoch, their colleagues who have remained honest, and ultimately themselves."

The evening sun is reflected in the window of Vennet's studio and this lights up the windows of the building opposite which in turn reflect Vennet's not particularly spacious studio, where his palette covered with bright splashes of paint and the worn paint-stained floor express for me the age-old essence of being an artist, and the smell of turpentine and paint change this spirit into a tangible reality; every time I visit a painter I get the feeling that the smells of the studio have soaked into my clothes, the same way cigarette smoke does after you've been sitting in a cramped bar.

"Incidentally, now that we're talking about the greens, I'd like to draw your attention to the fact that both feminism and green thinking are by their very nature structurally similar fields of activity with which artists and critics can achieve fame and earn money. Feminism is no longer a principle but a market niche. For the sake of money, fame, and power, people will simulate anything, even being homosexual or left-wing. The whole thing can be reduced to selling yourself, and it doesn't matter in the least under what label the transactions are carried out."

"Looking at your paintings, it seems that by the end of the Sixties you had already booked a place in the ecological or environmental niche and that you would fit perfectly into the present-day world of eco-criticism," I cannot help remarking with a smile, whereupon Vennet bursts into hearty laughter.

"But of course! I would be a roaring success with the right critic. Someone could make a name for themselves as a critic in this particular context with the help of my paintings, and I too could derive some gain from this as an artist, even though the environment isn't really my department.

"In October, I will be taking part in a four-man show called 'An Unending Landscape,' where apart from me there will be a painter, a graphic artist, and a photographer. The photographer is a well-known theorist and an apologist for postmodernism. The word 'apologist' is a silly, strange word, but it describes this man to a T. A large part of his energy is devoted to proving to himself and to others that he is an artist. His way of tackling the problem in a postmodernist situation is a little different from that of your friend Teodor, who wants to base himself on Beuys, i.e. claim that anyone can be an artist; this guy wants at all costs to prove that mechanically produced pictures are art to a greater extent than the 'crochet work' of the artist. In doing so he wants to show that he himself is a greater artist than those artists who have received schooling and training. His hobby-horse is social values. For him the beauty of a work of art is merely a danger that prevents the problems of society from coming to the fore.

"The focus of this forthcoming exhibition is the landscape, and I hope that between us we can manage to generate some kind of good dialogue on the walls of the House of Art. The photographer will look at the landscape as territory—anyone can turn whatever view into his own contextual territory; to put it bluntly, this is a dog raising its leg and peeing away, whereupon a new dog will turn up and mark out its own territory.

"For me, my own landscape is identical with myself, it has grown with me over the decades and I don't have to raise my leg to mark it out, it is my own creation and my landscape painting is such that the viewer sees at first glance that it is *different* from all other landscapes, its essence is *difference*. I want to demonstrate at this exhibition that difference is not finite, that it is without boundaries, that within certain boundaries art can and must be limitless, i.e. never-ending. There is nothing easier than collecting objects and thoughts and feelings that we see the neighbors already have. But when we stumble upon a object, thought, or feeling that we have never experienced before, and about which we cannot tell whether it is useful or useless, good or bad—should we then reject the object because we lack the guts to decide or judge and reject it, pretending that we have never seen it, or walk swiftly by? I personally do not want to be one of a thousand-strong flock on the song-festival stage, and open my mouth when the conductor makes a movement of his hand, and close it again following another movement. I want to be the only fool to be out of step on the parade ground!"

***

The sun is shining in the silent pale blue sky, nature does not yet show any signs of autumn, merely a slightly weary green and the gold of the fields of crops. There is something joyful about the idyll of the unending landscape, something so uplifted that it brings a song to your lips, as always at the start of a trip or a journey. *Bla-bla-blaaa*, is what I sing aloud, *bla-bla*, I bawl out the refrain, no one is wrinkling up their nose, and no one is looking or listening to the writer So-and-So, in his own little world on the late morning highway. Everyone is in a good mood because of the fine weather, the policemen at the roadside are happy and raise a hand in greeting to passers-by, cats and dogs wait patiently at the curb—not one of them wants to end up under a car, and I am truly sorry I couldn't persuade Vennet to come along. "I will come when my work allows, phone me when it's a good time for fishing, but I'm afraid that I probably won't have a free day until the beginning of October, and then you'll already be back, damn it, I'd love to throw everything into the corner and come along, etc.," Vennet's mouth was saying, but his eyes slid off to look at his half-finished work.

This Vennet is no longer the same Vennet as in times gone by, I think sadly. How would I describe the present Vennet if I needed him for some story or other?

I have used Vennet now and again, usually his chief traits, which are those of the buoyant (pretty stereotyped) and romantic type of artist, and have contrasted him on several occasions to the distinctly rational, calculating type of person that inhabited the Socialist camp in the 1980s. The likes of Vennet constituted a nostalgic nod to a world that was exuding cold and about to change.

Now Vennet is different. A knight charging windmills, who has forgotten his original purpose and meaning. I'm afraid that it won't take long for him to turn into his own opposite.

When I begin to write a longer story or novel at Teeriida Farm, in the country by the sea, then I should make room for both Teodor and Vennet on the (as yet non-existent) pages. The game (every book is a game in itself) could begin with some metaphor, where Teodor and Vennet have come to blows so that snot and blood are flying around, Vennet lies gurgling on the stony road, Teodor is kicking him in the face, in the ribs; the fight has lasted some time and no one remembers any more why it started. I can of course use the (implausible) scenario that Vennet will win, but then I would have to supply him with a more sporty background, and make him a good deal younger.

At the side of the road the third or fourth provocatively and seductively dressed woman hitchhiker is waving her arm (this time rather despairingly, as if it's a matter of life and death)—there have been lots of them on the roadside this summer, and they are not at all expensive. This one waving her arm makes me consider for a moment, I lift my foot off the accelerator (for a brief moment the picture flashes by of her slender fingers with nails cut short opening my fly, the cool fingers touching my hot skin), but an unpleasant experience has made me act with caution, and lets me pass the alluring bait with a sensibly hurrying look, I'd like to give the woman what she needs, what she's longing for, but when it's only for the money I know anyone can give it, and the woman's wishes have nothing to do with me.

I think that everyone has a special key that unlocks their sexual desires. For instance, a good friend of mine gets turned on when a woman limps. Something that would be sensible to hide is what excites my friend. I, for example, could never bring myself to rape a woman, but when I sense passion in her, and especially if she shows it, then I'm sold. If a woman just wants money from me, then I become impotent. I simply can't help it.

Above the road a helicopter is circling low, a couple of police cars whizz by, and an ambulance. Something has happened down the road, and I'd rather not think what. Usually my writer's imagination will first of all paint the blackest of scenarios. If someone I know is late, or fails to turn up at the appointed time, my poor brain starts inventing all kinds of possible accidents. In my texts I tend to write about how things go wrong for people. The worst thing is that I have no sympathy for my characters, I don't cross my fingers for them, I am more likely to be ironic about them and give a short laugh: Why are you what you are? That has been held against me time and time again, but it doesn't worry me, as there are plenty of colleagues who think positively. One decorates cakes, the other dresses Barbie dolls, a third does such well-appreciated work as making caskets or digging graves.

Ahead of me is a cluster of vehicles. The road has been blocked off, and I'll have to make a detour along dusty side-roads. A police officer stops me. "Take this girl with you," pointing to a young girl in a very short skirt and long legs standing at the roadside. It is not a request, it is an order, but when I drive nearer and see it is the same wayside prostitute as earlier, I smile wryly: who would have though that of the young policeman (?!).

"How did you manage to overtake me?" I ask the young girl as she sits in the car, and I'd like to ask her how much of her hard-earned money she has to hand over to the police officer, but I don't have time, since she says matter-of-factly: "An elephant never changes partners. He loves his partner dearly. He only mates with her every three years."

"Are there only women on the job?" I ask when the first stupefaction, surprise, and a suppressed chuckle have passed.

"Not only women," she says as if hurt. "But you know, it's not much fun for me to have to explain the love-lives of elephants to a stranger. If someone who doesn't know you should have to contact you, and picks the wrong person, and someone for whom the message isn't intended gets to hear it, i.e. that an elephant mates every third year, what would imagine about the person asking the question? Eh?"

"I don't know what he'd think," I say with feigned indifference. "It seemed to me to be a perfectly good password, one that Barbi wouldn't have anything against." (It's true that at first Barbi didn't want to hear about elephants mating, but I managed to convince her, skillfully and slyly, because I, for my part, would like to have some fun too; I can't take this work as an informer completely seriously, the whole business has to have some ambiguity about it, maybe by means of hints, or trivia.)

"Oh, forget it," she makes a vague gesture, and I imagine she doesn't often laugh. "I was put out there at the roadside and they told me that you were bound to pick me up. They didn't realize that it was swarming with girls. Let it be. You're being followed, and that's fine because it means they're interested in you. Now there's a gray Volvo behind us. Your friend Teodor Heamees is in it. Well then. What did he have to say to you yesterday? We don't imagine he was talking about culture. In case Barbi didn't mention it, I'd better tell you that we're keeping an eye on you all the time, to keep you out of danger."

"An ear on me, too?" I blurt out. "What I mean is, are my telephone conversations being bugged?"

"I'm not at liberty to say, but it's all for your own safety. Two nights ago some house burned down not far from where you'll be staying, and they found two charred bodies. We know that Ummal had often been seen with the owner of the house. When the fire took place he was in Finland, and he's still there. No clues about whose the bodies could be. And two hours ago there was a terrible accident involving an army truck and another one carrying logs, an accident that could have dire political consequences."

The gravel road comes to an end, and now we're driving along the old highway, which is potholed, but at least not dusty. Now I also notice the gray Volvo behind us, keeping a respectful distance. "Let's turn right," says my traveling companion. The piece of forest we're driving through suddenly opens out into a stretch of grass by a river.

"This is a fine mess," the girl says, in a bit of a funk. "Now they'll be able to keep an eye on us." I give her a surprised glance then I realize: I have driven into the woods with a roadside prostitute, and in order not to blow our cover we'll have to have sex together.

"How are we going to do it?" I ask in helpless innocence.

"We really are quite exposed here, but it wouldn't be logical to turn round and drive back immediately," she says indignantly, as if she has just trod in a cow pat. "Anyway, I'll put my head down on your lap and pretend to be doing it. You know what I mean."

I have nothing against her small hand touching my thigh, she has very well manicured (very soft?) fingers, and on one of them a tiny gold ring with a glittering stone. There's no wedding ring there, and I feel something swelling within me, I cannot (and don't want to) do anything about it, so that everything will appear more real, I stroke (with my own fingers) her hair, and her thighs are too bare, and her perfume floats like a whiff of smoke into my nostrils. "Maybe they're watching with binoculars," I say, expressing the suspicion that has entered my head.

"We tried to make contact with you yesterday, but you slipped the net. Where were you?"

"At Vennet the artist's place, then back home, I went to sleep early," I report, and I can't even get worked up about the fact that they have forced their way so crudely into my private life. The girl's fingers have moved slightly upwards and the shoulders hunched over my lap rise and fall.

"Tell me what you talked about with Mr. Heamees and how your meeting with Ummal went."

I explain that Teodor was my classmate at school, and I am surprised that they aren't aware of this fact; I express the opinion that Teodor is in cahoots with Ummal, working for him; as I start to describe my meeting with Ummal I feel that the swollen thing in my trousers has suddenly been released (those gentle fingers!), and it all feels indescribably warm and pleasant for a while; while my companion wipes my trousers with tissues, I describe the especially warm attention that Ummal paid me.

When we get back to the main highway, Marla (for me the never-heard-before Marla-Karla) has me stop the car. "This is where I get off," she says. "I may come to visit you—only as an exception, of course." Then she asks me to sign a slip of paper that looks like a receipt. At the surprised expression on my face she explains that she'll be paid extra for this. "For what?" I ask.

"For *that*," she nods her head as if talking to a dense schoolboy. As she gets out and walks away, I notice that she has the nice face of an innocent girl and a round bottom, as well as those delicious hands. I really hope I will be able to sign another, similar receipt. A few kilometers later, I see my schoolmate Teodor standing at the roadside with extended arm and the hood of the car open, and when I come to a halt he is demonstrably surprised to see me.

"Our car broke down," he says grimly. "I hardly suppose you know anything about car engines."

"It'd be nice if you could tow us," says the other man, whose fingers are oily and who does seem to know (or thinks he knows) something about engines. "A few kilometers from here there's a former sovkhoz workshop and I hope that they're still in business."

In the car, Teodor sits next to me—my old schoolmate, after all—and asks where I'm going. It seems odd that only yesterday he held it against me that I was going off on vacation to an expensive place and is now pretending so diligently that he knows nothing. I explain that I'm going to a village called Posti, which is near a small town called Hüürupea.

"Well, then we're going in exactly the same direction," says Teodor cheerfully. "In that same village called Posti lives the most contemporary artist in Estonia. It's true that only a few people know about him now, but he'll soon be a household name the world over."

At the workshop (which clearly does deal with vehicle repairs) they discuss the matter. While the others are sorting things out, I sit in the car with the newspaper on my lap—my light summer pants show visibly wet patches. I had noticed how Teodor was inspecting them and I don't like other men doing so. Finally Teodor comes out, chucks his bag onto the back seat, and is ready to go. I can't understand why they need to follow me and what benefit they will derive from doing so. It would be nice to think that Marla is imagining the whole thing to be more serious than it actually is, but there are clear signs that Teodor is in cahoots with Ummal. At least I know that he's following instructions from Ummal, and he doesn't know I know; but maybe he knows I know, but is pretending not to, and is letting me think that he doesn't know, that I know he knows.

"Do you know that I know Ummal, owner of the 'Full-Blooded Recreation,' pretty well? He's a really interesting guy, he was one of the founders of Fluxus back in the Sixties, and his wife is a pupil of Beuys's. I got to know him in Lithuania, when there was a big Fluxus exhibition there. By the way, their Landsbergis down there was the only living Fluxus member on Soviet territory. I wanted to write a series of articles about Ummal right away, but he didn't want to say a word about that period of his life. He wasn't even prepared to give the briefest interview. This obviously has nothing to do with false modesty, it's more likely that there are unknown conflicts in the art world that people want to keep out of the public gaze.

"Some while back Ummal phoned me and said that there was this amateur installation artist working out in Posti village. He suggested we drove out to take a look at the installations. At first, I couldn't really see anything special about them, but then I cottoned on. That guy—he's around thirty, a little simple-minded, in fact the village idiot—has a completely different background from all those highly-educated artists nowadays. Here a process is beginning to take shape where art enters life, and life art. Most of us have gotten our education by way of what's termed "culture," but he has learnt what he knows in the depths of the forest, and is a child of nature. Examining his work, I discovered that he isn't searching for symbols but for subjects, and he uses them not in the superficial way someone from the city does, but by employing his sensitive intuition. He's like a Sunday painter—a sailor who paints boats, a villager who conjures up village scenes. In the Sixties the boom in primitivism kicked off, but it began to wane after a while because those who were revealed to be Sunday primitivists began asking too high a price and turned into professionals. Primitivism simply turned into yet another commodity.

"I'm not so naïve as to regard everything connected with contemporary art as a nugget of pure gold. Recently I happened to watch a film about Louise Bourgeois, who represented U.S. art at the Venice Biennale in 1993. She was an 82-year-old! The film showed the half-crazy old woman's life, but even her basic daily activities were afforded great significance. She showed her own work and explained *why* she did this or that, her work was accompanied by pretentious and *significant* texts. One installation showed how human body fluids were stored in small phials: sweat, urine, tears; the phials were hanging like fruit from the branches of a tree, at first they would speak of fears, and then, higher up, of passions. Then a little blouse was shown, impregnated with fear and hanging neatly on a coat-hanger. That old girl is now a big name in the contemporary world of art, no major exhibition is staged without involving her somehow. She was married to an art historian and had tried in vain to break through during various waves of modernist art. Then you saw the sly faces of two young men flash on screen: the art agent or minder, and the biographer. I for one found it very hard to believe that the texts used in these trendy discussions had been thought up by this half-crazy old woman herself.

"In my opinion this was all a brilliant business concept conjured up by these gifted young men, an act which could in itself be interpreted as a work of art: they created a famous artist called Louise Bourgeois. I see no reason why I shouldn't adopt the same method in the village of Posti and make Joosep Vaino famous. They happen to call him Poiss—the Boy—in the village, and he's regarded as a nut, and indeed, isn't well endowed with mental gifts, although such things can be turned to people's advantage nowadays. At any rate, I have plans for him to exhibit in Vilnius, where there's going to be the Baltic Exhibition of Contemporary Art. The Lithuanians have gotten ahead of us. During Soviet times we overshadowed them, but now they are creating things which have the stamp of their own national ethos, their closeness to nature. It was quite a revelation for me to see Egle Rakauskaite's girls tied together by their plaits. I saw them in Warsaw, and at the moment we're unable to match Rakauskaite's performance piece, the one where she wallows stark naked in honey and breathes though a tube, like a baby in the womb!

"At present, we're doing a video of Joosep's project, called "Felling Trees All the Way to Vilnius". We drew a straight line from Posti to Vilnius on the map and along this line, in all the hamlets, villages, and towns, we saw down trees. Each tree has roots, a landscape in which it is growing—this is its concrete environment, recorded on the video, together with the sawing. The piece symbolically clears the way from the village of Posti to the city of Vilnius, and all the logs from the trees that have been chopped down are exhibited in the art gallery in anonymous stacks. You get it, don't you?:

trees that once stood in the soil have now been reduced to piles of firewood. Just like those anonymous apartment blocks in the cities where rootless people skulk. This is all about turning a natural structure into a rational one, which a stack of usable logs actually is. A few handfuls of sawdust can be added. Inside the stack of logs a screen is placed where the viewer can follow the process of "deracination"—the artist hard at work, the concentration on his face as he fells the trees and thus changes the landscape, creating a new reality. The Joosep Vaino Project will display our sensitivity to local issues, one that we're using to carve out a window in the art world of today, which is open to these sorts of trends."

"But the things this unknown guy has created—if they really are his creations—can they be successful?" I ask uncertainly.

"Obviously there will also be a catalogue of his earlier work, plenty of which is scattered throughout the village. With suitable captions, each of these installations will acquire a special meaning. He has, for instance, framed a number of pieces of upholstery. In his book *Ways of Worldmaking*, Nelson Goodman gives an example of how some old lady insisted in an upholstery store that she wanted a piece of cloth that matched exactly the sample she had brought in. The store indeed sent her small pieces of cloth that matched her sample exactly in size. Goodman comments on this with his famous sentence: 'My friends are different from other people, not because of a single identifying characteristic or group of characteristics, but simply because, at some point in time they are my friends.' You get it: when the Boy Joosep puts his pieces of cloth in picture frames they take on the characteristics of *paintings*, so he is demonstrating exactly what Goodman was driving at."

"This Goodman is your namesake," I say.

"In what way?" says Teodor, growing confused.

"Well, Goodman in Estonian becomes 'Heamees', which just happens to be your surname," and I am, in turn, surprised that he has never noticed the connection before, then realize that someone with a poor gift for languages would never think of translating a foreign name, although it seems to me that Teodor's profession does require knowledge of a foreign languages. I can't remember how he related to foreign languages back in our days at school. Some people simply never get a grip on languages, whatever efforts they make.

"For me, what's so splendid about this project is that the Boy Joosep is showing our highly trained and gifted people their place. I should be able to manage to get his project to the São Paolo Biennale. That really would be a triumph! From Posti, a clearing in the forest, all the way to São Paolo—an international project, where local and global sensibilities are united!"

"But what happens to Joosep when he's dragged into the international carrousel? What about him as a person? He isn't far from his ceiling of competence." I ask this because writers are used to posing questions about people. My imagination has once again conjured up the umpteenth depressing human fate, but I am not at all prepared when Teodor bursts into hearty laughter.

"Ha-ha-ha-ha-haaa! You do come up with things! Do you know, I've seen a few others like the Boy Joosep in my time. Before long they're no longer in any doubt that *they* are the greatest of artists. If you plant some idea or other in their minds, within a short space of time they will have *convinced* themselves that *they* thought of it. There is nothing more human than for people to become reconciled to success and fame. The bigger the bluff, the surer he'll become convinced that he has special gifts and powers that have never before been appreciated properly, that he has suffered because of the unjust world, and that he should have been given his rightful moment of glory ages before."

We drive past a building bearing a sign "Posti Store," and a road sign shows that the lighthouse is one and a half kilometers farther down the road. It has been raining here recently, the gravel road between the linden trees is wet and there are large puddles. Then the sea comes into view. Pale blue. No wind. At the end of the naze a white tower can be seen, at its foot a tiny house. A sheep fence blocks our way. Teodor jumps out and stretches his limbs. Bottles jangle in his bag. "The Boy Joosep likes his beer," says Teodor.

I too step out into the fresh sea air. My limbs have grown stiff from the journey, the stains on my trousers have dried and are now almost invisible. A small man emerges from the little house at the foot of the lighthouse. "Come on, let's go," says Teodor, inviting me. "The Boy has made an exhibition. The most fascinating item is called "Graveyard"—crosses that have a shard of mirror instead of a name, so that everyone can see themselves in it."

We open the rustic timber gate and put it on the latch again with a length of aluminum wire. The man, short in stature and with a large balding head, steps toward us, smiling all the while. So this is the Great Estonian Artist, I think to myself, disappointed somehow.

***

At some point, when Estonia's declaration of independence had been accepted, but the country was still a *de facto* part of the Soviet

Union, Vennet came up with the idea of creating a non-existent culture for a non-existent state. He agreed with a number of critics that they would write about non-existent artists, writers, composers, describe non-existent cultural events and analyze non-existent cultural policy in a serious way. This would have been a fantastic opportunity to acquaint the world with a non-existent, ideal cultural country, so long as critics were capable of creating ideal artistic people. In their overviews and critical articles they would get the opportunity to propagate the most fantastic ideas.

But it didn't work. Vennet never got anyone involved, he had neither the time nor the inclination, as he spend a good deal of his time in drinking circles and had no plans to go beyond the planning stage. Quite recently all of this came up in conversation, and Vennet said that the whole idea would never have succeeded back in 1988 anyway, because later analysis revealed that at the time none of our critics would have managed to present themselves in a global context. The result would have been laughable, since we would have been flirting with modernism in a postmodern world. "You can't jump over your own shadow" is how Vennet put it, adopting a worldly-wise facial expression. That phrase was Vennet's little joke. Ambiguous. Anyone overhearing him saying it would, however, take it as a deadly serious assessment of the state of our home country.

As I walk down the slopes of the sand dune to the water's edge and let my eye rove once more over the Boy Joosep's artworks (?), Vennet's old idea of an ideal cultural country springs to mind, and I think: Better late than never. Now that Estonia has shrunk from being the erstwhile cultural capital of the Soviet Union to a European cultural province, we should make great efforts to restore our self-esteem. Some decent hoax would be most welcome. But Joosep's installations would not be enough—their quality is poor, even the pieces of upholstery stuck in picture frames, and so praised by Teodor, look familiar: I've already seen something similar in a German museum, and although I don't remember the artist, it must have been an installation classic. I think that Teodor himself should start working on turning Joosep into an artist, as it is after all "the Boy Joosep, Artist," who is himself a multilayered work of art that will find its (honorable!) place in our (art) world, which lacks the ability to make value judgments.

I take off my shoes and walk on the hot summer sand. The water too is warm. I am astonished at how beautiful the sandy beach is here. The tall pine trees on the cliffs, the dark green wild rye. And not a soul around. My townie's brain associates summer beaches with half-naked bathers, I just can't imagine an empty beach on a sunny day. I'm in no hurry to go anywhere. I can take off my clothes and lie down on the sand. I can go swimming stark naked. I'm the master of the place, it's like my own private beach. On the horizon, a lone white sail can be seen. The sea birds are bobbing up and down on the shallow waves. I'm glad now that I've reached the beach, that I took the wrong turning and ended up by the sea instead of at Teeriida Farm. I hope that looking out over the sea will give me peace of mind, which I have (have I?) come to seek / obtain here in the countryside (away from the city) and to tell you the truth, all this had nothing to do with my own will.

The all-embracing feeling of bliss that filled me when I reached the sea begins to dissipate as uneasy thoughts wash over recent events, and I suddenly find myself asking again why Teodor had to travel with me. When the Boy Joosep was showing us his installations, Teodor said all of a sudden that he had lost his notebook, that maybe it had fallen out of his pocket in my car, and he went off looking for it. And it really was (according to his story) on the floor of the car.

In spy films there is the familiar scene where things are taken out of (secret documents, material evidence) or put into (a tape-recorder, a primed bomb) someone's car. I will have to check for both of these sorts of things—it would be inappropriate to smile, since there are so many pieces of evidence already suggesting that a serious game is being played. And what's worst of all: I myself have been drawn into this game (if it can still be called a game). My vision of myself as an impartial citizen who doesn't really bother about what happens in the country as a whole, whose societal involvement is limited to voting at elections, and the essence of whose life is creative work, is no longer accurate. I have become an Informer to the Estonian Republic—honest, faithful, and public-spirited, someone whose task it is not to question the honesty and loyalty of the state, of the people who recruited him as an informer. When I start seeking / finding justification for my actions (being an informer) I am obliged to repeat the words: honest, faithful, my Country, the President, the Estonian Republic (for the survival of which I would be prepared to eat nothing but potato peelings), self-sacrificing . . . and I have the grim thought that these words have suddenly become emptied of substance, that I'm no longer sure what they really mean. I am incapable (abruptly, all at once, just like that) of telling myself whether this republic actually is something worth selling your soul for.

I can think of several gifted young acquaintances of mine who have gone off to establish themselves abroad without making a big thing of it. I remember references to a Lilliput country run by *third-rate* former Soviet Estonian bureaucrats, are unable to rise above their mental and financial limitations. This republic has been shaped by the *lower* middle class world view. The fact that such government officials are prepared to sell themselves for such laughably *small* bribes or trifling gifts has already sealed the country's fate.

I put on my clothes and decide not to go swimming (I can imagine how I will regret my decision next winter: the image of the calm sea and the sunshine will haunt me as I lie there before sleep comes, wallowing in regret). I will now have to go to Teeriida Farm and search my car thoroughly. I start walking briskly through the wild rye, but suddenly see someone lying on the sand.

It's a woman—she's pulled up her bright yellow dress to expose her thighs, her naked legs are spread in the sunshine, and she seems to be asleep under a matching kerchief that covers her face. I am surprised at how her legs are covered in dark hair. Like a man from southern Europe, is what I am thinking, and I see in my mind's eye circus people with their hairy faces (like dogs' faces), the kind I once saw in a movie. I stand there goggling at the woman for some time, when all at once I hear loud panting: three men in camouflage suits are running toward me, I take a couple of steps back, one of them rushes past, brushing me lightly, the other one almost stumbles over the woman lying there—at the last moment he manages to jump over her—the woman sits up in confusion, she has short dark hair and her scared face isn't hairy.

I move off some distance before daring to look back. The woman has got to her feet and is watching, as I am, how the men throw off their clothes and storm into the water.

So much for an empty beach, I growl as I open the car door, but while I'm scrutinizing the map that "Full-Blooded Recreation" has given me, someone knocks on the car window. "Did you happen to notice which way they were running?" asks a fat man panting heavily and covered in mud up to the eyeballs. I understand who he's talking about. "Defense League people?" I ask in turn. He shakes his head vigorously. I say that some men went swimming. He goes running off in the direction I've indicated, ten meters further on he trips and falls. I've only just opened the door to go and see what's happened to him, when another man stumbles past—so I wait until he reaches the fallen man and crouches down beside him. Now there are two heads visible among the wild rye and neither of them can come to grief.

I decide that the best thing to do is to ask for directions at the store, and try to find out a thing or two about these strange people as well. These men have aroused my curiosity, I can't place them, give them a name.

Outside the village store in Posti some locals are whiling away the time on a bench, they're drinking beer and are in no hurry. I ask them the way to Teeriida Farm, but they don't know. "Teeriida?" asks one of them. "There's nothing with that name round here." "I've lived here all my life but the name Teeriida has never reached my ears.," says another. A man on a bicycle rides up. He's riding fast, and only just manages to stop in front of the store. "Here, have you heard of Teeriida?" the others as him. "Of course I have" he says. "Teeriida is the new name they've given to Värniku," he explains, and tells me how to get there. It's not particularly far. He appears to be proud that he knows everything there is to know about Teeriida, and mentions that the new owner gave the place a new name, saying that the new name was in fact the old one, but people just don't remember the older name, for them the place has always been Värniku.

I thank him and walk towards the door of the store to see what they've got on sale, I have to be prepared, to stock up on food, have to know the opening times and when the delivery truck comes; this isn't the city, where stocks are replenished 24/7. But my jaw drops when I see Kandiman in the doorway. He squeezes my shoulder with a broad grin, as if our meeting here is the happiest event of his life.

"What's happened to you?" I ask, rather startled because he has a black eye.

"Nothing special," he smiles. "Some guys in blotchy overalls wanted to demonstrate their strength, but luckily they didn't succeed."

I say that I've just seen them charging into the sea. "That's what they do, yes sirree," says Kandiman, and we walk over to his car where there is another guy sitting (and at the same time lolling) on the back seat, his face badly knocked around, and a sick look about him. "This is the work of 'Full-Blooded Recreation' guys," says Kandiman, handing him a beer. "Meet my old friend Siimon, who's paid good money to come out here to relax and get into shape. Now these guys have knocked his face out of shape." I don't understand anything. "You just don't get what's going on," laughs Kandiman. "Not far from here there's some camp or other called

'Full-Blooded Recreation,' where people pay to practice survival techniques. But the whole business has a catch: everyone who attends the week-long course signs a document that he will submit completely to their discipline and will do anything they consider necessary. This means that they sign away their freedom for a week, turn into soldiers or prisoners—and they pay good money for doing so.

"Our Siimon, poor guy, got fed up, he stuck it out for a couple of days, and when one morning they weren't even given breakfast, he called me up and asked for help. I've got a summer cottage out here. He's visited me before, and as I happened to have the time, I turned up and we had a party. And now, just imagine, while he was sneaking over to my place, these types followed him, and turned up in the night to arrest him. They have a strict rule about abstinence in the camp, and of course you're not allowed to leave the territory. There was quite a fight, but he couldn't put up enough resistance, and they took poor Siimon with them. Imagine paying to get beaten up! There are several houses belonging to 'Full-Blooded Recreation' out here. They've done up old farms and put them up for rent. Mostly to foreigners who are prepared to pay exotic prices for Estonian exoticism. But local guys turn up too. And why not—someone who toils away as a government official, or does business from morn till night, can spend his holidays here while learning the art of how to fight, shoot, and survive."

When Kandiman asks me what brings me to this neck of the woods, I explain that I've come to look up some relative of mine at Hüürupea (I would rather not mention that I've actually come here to use the services of this very same "Full-Blooded Recreation" set-up, and I'm afraid that Kandiman would invite himself to have a look around the place, and then a major drinking-session would be unavoidable). I tell him about how I had just gone down to the shore to admire the seascape—I could never have imagined that the county of Läänemaa could have such fine dunes and sandy beaches. Then I describe my run-in with those guys in their camouflage uniforms crawling half-dead through the wild rye grass, and how I saw a strange and impressive woman sunning herself, hairy as a man (I don't really know why I need to say this to Kandiman, it just slipped out, and I feel unexpected amusement, describing this woman covered in dark hair.).

"Fantastic!" cries Kandiman. "Years ago I used to have a hairy Russian girlfriend. I met her on the street, and wow, did it click between us! We went straight home to her place. She lived in some dorm or other, together with another girl in the same room. No unnecessary chatter! Oh boy! When I put my hand on her thigh and felt that hair, I felt like a sodomite. It was like being with a little animal. Slugged away the whole night. Her room mate was masturbating in the next bed. I could hear the squelching sounds the whole time and this turned me on even more. The girl herself was really ashamed of her body hair and was quite amazed that I liked it so much. She remained as white as a snowflake right up to the end of the summer—I called her Snyegurochka, my hairy Snyegurochka—because she didn't dare go to the beach and always wore dark stockings. She was afraid of shaving the hair off because someone had told her that this would only make it grow more thickly. You can imagine those dark stockings and above them her plump white skin, covered with coal-black hair!

"Could be that that woman on the beach was my ex-girlfriend?

I spend the summers in the next village, and hardly ever visit the beach here. Interesting, I wonder who she could be. If I had the time I'd stroll out there and have a look, could be the same girl—something happened back then, I don't remember why I lost contact with her. And even if it isn't her, it's interesting none the less. Pretty weird things happen in this village. At Teeriida Farm—that's one of the 'Full-Blooded Recreation' sites—a woman disappeared about ten days ago, along with her grown-up daughter. She'd been lecturing at the university. People went into the forest to look for them. Then it emerged that as they were driving away they'd had an accident, the gas tank exploded and they were turned to charcoal. Don't know whether it's all true, but that's what they say. Well anyway, fine, I really have to be going, have to be in town by two," he finishes his unbroken monologue. I watch him go rushing off toward town, then I open the door of my car and something wrapped in pink under the passenger seat catches my eye. I fumble about and pick it up. It's heavy. It's a pistol. I pull away my hand, as if bitten by a snake. *Must be Teodor*, is what flashes through my mind. Put it there when he was looking for his notebook. What if it's a weapon that someone's been shot with? What then? What were they planning to do with that pistol? I suddenly break out in a cold sweat. When I turn off the road a police car with flashing blue and white lights rushes by.

A rather poor road, stony and covered in grass, leads up to the farm, and you have to drive with care to avoid damaging your car. Behind a stone wall to the left the forest is filled with bushes, or the bushes have grown wild, and on the right there are strips of mown hayfield where one or two trees and juniper bushes make it look just like an English park. The landscape here is exactly like in a Vennet painting, and I keep feeling that it's a pity he didn't come along. For a short while I have managed to forget about the pistol or revolver (all the same to me) wrapped in pink cloth, as negotiating this rough road demands all my attention; then the road gets better and I no longer want to be carrying around that object (evidence?) wrapped in pink silk (a shawl? a kerchief?).

Sometime during my childhood (we were seven or eight years old) we found a revolver wrapped in oily newspaper inside a low hedge. I remember how we watched as it was unwrapped in the arbor in our back garden, where Leo, Teo, and I held our breath as *it* emerged from the paper for a second time. *It* emanated crime and mystery, conspirators and robbers. *It* was a world we had nothing whatsoever to do with. My father was the headmaster of a school, Teodor's was an important Soviet government official, Leo didn't have a father at all, though his mother was the director of the only restaurant in town. We came from decent homes, we were well-dressed and had been brought up to be polite. Like some instructor of a children's hobby group, my mother was perpetually making sure that we were having an interesting (and rewarding) childhood.

I don't remember what we talked about or thought. My memories are only of watching the revolver, silently and tensely. If I were to try to reproduce the event today, I would put words in our mouths and thoughts in our heads which would serve my more pressing, contemporary artistic aims—and you'd *have* to doubt them. When I say that I myself had the good idea of giving away the revolver, I have no doubt that I did. And if I were to describe the way that I pondered the relationship between the object discovered under the car seat and the object from my childhood, nothing would be achieved. Let us keep the two incidents quite separate.

I pull the wrapped object out from under the seat with two fingers. I don't look at it to see what *it* looks like. I'll hide it in the dry stone wall: I remove two medium-sized stones, put the bundle in the hole, put the stones back on top so that nothing shows. Once I'm back in the car, I ought to have a feeling of relief that there never was anything suspicious lying under the seat.

I can't tell why I suspect Teodor of having put the gun there. It could just as well have been Marla who had taken the pistol out of her ample bag while I was rinsing off the front of my pants—which had carelessly (or intentionally?) gotten stained—she could have had some motive for putting the thing in the car. At any rate it was a trump card against me, an opportunity for someone to get me. "Yes," I chuckle, "now the murder weapon is lying there in the dry stone wall and no one can associate it with me." I chuckle in a forced and clumsy manner—any theater director would have taken the role away from me on hearing it; when I light a cigarette, a feeling of unease gnaws at my soul like a little mouse.

I look at the surroundings and (like a camera) try to record the picture in my memory: a withered juniper bush, half-leaning over the stone wall; a tall spruce tree, surrounded by lindens like poor relations—and then, like a moose, a man charges over the dry stone wall and across the raspberry patch in his camouflage uniform, and runs right at me, comes to a halt a couple of meters from me, pants for a while before he's able to ask if I haven't seen similar men in the vicinity. I tell him that just moments ago I saw one slip past, I don't know why I trick him, pointing into the blue of the nether distance; he's having a rough time and I'm making it even rougher for him. He tries to make some sense of this with a compass and a map, but can't. Farther off, in a green forest glade, something glints, then again, as if the sun were reflected in glass. The man in his camouflage uniform runs off in the wrong direction, as indicated by me—he has no time to thank me, he hasn't got the intelligence to do so, and I feel relieved.

***

And there it is. Teeriida. It's not so very long ago that I heard the name for the first time (it was Barbi, yes, Barbi, who spoke of Teeriida, and I felt that I had heard a similar name earlier), but now this combination of letters has become a fixed entity for me— both the meaning of Teeriida and that of myself fuse into some kind of unit: mention the one and the other springs to mind. I don't yet know what my relation to Teeriida will be. I could think that arriving here means coming home—a place that fits in with my image of home, a place where I belong. I can stay there a few days, weeks, long months, imagining myself to be at home (because I have no choice), but one fine day I will discover that I have been harboring an illusion, and that Teeriida is the last place on Earth I ought to be. I should take this possibility seriously, as in fact Teeriida has been thrust upon me, I didn't take the trouble to seek it out. Maybe it's a trap which has been craftily placed across my road in life.

If I were to stop and describe Teeriida (which I am likely to do in some forthcoming book) I could start not with the farmhouse itself, but with the landscape that surrounds it. Then I would close in, step by step, moving first through the gate, and then into the house. I would spend some time describing how I unlock and open the door, then run quickly through all the rooms, and emerge again from the house; now I could go (one by one) through the various outbuildings, wrinkle my nose at the privy, and stop for a good while in the orchard with its dappled play of light. I would try to describe the alienation that Teeriida evokes in me—it is merely an (un)populated place. This uncertainty fades away once I have put my baggage in the (kitchen) corner. (Or when I have a pee outside at the corner of the house?) I make the place my own by my presence, but my presence here is like that of a Christmas tree brought into the room, which stands upright not thanks to its roots, but to the crosspiece underneath it.

When I stop the car to open the gate to Teeriida, I still can't say whether I've left home to visit Teeriida, or whether I've left home to end up at Teeriida. At this moment I can't make a decision, but feel that making such a (seemingly formal) distinction is very important, that the rest of my life depends on it, and that I should adopt a standpoint pretty quickly. I know (as a writer) that the best way to reach clarity is by way of a *text*. A text is not a result, it is a process—an aimless wander, whose aim becomes clear during the wandering itself. The time it takes for me to step out of the enclosed space of the car into landscape (which is practically limitless around me) becomes a text that I must cover with another text so as to produce a significant (third . . . or tenth) text. It is quite unimportant (!) whether the stacked texts cover (suit) one another, what is important is that the texts exist, the number of layers, points of view, from which we observe (not assess!) the thickness (or thinness) of these layers. I open the gate, and now there's nothing to stop me from changing my attitude, as I can cross at will the invisible boundary according to which I am *inside* or *outside*. Whether I have become a part of the unending landscape around me, or am inside the fence that has been erected to protect the house.

The first thing that strikes me is the verandah with its pink pillars—it isn't set symmetrically in the middle of the building, but disproportionately to the right; which ought to, but doesn't, balance the rather clumsily-built (as if designed to be a ruin) decorative stone wall that juts out onto the somewhat neglected lawn and looks rather bleak. The walls of the verandah are covered with imitation wood paneling made of white plastic, which suddenly (as if they had run out of building material) ends, giving a rather basic grey log wall the chance to enter the game, a wall that quite suits the newly thatched roof, but when you take into consideration the strangely bulging attic windows with their strange mirror panes sticking out of the roof, then it looks as if this log wall had been brought from another house. There is another decorative wall at the other end of the house, but it stands further off and its principal function appears to be to shield the view from the window and give passers-by a kind of shock, as if seeing ruins.

It isn't a house that looks inviting from the gate, but I console myself with the fact that in future I'll be mostly looking out from it and my view will be made more joyful by the neatly-mown lawn and the views of a landscape surrounding the house that seems to have been chosen with care.

I drive the car into the yard and stop near the decorative wall. A cat—its tail up—slips from the door of the shed and scurries towards me. It stops, afraid of me. Then sits down, waiting.

I imagine the cat belongs to the house. I have no experience of pets. My mother was allergic to animal hair (or so we were told), and although our house would have been suitable for keeping cats or dogs, I was forced to satisfy my love of animals (if that is the term) by stroking Teo's dogs (Laika, Tuks) or Leo's cats (Miisi, Liisi, Kiisi, all of which were she-cats, and regularly pregnant). It was Leo's job to get rid of the kittens, and he did so with grim determination. In those days we went around together a lot, but I don't remember ever participating in any animal massacres myself. When a cat got very fat, it was clear that offspring were on their way. One day Leo (with ardor) invited me to look at some kittens; but a few days later there was nothing left to see. This was a kind of "now you see it, now you don't" act that repeated itself every few months.

I don't know whether it was this mysterious disappearance of the kittens (only explained to me when I was older) or my mother's allergy that formed in me the firm belief that a city apartment was not the place to keep pets, but either way, despite my daughter's pleas, I stuck to my principles. I can remember the day we started to drive back into town from Vennet's place in the country, and stopped off at the milk woman's place. That particular farm had an enormous number of cats, and the woman showed us some little furry balls romping around in the hay under the shed. "Dad, we're going to take one with us, aren't we?" said my daughter, looking me straight in the face. I had never before seen such an urgent wish in her eyes. There was despair, fear, hope—in a word—every emotion was expressed in those eyes and that statement of hers (we're taking one) was the best simulation that a ten-year-old girl could muster. "No, we're not," is what I said. "Our apartment in town is not suitable for pets," I added in a firmer tone of voice, in order to cover up the uncertainty of my previous words.

When we were getting divorced, a couple of months after, my wife and daughter got a dog, and soon after a kitten. By then my daughter was twelve, and I was relieved that it wasn't too late. I couldn't change my opinion back then, although this would have been a good opportunity to do so. Only after the divorce did I understand that people have to have things smaller than they are. Someone or something to look after. Looking after someone else is really looking after yourself. You only understand this when you're left on your own.

I am sitting on the bench on the verandah, smoking and drinking beer. A bunch of keys is lying next to me—five keys, two of them large, for padlocks. The cat has done several rounds of the verandah, but I haven't paid any attention or disturbed it by calling out kitty-kitty-kitty, and now it's rubbing up against my legs, getting ready for a big leap, and jumps. The cat is unexpectedly heavy, its claws dig into my thighs as it purrs, the purring increases as I stroke it, then it looks me in the face and emits a little miaow.

I have to lift the door by holding the handle, before being able to turn the key in the lock. Through the still closed door to the entrance hall I can hear the dull striking of a clock, and I start to mechanically count the strokes: one . . . two . . . The third stroke is at full volume, and in the spacious kitchen there is a long table with a vase full of yellow flowers, and a rag runner leads to a large room where everything groans under a thick layer of varnish and there is a fireplace made of stone where firewood is stacked, ready for burning. I lean my arms on the writing desk and look out the window. There are dead flies on the plastic window-frame. A butterfly with a broken wing is beating against the pane. Through the window the gate can be seen, and through the irregular hedge, glimpses of the road.

The cat is rubbing itself against my legs all the while, and I am glad that it has immediately taken to me, but when I stumble over it I realize that behind all this attention could be an empty stomach. I go and get my food bag from the car, and take out a frankfurter; the cat snatches it out of my hand and vanishes under the shed with its booty. I take my typewriter from the back seat and my bag of books; when I put the typewriter on the desk and lay out my notebooks and pencils, I've furnished my room. The desk is covered in green baize, outside the window there is a green lawn, beyond the garden starts a field with faded or dried-out hay, and beyond that there are tall trees, and between them a whitewashed house whose dark windows with cross-shaped panes emanate unease. I drag the chair up closer to the desk and sit down. Now I can see the central part of the white house, the middle of the three windows, and feel I can make out a white face of someone inside.

There are three bedrooms on the second floor, furnished like hotel rooms, rationally and impersonally, they don't seem to belong to the house and I don't think I'll be going upstairs very much at all. From upstairs the view is more extensive. A woman in a yellow dress is walking along the road. It'll be a couple of minutes before she knocks at my door.

I haven't been here at Teeriida for half an hour, but already I have the irresistible urge to talk to someone, I want to put off being alone (being alone with yourself); I am seized with the fear that the woman in the yellow dress could simply walk past, go her own way without dropping in. I go into the yard and busy myself with the gate: I have left it open and should put it on the latch, so it won't swing open again. I could ask the woman something— introduce myself, then inquire where you can make a phone call to town. And if she's not in a hurry, I could invite her in for coffee. I realize that I (as a writer) should make the acquaintance of a lot of the villagers—infiltrate the village—so that later on I can use all the scenes, adventures, and people in my writing. This train of thought broadens out immediately to include my informer activities—I will infiltrate Ummal's world (Ummal is a sponge and I am a splash of spilled coffee on the table; Ummal is the blotting paper and I am the ink; Ummal is the soil and I am the rain; Ummal is an open book and I am water dripping from the ceiling), so that I can get subject matter for the novel that is going to reflect the situation at the end of the century. The environmental crisis (or, to be more exact, waiting for such a catastrophe to occur) is surely one of the most difficult burdens we will be dragging into the next century. Ummal is offering one opportunity and I should, in my novel, try to find out whether it is justified to abandon (the myth of) progress (I almost wrote: deconstruction) and gradually move step by step back to the Stone Age. I have already understood that Ummal's way of turning back is actually an arrival. The end of the myth is the beginning (of the history) of return.

I could give the novel that I write (could be writing) the title "Novel at the End of the Century," a title whose blatant pretentiousness could be softened somewhat with the (ambiguous) motto: " . . . contemporary art is like a symphony concert, where a group of musicians appear on stage who have no ear for music and cannot play their instruments, and on the conductor's rostrum stands someone wielding the baton who cannot read the score or convince the audience that the noise they are hearing is music . . ." Ambiguity is concealed within a hoax, as the author Richard Bonnaire doesn't actually exist, nor does his book, *Introduction to the XXI Century* (although I can well imagine that such a nice title has been around for ages). Contemporary art would be, in my opinion, a suitable metaphor for (an extremist brand of) the green movement, because art has already reached the level that the fundamentalist greens only dream about achieving.

I step out of the gate, and in a few paces reach the road that passes the house, but the woman in the yellow dress is nowhere to be seen, and neither is anyone else. It's quite impossible to imagine where she could have got to. It is not likely that she turned back—to my mind, people in the countryside always know exactly where they are going and don't tend to wander back and forth like people in town. I'm a little disappointed that I can't have a chat with anyone, and could even imagine that the earth has simply swallowed up this woman who was trying to get in touch with me, but my opinion doesn't change the course of events (ones that will never become clear to me).

I sit down in the grass, and a short while later roll over onto my stomach, my nose pushed in among the blades of grass, so that I can smell the soil. I don't remember sitting down on the ground before (on the floor, on asphalt), let alone lying down. I always sit down on a bench, a chair, a sofa, the edge of a table . . . I am enjoying the unusual nature of this moment, I inhale the smell of earth, and have the feeling that the earth is breathing beneath me, as if we are two weary lovers breathing quietly in each other's embrace. Something is crawling up my leg, is getting lost in the forest of hairs, I scratch vigorously with my fingers, a little while later the tickling feeling is there again and I sit up and pull up the leg of my pants—in among the hairs a large red ant is climbing, I tear it out with the tips of my fingers, then crush its brownish-red body by rubbing my fingertips together; a couple of dark pieces are left under my fingernails even after I wipe my fingers off on my pants.

Now I can think about what that Frenchman Richard Bonnaire actually looks like. He could have a large (or small) shoe-size, he could be tall (or very short), at any rate he should strike the eye immediately, and his wife could be Estonian. In fact (if we're honest) he was born in 1968 in Paris into a Maoist-poststructuralist family, and after a complicated and contradictory youth he moved in 1986 over into the Anglo-American cultural space, where he worked (1996-1999) as a visiting lecturer at various U.S. universities. RB's point of departure is the concept of a basic word *(underword)*: these are the words from which sentences are constructed. In his "Virtual Theory of Information" he places his bets on the concept of cogency: " . . . when we can present our inventions cogently in art / advertising / politics, they become truths." His *chef d'oeuvre, An Introduction to the XXI Century*, contains 7,462 cogently presented sentences.

I have the urge to smoke a cigarette, to lie with my face turned up to the blue sky and watch how the smoke disperses in the air, but to do that I would have to get up, go inside, and fetch the packet of cigarettes from the table. By the time I lay down in the grass again, everything would be different, I would probably no longer be dying for a smoke, and it is very likely that I wouldn't even have the energy to come back outside and would end up smoking my cigarette at the kitchen table. A crow flies (silently) across the sky. A plane marks its progress in the heights. The yellowish-white streak thins, spreads, thickens, thins, until there's nothing left. The plane can only mark out where it has flown for a short distance. Tirelessly, it grows a tail which someone is cutting off the whole time.

I take my things out of the car and bring them into the house. I suddenly (seem to have) decided to stay for some while at Teeriida, and I act decisively. I open the clothes closet in the bedroom and put in my few items of clothing. In the bed-linen closet there are sheets, towels, pillow-cases, I can smell the laundry that gives a feeling of being at home, and this is something quite different from a hotel room—the shelves show a definite trace of perpetual human care; it is a simulated impression of home, but I fall for it; when I open one of the drawers to put in my underwear, I see a set of woman's negligée, at first I am not surprised, later I run an eye over the bras and panties as if they belonged to my wife; only a few seconds later do I realize that those underclothes shouldn't be there.

(The previous occupants—a mother and daughter—have disappeared, so they say; their charred remains were found in a burnt-out car, in which they were on their way back to town.)

I think to myself: a woman would hardly leave her underwear

in a clothes closet.

I shut the drawer and go into the kitchen and pick up the packet of cigarettes lying on the table. The Zippo makes quite a crack in the silence. Through the window among the junipers you can see a wooden garden table faded to gray in the sun. There are some silver spangles on the table. A magpie is pecking at them. The sun is shining slantingly at the more distant woods which throw dark shadows. The wall clock strikes a muffled half hour. There is a glint out there among the green of the spruce tree crowns. I now remember that I've seen the same kind of glinting earlier. When I was hiding the revolver under the stones.

Whistling loudly, I stroll out through the gate, along the road past the house, then climb up onto a large rock and, basking in sunshine, look at the surroundings. Nothing suspicious anywhere. Nothing glints or twinkles. I slouch around among the raspberry bushes, find a late pinkish-red fruit, and pop it into my mouth. I look for another berry and happen to find myself by the dry stone wall, so I lift up one stone, then the other. The withered juniper bush has now drooped right over the wall, but the revolver, wrapped in its silk shawl, is no longer there.

***

"We have a lot in common."

These words that are rattling in my head are not associated with any specific person, I heard them just recently (I'm dead certain!) and remember them through a vague mist (like a brittle relationship between non-existence and existence). When I move, a painful throb shoots through my temples, when I open my eyes I begin to make out the silvery-blue window, the bright frame, and the ceiling that reflects the moonlight. My belly has cooled off, the naked skin of my stomach is ice cold and my hands glowing hot. I realize that I am and am not wearing pants—the stiff denim waist is digging into the backs of my knees. I am in bed; in a world of sheets, pillows, and blankets. I have ended up there seemingly without knowing it, I must have flopped into bed with my pants pulled halfway down. Something has gone very wrong, something is not as it should be.

I remember coming in from outside; the thought that someone had taken the revolver from the stone wall put me in a state of panic—it was a clear sign that I was now mixed up in something that I had no business with. My brain was looking feverishly for a way out, a way of refusing future proposals (I hadn't been told the rules of the game sufficiently, I did not realize that the first move would involve everything I had stored up in my subconscious), but I did realize that it was now hopelessly late and that the future would depend on me alone—whether I let myself be dragged on by my urge to play games.

I came in from outside, picked up the half bottle of beer standing on the table and poured it down my parched throat. I took a new one from my bag, thought I ought to put all the beers in the fridge as they had gotten warm in the car, then realized that there was no electricity in the house, as I'd already been told at the "Full-Blooded Recreation" office. So there is no light, no way of cooling things, no radio or TV, and to get any warmth I would have to light the stove with firewood. I had never lit a fire in a stove in my whole life. Never even lit a bonfire. I lit a cigarette and let the fine cloud of smoke waft toward the window-panes. I knocked the ash into the empty beer bottle. It was as if the world had made no progress. No picture, no sound, no ice cubes in a cocktail glass. I sudden felt terribly hot, suffocating, I felt as if I was dying.

"We have a lot in common," someone says.

I wake up, the moon is shining outside, and I have been asleep for a few hours. I am sure that someone must have put some sleeping draft or other in my beer. Someone needed me out of the game for some short space of time, and they succeeded.

I pull up my pants (why the hell were they pulled down anyway!) and go to the kitchen. The moonlight is bright. The outside door is ajar, a moonbeam cuts the kitchen floor in two. There is a candle beside the vase of flowers, the moonlight glints on the shiny surface of the Zippo. I know that I should now check my property like any normal person: see if my car is in the yard and my money in my wallet, but I watch the flickering of the candle flame reflected in the window pane and feel afraid.

A frightened person can react unpredictably. Fear changes one's value judgments. The world of fear is not a logical one.

Painful veins bulge along my temples, I press my fingers to them and feel the blood pounding under my fingertips.

On the corner of the table, to the left of the candle, lies an object wrapped in pink cloth, and in the candlelight the color seems lighter than it was during the daytime.

Gingerly, moving a few centimeters at a time, as if afraid to scare the object, I move towards the corner of the table. I am cold, I am sweaty, but above all cold, and to get warm I should take the jacket hanging over the chair back and put it on. The night is chilly, the twenty or so degrees during the day at the end of summer are long gone and have been replaced by a night knitting frost on the windless ground.

As I take hold of the corner of the piece of silk and lift it up, the weight of the object causes it to rotate on its own axis, the cloth comes away in my fingers, and with a muffled thump the metal object rolls onto its other side. Now a nickeled surface is exposed, the same sort as that of the Zippo lighter, and several candle flames dance on every facet.

All at once I realize that I am maybe not the only one staring at the (lethal) weapon. *Someone* could see exactly the same thing through the window as I am seeing. I hastily fill my lungs with air, and leaning slightly forwards I blow hard at the candle. Instantly darkness surrounds the glowing orange dot, which vanishes a moment later. The room slowly fills with moonlight. Total silence. I have seen exactly what I expected. A barrel, a trigger, a varnished, wood-covered butt. Everything is exactly as I imagined it. Frighteningly similar to what I saw in my childhood, which a moment ago turned from a vague memory into the precise here and now.

I put on the jacket and feel in my pocket for my car keys. I can't find them, maybe they're still in the ignition. Cautiously (and without leaving fingerprints) I wrap the pistol again in the pink silk and put it in my pocket. I fumble for my packet of cigarettes and lighter. When I hear the first strike of the clock, I freeze on the spot, counting . . . three . . . I have been asleep for nearly twelve hours. It is unimaginably bright outside, the junipers have become like theater props on a well-lit stage. The polished surface of the car reflects several moons in several skies, though the car is no longer standing by the decorative wall, but beside the open gate. On the seat is a large bundle. My fingers feel nylon, then hair and a cold face.

I rush heedlessly a hundred meters away from the place, then realize how futile it is to run away. You can flee from your pursuers, but it's pointless to try and run away from a complex or unpleasant situation. As if out of inertia I walk straight ahead and begin to feel how my thoughts are settling into some sort of order. Then I see a distant glow—it broadens, and all at once I see car headlights and hear the sound of an engine getting ever louder as someone drives in my direction. I swerve off to the right of the road, toward a large boulder some ten meters away. The car is making its way slowly along the poorly-surfaced road, then the engine cuts out and human voices can be heard. "Julia!" a man is shouting. "Juuuulia!" These are drunken human voices. Suddenly the car engine is switched on again and the lights vanish round the corner.

I lean back against the boulder, slowly, feeling *physically* how refreshing energy is flowing into me. I stand up and stretch out my arms to their full extent along the surface of the boulder in the shape of a cross. In the silvery darkness there are countless larger and smaller lights, some blink, some move with a dull persistence to the other end of the sky. The sharply outlined moon stands above the black silhouettes of the fir trees.

Suddenly I get it—it becomes clear to me that in fact no one has any reason to really wish me ill. This thought is a great relief. A thought I can calmly pursue. In the distance a dog begins to bark. It is a relief to hear this too, it is good to know that quite nearby (nearer than a kilometer) there are people who own dogs. I open my fly and have a pee. The moonlight sparkles on the stream of urine.

When I head for home (!), my recent flight seems quite ridiculous, I can hardly believe that I acted as I did. That person in the car isn't likely to be dead, just sleeping. But why would someone be sleeping in my car when the door to the house is open and the house full of beds? I thrust my hand in my pocket, my hand feels the cold of the metal through the silk and it unexpectedly adds to my sense of security. I take off the silk wrapping (I can always wipe off the fingerprints later) and point the gun at the moon. My finger gently presses the trigger, I feel its resistance, press harder, and then the trigger gives way and a bluish yellow flame lights up among a shower of sparks.

It's just a cigarette lighter, I think in disappointment, whereby the disappointment soon turns into relief. (But wasn't the little bundle I put under the stones in the dry stone wall actually heavier?—I am once again gripped by suspicion.) I shut the gate properly and open the car door in the faint hope of finding the seat empty, a hope that's extinguished when I again feel the hair and something wet and sticky. I step back a couple of paces (I don't jump, but step) and look at my own hand in the moonlight. I cannot see any dark streaks of blood there, I sniff it and smell the strong odor of vomit.

"Fucking bastards!" I swear aloud. "Fucking shitheads!" The person in there has puked up in the car and the stink has crept into every crack in the upholstery. I open the window on the other side, I grab the nylon coat, pull the bundle to an upright position, then I squat down, put a limp arm over my shoulder and haul the person out of the car. The drunkard proves to be amazingly light. I lug the bundle across the lawn and lay it down in the grass. It's a woman, muttering incomprehensibly. I shake her. "We have a lot in common," is what she says. "Me and you have a lot in common," she repeats like a scratched gramophone record.

She has puked all over herself. I fetch a bowlful of water and a towel from the house. When I start cleaning her hair and face, she repeats the sentence again, this time accompanying it with several sobs. I take off her coat, then pull down her spewed-upon pants. I don't know whether I wet her blouse myself, but just in case I take that off too. When I pick her up, she puts her arms around my neck.

I just haven't the strength to start cleaning up the car, I merely throw out the mats, open all the doors, and take away the keys. The woman's clothes lie there on the grass (I'm not going to start washing them!), and I stick my tongue out at the moon and go inside. If I had to describe what I'm feeling now, I wouldn't be able to. Sticking your tongue out at the moon is a metaphor which doesn't mean anything. I'm fed up with groping around and feeling my way across the ground (floor) with my foot, I light a candle, there is a petroleum lamp on the table in the main room which sloshes pleasantly when I shake it. I have seen (in a movie?) how to operate such a lamp, and now there's enough light for me to regard the pornographic picture sitting in the room's only armchair.

I take an eiderdown from the closet and tuck it around the woman. She no longer smells of vomit, but I think that maybe she's caught cold. I have some cold medicine in my bag, I open a bottle of cognac and pour out a glass. She doesn't splutter but swallows it, suddenly opens her eyes, then is gone again.

Is this the Julia they were calling after? I wonder as I sit back again at the table, drinking cognac in large gulps, straight from the bottle. When I flick my Zippo, I can see myself in the window pane, further away behind me a female face is glowing, the blanket has slid off slightly and bared her shoulder and the curve of her breasts. I want to get rid of that reflection but there are no curtains (on this window, nor anywhere else in the house, for that matter). I am unpleasantly exposed to the view of the whole village. I do not light a cigarette, I take the glass and try to get the woman to swallow some more, and again I succeed. She is wearing a wedding ring—not a country ring or a countrywoman's hand—this woman doesn't look like someone from the countryside, is more likely an up-market businesswoman or university lecturer, her dark (dyed?) pageboy style hair frames an intelligent face, and I already have the clear impression that I've seen it on TV or in the paper sometime or other.

I don't want any more adventures—I lift the woman from the chair and take her to a bed in the other room. The woman says something vague, her body is burning. I hope she's finished vomiting, but put a bowl by the bed just in case. I lock the outer door and blow out the light. That is a nice expression—I *blow out* the light—and I'm sure that I'll be using it soon in a text.

I can't get to sleep, the moonlight outside makes me restless, and I try to console myself with the thought that everything is fine, that I thought I was in a couple of sticky situations, but in reality . . . in reality this day has left a lot of question marks hanging in the air. I no longer want to think about my circumstances, I let my mind wander, and suddenly my own wife is there in my mind's eye.

(How should you picture a wife who has clearly let it be known that she has found someone else more handsome, someone with feelings and common sense, someone who's clever, rich, young, with a longer and thicker thing?)

I'd like to be able to imagine my wife as a stranger who, for some reason, has ended up among my circles of friends and acquaintances, and whom I therefore know better than the average stranger. I know things about her that others perhaps do not know. I have had relationships with a few dozen women, where the only thing that brought us together was physical pleasure. I don't know much about the characters of these women, I am not interested in what they did yesterday, or will do today, tomorrow. They were and have remained strangers. I cannot in any way imagine my wife as a stranger. During the life we've lived together, I have begun to think about her as I do about myself—nevertheless, it is the sexual (not mental) proximity that makes her different from other women.

Modernism—what else can we call our recent past—created (along with other myths) the myth of marriage based on sexual love. That is interesting to know in our times. You can imagine that the situation has now changed in this field of experience, too.

In marriage, love is one (principal) argument for manipulation, this thanks to its modernist context. We are (still) capable of referring to *loftier* feelings. But our (hypocritical) honesty, inability to compromise, faithfulness, etc., are exactly the same sorts of myths from the modernist era as those qualities that once made works of art lofty. In fact, the art of the end of our century lacks the category of loftiness, or is presented as a parody that appears to scoff at all the ideals of the previous generation. Contemporary art (marriage?) is therefore "good" when games are played that are threefold, fivefold, tenfold.

(In an economic context, a man's member can indeed be longer and thicker than it really is.)

I can play cynical mind games, but I can't shrug off the feeling of being a jilted man. It isn't easy to make do without something (a possession?) that you consider to be an inalienable part of you. Even more complicated is to accept the thought that all those intimate things that happened to me so recently are now happening (in exactly the same way?!) with someone else. From the point of view of a jilted husband, his wife's death is easier to take than her leaving with someone else. Death is in many respects also an abandonment, but in that case the hope (however tiny) that things will ever be the same again is lost.

The landscape through the window is like a theater set. Too beautiful, too still, too well-kept, to be real. It is an unreal landscape, one that makes you feel uneasy.

In actuality, what has been wounded (a wounded bird!) is my self-esteem—I am not irreplaceable, unique. I am an object tossed backstage, into the wings, behind the scenery (a beautiful moonlit landscape), I am despised, lost, gone; I don't even have a piece of rope with which to drag myself back from behind the curtain. Whereas before she at least saw an image of me when she thought about me (along with all my attributes), now I am nothing but a name to be uttered (when necessary). I have already dissolved among all those countless strangers she has met during her life, and perhaps my wife is at this very moment scouring and scrubbing away to remove the last trace of my muddy feet from her soul.

In the next room, the snoring has grown louder. Some strange woman has come into my life in order to snore. When I listen to the snoring, growing ever louder, I suddenly get the feeling that it is my own wife who is sleeping in the bed. I have to smile: a strange woman has snored her way into becoming mine. When I go and sit on the bed and put my hand on her forehead, the snoring grows less loud, then stops altogether, along with her breathing, and after a short period of silence she heaves a sigh and rolls over onto her right side in her sleep. In the bedroom, filled with the silver darkness of the moonlight, my wife stops snoring, my fingers brush her brow, cheeks, lips; I wonder why I can't sleep next to my wife. I get undressed and snuggle up next to her, her body soon adjusts to mine, *her fingers* brush my brow, nose, lips, jaw, throat, cross my chest hair, a nipple, *fingers* cautiously touch my stiff penis out of curiosity, they feel so familiar and now I am no longer in doubt that I am lying next to my wife.

***

The word is "murderman" I decide, and I picture a monstrous in-dividual with a bloody knife raised above his head. A murderman is a paid killer, a professional murderer, who deals in murder; the nature of this word resembles that of "beeman," the stereotype good-natured individual who talks kindly to his honey bees. In the 1990s, they made a movie where a small girl wants to become a murderman, she is a diligent pupil of a *good* murderman and no doubt sees her future in being a good murderman, but this idyll is ruined by a *wicked* police officer, who ends up getting the good murderman to kill him and himself too. In this movie, the profession of murderman is ennobled, as opposed to the bad policeman's horrible (greedy) cruelty. Superficially, everything is OK: the death of the murderman is a punishment (in fact a happy ending) for him killing a whole load of innocent policemen, which he has been forced to do in self-defense.

The movie shows an interesting phenomenon: in a certain context murder is noble. (In the case of an alcoholic it is natural that his drinking bouts are always justified - he always creates a context for his passion for drink.) Dozens of family fathers and honest front line police officers die by the bullets of the hired killer, but in the case of the bad policeman, the murderman does not perform an evil act, which would have branded him in the eyes of the viewer.

I have been thumbing through the books on the shelf here and someone has gone to a good deal of trouble to translate, copy and bind texts, and it becomes obvious to me that my previous (humane) values are wrong. When you look at the world from the point of view of limited natural resources, it would be better if there were far fewer human beings than there are now. In this context it is a sheer blessing that the total world population decreases on account of wars, and that those that cannot cope will die of starvation, and that those who are sick and crippled are left to the hand of fate.

"Four classes of school should suffice for someone to fight in the defense forces, only well-educated people can use up all the world's resources, only education can give humankind enough means which guarantee new technology for marketing new products. The amount of work, resources, and energy required by an engineer or university graduate is dozens of times more than that of a smallholder . . . For those starving in Africa what's needed isn't education, just a sterilization program."

(This reminds of a recent Minister of Defense who said that a four-class compulsory system of education should be created, which in his opinion should be enough for conscripts.)

"A society based on schooling does nothing more for humanity than tormenting young people—so that during the time they should be tramping through the meadows, rowing on the lake, collecting water lilies, watching flocks of cranes from boulders covered in reindeer moss, eating bunches of whortleberries, wandering through the primeval forest and singing, having sex and loving one another—all these years they are crammed into schools and universities or, what is more shocking, summer schools, where they learn things that they will never have any use for."

I push aside the books and now before me is a pure green rectangle. True, the green baize is stained with ink, coffee and wine, but only when you look closely. The sun is shining from behind the house and in front of the window is a dark green shadow extending in both directions and beyond my field of vision. The house between the trees is a brilliant white in the sunshine. I don't think that anyone lives there, as I have not seen any movement around the place. I plan to take a stroll over in that direction and nose around a bit, but later. A woman is now coming from among the trees and heading in my direction. I could try to imagine that this is the same woman I shared a bed with last night, but I don't believe it is.

When I woke in the late morning, the woman was gone. She had left no trace, the car had been scrubbed clean (or had there never been anything to scrub away in the first place?), and the pistol-cum-cigarette-lighter had vanished from my jacket pocket. Maybe I dropped it somewhere when bustling about—*or maybe it had never existed.*

The thought that everything—including the woman—had been very real figments of my imagination begins to seem plausible. When I started looking for concrete traces—a half-empty cognac bottle—I could not find one, but I found a *sealed* bottle in my pocket. Nothing betrayed last night's events. Even the car was near the decorative wall, exactly where I had left it the previous evening.

When I thought things over calmly, all that I could be sure of was that someone had given me a powerful sleeping draft. Put it in my beer, when I went to the dry stone wall looking for the pistol. I reckon they (who?) needed to rummage around in my things. Maybe attempts had been made to infiltrate informers into their group before, and they were now grown cautious. It was not for nothing that Barbi said to me that I shouldn't even have a dictaphone with me as it could raise suspicions. "I'm used to dictaphones," I tried to say to her. "What you should do is stick a notice on the dictaphone saying: writer's equipment, not to be used for secretly recording conversations," said Barbi, not without sarcasm.

A woman (or girl?) opens the gate. She is wearing a very short denim skirt, her jacket is slung over her shoulders, her breasts jut under her yellow blouse and her legs in black tights (stockings?) have strong and plump thighs. She is carrying a milk can, and is striding purposefully towards the door.

"Hi, my name is Maria Laakan," she says in a shrill and rather forced voice. "Ummal told us to look after you."

I reply that I have nothing against that; this woman is certainly dressed in a girlish way, although I reckon she must be over thirty, and is more of a city type than a country woman. (Indeed, later on she says that when their mother fell sick some three years previously, her brother Jaak came out to the countryside to run the farm, and that she lives partly in the local county town, partly out here, but has plans to soon make the countryside her permanent home.)

"I could cook you a hot meal once a day," Maria offers and asks me whether I am familiar with everything in the house. I shake my head, and say that I haven't had a chance to stick my nose in every corner yet.

"But you must," says Maria. "The whole idea is that you make yourself at home here and run the place."

I walked obediently behind her, and understand that soon it will be time to harvest vegetables. ("I'll come and help you," she laughs, seeing my startled face.) When she opens the door to the cellar (it would not have occurred to me to look for a cellar), my jaw drops at the sight of the huge amount of stores (even beer!). "If you decide to bottle any fruit or vegetables, remember that they should remain as property of the farm. In my opinion Ummal goes a little overboard with this, but everyone staying here has been happy with it, and they even compete to see who can make more jam."

The cowshed emanates a dry, somewhat musty smell. "Maybe starting next year we'll keep a cow and a couple of pigs. When you buy your voucher for coming out here, and you want everything to be genuine, then you have to have the opportunity to keep animals. This is especially good for children. People who consider keeping animals a chore should stay at some other farm."

When we go back into the house, I complain to her I can't get the fire going in the stove. Maria opens some flap, sticks a burning piece of paper into it, and the stove begins to roar. "The sun has warmed the top of the chimney and there's no wind," she explains. "You have to coax the chimney to draw," she says, looking at me with a crafty expression on her face.

"If you get a pike or perch and pick some mushrooms, I'll make you some 'dölööz-guatari,'" says Maria Laakan enthusiastically. "It's a fish dish from abroad, and the woman who was staying here before you taught me how to make it. She didn't know herself what country it comes from, she'd learned how to make it from some French professor or other, but I can assure you that this little 'dölööz' will appeal to every man's taste, since every mouthful gives you a different flavor."

"And where will I get a pike from?" I ask in surprise.

"Rolli will take you fishing this evening. Everybody who lives here has to catch fish, it's like an unwritten rule, and you also have to pick the mushrooms. Mushroom-picking and fishing will create the impression that you can handle things here, and that is something that Ummal thinks very important. Usually everybody makes their own food, but for some reason Ummal is making an exception in your case. Maybe you know why. I haven't got anything against earning a little extra."

I am beginning to become irritated by the woman's endless flow of words, and her bubbling energy remains inexplicable, as if she has not had a chance to talk to anyone for some good while. I don't want to be her victim who (though not in any way with malice) gets sprayed with words, so I excuse myself, saying I've broken off my reading and explain that I have come here to do some work and I would be very happy for her to make some coffee. I then flee to my baize-covered writing desk, where there's a stack of books I've chosen on green subjects.

I wonder what sort of confusion I would give rise to in my reader, were I to try to explain that the green movement embodies a concrete threat to mankind. It's just as inconceivable as was implementing the left-wing idea of equality in the inhuman socialist bloc. It was necessary to see tanks on the streets of Prague. Mao's cultural revolution was necessary. As was the "Gulag Archipelago." Manipulating people in the service of what seem to be the noblest of ideas, horrible crimes can be committed. For instance, the ideas of Pol Pot, a left-wing student at the Sorbonne, claimed the lives of some three million victims.

It's a sly business—it is left-wingers who have woven (crocheted) together the postmodern worldview of the end of the century. This epoch has arrived without grand narratives, without fixed values. We no longer believe in the illusion of progress, we can no longer believe in anything. The dismal future will be enlivened by "green ideas"—a utopian third way to make the world tolerable, to make it last. It is inevitable that some will be more equal than others in a "green paradise." It could happen that those who dreamed of power back in the 1960s will finally get it in the next century.

When Maria Laakan brings a cup of steaming coffee to my desk, I notice her hands for the first time. They are large for a woman but smaller than a man's, and I can see hairs growing on her fingers. I suddenly realize that this is the same woman who was on the beach and that her dark tights are concealing the hairy legs. I give a start inwardly—my discovery is just too unexpected, I wasn't prepared for this—and when I look at the woman, now disappearing into the kitchen, I *see* her shapely buttocks, which wiggle invitingly under the material of her skirt.

The woman's prattle is no longer disagreeable. I am already waiting for lunch to be ready (what a smell of roasting is wafting from the kitchen!) so I can ask Maria this and that about village life. Maybe she'll tell me what happened to the woman who was staying here before me.

"Lunch is ready!" Maria calls from the kitchen, and by that time Kandiman's tale has got me all worked up, so that I can't stop imagining how my hand would slip up the hairy leg, and the feeling has the same charm as when you stroke a cat or a dog (latent sodomy?), but this image gets me excited (something previously unknown!) and I don't want to deny it to myself.

The table has been nicely laid and even the table napkins have not been forgotten. The clock chimes three muffled strokes. "This is just the right time to eat lunch," I say as I clatter with my chair. A helicopter flies low over the house and for an instant I feel that it's going to crash into us. The cat rushes *whoosh-whoosh* into the room, stands there watching me, and is silently begging for food. "Well, well, look who's here!" says Maria in surprise, looking for something in the crockery closet, from which a white mug falls to the floor and smashes to pieces.

"I thought that it left with Marla," says Maria, crouching to pick up the broken pieces. The dark space between her open legs grows lighter further on. Stockings, I decide, then the name Marla reaches my consciousness, a rare name, and now I get a nervous feeling in the pit of my stomach.

"Who's this Marla?" I ask rapidly, maybe too rapidly.

"She's the professor who was here before you, she was beginning to like the countryside and had hired two rooms from Pulman, because who can afford the sky-high prices that Ummal asks."

"So she stayed here and didn't go back to work?"

Maria shrugs her shoulders, it's not any of her business what people do, she puts the pot on the table, from which the aroma of the vegetables and chunks of meat make your mouth water. They're begging to be eaten, gobbled down, so that someone will get the pleasure of scraping the pot clean. They are begging to cease to exist, why else would they be emitting that delicious aroma.

"To Teeriida!" I say, raising my frothing beer glass. "Cheers!" says Maria Laakan and after a long drink of her beer wipes the froth from her lips in a rather masculine way.

***

"A life like the king's cat," I mutter, and turn over the page of my notebook. I've managed to get a few things down on paper, although I'm not entirely sure I want to write. What has to be done first is like collecting all the construction materials you need— anything lying around, just bring it into the shed, might come in handy later. But the life of a king's cat is not very pressing, and one day I'll bundle everything together and go back to town.

When I try to work out how many days I've been out here in the countryside, now that one such day is drawing to a close, I can't actually be sure. I'm not sure whether it's a Tuesday or a Wednesday and however much I exert myself I simply can't get a grip on either events or time. Here another time holds sway. In each new place, situation (even in different company), time flows along slowly (like a locomotive pulling wagons from standstill), then the torrent of new impressions recedes and (if you're traveling) you get used to the constant new experiences and the days begin to flow at an even pace like wagons in a train going along at full speed.

Vennet once bragged that one early spring they had spent around ten days on the island of Vilsandi where there was no electricity, telephone, TV, radio, or even the correct time. "We had our own time, we said that now it's such and such an hour, and when in the end we happened to check the real time, it turned out that we were only off by a few minutes." When you come to think of it, this bragging is worth taking note of, because out there they were deprived of everything that seems *important*. The first few days I borrowed the newspapers from the Laakans, listened eagerly to the news bulletins on the car radio, but then one morning it went dead and the car wouldn't start (I still don't know what's wrong, some villagers will have to take a look, but it all takes time), and when Maria forgot to bring the newspapers I said that she needn't bother as I wasn't interested in what had happened in the world at large.

When I said *wasn't interested*, then in effect I *bragged* (it would be interesting to know why this word sounds just right). I had to convince myself that I was no longer dependent on the world and if I made this lack of interest know to others (Maria) then I didn't yet really believe it myself. What was important became unimportant later on, maybe that morning when the sunshine made the tiny drops of water on the spider's web glitter, or that evening when I sat outside the sauna, my body steaming on the bench, listening to the grasshoppers, or when I had whortleberries in my mouth and was watching the baby cranes.

I think that I consider my lack of interest as a temporary absence, I can't imagine tying myself to any place in the country for good; that would be like some *substance* going from one state to the next, figuratively speaking—like comparing congealed with melted fat. Here in the country I am a guest, a person who comes and goes.

Yesterday evening I went to see where Maria had got to. Her brother Jaak was at home and he was sitting in the untidy living-room drinking vodka. I was surprised how much he looked like his sister, and was of course depressed by the chaos that bachelors and old boys tend to live in. I accepted the glass of vodka I was offered and wondered why Maria, who seemed very tidy and organized, couldn't keep her own home neat and tidy. Jaak was pretty drunk and, quite unlike his sister, said little. I couldn't very well leave right away, so I sat at the table watching Jaak watching TV. Maria had apparently driven into town and would be back the following day. The wallpaper in the room was faded and full of blotches and the drapes at the windows were yellowed with cigarette smoke.

Jaak sat watching TV without moving a muscle, his lips were pressed together and this gave his face a robotic look and I was thinking that if you were to paint those lips and eyes (Maria was always carefully made up, which felt rather odd out in the countryside) and comb his hair differently, then he would be the spitting image of his sister. Suddenly, I heard a familiar voice behind me: "A growing gap between the traditional humanist concept of culture and the cultural state of affairs today makes us revise our standpoints. We have to understand that what was considered great art yesterday is no longer acceptable today, the context has changed, and in this new context notes have begun to sound which we would not otherwise have heard . . . "

I turned towards the TV screen and saw Teodor. How he waffles, was my immediate thought; then I realized that this was a TV set bringing the close-up of Teodor's face and his voice into the room. I took the TV as something ordinary, something I didn't have to pay any special attention to, and yet by now I was used to living in the country, living without talking pictures in the livingroom, and when I again encountered my lost plaything, no cry of joy came to my lips. I now *saw* that the room was lit up by an electric lamp, but I didn't exclaim, Oh how nice to see electricity after such a long absence! It would seem that important things aren't as important as they seem to us.

On the TV screen Teodor was replaced by a short man with a

big head, who was toddling around a stack of logs to the accompaniment of mystical sounds; then they showed him felling trees, and finally declaring in a theatrically forced voice: "I am a part of nature and this sets a special stamp on each one my actions . . . " The words stopped, while a slightly foolish smile remained on screen for a couple of seconds.

"That man's from your village," I said in excited recognition.

"God rest his soul," said Jaak Laakan, and crashed to the floor along with his chair. He was now blind drunk, and it took me quite some effort to get him to bed.

On my way home—following the flashlight's beam as it penetrated the pitch darkness—I thought with some malice that this had been some parabiennale, a competitive exhibition that they'd modeled on the paralympics. Where cripples compete with one another—blind people, color-blind people in their own contexts; I once happened to see a documentary where a disabled young man was painting, holding his paintbrush between his toes. He was a famous artist and people would pay high prices for his paintings.

Living like the king's cat, I'm thinking, as I spot the cat, tail up, crossing the yard. I haven't felt so at ease for quite some time, I watch the cat and wait for Julia to turn up in my field of vision. Julia was going to come and help me empty the nets. She, her husband Rolli, and I go out to get our staple food (the fish) out of the sea. The last time the wind changed during the night and drove wrack (seaweed) into the meshes (nets), and it's a nuisance to get the "fur" out.

Julia is punctual, she leaves her bicycle by the gate at three (dull strokes of the clock!) and walks towards the shed wall where the nets have been left to soak. I have some coffee ready brewed, I like to have a chat at the kitchen table before getting down to work, so that I can reduce the feeling of strangeness / uncertainly that I (clearly) cause in Julia.

"The funeral is on Saturday," says Julia when I light her cigarette. She smokes a lot. She seems to have grown old prematurely, and her face, weathered by wind and sun, is inexpressive, like a mask that this manly woman wears to shield her inner life.

Maria said that they had come to live here only five years ago. She didn't say much about their past, but some say that Rolli, others Julia, is supposed to have been in prison. They don't seem to do anything but fish and mend nets. They don't even have a cat—as Maria said, somehow irritably.

If Julia doesn't say whose funeral it is I'll have to ask her, get acquainted with village life and definitely go and have a look at the graveyard (in order to reproduce it later, colorfully or in monochrome in a text).

"I imagine that idiot Joosep must have jumped from the lighthouse yesterday. Ants found him this morning. Fell straight on his head—no wonder, it was too big and heavy there between his shoulders."

"I see," I say, and think that that's the end of the story of the Great Estonian Artist.

"What makes things more complicated is that yesterday afternoon, Pulman's old woman happened to catch them at it. At first she thought they were wrestling, but then it emerged that they were naked from the waist down, and she started shouting horribly. The old woman didn't really understand anything, poor dear."

"Hang on, hang on, who did this old woman happen to come across?" I ask, now gripped by her tale.

"Oh, Joosep and that man from town he was always drinking beer with. There'd been talk in the village some time ago that he was a queer. Ants promised to wallop him one with a cudgel if he ever clapped eyes on him."

I gasp for air, I'm suddenly a fish out of water, thrashing about helplessly at the bottom of the boat. Teodor a queer! I find it hard to believe, but hell, there certainly is something perverse in his gaze . . . but I would have heard something in town long time ago . . . or maybe a wolf doesn't strike near home . . .

"We might think all sorts of things, but Joosep left a note. 'I'm going to die *a free deth,*' he had written there, that's true, he couldn't even write one sentence properly without errors. And last night he was on TV. The whole village watched it. Ants went to look the next morning to see where the Boy was, as he was supposed to have come to watch the program."

I would like to know more details, but at the same time I'd rather not. I want to try and keep this tale at arms' length, because the childhood I shared with Teodor means I'm involved as well. As if someone wants to put us in the same boat. As if I too am a marked man. "Has Rolli already cleaned his nets," I say, fleeing to another subject and making it impossible for Julia to continue on the subject of the suicide of the village idiot.

I hear, but do not listen to what Julia replies. Teodor's self-important face as I saw it yesterday on the (live?) broadcast looms before me, and I realize all at once that he cannot have known, then.

Poor Joosep was lying there, his head smashed, on the rocks at the foot of the lighthouse, while at the same time the foolishly smiling Boy Joosep appeared on TV, saying he was a Part of Nature. It could well be that his death occurred at the same time the whole nation was watching him, when someone might have spat angrily in a corner, saying, Look what an important man they've made him into. Not *he's become*, but *they've made him*.

I go with Julia over to the shed, and we beat the nets like sheets, and little pieces like snot spray out onto your clothes and into your face. Julia explains that for a long time men refused to accept her method of cleaning the nets, they picked it all out piece by piece, the way hens peck at shit. "The way a woman thinks is somehow more direct than the way a man does," she continues seriously. I try to conjure up the picture of what Pulman's old woman saw, but the movie theater of my brain refuses to show the film.

I can suddenly hear Jaak Laakan saying, "God rest his soul." Did he merely say this because he was drunk, or did he actually know that the Boy Joosep was dead? Had he stumbled upon the corpse at the foot of the lighthouse and not reported the death for fear of getting mixed up in the affair—or was he *mixed up in it himself*? When someone has read a couple of hundred crime novels over a lifetime, and seen hundreds of crime movies, he just has to think like a village detective, to construct the motive that made Jaak Laakan kill the village idiot and then forge the message himself, complete with spelling mistakes. "What sort of people are the Laakans?" I ask Julia while we are having a smoking break.

"As far as I know *only one of them* actually lives there—Jaak. When the old Laakan mom fell sick, three years ago, both the twins, Jaak and Maria, left town. Last spring Maria met with an accident—a tractor crushed her—and she was killed instantly. It would seem to have been Jaak's fault, but he wasn't charged with anything. At any rate, since then Jaak has shunned company, and become a little strange. On a few occasions he's been seen wearing his sister's clothing. But it's a man's own business what he goes around wearing," ends tolerant Julia's description. She spits on the still glowing cigarette butt and gets up to start beating the next net.

***

In my field of vision—whose every detail I have memorized now from sitting at my writing desk—something strange is happening today. The whitewashed house has suddenly sprung to life, and people in camouflage or military uniforms are swarming around. I don't know whether they're from Ummal's encampment—businessmen learning partisan skills—or real soldiers. A truck whose body is covered in sailcloth drives up to the house, and men start carrying things inside like ants. I'm very glad that there's a large distance between the houses, as otherwise I'd catch snatches of their shouting, and this would occasionally dispel my own thoughts. Then a woman (who ought to be a man) enters the scene before me and walks between the men in camouflage, and I can imagine their obscene remarks and shouts as she passes by. Maybe she's being coquettish in a feminine sort of way, and her butt is beginning to waggle even more as she walks away from the men and approaches the house where the writer So-and-So is sitting at his desk, trying to concentrate.

"You're going to have visitors," says Maria (Jaak) Laakan excitedly. "Ummal called and said they'd be here in two hours. He has a lot to tell you, and if you don't mind, they'd like to stay the night. But he said that if you wanted to do some work, they'd be over at the encampment."

I say that I have nothing against visitors, and realize (with embarrassment?) that it's high time I started doing my job as an informer. That is to say, I've got to justify my time here and get down to work (though it's not my fault that I've had little opportunity up till now).

"I'll go upstairs and tidy the rooms up there and with luck we'll be able to make some "dölööz-guatari" for them, because we've now got fillets of pike and boletus mushrooms."

What the hell, we're going to have a party today, and that puts me in a seriously good mood—for a couple of days now I've felt that I'm at some indescribable pre-writing stage, where my texts are like water welling up behind a dam, wanting to rush out of me, and yet at the same time my writer's fantasy hasn't yet matured. It is an intolerable state of affairs, but I'm sure that the tension will ease once I've downed a glass of vodka and spoken my mind.

I tidy my writing desk (there are going to be visitors, after all!), I stack the books neatly one on top of the other, then back on the shelf, and run my eye over the last pages of the book I was reading (how does a colleague of mine tie up the loose ends?)—it isn't actually a book, but a photocopy of an edition published in 1936; someone has taken a good deal of trouble, so that children would have something to read as well.

The Land of the Green Sun is its telling title, and the story is about two abandoned dolls that mainly mix with deer, frogs, bugs, grasshoppers, ants, and some green princesses from the Land of the Green Sun, who are descended from *higher* beings. In this story, human beings are *bad* creatures. The concept is rather strange in that even dogs are regarded as bad humans—they destroy the *good* mice and gnaw at the legs of Market-Reet (the hen).

It is a poorly written book, no verve, no excitement, it plays with the idea of being *small* and helpless, which ought to give rise to feelings of (empathetic) superiority in a child. In places the book seems to be one long meditative repetition of things: this is good, this is bad. On the last page, my eye suddenly falls on this stretch of dialogue: "Listen, Moon, I would also like Mari to get to know about our remarkable journey. I don't know how to tell her." "Don't worry. It's quite easy for me to do. When Mari is asleep, I will let your journey appear in her dreams. Mari can write fairy tales for children. Maybe she will write it down for children."

This play on ambiguity is very modern, and I can't help thinking that the whole text actually simulates a naïve description. At the end of the book, a child's hand has written: Toomas, 28ᵗʰ December 1950, which is likely to mean that on that day he finished reading the book, and started defending the good mice from the bad cats and from traps and doses of poison laid out by human beings.

From the kitchen, Laakan (it is simpler to call Jaak's Maria that) is clattering with the pots and pans, the clock strikes the half-hour, and I think that Laakan doesn't know that I know that he isn't who he thinks I think he is. It would be interesting to slap his bottom and tickle his tits and see how the man reacts. (Truth be told, it never entered my head to doubt the fact that he was a woman.) Once—I must have been in my third year at university—a girl came home with me after a dance. My roommates were away and everything looked promising. We snogged like anything, but the girl wouldn't let me put my hand down her briefs, and after a lot of wriggling about she explained that she was having her period, but she'd give me a blow job, which of course I had nothing against. But suddenly I felt *his* erect member pressed against me. I cried out. I clearly don't have any homosexual tendencies, because I could have killed him. (You tend to be hot-tempered when young, tolerance comes with the years.) But my girlfriend / boyfriend did not understand my state of mind: "If you don't want that, let me at least do your washing for you, your socks and underpants are dirty," he / she begged me.

That little anecdote from years gone by comes to mind when I enter the kitchen and ask how you prepare "dölööz," and it shocks me to think that I never realized earlier that Maria is a *man*. Now (knowing this) I see him as a man, because the scales have fallen from my eyes. (This is exactly the same kind of stupid situation as when you see some item of contemporary art, *not knowing* it to be a work of art.) It is depressing how easily I let myself be manipulated, but there's nothing left for me to do except spread my arms helplessly, wring my hands, spit on the floor in anger.

"First the pieces of fish have to be browned in the pan, then they should be removed, and in the same oil you should fry the onions and garlic, then add the mushrooms, tomatoes, paprika slices, peas, pieces of smoked sausage and ham, raisins and chopped nuts. The rice has to be boiled in the fish stock and now the pieces of fish and shellfish have to be folded in. It is essential to squirt grapefruit juice on the food before eating. Marla stressed that the shellfish round off the dish, and we don't have to tell people what's in it. Marla also said that you could throw in garden snails as well, but they're rare in these parts—and I don't know whether you eat shellfish, but I'd suggest you try. There are a couple of jars left over in the cellar from Marla's time here." Once there was Marla's time, now it is the writer So-and-So's time—Maria's (Maria again!) words make me smile. I say that I can eat any sea food, and what I don't fancy I can always wash down with a drink. This joke seems to amuse Laakan, and he laughs, *huh, huh, huh*, he is in a very good mood today, and I now think that those words—i.e. God rest his soul—slipped from his mouth quite by chance, and that he has nothing to do with the Boy Joosep's death.

And besides—this whole business has nothing to do with me.

I discover that there are no more cigarettes, there isn't even a half-smoked stub in the ashtray, and now that there are no cigarettes I get a craving for one. I say that I'll go to the store and get some, and ask if I can fetch him anything. "No, we've plenty of everything, and Ummal promised to see to drinks," says the woman / man, and now I simply cannot believe that the person standing at the stove isn't the efficient housewife she's pretending to be.

As I pass my car I remember that there might be a packet of cigarettes lying in there. In the glove box there's something wrapped up in pink silk. I cry out in surprise (not joy), but for some reason I don't want to touch it, even though I know it's *only* a cigarette lighter. That woman—whoever she was, she *was* at any rate a *woman*—probably found it on the ground and put it away in the glove box when she was cleaning the car, but I have a feeling of unease that I can't explain—as if the pink silk reminded me of something depraved, sinful, indecent.

I can't simply pass the boulder that crouches like a camel's hump about ten meters from the road without stopping. I don't really believe in the sorts of games where super(un)natural forces are at play, but when I lean back against the boulder I *feel* an inexplicable energy flowing into me, my head clears and the thoughts line up like platoons of soldier ready for battle. Even my groin throbs and my member swells, ready for action. Looking up at the high, fibrous clouds, I remember that nameless night woman, and I can already see her dozing there in my armchair by the light of the petroleum lamp. Her head is drooping slackly on her shoulder, she is a vivid white in the dark room, defenseless, pornographic; the nipples of her small round breasts protrude as a challenge, the little shaven pillows around the crack between her legs, like pouting cherries, entice you to touch them with your lips, drink from them as if they're milk, dive into them as if into water, read them as if they're a book.

This woman could well be that same Marla, the one who lived at Teeriida before me—but then, those men shouting in the night were calling the name Julia. Now I remember the time I stood at this very boulder and experienced the energy flow for the first time. I must ask Laakan where this Marla lives now. I cannot explain why I haven't asked before, and suddenly I feel a stab of pain in my heart at the fact that tomorrow (or the day after) my stay at Teeriida will be coming to an end and I'll be driving back into town.

I buy a sleeve of cigarettes and a bottle of beer, so as to enjoy little pleasures of life near the shop in the fresh air. I light the cigarette, take a long draw on it, and release the stream of smoke gradually from between my lips. Then I swallow a mouthful of the cool beer. A black limousine races past.

"Look, there goes the Minister of Defense," says one of the villagers who seems to live near the store. I think with disappointment that I haven't gotten to know any of the real village men out here. Those people who've dropped by were townspeople until recently, but then, maybe a real countryman wouldn't accept me so easily. A crack or gap opens up that can't be filled with anything.

"Well, the top brass are turning up as well," says a second man as two more cars whizz by.

Then Kandiman turns up, screeches to a halt, and runs over to me to squeeze my shoulder: "You again, have you settled here?" I tell him how things stand, there's no longer any point in hiding the fact (now such a short time before I return to town) that I'm the tenant of Teeriida Farm. When Kandiman has got himself a beer we sit down in front of the store in the sunshine like two drone flies. I ask him what those fancy cars are doing in these parts.

"Always whizzing past—for them driving at a normal speed would be beneath their dignity. They're likely to be arranging some weekend party or other. There are two encampments here, one that Ummal is running, and the other for members of the defense forces, and they arrange all sorts of family days and festivals. Listen, I'd like to drop in at your place afterwards, I know exactly where that farm is situated, it would be interesting to see what this architectural wonder actually looks like. Fuck, nowadays every amateur bastard builds what he likes and then calls it jewel of postmodernist architecture. And what's strangest of all—no one gives a squeak, because the bastards' blethering has such force that anyone making critical noises will look a fool."

I mention that today we're having a party too, that Ummal himself is supposed to be turning up.

"So you know this Ummal, you have to because otherwise no

writer could afford to stay at Teeriida. This Ummal of yours is a crafty guy, I wouldn't mind meeting him. I was just thinking the other day that he operates out here as if running a training camp for terrorists, and since there are elite members of the armed forces in the other camp right now and some ministers with their families, he could capture the encampment with his own men. That would be a laugh. And it would be very interesting to know how our fledgling republic would manage to wriggle out of that mess."

I say (feeling strangely uncomfortable) that it would be best if such a plan didn't pop up in Ummal's head. Then (I don't know what sort of bug of spite has just bitten me) I say, as if in passing, that that hairy woman I saw sunbathing on the beach will be making the food for today's party.

"So, what's she like?" asks Kandiman and I can see clearly that his eyes *light up*.

"A really nice talkative woman, who makes heavenly dishes," I say matter-of-factly, just to work Kandiman up.

"Well then, have you screwed her yet?"

"I don't know, never entered my head, why not?" I say thoughtfully, as if weighing this up seriously.

"Listen, I've got to get back to my summer house, but I'll be at your place in two or three hours. I'd come right away, but I've arranged for this man to mend the stove. Damn, it might take at least four hours."

"You know best," I say, hardly able to suppress my laughter. Kandiman is about to climb into the car, when he turns back. Only a moment ago he was in a hurry, now he has all the time in the world. "You probably don't watch TV here?" he asks cautiously.

I say that there's no electricity out there.

"A couple of days ago some man from this village was shown on TV because he'd won the Baltic States' Contemporary Art Exhibition prize. Maybe you know the art critic Teodor, he was bobbing about and crowing like a rooster on a shitpile, but what that Teodor doesn't know is that it was me who produced all those things the Boy Joosep was supposed to have made. I was bored during the summer, and since I had nothing better to do, the Boy and me started to do contemporary art. Once he got excited, I had the feeling that I'd taught him something indecent. Like in Bunin's short story, "The Village," where an idiot's taught how to masturbate and amuses the villagers with his new skill . . . Now I'm a nobody, while the Boy is a famous artist."

"*Was*," I say, realizing that Kandiman hasn't yet heard the tragic news.

"What do you mean 'was'?"

I tell him what happened. When I get to the part about how that old local crone stumbled upon the Boy and Teodor together, I feel like a wretched gossip, but imagine he'll hear the story many times around the village.

"Fucking hell," swears Kandiman thoughtfully. "What a cracking article that'd make! I'd come round right away, but I can't, I've got that appointment with the builder."

I'm in no hurry, from what the villagers are saying I understand that last time, when the Defense League had had a party, a local young man was arrested as a dangerous spy: he'd taken a short-cut through the camp, but the Defense League men had shown drunken *bditelnost'* (i.e. vigilance), something they had learnt during Russian times.

"They're all ex-Komsomol leaders in the League," says a young-ish man in oil-stained overalls, and spits angrily.

"No, well, some of them are OK," says another and spits next to his friend's. There are bottle tops and cigarette ends lying on the ground and it never entered anyone's head to sweep the area in front of the store clean.

"Nothing to be done," says a third, whose turned down fisherman's rubber boots are full of silver fish scales that look like coins.

***

I can't believe my eyes when, out of the car that has stopped at the gate, jumps not Ummal but Teodor. If he shows his face in the village he could get bumped off, is what flashes through my mind, yet he seems unconcerned and yells joyfully for me to come and help him carry the crates of beer to the cellar.

"Ummal drove to the camp and will be here in an hour. I'll have to make an inventory of what's in the Boy's room so that I can lay my hands on every little thing worth anything. You can't trust the villagers, they might run off with things not realizing that they have museum value."

I'm speechless. I pick up a crate, and between us we lug it down into the cellar. "In the cellar, beer gets to just the right temperature," explains Teodor, taking (without asking my permission) a beer from the shelf and opening it with a practiced flick of the hand.

"Actually, it's a really good thing that that crazy Boy jumped from the lighthouse," says Teodor quietly, taking a seat on the bench outside the cellar and sipping his beer. "In Vilnius he was quite a handful, since he understood immediately what his role was and it went to his head like wine or vodka. He himself *believed* that he was the greatest artist of the Baltics. He wasn't such an idiot that he didn't suss that, but the words that came out of his mouth made you want to vomit. He just didn't realize that he had to cut the crap or it would ruin everything.

"But now, by a happy coincidence, I am in an even stronger position than before: I can link his work with the conflict that emerged between him as a defenseless homosexual and society at large, and his tragic death is the ace I hold at the start of the game. In this new context, the Boy takes on an even greater significance—he'll link up with global culture. Imagine a tunnel: you enter, and there's a curtain before you, and when you open it you meet a new curtain, and a new curtain after that, and you hope there's going to be a way out as you approach each curtain, hope for understanding, for the recognition of homosexuality, but society puts up curtain after curtain—so that you walk forever down this tunnel; forever, but each and every time you come to a curtain, you open it in hope. You can imagine how you could pad out this curtain project, adding more moving details, even sentimental ones—it should be a big thing at the São Paolo Biennale. In Russian times, homosexuality was a punishable offence. The Soviet Union was one of the few countries where they had such a paragraph in the law. But even now plenty of our fellow citizens would like to bludgeon all queers to death. You can't change attitudes just like that. What has become normal in other parts of the world, is still regarded as abnormal over here."

"But you don't have to praise homosexuality to the skies, either," I say with undisguised sarcasm—I am listening to Teodor with my eyes wide open, my (untempered, old-fashioned, stupid) mind cannot believe that anyone could be so cold-blooded and cynical about the death of his lover (for what else was the Boy to Teodor). Suddenly the idea occurs to me that maybe Teodor paid some villager (e.g. Laakan) to push the Boy Joosep off the lighthouse. The note with its misspelled words doesn't count for anything. And nothing can be proven, while the homosexual episode could have been mere simulation, upon which the murder (and later, the myth of the artist) was built . . .

"Anyway, you are not getting my point. We must take local problems into a global context and vice versa, this is one of the advantages of entering the world from the periphery these days. Nobody's talking here about ass-fucking, the game is kept at a theoretical level and homosexuality is examined as one possibility for human existence, which must have equal opportunities with other models for existence."

All at once I feel an indescribable feeling of antipathy toward Teodor—as a kid he wasn't a bad boy, he's smart and has a god-given ability to write, but what use is all this now that he's concocting a project that flies in the face of all existing value criteria?

"What you intend to do seems to me like the desecration of the corpse," I can't help saying, and turning my back on Teodor I go to the verandah. A group of young men in camouflage are running past the gate. "Listen, old man, where is there a store round here?" yells one of them, I look searchingly around me, then I understand and point and the group changes direction.

Teodor comes strolling toward me. "You do understand that the myth that we have an internationally recognized artist is necessary for the Estonian nation, which has always had great self-esteem. And in the context of a free republic it all has to be coddled and supported, if we want to survive. The Estonian nation is like a diligent schoolboy who's always in need of praise. Punishment achieves nothing. Just think how many Estonians have nationality as their only praiseworthy quality. You've just *got to* do something for them. That snatch of song about national pride may be the only thing that the man driving the state mail van knows. As long as such simple notes remain on its lips, nothing bad will happen to our nation, quite the opposite—we can adopt the sort of position on the world stage that we didn't even dare to dream about before."

I say nothing back. When he has driven away, gone off to meddle in the things of the poor Boy Joosep (I wouldn't feel in the least bit sorry if some villager took a swipe at him with a cudgel, as one already promised to do), I go back inside where Laakan is just putting some fish pie in the oven. "Who was that man," he says inquisitively. I say it was an art critic.

"Was that the same one that turned poor Joosep into an artist?"

"Yes, the very same," I reply curtly and walk toward the other room.

"This summer, the townies were swarming around poor Joosep like flies. First someone called Kandiman, then another man from town called Mihkel and now this famous art critic."

I turn back when I reach the door and ask who this Mihkel is.

"Oh, that was the one with the Boy when Pulman's old crone happened to stumble across them. Some scientist, maybe historian, he was here last summer too, but now the men here are really angry with him, because they say it was because of him the Boy Joosep committed suicide. Look, those men from the town have neither honor nor shame, but things are a teeny-weeny bit different out here in the countryside. It's not easy for a known pederast to live out here. As soon as the menfolk get drunk, they'll start tearing him down. People might do all sorts of things in the countryside as well, but you just have to avoid getting caught."

"I see . . . " I say slowly between my teeth. When I light up a cigarette at my writing desk, I feel that my mood has suddenly taken a change for the better—as if a heavy burden has been lifted from my shoulders, as if I've struggled my way out of a bog onto dry land. Now I can meditate on this comparison: out of a bog— it would suggest that I've actually experienced this, though even without any experience I can afford this comparison, as it's instantly understandable to everyone without further explanation. Thanks to literacy and the art of the movies, everyone nowadays acquires countless experiences by proxy. Writers like me manipulate other people's experiences, they alter and adjust them and represent them as things they've experienced themselves, things whose truth no one usually calls into question. In this way each experience moves away from reality and gradually becomes a myth. In the end, people no longer have direct experience of anything, they identify with what they've read and seen in the movies with reality, and one fine day they will regard reality as something unreal.

It is natural that the further we travel, the more we *move away from* the original source. So the source takes on the meaning of a symbol, and you can manipulate any aspect of it you like (compare freestyle in sport). It is, of course, possible that after numerous games you'll arrive back at the source, get a couple of mouthfuls of crystal-clear and refreshing water, and then go off in a new direction, away from the source.

I think that when Joseph Beuys wrote that anyone can be an artist, what he meant was that anyone can be a *creative* person, and that creativity, whether it be in economics, politics, or religion, gives someone's life a special meaning. When he talked about art, he wasn't thinking of the sparkling attributes of institutionalized art, or of the *art world*, where you earn money and become famous. On the other hand, when the likes of Teodor say that everyone is an artist, they're thinking of personal ambition, and have no qualms about mercilessly exploiting Beuys to achieve their aim.

Teodor can go very far. The death of the Boy—which occurred at a most convenient moment for him—offers great new opportunities. Even if it turns out that the majority of the installations were actually created by the art critic Teodor, nothing will go wrong, because it will have become possible to present the Boy Joosep as a conceptual mystification, a piece of art.

My mood is already pretty good when I see Ummal coming through the gate, and I think to myself that games should be played in a good mood, and that my game as an informer will take off today, will become productive. Laakan goes up to Ummal, Ummal embraces him (what if I told him that Maria was really Jaak?!), his companions, three men and women, hold back. The cars are neatly parked in the yard, and the cat runs up to Ummal and rubs itself against his legs. One of the men is a well-known face (from TV), a politician, and one of the women a female journalist who has become famous for her feminist articles. She has her arm round another woman and they're conversing in a lively mood, not paying attention to the surroundings. For some reason I am convinced that this other woman is a Finn, and later on it transpires that I'm not mistaken. I like both women, their bodies are very attractive—they're almost harassing me sexually. At the sight of such women, men have a hard time keeping themselves under control, it can't be helped if chemical processes in the male body lead to indecent suggestions or wandering hands.

It's nice to be looking out the window, but the master of the house (I am after all the master of Teeriida Farm for the time being!) should, with a smile on his face and his arms spread wide, be welcoming his guests and exchanging ideas with them—welcoming everything they choose to tell me and abandon my own (precious) thoughts without any words of praise.

"How do you like Teeriida, Mr So-and-So?" asks Ummal, as he shakes my hand long and heartily. He emanates human warmth and an assurance that reaches and even penetrates me, and I cannot believe that such a person could be a conspirator or terrorist. Somebody must have got it all wrong. Projecting their own ambitions onto him.

"Even more pleasant than expected," I say, smiling broadly. "My habitat has always been the city and, to tell you the truth, I was a little afraid at first that country life wouldn't appeal to me, work for me. But now the prospect of returning to city life is rather daunting."

***

"Humanist prejudices simply don't allow people to see situations for what they actually are. We're not allowed to say straight out that there are perniciously many people on Planet Earth. We're not even supposed to think about possibilities for reducing this population. Mankind is liable to take care of just about any other species—he distributes hunting licenses without feeling any pangs of conscience, knowing that in any natural system there are too many species of one kind, unable to feel themselves. But he is driving his own species quite cold-bloodedly to the point of extinction," says Ummal slowly, stressing the various words that are more important to him, and his clear, bright eyes are staring into the flickering flame of the candle. He's leaning forward, supporting itself on both elbows, his fingers—powerful, very manly—are crossed, resting, out of the game for the moment. They are not the hands of an intellectual, though the clean and well-trimmed fingernails tell the opposite story, and I think that the hands lie in each others' embrace as if in suspended animation.

"If you press the population to adopt zero growth, then no one will listen to you, because people don't approve of prophets that want them to stop having children, eating food, enjoying other creature comforts, cutting down on things at all costs, and all in order to avoid some future disaster. When the Nazis promised the people _Lebensraum_, strength, the opportunity to propagate, and all of it at the expense of others in their species, people listened to the truths they were longing to hear. Human rights, democracy, equality, and quality of life, don't fit together in the long run. When you increase one, the other diminishes. If Asia reached a

European standard of living tomorrow, then the day after a total environmental catastrophe would ensue. These are simple truths, but no one wants or dares to utter them.

"I can imagine that war, famine, and sickness are a prerequisite for saving mankind as a species, but I cannot say so aloud. My message must first of all conform to the norms of living together, as each and every individual's struggle against the rest to maintain personal survival inevitably leads to disaster in the same way. I *can* look after *my own* family, relatives, nation. Everything that is beyond such narrow boundaries is just too much. We cannot all get through the pearly gates together.

"When I lived in Germany, we couldn't even think about *our own* German nation. That variant had been lost in the 1940s. Influencing the course of things by way of parliament seemed realistic at some point, but once the European Union arrived that idea was crossed out. Now we even have to support the Greeks.

"I was in Japan for a couple of weeks in the spring, and their cities are a salutary warning of what can happen to people if you depend on technology for progress. I don't want that kind of existence for myself or my children—a way of living where a person becomes like a cell in a huge organism, whose goal is for the organism, not the individual, to survive.

"The Estonian nation now has its last chance to drop out of the game, the European Union fanfares have not yet sounded, and we've created very good conditions for maintaining our children and families. Instead of leaping around like an economic tiger, it would be advantageous for Estonia to be transformed into a park state independent of the European Union—the principle being that small is beautiful. And that should become the norm for Estonians. What the rest of the world is rushing after is something we should ignore. We can offer the world, maybe those Japanese, what they're looking for, and for good money."

There are loud voices outside. I excuse myself and—in my role as master of the farm—I go out to see what's the matter. Teodor bumps into me in the doorway, and his face is bloody. I fill a bowl with water and ask him what happened. "That fucking Kandiman called me a pederast, and said that it was my fault that the Boy Joosep killed himself. I screw my own wife dutifully, not village idiots! I loathe pederasts! Fucking hell, why did he think I was one?" I hand him a towel—at least in the not-very-bright light of the petroleum lamp, he doesn't look too awful. Only his lower lip is cut. "But I gave him a thrashing," boasts my childhood friend, who was well known in the past for being a coward. "Can you imagine, he even bragged that it was he who had put together the Boy's installations."

I imagine poor Kandiman sitting hunched in pain by the bonfire, or even knocked unconscious, but in fact he's sitting inside as if nothing has happened and trying to explain something or other to Laakan. I fill one of the glasses with vodka and hand it to Teodor in the kitchen, but when he says he wants to go into the living room, I tell him that Ummal and myself are still discussing things, and it surprises me how submissively and reverentially he steps back from the threshold.

"Oh, nothing special," I say soothingly, replacing a nearly burnt down candle with a new one. The room grows lighter and moths fly in through the open window and dance around the flame.

"I've had a long talk today," Ummal continues, "with the Minister of Defense—he's staying near here at the encampment, they've got some family festivities or other—and he doesn't want to give up the area that's been assigned as a military zone, but I don't want to give it up, because I want to sell untouched nature to my clients. I personally have a positive attitude to the defense forces—they consume state money which would otherwise be used to raise the standard of living, which in turn would lead to a greater environmental burden. I know full well that the minister has personal interests at stake regarding the military zone, and he's not afraid of admitting them publicly. 'It's all sewn up,' he says. 'Look, Juss,' I say to him, 'I've got forty men a couple of kilometers down the road and we can do what we like with the likes of you and arrange all kinds of unpleasant accidents, but that won't happen as long as you keep your own private interests out of it and do what is good for the Estonian people.'

"You should have seen his face! His mind began to work, or maybe he finally understood that he isn't some baron or other, whom the nation serves, but that the situation is quite the reverse. I'm an unpleasant and irritating factor to them, but I'm also a force to be reckoned with. When all this European Union stuff gets nearer, it will become clear that two thirds of the Estonians in parliament will vote in favor of joining, but that two thirds is split between three or four political parties; on the other hand, the other third will be voting for the one Euroskeptical party—and that will decide the issue. It's perfectly possible to vote in a Green Republic in a parliamentary way.

"It's still too early. The new party should emerge about six months before the elections, maybe even later, but until then preparations must be made, keep all your irons in the fire. I read a review of your latest book, and was pleasantly surprised by how profoundly you've examined global problems. Unfortunately, I've not yet had time to read the actual book. But never mind. Have you gotten acquainted with *those* yet?" he asks, and runs his finger tenderly across the spines of the green books on the shelf.

I tell him that at first, such radical green ideas were alien to me, horrified me, but that on thinking it over I began to feel that you have to accept the bitter and unpalatable truth.

"Exactly, the truth that people will have to face is bitter, but it's impossible to publish the real solutions anywhere. It would be a crafty move if some writer or other were to air such bitter but justifiable truths in some work of fiction, where he could simulate being part of the struggle against green terrorism or fascism . . . ."

"And you, Mr Ummal, are hoping that the writer So-and-So is crafty enough to carry out this plan."

"Call me Enniver," suggests Ummal. "Estonia is so small that we can all be on first-name terms. We will, of course, help publish the book, and the fee will be worthy of the labor put into it, and I can imagine that living for nothing at Teeriida would be conducive to working on it."

"I don't want to write something lightweight, something that doesn't really interest me, but if I write anything too complex, no one will read it and your plans will be in vain. Besides, I'm not entirely sure that my interpretation will meet with your approval."

"Knowing the present intellectual climate here in Estonia, a book critical of fundamentalist green thinking would generate a good debate. It has to be taken into account that it's here in Estonia that the only foreign translation of works by my Finnish friend

Pentti Linkola have appeared," says Ummal, rubbing his hands together. "We have the perfect soil to sow our seed in, and there are plenty of people just waiting for the sign, so that they can come out with their daring standpoints."

I still don't want to join his project, give him my three drops of blood, sell my soul to the green society of the future; I must wriggle and wiggle like a prostitute who's paid to pretend to be an innocent girl; I must put a brake on both him and me, give the impression that the decision must be made (though in fact the secret police have already made it) as a result of gradual inner enlightenment rather than in one fell swoop.

"I'll have to think the matter over. I'm not sure that I'll be understood correctly. Estonia has an unambiguously warm attitude toward things green. If I make things come to a head, I could be courting disaster. I could be ground to dust, scattered to the four winds."

"Don't fret, *we* will make sure that your book is properly understood," says Enniver Ummal, squeezing my shoulder as he stands up.

"I can't promise anything right now," I say, wishing he'd take his hand, which has been there a few seconds *too long*, off my shoulder; but I *mustn't* shrug it off. "I'll try a thing or two," I say vaguely.

***

The sea is stormy for the second day now, the wind is ripping the leaves off the trees, whirling them up in the air, then the next gust flings them back to the ground. The large maple at the edge of the forest has gone red, lots of its leaves are flying around, and flocks of cranes, tens of them (or the same flock ten times over), are sweeping across the gray sky.

I've stoked the stove too much and the heat is making me sleepy. I rip the umpteenth sheet of useless text out of the typewriter, light a cigarette, and look sadly at all the stubs in the ashtray. A car stops outside the gate and a short while after I see Kandiman fumbling with the latch. I swear under my breath; just when I could be doing some serious work, someone comes and disturbs me, though (on the other hand) I am happy that I can take a short break from my wearisome task, that I can find an excuse to extend my free time, escaping from the pressures of writing (maybe until evening).

"Listen, is Maria here?" asks Kandiman by way of a greeting. I tell him I haven't seen her for a couple of days.

"I'm at my wits' end," sighs Kandiman, and sits down on the wet lawn as if his legs will no longer support him.

I suggest he come in and drink some coffee. Kandiman drags himself reluctantly to his feet, his face looks pale and exhausted.

"I'm in love," he confesses. "I am forty two years old and have fallen in love like a green young thing."

I don't ask him who it is, I know that Kandiman (suddenly I try to remember what his first name is, and I get the feeling I've never heard it) will soon mention it, that this theatrical prologue will ultimately lead to a (ritual) introduction.

"Heard the news?" he cries, jumping up quite unexpectedly from his chair. "Ummal's been arrested! It was on the radio yesterday evening, and now it's in all the papers. He's already been charged—plotting to stage a coup d'état! Who would have thought it of him!"

I don't look Kandiman straight in the face, I look down at my fingers, which are trembling as they hold my cigarette, I click the Zippo, but no flame emerges—the fuel has run out. There is a box with a few matches in it on the edge of the stove, and no other matches in the whole house—maybe I ought to go and fetch some from the store before it closes, maybe Kandiman has matches, even though he doesn't smoke (has a negative effect on your erection, as he eagerly tells everyone), but you never know.

"When they searched his place they found detailed plans for a coup d'état, but he was arrested on the strength of the testimony of the Minister of Defense. I can imagine he'll be found guilty, since the Minister has weighty evidence, and another man was recently found guilty of insurrection on the evidence of what just one high-up official gave in evidence."

"And what other news is there from the city?" I ask in an indifferent voice, thinking that now they'll be wanting me to give evidence in the Ummal case. That was, after all, what they sent me out here for. I'm not at all sure that I'll be giving any evidence, as no one but the two of us know about the conversation where Ummal talked me round to writing that book. *For them.* Apart from Ummal, there are other people involved, and *they* are still at large.

"Vennet opened an exhibition—actually, there are several people exhibiting. I saw the opening on TV, everything revolved round some photographer or other who talked incessantly, while no one really took much notice of Vennet himself. Yesterday there was an article by Teodor introducing the exhibition, and he said straight out that Vennet ought to start earning his keep with something else, that this pushiness—he's been trying to be topical for thirty years now—makes you sick, that it's incomprehensible that the paradigm shift somehow doesn't penetrate the brains of the likes of Vennet, and that now is the time to rewrite the history of Estonian art, to show the current classics their place outside history."

"So much for Vennet," I say wearily. I can't be bothered to inform Kandiman about my own views, and he would hardly bother to listen, so I ask him about how he managed to fall in love again. "It isn't possible for someone to keep on falling in love again and again for a quarter of a century," I say.

"Oh, but it is, and besides, falling in love isn't the same as figurative art, and this time it's all your fault," says Kandiman.

"Me! Guilty of the fact that Mr. Kandiman has fallen in love!"

"Well, you did, after all, extol Maria—otherwise I wouldn't have looked at her once. But now I don't know whether to be angry with you or praise you to the skies."

"Maria?!" I ask, and my voice sounds alien to myself.

"You could never imagine. A fantastic woman!"

After a short pause, I ask whether he doesn't happen to have any matches, and he doesn't. "You don't even have matches," I say.

"Don't bawl me out. You don't have any either," says Kandiman.

When Kandiman has gone ("I'll drop in and see if Maria has come back, and if not I'll have to arrange the stove-repairing at my summer house again.") I sit down at my writing desk and look thoughtfully out at the autumn landscape. Soon, the cold will arrive, but I have plenty of firewood. It is completely silent all around. I no longer have any obligation to write any green tract, neither to condemn nor praise them. I don't need to write about the weird state of affairs in figurative art, in order to investigate other positions that *Fin de siècle* culture has taken. I have no need to go spying or informing on anyone, and until they turf me out, I'm going to be quietly getting on with my writing out here.

I roll a sheet of paper into the typewriter and type, in the middle of the page:

A NOVEL FOR THE END OF THE CENTURY

I want to enjoy the title, enjoy the new (new) beginning, enjoy a cigarette, but when I reach for the matchbox, I realize there is only one match left, and that it's a spent one. I remember that there's that pistol-shaped lighter in the glove box of the car. Indeed, there is a heavy object in that silk shawl. The events of that night flash like a movie before my eyes, and I am surprised (in stereotypical fashion) how long ago the first day I spent at Teeriida now seems. I think (lustfully) that tomorrow, tomorrow already, I will seek out that mysterious lady who came to live in these parts, in order to stay.

I put my cigarette between my lips and lightly press the trigger of the pistol, it does not give, but when I press harder, there is an ear-splitting roar and the powerful blow knocks my hand to one side.

****

A Novel for the End of the Century

". . . and everything felt so light and pleasant."

ANTON CHEKHOV
"The Lady With the Lapdog" (1899)

When Enniver and Alma Ummal returned to their native land in the early nineties and used a large part of their wealth to found "Full-Blooded Recreation," many people shook their heads in pity: the idea of buying up and renovating houses and pioneer camps that were falling into disrepair seemed simply too strange (if not "crazy") for practically-minded Estonians. The couple returning from Germany were regarded as weirdos as well, people who ignored common sense and went about their business with deadly seriousness, refusing to listen to competent advice and come to terms with their striking ignorance of local matters. "Nonetheless, it is ultimately your own business what you do with your money," people finally said, shrugging their shoulders.

However, the business success of "Full-Blooded Recreation" was beyond the expectations even of the Ummals themselves, though Enniver tried in every interview to give the impression that everything was going according to plan, and that he'd been convinced right from the start that in a post-socialist society people were yearning for nature and would agree to pay good money for living an uncomfortable existence. And indeed, in the "Full-Blooded Recreation" houses there was no electricity, and often people would hand over their car keys, so that all their comings and goings would be on foot.

One fine Indian summer morning—this year early September was amazing, the sun shone as it had in summer, and the temperature rose to twenty-five degrees Celsius during the daytime—Celia was sitting alone in the "Full-Blooded Recreation" office waiting for customers. She had come to work there the week before, and still felt a little unsure of herself. The chunky rustic furniture, the walls in dark tones, and all manner of old junk—everything added to her depressed mood, and since the office was situated in a narrow street with high buildings on either side, the room was always filled with gloom, and you had to have the lights on even in the daytime. When she'd stepped for the first time into this room, she had had the urge to turn round and flee forthwith as far away as was humanly possible, but she summoned up a smile and greeted her future employers respectfully. Celia needed the money, and as good jobs weren't two a penny she was very lucky to have received this opportunity. The name of Celia's lucky break was Enniver, Uncle Albert had introduced them, and on that occasion it didn't bother Celia a bit that the man was forty years older than she was. The man smelled nice and expensive. When he invited her to work at his firm, she gave it a good deal of thought. It was almost like an offer of marriage, or rather an offer to become someone's permanent mistress. This could change Celia's whole life. After debating with herself for a good while she decided to risk it, to play a bold hand.

The previous summer Celia had fallen in love, and it seemed to her that this was a firm enough foundation on which to build a family. The future unrolled slowly and gently before her eyes. Verner was a thirty-two-year-old bank clerk, strong and slim, he was admittedly a little cross-eyed, but it felt nice and dignified to be beside him. Marriage was in the offing, but at that point Verner made it known that Celia would have to leave behind her dog. "Listen, come to your senses," she'd shouted at him. "You could get rid of that revolting cat of yours." Verner's cat was an ordinary tabby, the town was full of them. For a while they kept off the subject, but when Celia went to visit Verner at home, the Dobermann would lie whining and whimpering, tethered to the radiator, for hours on end, while the cat lay snugly in the armchair, purring. They couldn't let these animals loose, or the furniture would be scratched to pieces.

The marriage didn't happen, and she grew ever more fond of her dog. "A man here or a man there," she boasted, but it did sadden her that Verner preferred some striped monster to her. Her financial situation had become ever more pressing, and that winter she had slept for the first time with Uncle Albert. Albert wasn't her real uncle, just an old friend of her mother's, and when she wanted to borrow a largish sum of money, they both know where they stood with regard to giving and taking.

The town hall clock chimed eleven and the dull strokes reached Celia through the window or door, bringing to the uncomfortable world surrounding her tidings from the colorful and bustling city center that lived its full-blooded life only a hundred meters away. And this is what they call "full-blooded," said Celia to herself, wrinkling up her nose in contempt, thinking about those poor souls who, instead of lying on the beach, on the warm sand of a seaside resort, were paying large sums of money to live in some godforsaken hellhole. But isn't it up to people what they spend their money on, thought Celia ironically (exactly like the majority of her compatriots), and wondered where Enniver and Alma Ummal, who always arrived at the office promptly at eleven, had got to. When she had first seen Alma, she'd gotten nervous, as if the woman was boring her lively brown eyes right through her, bringing all her secrets into the light of day, but this penetrating and investigative gaze didn't lead to any suspicion. The day before yesterday, Celia had happened to see Alma sitting in a café with a very handsome young man. Maybe she and Enniver both had their separate love lives by now. Maybe that was inevitable. During her twenty years of life she had seen dozens of marriages survive without (the logic of) love. When I am old and rich, why shouldn't I too use the services of a young man on occasions, thought Celia dreamily, imagining how he'd sit up and eat out of her hand, but just then her attention was drawn by someone coming in through the office door, a middle-aged gentleman whose face she seemed to have seen before—no doubt on TV.

"Like a village inn," the man uttered, letting his eyes rove round the room.

"Excuse me?" asked Celia, thinking she had misheard.

"This looks like the way village inns do in the movies," said the man, stepping closer.

"We wish to give our clients their first vivid impression of the world they will be entering," said Celia, as she had been taught, and then she remembered that she'd seen this man talking on TV about a book he'd just written. This was a famous writer, and Celia had at some point read one of his novels. It was about a young man who falls in love with a much older woman. The novel had been written with indecent candidness, and she remembered one episode that had gotten her moist. Celia conjured up her irresistible (as Ummal liked to put it) smile and added: "We send our clients out into a full-blooded world. Only when someone has to draw water from a well, and chop firewood with an ax to keep warm, does he feel that blood is flowing in his veins, not Coca Cola."

"You have a wonderful smile. I'd really like to know how much you're paid a smile like that."

Celia named the sum mechanically, suddenly wondering whether she was supposed to reveal such information to clients.

The writer (if indeed this is who he was) gave a low whistle. "Then what you're selling must be pretty popular."

"It is indeed. Our vacation homes are full all year round. There are lists of people waiting to join our survival courses. The fishing and hunting trips are also sold out for the high season in the fall."

"Well, in that case I've come in vain," said the man with a smile. "But you could describe to me what your vacation homes are like."

"Things aren't that bad," smiled Celia and began to paint impressive verbal images of things, though she had only a vague notion of things she was describing.

"I imagine you meant that your clients must feel like they've suddenly been cast out of civilization. That suits me fine, I've been hoping for a good while to be cast out of somewhere. I'm the writer So-and-So, and what I need is the peace and quiet of the forest so that I can get on with my work."

When Celia heard that the writer would like—today, the very next hour, minute, second—to leave the city behind, she knew that she couldn't help him, since all of the homes were hired out until the end of the year; but she didn't say so immediately, and *pretended* to be looking at lists on her computer—she had to give the client *the impression* that she was trying to do the impossible for him, although impossible *did mean* impossible. Quite unexpectedly, she noticed that Teeriida Farm was free at the moment, and that there were no bookings for it. It was like a miracle, because only the Friday before, no location of that name had been on the list.

"You're in luck," said Celia, and went to drawer number 13, where the keys were deposited along with the instructions—in other words, everything that was needed for the vacation home. "You really are in luck," repeated Celia handing the client the file marked "Teeriida."

The telephone rang: "I'm terribly sorry but I'll have to cancel my booking," said a penitent voice. "Things have changed, I'm going to have to fly to Peru tomorrow, so my vacation's off." Well, thought Celia, this writer would have been in luck anyway.

"And what do these surprises consist of?"

"I can't reveal the surprises, otherwise they wouldn't be surprises. But you'll get a surprise alright," smiled Celia. "We try to make life as interesting as possible for our clients."

"I would have nothing against such a surprise, if it were that you yourself drove out there for the weekend," joked the writer, and it was clear that he indeed would have nothing against such an event. A hopeless ladies' man, thought Celia, the kind that'll have obscene thoughts in his head even on his deathbed.

Once the new tenant had been registered for Teeriida Farm, silence reigned for a while at the office; then the bells of the Town

Hall chimed the half hour. What a funny business time is, soon we'll be writing the year as 2000, as if that much time has passed since the Beginning, but in actual fact it's a mere convention. It could be any number, and nothing would change. Celia would have been glad to carry on thinking about the turn of the century, but in walked the Ummals—Alma and Enniver—the owners of the firm "Full-Blooded Recreation."

"Did the writer So-and-So drop round?" asked Enniver.

"Yes, he left a few minutes ago. I've booked him in for two weeks at Teeriida."

"Teeriida?!" cried Alma in astonishment and Celia noticed the couple exchange knowing looks, of which she understood nothing.

"I was rather surprised that Teeriida was free, too," added Celia, feeling a slight pang of guilt.

"But weren't they supposed to cancel for Tammsaare Farm?"

"Yes, somebody phoned and said he had to fly to Peru, but I'd already offered Teeriida by then."

"What a devil of a nuisance! Teerrida should never have been on the computer list in the first place," said Enniver, and Celia understood that something wasn't right.

"But it could prove useful in some way," said Alma, and deleted the writer So-and-So's details. Everything was now back to exactly as it had been half an hour before, when the writer had stepped in to the sound of the jangling of the doorbell.

Enniver Ummal went over to the window and looked out. His chest ached, he raised his handkerchief to his mouth and coughed, looked at his own phlegm before putting the handkerchief back into his pocket—there were more streaks of blood today than usual. He knew—in a couple, maybe three months he would be done with this world. He believed in neither hell nor paradise, nor any form of reincarnation. He knew that the only way to live on was in his own children, everything else was a mere fairy-tale with no guarantees. He had thirty-two children, each with a different mother, and maybe there were more, but he only counted the ones he was certain about. He hoped that before his death he would have the opportunity to procreate again. With Celia, for instance. Children were his secret vice, which he hid from everyone. If it came out how he was spreading himself demographically, none of the people holding his views would take him seriously any more. At present, only his lawyer knew, whose job it was to make sure that none of these children married one another by accident.

The thought of his impending death made Enniver sweat. The wave of perspiration moved from the palms of his hands to the rest of his body, and a terrible fear, not yet linked to anything concrete, darkened his mind.

As a child he had been sickly and had suffered from weak health—the physicians had made great efforts to pump the spirit of life into him and keep it there. He was mollycoddled, he'd learned to regard himself as the center of the world, yet his coevals achieved greater success for some reason, and in the end he gave up, using his sickness as an excuse, which everyone seemed to understand. He grew up in an academic environment, and when it transpired that he was unsuited to such, hatred had made a visionary of him. Or to be more exact: suddenly he began to grasp the nature of things around him, to realize that culture was in diametric opposition to nature. That all the world's ills stemmed from literacy.

He loved to stress that, according to the laws of nature, the sort of sickly child he'd been had no right to live; it was only due to the brutal interference of medical science that this miserable creature could live and—most cynically of all—beget offspring. He called himself a paradox of civilization: the fact that the physicians had kept him alive gave him the chance to devote himself to the rehabilitation of natural choice. He hated surgery, technology, and humanism in equal measure, things that idolized an unstoppably greedy human being. He never wearied of repeating that the *last* important values of mankind had been snatched away during his lifetime and under his very eyes.

Now, as a sixty-two-year-old, he had no visible reason to allow himself to die. He loved life, the struggle for fundamental values gave his life a special meaning; he would even have agreed, against his own views, to consult a physician, so that he could thereby cheat fate by a year or two, if possible, but who would believe in his standpoint after surgeons had performed a successful operation on him. He was a fundamentalist, and demanded of himself that every *word* he uttered with regard to the past, present, and future, corresponded to reality.

"Listen, I feel rather worried about that writer, we should really try to do something," said Alma in a low voice.

"Let's see how things develop," said Enniver, thinking that a secret police informer deserves a few nasty surprises. Teodor had said that the writer So-and-So had been sent out to spy on him. Handy to know when someone is an informer, while at the same time the informer himself has no idea that he is suspected of spying on people. "If that writer doesn't suffer an accident, then I'll pay him to write a book on environmental terrorism. That would be an amusing way of acquainting people with our ideas. Very likely he'll fall for it," said Enniver, and his face took on the expression of a schoolboy hatching a plot, and soon he was smiling broadly.

Alma Ummal poured herself a small cup of coffee. She didn't bother offering Enniver any, knowing that it would give her husband palpitations. He shouldn't smoke at all, thought Alma worriedly, he's got such a bad cough. But cigarettes and other damaging pleasures were part and parcel of Enniver's system: he was in the habit of saying that every means that can reduce the population, should be encouraged, When they had met in the late 1960s—Alma was then studying painting in Düsseldorf—what charmed her was the man's devotion to his idea. They all thought at the time that the world would not survive as it was, that a new way to salvation had to be found. While the Marxists and Maoists were thinking of the present day, Enniver and his friends were already thinking about tomorrow. The future of the world looked bleak. It was like a huge creature that had begun to eat itself from the tail upwards.

Alma lived selflessly for Enniver, who lived selflessly for the idea. Despite the fact that Enniver devoted a large amount of his time to saving the world, their finances were in good shape. One especially profitable enterprise, begun in the early 1970s, demolished houses, factories, and other buildings that were no longer needed: one day a factory with two chimneys was standing, but a couple of days later it had been razed to the ground, leaving a level area where grass seed could be sown. The only thing that darkened their life together was Enniver's insistence on not having more than one child. Alma would have liked three, two at least, but she had to make do with the one boy, who nevertheless made them both happy by following in the footsteps of his father.

When they started the firm called "Full-Blooded Recreation," they at first regarded it as a summer pastime—Enniver's plaything. But as time went by, the firm began to bring profits, both financial and spiritual. "It constitutes the foundations of the 'green realm,' upon which green walls will rise. When one day I buy up their power station and only sell electricity to the 'green realm,' then the roof will have been put on this building," dreamed Enniver.

When the fact that the secret police were taking an interest in the Ummals first reached their ears, the amused Enniver explained that Estonians have one national characteristic in common—envy, which causes them to regard those who lead successful lives as having committed a mortal sin. And yet this ruined Alma's sleep. A few days before she'd had a serious talk with their son, and some stray sentences that he'd uttered made her heart ache even more. She had only a vague idea of what her husband had been dealing with all these years. In France, Enniver had made friends with Pol Pot and later, when he had come to power, Enniver went to visit him several times; as far as she remembered, they'd even done business together. The thought of all this did not encourage her right now, and what also worried her was that Andreas Baader had at one time visited their family quite often.

Alma was only able to say anything definite about her husband when they chanced to be together (such as now), and that didn't happen often. Here in Estonia they had the habit of dropping in at the firm in the morning, and then (often) living their own separate lives till the next morning. Alma put her cup on the saucer with a quiet chinking sound, went up to her husband and took his cool and feminine hand in hers: "Do try to smoke a couple of cigarettes less each day," she said.

I

The Estonian writer So-and-So drove out of town around lunch-time, headed for the farm on the west coast that he'd hired for a couple of weeks with the connivance of the secret police. The whole business was in itself unpleasant—it wasn't a writer's job to spy on people, but taking a number of factors into consideration he simply could not refuse the assignment. He would just make the best of a bad job and use the opportunity to start writing a new novel.

He was worried. What was worrying him was not so much the ethical aspects or the danger involved in being an informer, but the fact that he had received a phone call from his wife hinting quite unequivocally that from now on she was going to continue to live her own life in the States.

He understood from what she said that some man had come into her life, and this was a cold shower for him. He was financially dependent on his wife, and while in the past he had been able to make ends meet with his writing, under present circumstances he could not imagine maintaining his standard of living without his wife's income. His wife had three nice houses in the center of the city where the writer could work happily and quietly. But now, unexpectedly, dark clouds had appeared on the horizon.

He was forty-one years old, his fifteen-year-old daughter was in the United States, studying to become an American; the twin boys, however, were studying at Tartu University: the one law, the other economics. He had married early, when he was a sophomore, and now his wife looked one-and-a-half times as old as he did. She was tall, with dark eyebrows, important and respected, and—as she said of herself—a modern businesswoman. She was always doing something, always occupied, never called her husband by his name, just that author gentleman, and secretly the writer So-and-So thought of her as narrow-minded, strait-laced, and in no way elegant. He was afraid of her and hid in his study at home, on the pretext that he was writing. He'd started cheating on her early, did it frequently, and maybe that was why he nearly always said bad things about women, why, when the topic came up, he'd call them brainless chickens.

The writer So-and-So felt he'd enough bad experiences to call them whatever he liked, although he would have been unable to do without his "brood of chickens" for two days at a time. In the company of men he felt bored, and uncomfortable, he was taciturn and cool with them, but when he was among women he felt free, and knew what to say to them and how to behave. It was also easy to remain silent in their presence. His appearance, nature, and behavior had something attractive about them, something intangible, that aroused sympathy in women, charmed them. He knew this, and something drew him to them as well.

Recurring experiences, in fact bitter ones, had soon shown him that every close relationship that so pleasantly enlivened life and seemed like a nice and easy adventure would turn, in the long run, for decent people—especially Estonians, who had a difficult time getting going, and then tended to falter—into an extremely problematic situation, one which in the end would become a burden. And yet, with each new interesting woman he met, those experiences would vanish from his memory, and what remained was the urge to live life to the full, and everything seemed so simple, such fun.

His wife's phone call could of course be taken as one of her whims, and he could interpret her words as encouragement or consolation, and yet the writer So-and-So now had nagging doubts about the future, and this was made worse by the fact that he had the previous day given incautious hints to Teodor about how the secret police had recruited him as an informer, and he was worried what such frankness could lead to in the very near future.

He had an inkling that there was something askew in all of this, that something had gone wrong right from the start. He was supposed to meet the director of the firm "Full-Blooded Recreation" at eleven to discuss going out to Tammsaare Farm, but instead there was a blonde young thing in the office, who managed to sell him a two-week stay at Teeriida. He had no opportunity to sort out the mess, because the secret police had warned him off contacting them. In case of need, their people would look him up, but how would they manage to find him when he might be hanging out at the other end of Estonia?

But that's their lookout, he repeated to himself for the umpteenth time.

The writer So-and-So had lunched with Vennet the previous day at the Artists' Club. They had just finished eating their jellied meat when the artist Tõnis Vint joined them. He was in a foul mood: "No one wants to finance us if we intend to build a kennel for our dog. It makes people smile. A big project always needs financing," he said suggestively, his voice full of fire.

Vint had just discovered some documents where it was written in black and white that the Estonian Republic was going to hire out the whole island of Naissaar, to the north of Tallinn, for one kroon (!) to someone called Enniver Ummal, who would be building an international ornithological center there.

"You know, some years ago in Shanghai they started a new business center on a plot of land the size of Naissaar. Already in the first year alone the necessary investments amounted to more than the investments for the whole region over the previous ten years. The project will be complete by the year 2000, and it could just as well have been located on Naissaar and been just as successful, since the business interests of East and West would have been able to find direct and profitable solutions there together. But no, all they do even in our capital city is build cheap Finnish shopping malls. Tallinn is turning into Helsinki's East End, because it won't ruin the interests of our friends who want to see Estonia as a kind of workers' district of Finland, at a lower stage of development. Estonia is becoming a model Lilliput state, with all the foibles of such," said Vint pulling some photocopies of official documents out of his briefcase.

"Listen to this. Here we have the intended development project of the 'jewel' near Tallinn:

"On the island of Naissaar, it is considered suitable to develop a visitors' center, an administrative center, a bicycle rental facility, lookout towers, picnic spots, roofed-in picnic locations, a ski rental facility, a history museum, accommodations in the right location, a restaurant in the right location, and an environmental teaching center. It is permitted to camp in the right location, to watch birds in a specific location, as well as to bathe, and paths will be marked out; in addition, a harbor will be constructed in the right location.

"Unsuitable: the shops, sanatorium, and year–round residents.

"Only year-round residents should be: a permanent staff of 3 persons, 5 family members, 15 coastguards, 10 others (?).

"Colors resembling those of nature should be used when building. No tall buildings or glass surfaces.

"Fighting forest fires. Although there is a view that forest fires constitute a part of nature, this *philosophical* way of thinking does not suit Naissaar, so the following three components are necessary: 1. Quick observation (!). 2. Accuracy in establishing the locations of fires. 3. Fire-fighting equipment. The present harbor will be of interest to foreign tourists if not to Estonian ones, giving an impression of a Soviet restricted military zone, which indeed the island was at an earlier point. This impression should be retained. For this reason a number of military buildings should be left in their ruined state. On the side of the island facing Tallinn, there should be a statue evincing the name of the island—Naissaar meaning women's island as it does. Something is needed that will leave the visitors with a particularly vivid impression. This could be a musical performance or a play devoted to the history of Naissaar."

Vint finished reading and looked up at our (dismayed?) faces with an ironic smile. "This is the reality of Estonia today—i.e., a project for the end of the century, Estonian style. This island, which is in the perfect location, economically speaking, is simply being given away to the émigré Estonian firm 'Full-Blooded Recreation,' run by someone called Ummal, who will teach schoolchildren a green way of life in addition to bird-watching. It would seem that the powers that be are enchanted by Malthus's theory, and are trying together to stop mankind's development, to begin, with their chosen group of people, the journey back to the Stone Age. The very way this Naissaar project is worded shows the authors' level of thinking, and it wouldn't surprise me unduly if the ideology governing us soon becomes neo-Marxism, with its crude hatred of intellectuals."

"Well, you have to maintain the distinction: at present we are being ruled by the Soviet Sixties generation, which drank Soviet Marxism in with their mother's milk, while the neo-Marxists are still consolidating their power—so maybe what played out elsewhere at the end of the Sixties still lies in store for us in the new century," said the art critic Teodor, who had just joined our table unobserved.

"So you mean everything will repeat itself up to Baader-Meinhof, but in an even more radical guise, or clothed in the religiosity of 'The Greater Truth'—literally the Third Way of the chosen ones. Whatever happens, this will lead to the disappearance of literacy, whether it be called the Religion of Taara, neo-Shamanism, or the Earth Mother Movement. The thought that education and a new spiritual and ethical level will enable truly great leaps forward must be nipped in the bud by using scenarios of fear and horror," said Tõnis Vint, who had started out in the early 1960s as a classical Modernist and deliberately subverted the pillars of Socialist Realism that held sway at the time, and who, in the Postmodernist climate of today, still believed as a true Modernist in progress and lasting values centered on the individual.

The writer So-and-So recalled how his childhood friend and classmate Teodor had clung to him as they left the Club. Although they belonged to the same circles, their relations were not particularly warm, and the writer So-and-so was surprised that Teodor, who was well known for being stingy, now invited him to an open-air bar to have a few beers. The weather was warm enough for outdoor drinking, and there was no wind, so he had no reason to refuse the offer.

Teodor had immediately steered the conversation toward Tõnis Vint and wanted to know what had been said about renting out Naissaar before he himself had turned up. When the conversation moved on to Enniver Ummal, the writer So-and-So told Teodor, in colorful terms and half in jest, how their mutual school-friend, the current minister Specs-Theo, had recruited him as an informer. He was now in full swing with his tale and didn't notice the change of mood that had come over his friend until it was too late. He now realized that Teodor could be in cahoots with Ummal.

They hadn't been sitting long when all of a sudden Teodor was *in a hurry*, and the writer had grown depressed at the thought that after recruitment he had given the game away to the first best person he met. He could not anticipate what repercussions his indiscretion would have. He had never been involved in any type of crime in his life, but had instead picked it all up from books and movies, and on the basis of *such alone* could feel real fear.

After his wife's night call he couldn't get to sleep for a long time, and he sat at the kitchen table, smoked and brooded. Across the street Parasoolin's windows were the only ones lit up. They were drinking vodka. While still at university Parasoolin was already making a career for himself, and by the end of the 1980s he had reached the top rung of the promotion ladder, so that every morning he would be driven in an official car to his important state job. Then came the sudden and complete fall from grace, by way of which he descended to the level of rummaging in garbage bins. Parasoolin knew full well that their windows were opposite, and at times the writer So-and-So wondered whether he was being offered a free performance: in the uncurtained apartment a tragedy was being acted out, so that he, as a writer, could note it down. This time a quarrel had flared up. Parasoolin's wife was struggling with her husband on equal terms. There was no sound, but you could see how smaller items of crockery flew about, how blows to the face drew blood. Now and again, the wife would go into the other room to take a break, then returned to the kitchen to attack her husband once again.

The writer So-and-So can imagine that the fall in fortunes of this family was caused by more than ordinary alcoholism, he can even gloat about the fact that someone from "former times" has fallen from his high perch, but alongside his own worries there is actually no room for those of others, so he watches indifferently how the woman falls to the floor, bringing the crockery down with her, and remains there, and how Parasoolin is getting ready to hang himself from the hook in the other room, where once a glittering chandelier had hung. So-and-So draws the curtain and nervously lights another cigarette. The next day he will have to meet someone called Ummal, someone who presumably already knows that the writer So-and-So has been recruited to spy on him.

When he turned off the highway and began to drive along a dusty gravel road in the direction of the shore, he started to think seriously about double-dealing. He felt no real motivation to risk something (maybe even his life) for someone else's sake, but at the same time it might interest Ummal a good deal to know what the secret police knew about his activities. He could tell Ummal straight out that he has been placed there to spy on him. It is useful for every suspect to know what the person suspecting them is thinking. Now he had become an informer, he was told more or less everything there was to know, so as an informer (if a deal is struck) he could trade what he knew and tell (sell) his information.

He studied the map, asked the way several times, but had obviously driven past the right road, and had now ended up by the beach, and could simply drive no further. The summer was coming to an end, and he had not been to the seaside once this year. A real townie just didn't feel the need for nature. I need it inasmuch as I can use it for some episode in a story, he liked to tell people. He even occasionally bragged that he had never sat round a camp fire (which was almost the truth), and once, when Vennet was telling in colorful terms about how they went on a kayaking vacation, the very idea of spending a night in a sleeping bag or tent sent shivers down his spine.

He turned the car around and climbed out. The sun was shining on the shimmering sea beyond the juniper bushes. A white bird flew with measured wing-strokes over his head. There were butterflies. He pulled a couple of bluish berries off a juniper bush and popped them into his mouth. The sand got into his shoes, he took off his shoes and socks, but the ground was strewn with sharp objects. For quite a while he remained where he was, unable to decide whether to go back to the car or proceed to the beach. In the end he put on his shoes and walked toward the sea. Each step that he took closer to the water filled him with inexplicable energy, a quiet warm wind cooled the sweat on his back, stroked his cheeks like the back of a soft hand. Right by the water he felt an even more inexplicable sense of liberation, and a loud cry forced its way out of his mouth: "Yeuheeeiii," as if this was something that had been bubbling up for ages, searching for a way out, and had now found one and was flying across the surface of the sea like a bird. All at once he noticed that he was not alone on the beach; some dozen meters away he could see a woman leaning against a large rock and observing him, and next to her, at the end of a reddish brown leash, sat a Siamese cat, looking out to sea.

The writer So-and-So blushed like a schoolboy caught in an indecent act, but pulled himself together when he saw that the woman was by no means looking at him ironically. He lit a cigarette, his sweeping gaze across the panorama ended on the woman's face, and he satisfied himself that the woman was *very* young and pretty, that she was here on her own and bored . . . The stories that circulated nowadays about the loose morals of youth were lies, for the most part. The writer So-and-So scorned them, knew that they were told by people who were themselves too old to do anything sinful, but when he ran his eyes over the banana-yellow blouse with its top buttons loose, so that the curves of her pert breasts were tantalizingly visible, tales sprang to mind of how schoolgirls sold themselves, of the orgies that teenagers organized in summer houses, of easy victories that one or other coeval would have with the girls in a haze of narcotics, and the enticing thought gripped him of a swift, brief affair, a romance with a woman a couple of decades younger than himself, whose name he didn't even know.

He walked nearer, crouched down, wanting to stroke the cat, but it raised its paws and tried to catch the writer's fingers.

The woman (girl or young miss) looked at him, then lowered her eyes immediately.

"He won't scratch you, his claws have been trimmed," said the girl and blushed.

"Can I pick him up?"—and when the girl nodded in assent, the writer So-and-So asked in a friendly sort of way: "Are you spending the summer round here?"

"I have to write my master's dissertation."

"I've also come here with work in mind."

Silence fell for a brief while.

For some reason the writer So-and-So felt happy that he was not dealing with a schoolgirl, but at the same time troubled and excited that she wasn't trying to adjust her cleavage. "I'm more of a man from town who spends most of his time at home, and now I'm here at the seaside I was feeling like a calf in early spring. Something of our hidden essence has always remained true to nature."

The girl burst out laughing, stood up, and walked, her cat tripping along on the leash beside her, along the sandy beach. The writer already wanted to go back to his car, but then he saw that the young woman had stopped and turned back. He waited for her to come up to him, then asked the way to Teeriida Farm, after which they walked alongside each other a while—and the playfully light conversation of free and easy people ensued, people who don't care where they're going or what they're talking about. They walked along and conversed about how strangely the light fell on the sea: the water looked as if it was covered by a silver membrane, and the horizon merged with the sky. They talked about what an extraordinary September they were having, as if the summer had done an about turn, or had simply sat down and refused to budge. The writer So-and-So told her he was just starting to write a new work, presumably a novel, which was going to rub the spirit of the end of the century the wrong way, and that he already had the title: "An Unending Landscape," but that getting the book going was always the hardest, finding the right tone of voice, and sometimes—with a bit of good luck—all you needed was one sentence for the novel to take off in all directions . . . From the young woman he learned that she had grown up in Tallinn, but was now living in a country town with a girlfriend, and that the summer house by the sea where she forced herself to work every day belonged to that girlfriend, who would be coming to stay for the weekend. The young woman was unable to make clear what her girlfriend did for a living—something to do with real estate or movables—and it seemed funny even to her. When the writer asked about the topic of her dissertation, she didn't want to say, but finally, when the writer pressed her, she admitted coyly (and blushing!) that she was interested in feminist discourse and wanted to look at Estonia's recent literature from that angle. And the writer learned that the young woman's name was Evelin.

It turned out that the distance from Teeriida to the summer house where she was staying was only a few hundred meters. "I'm your nearest neighbor," said Evelin. "If you need to borrow matches, all you need to do is come and ask."

Later, when the writer So-and-So had taken his belongings indoors and was sitting drinking beer at the kitchen table, he thought that they would surely meet the next day. It had to be so. They could go mushroom-picking together. Or row out to sea.

He mooched about the house thinking how odd it was that he would be playing the role of master of the house for a couple of weeks. The apples were beginning to ripen, the plums were already ripe and were falling down from the tree. The house needed a mistress, thought the writer as he sunk his teeth into a plum that had grown warm in the sun and was as juicy as a kiss, the juice dribbling out between his lips and running down onto his shirt front.

He had been no longer than a couple of hours at Teeriida when he sensed how bored he was. The unusual silence rang in his ears, and when he listened he could hear the twitter of birds, then a very distant plane; he would have liked to switch on the radio or hop from one TV channel to the next, and with growing unease he thought that once it began to grow dark outside he would only be able to read by the flickering light of a candle, and that there was nowhere to go to stave off boredom and, when he was in a chatty mood, no one to talk to.

When it did begin to grow dark he felt tired, and without lighting a candle he climbed between the slightly damp sheets of his bed. The crickets had begun to chirp outside, and could not be switched off. The horizon glowed red and a few pale stars had come out. The sleeplessness of the previous night made itself felt, his eyelids drooped, but an inner restlessness kept the arrival of sleep at bay. It occurred to him that Evelin had only recently been an undergrad, just like his own boys, he remembered how much timidity and awkwardness there still was in Evelin's laugh, in her conversation with a stranger—she was presumably alone for the first time in her life, and in a situation where someone had come up to her, looked at her, and spoken with only one secret aim of which she was not unaware. The writer So-and-So remembered her slender, delicate neck and beautiful grey eyes.

"There is something sorrowful about her," he thought dreamily.

II

The next day, the weather was just as sunny and warm as on the previous day, but the wind had shifted to the south-east and wanted to blow through the skin that the sun had made sweaty. In the afternoon the writer So-and-So took a basket and went to see Evelin, to invite her to go mushroom-picking. Neither of them felt at home in the overgrown woods, they didn't dare to go far for fear of losing their way. They found a few chanterelles and were happy and excited about that. Once they were safely out of the woods and in an open hayfield they breathed a sigh of relief, and inventing suitable excuses left the woods far behind, fleeing to the safety of their home walls.

In the evening, when the wind had died down somewhat, they went to the shore to look at the sunset. To their great surprise, the beach was swarming with people who were taking part in some sort of weird exercises to pass the time. The younger ones were noisily drunk, while the older ones looked ridiculous doing more demanding physical exercises.

"This must be one of those family days that the military holds," said Evelin and explained that there was a former Pioneer's camp nearby, where they often arranged all sorts of meetings and get-togethers. Owing to the billowing sea and the frizzled sky, the sunset was nervy somehow. It lacked grandeur and peace, and the writer was seized by a vague feeling of disappointment when the last glowing spot vanished beyond the horizon. Evelin was still watching, her eyes narrowed as she looked into the distance, as if hoping that what she was waiting for would surely come about. She had spoken a lot all day, her questions were fragmented, and she immediately forgot what it was she had been asking.

The people on the beach were now thinning out, their faces could no longer be seen in the dusk, the wind had almost abated completely, the writer So-and-So and Evelin were still peering at the horizon, as if able to detect yet more nuances in the sunset, a tiny change of mood that the others couldn't see. Evelin fell silent and sniffed the heady fragrance of the little flowers that were glowing in the dark.

"The weather's gotten better," said the writer So-and-So. "Where are we going now? Or shall we drive somewhere?"

Evelin did not answer.

Then the writer So-and-So looked her straight in the face, embraced her roughly and kissed her on the lips. He could smell the burgeoning fragrance of the flowers and the dampness, then looked fearfully around him—was anyone watching?

"Let's go to your place . . . " he said softly, picking up the cat.

Both quickened their pace.

Evelin's bedroom was stuffy and smelled of the smoke that was rising slowly from a joss stick. Looking at her now, the writer So-and-So was thinking: "What coincidences life presents us with!" From the past he had retained the memory of carefree good-natured women for whom love was fun, and who were grateful to him for a moment of happiness, however fleeting it was. Or of those others—like his wife, for instance—who made love without sincerity, with a surfeit of chatter, coquettishly, hysterically, with an expression on their faces that said this is not love or passion, but something greater. And one or two very beautiful and cold women across whose faces would flash the expression of a predator, the stubborn desire to take, to snatch from life more than it could offer—and these were usually no longer very young, willful, thoughtless, power-hungry, and stupid women—and when the writer So-and-So cooled off, he felt only contempt, and the frills of their underwear would remind him of fish scales.

Here there was still the timidity of youth, an awkwardness, an uncomfortable feeling, plus confusion, as if someone had suddenly knocked on the door. Evelin, the "lady with lapcat," reacted rather unusually to what had happened, very seriously, as if reacting to her fall—as she thought of it—and this was odd, and didn't quite fit. The contours of her face slackened and seemed to wilt, and her long hair hung mournfully on either side of her face. She mused in a sorrowful pose, just like a sinner in an old master.

"A bad business," she said. "You'll be the first one who doesn't respect me now."

On the bedside table lay a water melon. The writer So-and-So cut himself a slice and began to eat hastily. At least half an hour passed in silence.

Evelin was a touching sight: she seemed to be the decent, naïve, inexperienced picture of female purity. The single candle burning on the table hardly lit up her face, but it was plain to see that her heart was troubled.

"Why should I have stopped respecting you?" asked the writer So-and-So. "You don't know what you're saying," he added. But all at once the scales fell from his eyes—Evelyn was a *lesbian*—he had been surprised that the young woman had shaved her pubes, but in a fit of passion he hadn't given it much thought, forgot about it instantly . . .

"May God forgive me!" said Evelin and her eyes filled with tears. "It's horrible."

"You seem to be trying to forgive yourself."

"What is there for me to forgive? I am a wicked, vile woman, I despise myself and I don't intend to forgive myself. I have betrayed not only my girlfriend, but myself as well. And not only now, in my thoughts I've been betraying her for a long time. My girlfriend is maybe an honest, good person, but she is a committed feminist. I don't know what goes on at the bottom of her heart, but she *loves* me. When I started living with her I was twenty, the curiosity was killing me, I wanted something better. There's something there, I told myself, a different sort of life. I wanted a taste of life! Only a taste of life . . . I got burnt by curiosity . . . You won't really be able to understand me when I say so, but I swear to God that I could no longer control myself, something inside me happened and I couldn't hold back. I said to my girlfriend that I had to work on my dissertation and so I traveled out here . . . Then I wandered about the empty beach completely stupefied, like a lunatic . . . and now I've become an ordinary, wretched woman, exploited by the first man she comes across."

The writer So-and-So was already bored by her talk, the naïve tone of voice irritated him, and the unexpected and unfitting regrets about her transgression. If tears hadn't flowed, it would have almost been as if she had been joking or pretending.

"I don't get it," said the writer So-and-So. "What is it you want?"

Evelin hid her face on his chest and pressed hard against him.

"Believe me, believe me, I beg you . . . " said Evelin. "Up to now I've been a committed feminist, I thought a man's phallus was something disgusting, and I really don't know what I'm doing now. Simple people say—you've trodden in a pail. Now I too can say that I've trodden in a pail."

"There, there . . . " muttered the writer So-and-So.

He looked at Evelin's fixed and frightened eyes, gave her a kiss, talked quietly and soothingly. Evelin gradually calmed down and her former jolliness was restored. They both burst into laughter and decided to go and have a walk to the seashore.

Evelin popped upstairs to change her clothes and the writer So-and-So stayed in the living-room along with the large Siamese cat. He didn't harbor any particular sympathy for the cat but knew that the young woman doted on it. And so he took a seat in an armchair and reached for the creature mechanically, absorbed in gloomy cogitations, imagining it his duty to stroke the cat. But the cat gave a snarl and it sank its teeth into the writer's hand. This bite added to the concatenation of worries that had overcome him these last few days, and whose pinnacle was the embarrassing, awkward scene that the young woman had caused quite unexpectedly, so that by now he was seized by rage and jumped up from his chair to scare the creature away. The cat leapt into the corner, hunched up, and began to hiss threateningly.

Then the writer So-and-So turned round and saw Evelin. She was standing on the stairs and it was obvious that she had been following the whole scene. She said: "No, you mustn't punish it. It was completely in the right."

The writer So-and-So looked at the young woman in astonishment. The bite was hurting, and he had expected of her that, while maybe not siding with him against the cat, she would have at least made some elementary gesture of emotion in the direction of justice. He had a strong urge to go up to the cat and give it a good kick, so that it would end up stuck flat on the ceiling like a pancake. With great self control he held back.

Evelin added, stressing every word: "The cat demands that anyone who strokes it be fully focused on it. In the same way, I can't stand it when someone is with me, yet thinking of someone else."

When they left the house, the beach had emptied, but the sea was making rushing sounds and the moonlight turned the crests of the waves silver. On the distant naze, a lighthouse flashed.

They got in the car and drove to the lighthouse.

"I figured out your girlfriend's name, there was an *ex libris* sticker in some of the books with the name von Diderits," said the writer So-and-So. "Is your girlfriend a German?"

"Not altogether. Her mother is Estonian and she calls herself an émigré Estonian."

They sat on a bench by the lighthouse, looked out over the sea and held their peace. Across the cove there were juniper bushes and a few taller trees in the banks of mist and slowly a red sun rose among them, which was *very* red and round like the disk on the flag of Japan. The landscape itself was somehow special, like a work of art, resembling an oriental engraving, and the monotonous dull soughing of the sea, which sounded as if it came from somewhere underneath, spoke of the peace and eternal sleep that await us all. Thus the sea had soughed when on this white mound of somewhat faded rocks there had been neither the lighthouse nor the well-worn bench they were sitting on; the sea was now rushing and soughing as indifferently and darkly as it would when they'd no longer be here. And this immutability, this total *indifference* to our lives and deaths, might in fact contain the guarantee of our salvation, of the unceasing movement of life on this Earth and of eternal perfection. Sitting next to the young woman who seemed so pretty, tranquil, and attractive at sunrise in these fairy-tale surroundings—the sea, the wisps of mist, the open sky—the writer So-and-So thought about how beautiful it all is, when you think about it, everything here on earth, everything beyond what we ourselves think and do, when we forget the higher aims in life and our human dignity.

A man of short stature and with a disproportionately large head was approaching, no doubt the lighthouse keeper. He took a look at them and went on his way. And this tiny event seemed mysterious yet beautiful. A large white ship could be seen on the horizon that moved as if gliding or flying along slowly—lit up by the dawn, its lights already extinguished.

"There's dew on the ground," said Evelin, breaking the silence.

"Yes. Time to go home," uttered the writer So-and-So, and the word "home" rang in his ears like a word from an alien language that he was incapable of translating for himself right now.

After that they met at midday each day, prepared and ate lunch together, walked a lot and were enraptured by the sea. Evelin would lament the fact that she slept badly and that her heart was beating wildly, she would put the same questions again and again, agitated—now from jealously, now from fear—that the writer

So-and-So did not respect her for being a lesbian. Quite often the writer would pull her towards him and kiss her passionately. Complete idleness, making love on the beach in broad daylight, looking out of the corners of their eyes to see if the young men in camouflage uniforms had noticed them—all of this had somehow transfigured the writer: he told Evelin how pretty and attractive she was, he was impatiently passionate, did not stray a pace from her, while Evelin was often engrossed in her thoughts and kept asking him to admit that he didn't love her one bit, and instead regarded her as a vulgar woman.

They awaited the arrival of Evelin's girlfriend. But then a telegram came in which she said that she had fallen sick, and asked Evelin to come home. Evelin began to make ready for departure.

"It's good that I'm going," she told the writer. "Fate itself is calling me."

When Evelin was already seated in the car, she said:

"Let me look at you one more time . . . One more time. Like this."

She did not cry, but was grim, as if sick, and her faced trembled.

"I will think of you . . . remember you," she said. "You stay here, God be with you. Keep good memories of me. We are parting forever—it has to be so, we didn't ever need to meet. Well, may God be with you."

It was growing dark, the red lights of the car disappeared rapidly round the bend, and soon the roar of the engine could no longer be heard, as if it was willed that this sweet dream, this craziness, should break off. Left alone in the garden of the strange summer house by the sea and looking into the darkening distance, the writer So-and-So listened to the crickets, feeling he had just awoken. And thought that now in his life there had been yet another adventure, and now it was past, and all that was left was memories . . . He felt wistful, sad, felt slight regret: that young woman (who had never gotten on first name terms with him despite being asked dozens of times) whom he would never see again, had not been happy with him. He had acted in a friendly and hearty way toward Evelin, and yet in his behavior, tone of voice, embraces, there had been light mockery, the coarse superiority of a man twice her age. Evelin had always said he was good, unusual and noble. He clearly appeared to her as something he was not, i.e., he had cheated her unintentionally . . .

III

The warm and sunny weather came to an abrupt end. The next morning the writer So-and-So woke up to the patter of rain, and in the afternoon he decided to light the stove to drive away the damp that made him shiver. He couldn't understand why it wouldn't burn—the paper and sticks would light, then smoke would begin to blow back into the room. It was the same with the kitchen range, and in the end he went off to seek help from the neighbor. Maria Laakan, that was the name of the neighbor, came without further ado and looked at him as if he were a freak, because he had tried to light the fire without opening the flue. The writer So-and-So shrugged his shoulders helplessly.

Maria Laakan was prepared to cook his meals for a small fee, and gradually he began to get into the swing of life in the country. Some days later, when the rain had subsided, and the sky had become silent and clear, he saw, looking out of the window on waking in the morning, that the whole yard was covered in hoarfrost. He lit the kitchen range, made some coffee, fried a couple of eggs, and started writing right away, as was his habit. His work progressed rapidly. He had never felt such lightness when writing; the words and sentences bubbled or simmered inside him like water coming to the boil and he worked for six or seven hours, was then dog tired but happy and went to bed early, wishing the morning would come round quickly so he could get back to sitting at his typewriter. The composition of the novel hovered there in his thoughts with inexplicable clarity—a complex, multi-layered and ambiguous work that was to consist of three separate novels, where the characters appear in changed circumstances and quality. In developing the novel (which in his imagination resembled a potato which grows a fine network of roots, which spread underground and grow new tubers there) he resorted to other authors, their writings, but transformed them; he wished the reader to stop now and again and listen to something else than what was before his eyes; his novel had to become like a performance of a play that the audience themselves were staging; his novel had to become a surrogate sexual partner against whom the lustful reader rubs his member, and at the moment of orgasm his sense of reality would leave him and he would think that he had attained satisfaction in the most natural of ways. It would be as if the reader were creating the novel himself, but it would keep breaking off halfway, and each new reader longs to finish it, but it is like the labors of Sisyphus—unending, never finished.

The title of the novel was to be "An Unending Landscape," and this title haunted his imagination; it was the key that fitted the lock exactly, all you had to do was turn it and kick the door open.

When writing the novel he was like an angler, walking along the bank of a river, casting in his hook and seeing what will bite; he thought to himself with a chuckle that if even small fish wouldn't sniff at the bait in these river pools, deeps, river bends, rocky stretches, let alone some bigger catch, then perhaps some assiduous critic would bite at and swallow the bait and end up writhing on the hook.

One afternoon he was involved in a spot of real fishing—a local fisherman called Rolli took him out to sea. Rolli and his wife Julia had moved to the countryside some years previously and this man from the city had now turned what used to be a pastime into a profession. For him, catching fish was a pleasurable pursuit for the most part. He never grew tired of philosophizing about it. He said that when you were fishing with a trolling line, the fish catches the fisherman. Only when the fish has got the simulated bait (the troll)—which is in effect an extension of the fisherman—between its jaws, does the former catcher (the fish) suddenly turn into the catch, and the fisherman becomes the fisherman. Rolli's wife Julia, however, just couldn't get excited about fishing. For her fishing was principally a practical activity for making a living. For her there was nothing romantic about it. "A good net means a good catch," she would say—and indeed the nets she put together were always filled with fish.

The day before the writer So-and-So was to return to the city, two cars came to a halt in front of the house, out of which emerged a whole company of people, of whom he only recognized the smiling blonde from the "Full-Blooded Recreation" office. He had just pushed aside his typewriter and was genuinely pleased to see guests. Enniver Ummal turned out to be a friendly and lively man, who, despite his decrepit and sick appearance, seemed to be driven by some inexplicable inner energy. When just the two of them stayed behind—the rest went off into the forest to pick mushrooms—Ummal told him that if his writing was going well here at Teeriida, he could stay for nothing as long as he wanted. "I know that a writer's lot nowadays is no joke. This would be sponsorship on my part, but if you have no objections, you could give our journalist an interview, which would serve as publicity for the firm," Ummal said.

The idea of "our" journalist put the writer on his guard, but the questions were quite ordinary ones, just a little tinted with a "pale green" undertone. By the end of the interview, when the journalist put aside the dictaphone, he asked the writer So-and-So whether he ever felt afraid at Teeriida. "What is there to be afraid of?" asked the writer in astonishment. "Well, the place is haunted by ghosts and poltergeists," said the journalist, realizing with concern that the writer had never heard of such things. "The farmhouse is actually no longer used," explained the journalist later, now in a drunkenly slurred voice. "Last spring a UFO landed on the grass behind the house and little green men had seized a woman and her teenage daughter and raped them on some unknown planet."

A grand feast was prepared—just as if it had to be so—the sauna was heated up, and Maria Laaakan prepared the food. When it grew dark, another group of guests arrived, including someone the writer recognized as the Minister of Defense. Ummal and the Minister squabbled loudly round the bonfire, neither minced their words, and no one dared to try and placate them. When it got too noisy, the writer So-and-So took a flashlight and walked along the forest path down to the sea. The summer house where he had been with Evelin stood deserted and dark. In the cloudy starless sky a bunch of colored airplane lights flew past, coming closer, then moving off again. The sea sent the waves, one after the other, up onto the sandy shore.

When he finally returned to Teeriida, the party had finished, the eternally smiling blonde was sleeping in his bed along with Ummal, and the other beds were also occupied by guests, and there was nothing to be done but to take the old sheepskin coat from the porch and roll up into a ball on the floor of the sauna. When he awoke the next morning, the house was empty, the guests had driven off, and it was as if no one had ever been staying there. "So you see, I never got the opportunity to confess to Ummal that I'd been recruited as an informer," thought the writer So-and-So to himself, but when he sat down at his desk he noticed next to the typewriter a book written in Finnish. This was Pentti Linkola's "Toisinajattelijan päiväkirja"—"From the Diary of a Dissident," with the author's autograph. In the bottom corner of the title page was written: *To my dear Informer to the Estonian Republic, the writer So-and-So, E. Ummal.*

Days filled with work ensued, one after the other, the novel grew thicker and longer page by page, and Evelin was supposed to become hazier by the day, and would ultimately fade into the mists of time like so many other women, who had been before her and would come after. A good while had passed since their last meeting, the trees had meanwhile become red and yellow, were then stripped virtually bare by the wind, yet in his memory everything was as clear as if Evelin had only left the day before.

The memories grew ever more vivid. When the unabated roar of the sea reached the room, or the cries of the departing flock of storks, the wind howling in the chimney, or when mysterious creaking sounds descended from the attic, everything suddenly came alive in his memory: what had happened on the beach, and when they went to the lighthouse in the early morning, the flag of Japan rising into the sky, their kisses. He paced the room, smiling to himself all the while, then his memories grew into reverie and the past merged with what was to come. Evelin did not appear in his dreams, instead followed him everywhere like a shadow, observing him. On shutting his eyes, he could see her, as if she were there before him, and she seemed more beautiful, delicate, younger than she had actually been. And the writer So-and-So himself felt better than he had a couple of weeks before. Evelin looked out at him in the evenings from the bookshelf, the fireplace, the corner of the room, he could hear her breathing and the friendly rustle of her clothing.

Now he was already tormented by the wish to share his memories with someone else. On one occasion he met Kandiman by the store, a man who would usually only be seen sitting around in the Artists' Club, but whose fifth wife had a summer house in the vicinity. They sat there on the bench in front of the store, drank their beer straight out of the bottle, and suddenly he couldn't help but blurt out:

"If you only knew what an attractive woman I got to know on the beach!"

Kandiman put his empty bottle in the garbage bin, went over to his car, but turned round abruptly and shouted:

"You were right—the beer tasted quite stale!"

For some reason, these ordinary words vexed the writer So-and-So, he felt that they humiliated and befouled him. How tedious and tiresomely familiar the people he mixed with really were. Pointless activities and talking about the same subject over and over again waste the best part of our time, and in the end all that is left is a plucked, wingless life, nonsense, and it is impossible to escape, as if we are all in a madhouse or prisoners' labor gang! Still annoyed, the writer So-and-So couldn't get to sleep for half the night, and when he woke up in the morning he had a headache. Suddenly, writing, which had so inspired him only the previous day, which had offered the prospect of great pleasure, now bored him. But all at once he seemed to get a handful of energy from somewhere, shaved, and drove into the nearby market town.

At a bar on the main street, where he drank coffee, he heard from the barman that von Diderits lived in a house given back to the owners, near the town park, lived well, was pretty rich, had two limousines, and that everyone in town knew him. The barman pronounced his name—Dreederits.

The writer So-and-So strolled unhurriedly through the park looking for the house. Straight across from it was a row of booths. He peered now into the windows of the house, now at the booths. He reckoned that as this wasn't a working day, the girlfriend was likely to be at home. It would be tactless to go to the house and cause a fuss. Best to hope for a lucky break. So he kept walking up and down the street, waiting for such a break to transpire. All at once, the front door opened abruptly and out came an old man, after him tripped the familiar Siamese cat. The writer wanted to attract the cat's attention, but suddenly his heart began to pound, and on account of his excitement he couldn't utter a word.

He walked along, hating those booths more every second and already thinking irritably that Evelin would have forgotten him by now and be amusing herself with others. This would be quite natural in the case of a young woman who was forced to look at those damned booths from morning till night. He went immediately back to the bar where he had drunk coffee and joked with himself bitterly:

"So there you have it, mate . . . a young woman with a cat . . . This is your adventure . . . You might as well just stay sitting right here."

He had already spotted a poster by the bar publicizing a performance of Anton Chekhov's "The Cherry Orchard" by a company from the capital city. He whiled away the time, then went to the theater.

"Quite likely she attends guest performances," though the writer So-and-So.

The theater was jam-packed with people. Every time people came into the auditorium to take their seats the writer looked eagerly up. Then Evelin too entered. She went and sat down in the third row, and when the writer So-and-So saw her his heart gave a leap and he realized that there was no one closer, more dear and important to him in the whole wide world. Evelin, who disappeared unnoticed among the people of the provincial town, this small, not in any way striking woman, holding a vulgar little handbag, now filled his entire life, was his sadness, the only joy and happiness that he now wished for himself. In the buzz of the auditorium he thought how pretty Evelin was. Thought and dreamed. A tall and dried up middle-aged lady came in along with Evelin and sat down next to her. She seemed to be nodding greetings to all and sundry, but her nods were arch, as if she were bestowing charity. This was presumably Evelin's girlfriend, the one she had called a feminist. And her stately carriage really did have something feminist about it. She smiled confidently and her costume seemed to conceal rather than accentuate her femininity.

During the first interval, the girlfriend went out for a smoke. Evelin stayed seated. The writer So-and-So, who was also seated in the stalls, went up to her and said in a quavering voice, forcing a smile:

"Hi."

Evelin looked up at him and went pale, then looked again in fear, not believing her own eyes, and clutched her handbag, clearly trying to prevent herself from falling into a swoon. Neither said anything. Evelin sat there, the writer stood taken aback by her discomposure, not daring to sit down next to her. The audience started to come back. Suddenly he felt afraid, as if they were all watching him. But at that moment Evelin rose and went hastily toward the door, the writer followed, and they both rushed heedlessly along corridors and up and down stairs, a few greeting acquaintances flashed past their eyes, coats and hats on pegs in the cloakroom, there was a draft, bringing with it the smell of cigarette smoke. And the writer So-and-So, his heart beating violently, was thinking:

"Oh heavens! Why all these people, this theater, this play . . . "

At this moment he suddenly remembered that when Evelin had left he had said to himself that all was over, that they would never meet again. But how far they were from the end!

On a narrow dark stair, where a notice proclaimed "Official Staff Entrance," Evelin came to a halt.

"How you frightened me!" she said, panting heavily, still pale and shocked. "Oh, how you frightened me! I'm hardly alive. Why did you come? Why?"

"But you must understand, Evelin, understand . . . " uttered the writer in a low voice, hurrying along. "Please understand, I beg of you . . . "

Evelin looked at him in fear, pleading, lovingly, looked hard at him, so that she would better remember his features.

"I have suffered so greatly!" Evelin continued, not listening to him. "I was thinking about you the whole time, I lived on those thoughts. I wanted to forget, forget—but why, why did you come?"

On a higher landing a couple of schoolboys were smoking and looking down, but the writer So-and-So didn't care, he drew Evelin toward him and kissed her face, her cheeks, her hands.

"What are you doing, what are you doing!" said Evelin in fear, pushing him away. "We're out of our minds. Leave this town, leave right away . . . I beg of you in the name of God . . . There's someone coming!"

Someone was ascending the stairs.

"You must leave town . . . " Evelin repeated in a whisper. "Listen. I'll come and visit you in Tallinn. I have never been happy, I am unhappy now, and will never become happy! Don't make me suffer even more! I shall come to Tallinn, I swear. But now we must part! My darling, my dear one, let us part!"

She squeezed the writer So-and-So's hand and ran down the stairs. When the writer called after her that he was still staying for a couple of weeks at Teeriiida, Evelin glanced back, and he could see in her eyes that she truly was unhappy. The writer So-and-So stood there for a moment, heard how everything had gone silent, took his coat from the cloakroom, and left the theater.

IV

And Evelin started visiting her girlfriend's summer cottage in order to meet the writer So-and-So. Every three or four days she would leave her market town, saying to her girlfriend that she had to consult her supervisor about her dissertation—and the girlfriend believed her, but at the same time did not. She would drive past Teeriida but didn't stop off at the writer's place, and went on to the summer cottage near the shore. The writer So-and-So would go to visit her there, and no one in the village knew.

One afternoon in early winter, when he was stoking up the sauna and looking after Maria Laakan's six-year-old boy, as Maria had driven into town, Evelin's car suddenly appeared at the gate—she sounded the horn, and when he came to the door, she drove on. The writer thought he should go to the sauna and only then to see Evelin. Besides, he couldn't leave the child on its own until Maria returned. Wet snow was falling. "It's three degrees outside, and yet it's snowing," said the writer So-and-So, more to himself than to the child. "But that's only the temperature at ground level, in the higher layers of the atmosphere it's quite another temperature."

"But uncle, why aren't there any thunderstorms in winter?"

He explained that too. He thought about how he would scrub himself clean, then go to see Evelin, and that no living soul would ever know. Again (for the fifth or sixth time) he had two lives:

one, the public one everyone sees and hears about, full of conventional truths and conventional deceit, exactly the same as that of his friends and acquaintances; and the other, lived out in secret. For some strange reason, maybe because of the coming together of chance occurrences, everything that was important, interesting, necessary, where he was sincere and did not deceive himself, which constituted the core of his being, was in the shadows, hidden from view; while the other life, where everything was a lie, in which he hid himself in order to conceal the truth, such as for instance the foreign texts he translated, arguments at the Club, going with his wife to anniversaries—all this was open to public gaze. He also decided for others on the basis of himself, did not believe what he saw and always assumed that every human being has his *true,* and most interesting, *life* under the cover of secrecy, as in darkness.

When the writer So-and So was ready to go to the sauna, the boy wanted to go along and wash himself too—as a child growing up fatherless, he would attach himself to him, often he got in his way, but he hadn't the heart to tell Maria that she shouldn't bring along her child. When they were undressing in the vestibule to the sauna, the child came up to him unexpectedly, touched his penis hanging between his legs and asked what it was. The writer So-and-So became confused, pushed the child's hand quickly away and said that you peed with it and that the boy must have the same thing, only smaller, and that if he didn't believe him he should go and have a look in the mirror. "Uncle's lying," said the little Laakan. "I don't have one, and neither does mom . . . Maybe somebody's cut it off," the child added sadly a few moments later. When the child undressed it turned out to the writer So-and-So's consternation that Maria Laakan's son was in fact a girl. Yet the child's name was Jaak—he snatched at this name like a straw. Later, when Maria came to fetch the child, he would have a serious talk with her about the matter, he thought, shrugging his shoulders.

Evelin was wearing the grey dress that the writer So-and-So liked most of all. She had grown tired of waiting for him to arrive, was pale, looked at him and didn't smile, and as soon as they were inside she threw her arms round his neck. They kissed for a long time, as if they had not seen one another for a couple of years.

"Well, how's life?" asked the writer So-and-So. "What's new?"

"Hang on, I'll tell you in a minute . . . I can't," and handed him a newspaper, opened at the center spread.

Evelin could say nothing, because she was crying. She turned aside and pressed her handkerchief to her eyes.

"Let her cry a bit, I'll read this in the meantime," thought the writer So-and-So to himself, and let his eyes run up and down the columns.

"The Minister of the Interior is personally recruiting informers. Is this a police state? The writer So-and-So claims to have been blackmailed into spying for him."

The only true item in the reportage was his photo, but all the rest had been made up by some spiteful person. Or maybe not everything . . . ? He remembered joking to Teodor about how he'd been recruited. His sudden anger subsided and rapidly turned to indifference. He couldn't even be bothered to read the article right to the end. Sure, it was part of some obscure political game, where they were manipulating someone, using his name, he decided.

And surely Ummal has a strong backing and an attempt was being made to back him up even more.

From the arts page he learned that the artist Vennet had won first prize at the first Düsseldorf Biennale of Painting. "Painting on canvas and figurative art are conquering Europe. Will the USA be next?" This was the headline in bold type above Teodor's article, which claimed there was nothing more interesting than old things that had fallen into oblivion. When the writer So-and-So put the paper aside, Evelin was still turned facing the window . . . She was crying at the agitating and sad knowledge that their life had turned out so badly: they would only see one another in secret, would hide themselves from other people like thieves! Did this not mean that their lives were ruined?

"Come on, stop it now," said the writer So-and-So.

He was clear in his mind that their love would not come to an end this soon. Evelin clung to him even more, adored him, and it was impossible to tell her that everything comes to an end one day. Nor would Evelin even have believed it. He went up to her and put his arms round her shoulders to embrace her, and at that instant he saw himself *in the mirror.*

He was already going gray. It surprised him that during these last few years he had begun to look much older and uglier. The shoulders on which his hands were resting, were warm and convulsing. He felt sorry for that life that was still so warm and beautiful, but no doubt quite near to growing yellow and withered, like his own. Why did Evelin love him so much? He had never appeared to women as he really was, and in him they were loving not the person they thought he was but someone of their own making, someone they were passionately searching for. Even later, when they realized their mistake, they would continue to love him. And not a single one of them had been happy when with him. Time passed, he got to know somebody, became friends, separated, but never loved—everything anyone could want was there, except love.

And only now, now that his hair was gray, he was really in love, truly—and for the first time in his life.

"Leave off now, my darling," he said. "You've had your cry—enough now . . . Let's have a little talk, think something out."

After that they had a long discussion, spoke about how they would free themselves in the future of the need to hide and deceive, the need to live in separate towns without seeing each other for long stretches of time. How were they to free themselves from the intolerable fetters?

"How? How?" asked the writer So-and-So, his head in his hands. "How?"

It felt that with just a little more effort the solution would be at hand, and then a beautiful new life would begin. And both knew quite clearly that the end was still far, far away and the most difficult and complex part was yet to come.

Epilogue

". . . actually his wife was his son."
SUSA MACHABEES, *Edmund, Alfred* (1996)

The writer So-and-So's wife, Mrs. So-and-So, returned from the United States on a Thursday afternoon. It was mid-December, rainy, muddy, and the Christmas snow was waiting up in the heavens to descend. At the airport she did not meet anyone she knew, she was helpless and confused—she felt that she was more of a foreigner in her home country than abroad. During her several months of absence she had begun idealizing Estonia, she felt she had not been able to appreciate what she should have appreciated, but from the moment she came back she grew irritated, even angry at trivial matters, things she should not even have noticed.

At home, as she had feared, the furniture was under a thick layer of dust, and it looked as if the apartment hadn't been lived in for a long time. The plants had, admittedly, been watered properly, but there was a great pile of newspapers and unopened letters on the kitchen table. She did not know what to think about it all. She sat there a good while, watching the street wet with the rain, and the people who leapt over puddles and were hurrying off somewhere. Last time, it must have been at the beginning of September, when she talked with her husband on the phone, he had announced that he was going away for a couple of weeks. He had not said where to. He had not said say why. Since then the phone had remained stubbornly silent.

In the end she got a grip on herself and rang the neighbor's doorbell. A dog barked for a long time, then Barbi came to open it. The neighbors' girl had blossomed these last few months, she was happy at her return and at the presents, she shone like a dewdrop in the morning sunshine, was as restless as a drop of mercury spilt on the floor. "I thought he'd gone to America," said Barbi, dismayed, when Mrs. So-and-So asked after her husband. After searching a while she found a letter that he'd left. "I have gone to Never-Never Land, please be so good as to water the plants."

"I thought it couldn't have been anywhere else but America," Barbi explained.

Not really, no, thought Mrs. So-and-So. There is no such thing as Never-Never land, people, language, food, car, fur coat, book, but she wasn't going to start explaining all that to fifteen-year-old Barbi. She felt gloomy and couldn't imagine what had happened to her husband.

She phoned a few people, tried to ask in a roundabout way, as she didn't want to let on that she had known nothing of her husband's whereabouts for quite some time, but in the end she could care no longer and asked straight out—yet no one knew where the writer So-and-So had gone, and nearly everyone was talking about Chekhov's "Cherry Orchard," which seemed to be playing at every theater at the same time.

As a last resort, she started looking through the mail on the kitchen table, but didn't find a clue to latch onto there either.

Suddenly, and quite unexpectedly, she saw her husband. The writer So-and-So was standing on the stoop of some farmhouse holding a large salmon, and he looked *happy*. Mrs So-and-So had not often seen him happy, she *couldn't even imagine him* happy. When she saw her sons growing up to resemble their father she thanked her lucky stars that her daughter *couldn't* end up looking like him.

The newspaper had printed a cynical and intriguing interview with the writer, who was said to have allowed himself to be recruited as an informer by an old schoolfriend of his, now The Minister of Home Affairs; he was now supposed to be writing a novel called "Informer to the Estonian Republic" at some farm called Teeriida, but the words which had been put into the writer's mouth were not his own. Someone had simply cobbled together the abominable text.

At midnight the boys phoned from Tartu; they had received her message, but they had no definite news about their father either.

"We read in the paper that he was writing a novel out in the countryside. He's almost become a kind of folk hero like, well, Kalevipoeg—he started a whole avalanche of scandal with his interview. We have no idea why he suddenly had the urge to get mixed up in Estonia's multi-layered postmodernist political games."

The next morning, Mrs. So-and-So phoned the "Full-Blooded Recreation" office, but she was told that no one knew anything about her husband. She went there personally, and some smiling, fish-eyed blonde refused to give any details, but at eleven o'clock exactly (she counted the strokes in order to keep her temper) a very pleasant gentleman entered, and even gave her a map which showed how to get to Teeriida. "Give him Mr Ummal's greetings," said the gentleman shaking Mrs. So-and-So's hand very warmly.

She borrowed the neighbor's car and drove away without further ado to find her husband.

That was a fox, she thought, when she saw something russet slipping into the bushes at the side of the road, or perhaps a cat, she decided a moment later, and let her gaze range over the many bright colors of the bog under the clouds that promised snow, up to the horizon, and she thought that she had seen this landscape before, and then the artist Vennet's painting appeared before her eyes, with its range of colors surprisingly similar to what she had just seen, except for the fact that Vennet had birch trees in the foreground, a couple of white trunks, which gave the picture an oppressive atmosphere (though there was in fact no reason for this), a foreboding, drawing your thoughts to an impending disaster, an inevitable catastrophe, which was quite impossible to avoid—all you could do was press your hands over you eyes and wait humbly for it to happen.

There seemed to be people on the road ahead. She gradually slowed down, and there was reason enough—two youths were kicking a third who was lying on the ground, then (presumably noticing her) they dragged the youth toward the edge of the road, and as she passed they *waved* to her. Behind them was a hamburger kiosk (open 24/7), and she thought that the windows had been smashed.

Nothing to do with me, she thought listlessly, and an ominous foreboding began to gnaw at her heart—just like that—it was a typical sensation when encountering some horror and knowing that you cannot stop *the process* from happening. You feel your powerlessness very clearly.

Then there was a shower of sleet right across the landscape.

The sky was growing ever darker as Mrs. So-and-So, after briefly losing her way, arrived at Teeriida. She looked around her: a juniper here, a juniper there, a third farther off, a fourth to the left of her, a fifth to the right, and between these a sixth, a seventh, and yet more. Between the junipers, meadows, a few buildings, with the wall of the forest beyond.

She wondered whether or not she, a woman still sitting in her car, and her husband could not live out their days in tranquility among the juniper bushes.

For some reason her chest contracted in pain. The pain spread downwards, reaching all her organs, which seemed tightly clustered around her navel.

The house was dark and seemed abandoned, but a familiar car stood there in the fallen snow. There were tracks leading through the slush to the sauna, someone had bathed there only recently. When Mrs. So-and-So knocked at the door (an alien place, after all!), she did not hear the familiar whoops, and imagining that her husband must be sleeping in the house, she entered, and was met by a pleasant wave of warmth. She groped around for the light switch a good while and then understood that there was no ceiling lamp, just candles—half-burnt ones, stubs, and unburnt ones—in every place you could possibly imagine. She lit about ten of them, the writing desk was in chaos as usual, on the corner of the desk lay a stack of typed sheets. "Well, well, he is indeed writing a new novel," thought Mrs. So-and-So, sat down next to the hot stove, and watched the quivering candle flames in the mirror of the window.

She imagined her husband could step in through the door at any moment, and wondered why this moment was taking so long to arrive, being continually postponed. In the end, in order to drive away impending boredom, she went to the car and fetched the book she had been reading on the plane. This was Susa Machabees' novel *Edmund, Alfred*, that had caused a sensation throughout North America, and in which the author had taken pains to describe life at the end of the century as accurately as possible. "Now the Europe of the 1960s has been carted over to America, down to the last shingle, and then sold back to the Europeans at a profit," is what Erwin—the man with whom she had almost tied up her life—had said about the novel. *Almost* was just the right word to describe the wave of passion that had overwhelmed them both one rainy evening, when the pregnant Arnold Schwarzenegger was just about to give birth on TV.

On that occasion—during her first month in America, when the real America had not yet gotten through to her—her previous life had seemed a pointless waste of time. She was like a ripe apple near the top of the tree, ready to fall into the lap of the first person to come along, who would help her to start a new, fuller life. It took a good while before she realized that the biggest problem the Americans have is that they do not have any obvious problems.

It became clear to her that it was impossible to live among people whose value judgments and opinions about life had frozen up. If you tried to tell them of anything that *differed* from the accepted stereotypes, they would refuse to listen to you, and they would feel really sorry for you only as long as you were having a worse time than they were. When she went visiting people with Erwin, they would tend to ask her when she had arrived, and then a little later when she was going back home to her country. One day she said, as a joke, "Tomorrow," and two days later she took a flight home.

At first she had an inkling, then she knew for sure, that she had managed to weather the latest crisis of her marriage. There was no point in expecting something special from life—the very life she had been living was, in fact, special; the country where she was born, the people she had grown up among—it was this that was special, irreplaceable, and the man—that man of eternally gloomy mien, the writer So-and-So, with whom she had spent twenty years of her life—the thousands of tiny things that seemed so unimportant, constituted history. They constituted the mutual affection of mature individuals, which could even be called love.

She waited, there was not yet the sound of snowy feet on the steps, just the sound of the wind getting up in the chimney, the novel with its bright cover had slipped from her lap and she let it lie there on the gray floor, and she picked up the manuscript lying on the desk—she wanted her husband right now, immediately, the very next moment, even if only one tiny piece of him, maybe just one sentence that had moved in his head, and she read:

AN UNENDING LANDSCAPE.

Acknowledgements

The author of this book would like to thank the authors of other books, but would especially like to credit the following authors who provided direct help: Irma Truupõld, Vladimir Nabokov, Iris Murdoch, Anton Chekhov, Tõnu Õnnepalu, Roland Barthes, Milan Kundera, Tõnis Vint, Virginia Woolf, John Fowles, Anton Tammsaare, Pentti Linkola, Jacques Derrida; and of course, my sincere thanks should stroke your ears, Good Reader, the most remarkable of all authors.

Translator's Acknowledgements

I would like to thank Tiina Randviir for her thorough and invaluable checking of the translation, so that mistranslations and clumsy expressions have been eliminated.

TOOMAS VINT was born in 1944 in Tallinn, Estonia, where he still lives today with his wife Aili. Since 1971, Vint has earned his living as a freelance writer and painter. Vint's novels and short stories have been nominated for several literary awards; he has won the Friedebert Tuglas Short Story Award twice, as well as the Estonian Prose Award.

ERIC DICKENS is a translator of Estonian, Swedish, and Finland-Swedish literature. He has translated *Things in the Night* and *Brecht at Night* by Mati Unt, both published by Dalkey Archive.

PETROS ABATZOGLOU, *What Does Mrs.*
Freeman Want?
MICHAL AJVAZ, *The Golden Age.*
The Other City.
PIERRE ALBERT-BIROT, *Grabinoulor.*
YUZ ALESHKOVSKY, *Kangaroo.*
FELIPE ALFAU, *Chromos.*
Locos.
JOÃO ALMINO, *The Book of Emotions.*
IVAN ÂNGELO, *The Celebration.*
The Tower of Glass.
DAVID ANTIN, *Talking.*
ANTÓNIO LOBO ANTUNES, *Knowledge of Hell.*
The Splendor of Portugal.
ALAIN ARIAS-MISSON, *Theatre of Incest.*
IFTIKHAR ARIF AND WAQAS KHWAJA, EDS.,
Modern Poetry of Pakistan.
JOHN ASHBERY AND JAMES SCHUYLER,
A Nest of Ninnies.
ROBERT ASHLEY, *Perfect Lives.*
GABRIELA AVIGUR-ROTEM, *Heatwave*
and Crazy Birds.
HEIMRAD BÄCKER, *transcript.*
DJUNA BARNES, *Ladies Almanack.*
Ryder.
JOHN BARTH, *LETTERS.*
Sabbatical.
DONALD BARTHELME, *The King.*
Paradise.
SVETISLAV BASARA, *Chinese Letter.*
MIQUEL BAUÇÀ, *The Siege in the Room.*
RENÉ BELLETTO, *Dying.*
MAREK BIEŃCZYK, *Transparency.*
MARK BINELLI, *Sacco and Vanzetti*
Must Die!
ANDREI BITOV, *Pushkin House.*
ANDREJ BLATNIK, *You Do Understand.*
LOUIS PAUL BOON, *Chapel Road.*
My Little War.
Summer in Termuren.
ROGER BOYLAN, *Killoyle.*
IGNÁCIO DE LOYOLA BRANDÃO,
Anonymous Celebrity.
The Good-Bye Angel.
Teeth under the Sun.
Zero.
BONNIE BREMSER, *Troia: Mexican Memoirs.*
CHRISTINE BROOKE-ROSE, *Amalgamemnon.*
BRIGID BROPHY, *In Transit.*
MEREDITH BROSNAN, *Mr. Dynamite.*
GERALD L. BRUNS, *Modern Poetry and*
the Idea of Language.
EVGENY BUNIMOVICH AND J. KATES, EDS.,
Contemporary Russian Poetry:
An Anthology.
GABRIELLE BURTON, *Heartbreak Hotel.*
MICHEL BUTOR, *Degrees.*
Mobile.
Portrait of the Artist as a Young Ape.
G. CABRERA INFANTE, *Infante's Inferno.*
Three Trapped Tigers.
JULIETA CAMPOS,
The Fear of Losing Eurydice.
ANNE CARSON, *Eros the Bittersweet.*
ORLY CASTEL-BLOOM, *Dolly City.*
CAMILO JOSÉ CELA, *Christ versus Arizona.*
The Family of Pascual Duarte.
The Hive.
LOUIS-FERDINAND CÉLINE, *Castle to Castle.*
Conversations with Professor Y.
London Bridge.

Normance.
North.
Rigadoon.
MARIE CHAIX, *The Laurels of Lake Constance.*
HUGO CHARTERIS, *The Tide Is Right.*
JEROME CHARYN, *The Tar Baby.*
ERIC CHEVILLARD, *Demolishing Nisard.*
LUIS CHITARRONI, *The No Variations.*
MARC CHOLODENKO, *Mordechai Schamz.*
JOSHUA COHEN, *Witz.*
EMILY HOLMES COLEMAN, *The Shutter*
of Snow.
ROBERT COOVER, *A Night at the Movies.*
STANLEY CRAWFORD, *Log of the S.S. The*
Mrs Unguentine.
Some Instructions to My Wife.
ROBERT CREELEY, *Collected Prose.*
RENÉ CREVEL, *Putting My Foot in It.*
RALPH CUSACK, *Cadenza.*
SUSAN DAITCH, *L.C.*
Storytown.
NICHOLAS DELBANCO, *The Count of Concord.*
Sherbrookes.
NIGEL DENNIS, *Cards of Identity.*
PETER DIMOCK, *A Short Rhetoric for*
Leaving the Family.
ARIEL DORFMAN, *Konfidenz.*
COLEMAN DOWELL,
The Houses of Children.
Island People.
Too Much Flesh and Jabez.
ARKADII DRAGOMOSHCHENKO, *Dust.*
RIKKI DUCORNET, *The Complete*
Butcher's Tales.
The Fountains of Neptune.
The Jade Cabinet.
The One Marvelous Thing.
Phosphor in Dreamland.
The Stain.
The Word "Desire."
WILLIAM EASTLAKE, *The Bamboo Bed.*
Castle Keep.
Lyric of the Circle Heart.
JEAN ECHENOZ, *Chopin's Move.*
STANLEY ELKIN, *A Bad Man.*
Boswell: A Modern Comedy.
Criers and Kibitzers, Kibitzers
and Criers.
The Dick Gibson Show.
The Franchiser.
George Mills.
The Living End.
The MacGuffin.
The Magic Kingdom.
Mrs. Ted Bliss.
The Rabbi of Lud.
Van Gogh's Room at Arles.
FRANÇOIS EMMANUEL, *Invitation to a*
Voyage.
ANNIE ERNAUX, *Cleaned Out.*
SALVADOR ESPRIU, *Ariadne in the*
Grotesque Labyrinth.
LAUREN FAIRBANKS, *Muzzle Thyself.*
Sister Carrie.
LESLIE A. FIEDLER, *Love and Death in*
the American Novel.
JUAN FILLOY, *Faction.*
Op Oloop.
ANDY FITCH, *Pop Poetics.*
GUSTAVE FLAUBERT, *Bouvard and Pécuchet.*
KASS FLEISHER, *Talking out of School.*

FORD MADOX FORD,
The March of Literature.
JON FOSSE, *Aliss at the Fire.*
Melancholy.
MAX FRISCH, *I'm Not Stiller.*
Man in the Holocene.
CARLOS FUENTES, *Christopher Unborn.*
Distant Relations.
Terra Nostra.
Vlad.
Where the Air Is Clear.
TAKEHIKO FUKUNAGA, *Flowers of Grass.*
WILLIAM GADDIS, *J R.*
The Recognitions.
JANICE GALLOWAY, *Foreign Parts.*
The Trick Is to Keep Breathing.
WILLIAM H. GASS, *Cartesian Sonata
and Other Novellas.*
Finding a Form.
A Temple of Texts.
The Tunnel.
Willie Masters' Lonesome Wife.
GÉRARD GAVARRY, *Hoppla! 1 2 3.*
Making a Novel.
ETIENNE GILSON,
The Arts of the Beautiful.
Forms and Substances in the Arts.
C. S. GISCOMBE, *Giscome Road.*
Here.
Prairie Style.
DOUGLAS GLOVER, *Bad News of the Heart.*
The Enamoured Knight.
WITOLD GOMBROWICZ,
A Kind of Testament.
PAULO EMÍLIO SALES GOMES, *P's Three
Women.*
KAREN ELIZABETH GORDON, *The Red Shoes.*
GEORGI GOSPODINOV, *Natural Novel.*
JUAN GOYTISOLO, *Count Julian.*
Exiled from Almost Everywhere.
Juan the Landless.
Makbara.
Marks of Identity.
PATRICK GRAINVILLE, *The Cave of Heaven.*
HENRY GREEN, *Back.*
Blindness.
Concluding.
Doting.
Nothing.
JACK GREEN, *Fire the Bastards!*
JIŘÍ GRUŠA, *The Questionnaire.*
GABRIEL GUDDING,
Rhode Island Notebook.
MELA HARTWIG, *Am I a Redundant
Human Being?*
JOHN HAWKES, *The Passion Artist.*
Whistlejacket.
ELIZABETH HEIGHWAY, ED., *Contemporary
Georgian Fiction.*
ALEKSANDAR HEMON, ED.,
Best European Fiction.
AIDAN HIGGINS, *Balcony of Europe.*
A Bestiary.
Blind Man's Bluff
Bornholm Night-Ferry.
Darkling Plain: Texts for the Air.
Flotsam and Jetsam.
Langrishe, Go Down.
Scenes from a Receding Past.
Windy Arbours.
KEIZO HINO, *Isle of Dreams.*
KAZUSHI HOSAKA, *Plainsong.*

ALDOUS HUXLEY, *Antic Hay.*
Crome Yellow.
Point Counter Point.
Those Barren Leaves.
Time Must Have a Stop.
NAOYUKI II, *The Shadow of a Blue Cat.*
MIKHAIL IOSSEL AND JEFF PARKER, EDS.,
*Amerika: Russian Writers View the
United States.*
DRAGO JANČAR, *The Galley Slave.*
GERT JONKE, *The Distant Sound.*
Geometric Regional Novel.
Homage to Czerny.
The System of Vienna.
JACQUES JOUET, *Mountain R.*
Savage.
Upstaged.
CHARLES JULIET, *Conversations with
Samuel Beckett and Bram van
Velde.*
MIEKO KANAI, *The Word Book.*
YORAM KANIUK, *Life on Sandpaper.*
HUGH KENNER, *The Counterfeiters.*
*Flaubert, Joyce and Beckett:
The Stoic Comedians.*
Joyce's Voices.
DANILO KIŠ, *The Attic.*
Garden, Ashes.
The Lute and the Scars
Psalm 44.
A Tomb for Boris Davidovich.
ANITA KONKKA, *A Fool's Paradise.*
GEORGE KONRÁD, *The City Builder.*
TADEUSZ KONWICKI, *A Minor Apocalypse.*
The Polish Complex.
MENIS KOUMANDAREAS, *Koula.*
ELAINE KRAF, *The Princess of 72nd Street.*
JIM KRUSOE, *Iceland.*
AYŞE KULIN, *Farewell: A Mansion in
Occupied Istanbul.*
EWA KURYLUK, *Century 21.*
EMILIO LASCANO TEGUI, *On Elegance
While Sleeping.*
ERIC LAURRENT, *Do Not Touch.*
HERVÉ LE TELLIER, *The Sextine Chapel.*
*A Thousand Pearls (for a Thousand
Pennies)*
VIOLETTE LEDUC, *La Bâtarde.*
EDOUARD LEVÉ, *Autoportrait.*
Suicide.
MARIO LEVI, *Istanbul Was a Fairy Tale.*
SUZANNE JILL LEVINE, *The Subversive
Scribe: Translating Latin
American Fiction.*
DEBORAH LEVY, *Billy and Girl.*
*Pillow Talk in Europe and Other
Places.*
JOSÉ LEZAMA LIMA, *Paradiso.*
ROSA LIKSOM, *Dark Paradise.*
OSMAN LINS, *Avalovara.*
The Queen of the Prisons of Greece.
ALF MAC LOCHLAINN,
The Corpus in the Library.
Out of Focus.
RON LOEWINSOHN, *Magnetic Field(s).*
MINA LOY, *Stories and Essays of Mina Loy.*
BRIAN LYNCH, *The Winner of Sorrow.*
D. KEITH MANO, *Take Five.*
MICHELINE AHARONIAN MARCOM,
The Mirror in the Well.
BEN MARCUS,
The Age of Wire and String.

SELECTED DALKEY ARCHIVE TITLES

The Princess Hoppy.
Some Thing Black.
LEON S. ROUDIEZ, *French Fiction Revisited.*
RAYMOND ROUSSEL, *Impressions of Africa.*
VEDRANA RUDAN, *Night.*
STIG SÆTERBAKKEN, *Siamese.*
LYDIE SALVAYRE, *The Company of Ghosts.*
Everyday Life.
The Lecture.
Portrait of the Writer as a
Domesticated Animal.
The Power of Flies.
LUIS RAFAEL SÁNCHEZ,
Macho Camacho's Beat.
SEVERO SARDUY, *Cobra & Maitreya.*
NATHALIE SARRAUTE,
Do You Hear Them?
Martereau.
The Planetarium.
ARNO SCHMIDT, *Collected Novellas.*
Collected Stories.
Nobodaddy's Children.
Two Novels.
ASAF SCHURR, *Motti.*
CHRISTINE SCHUTT, *Nightwork.*
GAIL SCOTT, *My Paris.*
DAMION SEARLS, *What We Were Doing*
and Where We Were Going.
JUNE AKERS SEESE,
Is This What Other Women Feel Too?
What Waiting Really Means.
BERNARD SHARE, *Inish.*
Transit.
AURELIE SHEEHAN, *Jack Kerouac Is Pregnant.*
VIKTOR SHKLOVSKY, *Bowstring.*
Knight's Move.
A Sentimental Journey:
Memoirs 1917–1922.
Energy of Delusion: A Book on Plot.
Literature and Cinematography.
Theory of Prose.
Third Factory.
Zoo, or Letters Not about Love.
CLAUDE SIMON, *The Invitation.*
PIERRE SINIAC, *The Collaborators.*
KJERSTI A. SKOMSVOLD, *The Faster I Walk,*
the Smaller I Am.
JOSEF ŠKVORECKÝ, *The Engineer of*
Human Souls.
GILBERT SORRENTINO,
Aberration of Starlight.
Blue Pastoral.
Crystal Vision.
Imaginative Qualities of Actual
Things.
Mulligan Stew.
Pack of Lies.
Red the Fiend.
The Sky Changes.
Something Said.
Splendide-Hôtel.
Steelwork.
Under the Shadow.
W. M. SPACKMAN, *The Complete Fiction.*
ANDRZEJ STASIUK, *Dukla.*
Fado.
GERTRUDE STEIN, *Lucy Church Amiably.*
The Making of Americans.
A Novel of Thank You.
LARS SVENDSEN, *A Philosophy of Evil.*
PIOTR SZEWC, *Annihilation.*
GONÇALO M. TAVARES, *Jerusalem.*

Joseph Walser's Machine.
Learning to Pray in the Age of
Technique.
LUCIAN DAN TEODOROVICI,
Our Circus Presents . . .
NIKANOR TERATOLOGEN, *Assisted Living.*
STEFAN THEMERSON, *Hobson's Island.*
The Mystery of the Sardine.
Tom Harris.
TAEKO TOMIOKA, *Building Waves.*
JOHN TOOMEY, *Sleepwalker.*
JEAN-PHILIPPE TOUSSAINT, *The Bathroom.*
Camera.
Monsieur.
Reticence.
Running Away.
Self-Portrait Abroad.
Television.
The Truth about Marie.
DUMITRU TSEPENEAG, *Hotel Europa.*
The Necessary Marriage.
Pigeon Post.
Vain Art of the Fugue.
ESTHER TUSQUETS, *Stranded.*
DUBRAVKA UGRESIC, *Lend Me Your Character.*
Thank You for Not Reading.
TOR ULVEN, *Replacement.*
MATI UNT, *Brecht at Night.*
Diary of a Blood Donor.
Things in the Night.
ÁLVARO URIBE AND OLIVIA SEARS, EDS.,
Best of Contemporary Mexican Fiction.
ELOY URROZ, *Friction.*
The Obstacles.
LUISA VALENZUELA, *Dark Desires and*
the Others.
He Who Searches.
MARJA-LIISA VARTIO, *The Parson's Widow.*
PAUL VERHAEGHEN, *Omega Minor.*
AGLAJA VETERANYI, *Why the Child Is*
Cooking in the Polenta.
BORIS VIAN, *Heartsnatcher.*
LLORENÇ VILLALONGA, *The Dolls' Room.*
TOOMAS VINT, *An Unending Landscape.*
ORNELA VORPSI, *The Country Where No*
One Ever Dies.
AUSTRYN WAINHOUSE, *Hedyphagetica.*
PAUL WEST, *Words for a Deaf Daughter*
& Gala.
CURTIS WHITE, *America's Magic Mountain.*
The Idea of Home.
Memories of My Father Watching TV.
Monstrous Possibility: An Invitation
to Literary Politics.
Requiem.
DIANE WILLIAMS, *Excitability:*
Selected Stories.
Romancer Erector.
DOUGLAS WOOLF, *Wall to Wall.*
Ya! & John-Juan.
JAY WRIGHT, *Polynomials and Pollen.*
The Presentable Art of Reading
Absence.
PHILIP WYLIE, *Generation of Vipers.*
MARGUERITE YOUNG, *Angel in the Forest.*
Miss MacIntosh, My Darling.
REYOUNG, *Unbabbling.*
VLADO ŽABOT, *The Succubus.*
ZORAN ŽIVKOVIĆ, *Hidden Camera.*
LOUIS ZUKOFSKY, *Collected Fiction.*
VITOMIL ZUPAN, *Minuet for Guitar.*
SCOTT ZWIREN, *God Head.*

FOR A FULL LIST OF PUBLICATIONS, VISIT:
www.dalkeyarchive.com